309 pgs

I'm too young to dream about the '60s.

But I know my history. Toby made sure of that. He's the one who told me about all those Vietnam War protests.

"We did a lot of marching, Melora. Marching, burning draft cards, singing, *All we are saying is give peace a chance!*"

But singing didn't do shit to stop that war.

Maybe the drugs kept them from finishing the job. For all I know it was the music, or the dancing, or those stupid beads they used to wear. Or maybe it was because they did whatever the fuck their men wanted.

None of that will stop me.

Books by Mendy Sobol

VIRTUAL FIRE

*THE SPEED OF DARKNESS—A Tale of Space, Time,
and Aliens Who Love to Party!*

VIRTUAL FIRE

MENDY SOBOL

FictionFire
www.mendysobol.com

FictionFire

http://www.mendysobol.com/

First Edition: July 2019

Book cover design by Ana Grigoriou-Voicu

https://www.books-design.com/

Virtual Fire/ Mendy Sobol. – 1st ed.

ISBN 978-1-73370-440-3 (print)

ISBN: 978-1-73370-441-0 (ebook)

Printed in the United States of America

For my mother, Betty M. Sobol, M.D., who read every word I ever wrote.

Hold fast to dreams,
For if dreams die
Life is a broken-winged bird,
That cannot fly.

Langston Hughes

Prologue: Melora

I'm too young to dream about the '60s. But I know my history. Toby made sure of that. He's the one who told me about all those Vietnam War protests.

"We did a lot of marching, Melora. Marching, burning draft cards, singing, *All we are saying is give peace a chance!*"

But singing didn't do shit to stop that war.

Protests aren't the only things Toby told me about from the '60s. He talked a lot about how girls wore their hair long and free. He showed me pictures from *Life* magazines he'd checked out of the library, pictures of shaggy-haired, denim-jacketed boys marching arm-in-arm with angry girls dressed in jeans and Navy pea coats. "Look," he said, "it's like a casting call for *Hair*!" I didn't know what *Hair* was, but I flipped through the old magazines, looking at photos of white girls with rivers of brown, gold, or red flowing over their shoulders and down to their waists, and black girls rocking naturals backlit like angels' haloes.

He keeps two framed pictures from those times on his desk. One is blurry, but I can tell it's Toby, towering over his best friends Tesla and Meg in front of what looks like some ancient Greek temple, all three of them dressed about the same, all three flashing peace signs. The other is crisp and clear—Toby and his pals standing next to a huge black horse. Only Meg's flashing a peace sign in this one. Flashing a peace sign and a big, sunny smile. From Toby's bed I can see her clearly. And her hair is long, lush, and beautiful.

Not like mine.

But those '60s girls didn't wear Net interfaces riveted to one ear with surgical stainless and looped across to the other by epoxied fiber optic threads. I mostly cut my hair to get it out of the way.

Sometimes I think Toby wants me to be more like them, all soft curves, smiling eyes, and brushed-shiny hair. I think he loved those women—even though they couldn't do shit to stop their war.

Maybe the drugs kept them from finishing the job. For all I know it was the music, or the dancing, or those stupid beads they used to wear. Or maybe it was because they did whatever the fuck their men wanted.

None of that will stop me.

PART ONE

DREAMS

Chapter One: Paul

Last night the dream came again. It's always the same. May 6, 1970. Senior year. A dozen Wellston University students sit in Franklin Hall's one-armed desk chairs facing each other in a circle. I look up at the arched gothic ceiling, then around the circle at the others, their faces framed by long, shaggy hair, black and brown, copper and gold. Pot smoke and frigid air drift inside as two freshmen pass a joint near the open doorway. I smell the smoke, feel the chill of the cold New England night, button the top of my wool CPO jacket.

Two days since Kent State. Cambodia invaded, the strike vote passed, Jackson State yet to come. We are cold. We are serious. We are deciding whether to set a fire, commit a crime.

Then in walks Toby. Toby with the dark hair and bushy beard. Toby with the black beret and red star. Toby with the wizard's eyes and quick smile. Big as a bear he towers over us. Spotting me on the far side of the circle, he raises his hand in greeting. "Hey, Tesla!" he says, his warm Virginia drawl sounding light, out of place. "What are y'all up to?"

I'm silent. Everyone's silent. Then Meg answers, looking angry, looking beautiful, but avoiding Toby's eyes. "Paul and the rest of us are deciding whether we should burn the ROTC building," she says, pointedly using my real name, not the nickname, Tesla, given me by my best friend Toby when we were freshmen.

Toby relaxes his posture, resting back on his heels. He looks around the circle. "Hey, when we want to play, we stay here at Wellston. When we want to burn things down, we go up to Harvard." And though to outsiders this would sound ridiculous, to most of us, it's persuasive. Heads nod, and on the strength of two short sentences, Toby carries the day.

Talk moves on to tomorrow's peace march. Toby smiles at me, winks at Meg, but her face flushes red and she quickly lowers her eyes. I watch as Toby's smile fades and he turns away.

I wake before the dream ends, and I'm glad. Soaked in sweat and shaking, but glad I wake up before the end. Because the end is Toby walking out of Franklin Hall and across Taylor Street. The end is a hit-and-run driver, speeding, swerving, losing control. The end is Toby dead, three days before his twenty-first birthday. And as I pass through the time when the dream is more real than the place I wake, feeling sad and happy and confused all at once, I think, *It was good seeing you again, Toby. Even in a dream.*

I've had the dream ever since that cold May night. Sometimes a year or more passes without it. Sometimes it comes two nights running. The dream comes more often now because of where my work is leading. I'm so close.

Toby and I were in the vanguard of those who'd soon become a mighty global force. We were computer nerds, college students spending every spare minute on Wellston's lone IBM 650 computer, a temperamental behemoth named Bruin. I was the technician, dotting "i's" and crossing "t's" in the long programs we wrote using the clumsy, arcane computer languages of the day. Toby was the math genius, the visionary, the first person I ever heard talk of linking computers, not just between two buildings, but around the world.

That's what we dreamed of in those days. Computers as small as refrigerators, linked so dozens of people could share their ideas. And Toby's dreams were much bigger.

The Vietnam War changed that, as it changed everything.

Chapter Two: Paul

Toby and I met on the first day of freshman year in the only place on campus either of us was interested in finding, the Physics Department, home to Bruin. While other freshmen decorated dorm rooms and planned panty raids, we sat glued to Bruin's keyboards and screens, spellbound by its incredible speed and limitless power.

Within days we talked our fraternity-pledging roommates into switching rooms, so without seeking official permission we could live together. From our bay window on the top floor of Parker House in the Freshman Quad, we could see all of downtown Butler, the New England mill town where Wellston University first opened its doors in 1770. The old Baptist church where the Wellston family worshiped, the white marble dome of the John Fitzgerald Kennedy Federal Courthouse topped by its gold statue of *The Spirit of Liberty*, the crumbling Amtrak station, and the tall 1950s office tower we called the Superman Building because it looked like the one on the TV show, the one George Reeves leaped "in a single bound."

A month into our freshman year we cashed in our cafeteria tickets, taking our meals in the front room of the Beef 'n' Bun restaurant on Taylor Street, our recreation at the pinball machines in back. The rest of our time we spent with Bruin.

I majored in engineering, Toby in physics and applied math, but only because the Computer Science Department didn't yet exist. We filled our semesters with courses about computing, and in required courses, like Western Civ and English Literature, we talked our professors into letting us evaluate Martin Luther's impact on Europe and analyze the works of Shelley and Keats using the powerful new technology of Bruin.

Toby and I quickly became among the most recognizable pairs at Wellston. Toby—dark-haired, full-bearded, blue-eyed, Baptist, a few inches over six feet and more than a few pounds over two-forty. Paul—dirty-blonde, clean-shaven, green-eyed, Jewish, an inch or two under six feet and a pound or two shy of one-fifty. Toby—gruff voice tempered with rhythms of the south. Paul—all north Jersey nasal. Paul's Old Spice deodorant announcing his arrival before he enters a room, Toby's lack of deodorant broadcasting his. Straight-haired Toby, bushy-haired Paul. Mets' capped Paul, black-bereted Toby. Always-joking Toby, always-serious Paul. Always interrupting each other. Always waving our hands for emphasis. Always together. On the surface we seemed like opposites who each lacked something without the other, and first students, then professors took to saying, "There goes Toby Jessup and Paul Simmons, Yin and Yang."

One day early in our freshman year while Toby was playing the *Fireball* machine after our usual cheeseburger lunch, I asked him, "How come you never call me Paul, only 'Buddy', or 'Guy', or 'Hey You'?"

Toby's fingers stayed on the flippers, his eyes on the machine. But as the metal ball bounced from bumper to bumper, clanging, banging, and racking up points, he smiled his quick smile. " 'Cuz I'm waitin' till I think you up a nickname."

With one last flick of a flipper and two expert bumps just light enough to avoid a tilt, *Fireball's* rotary numerals clicked from 999 990 to 000 000, and the beaten machine sounded the familiar wood-block knock of Toby scoring a free game. Hands dropping to his sides, he watched the ball drain neatly between the flippers. Still smiling, he turned to me. "And I think I've got one. How do you like 'Tesla'?"

At first, I was stunned. I hadn't cut my hair since the day before my high school graduation and was beginning to look like I'd stuck my head in the middle of one of Nikola Tesla's high-voltage experiments. But Toby never made fun of anyone's looks, and I realized in an instant he chose the nickname from our lunchtime discussion, a discussion we'd had a dozen times since school began. The "Who's the bigger genius?" argument went like this:

Toby (smiling as he looks up from his cheeseburger, chewing with his mouth open, changing the subject from whatever we've been discussing) "Einstein, definitely Einstein."

Me (feigning ignorance) "Is that the name of a new band?"

Toby (still smiling) "No, buddy. Einstein was definitely the biggest genius of all time."

Me (still under control) "Are you talking weight, or height?"

Toby (patiently, as if speaking to a small child) "No, I'm talkin' brains."

Me (getting irritated) "How can a guy who sat around thinking up theories in his head possibly be a bigger genius than Tesla? Tesla built real things that really worked in the real world!"

Toby (big smile stretching across his big face) "Oh re-al-ly? Well y'all be sure and tell the Russians 'The Bomb' isn't real!"

Losing all control, I'd angrily recount every fabulous experiment Tesla conducted, with Toby all the while laughing harder and harder, until I'd start laughing, too.

Toby knew I loved Tesla, and the power, beauty, and enduring impact of his wild experiments. So he wasn't calling me Tesla as a put-down. He meant it as a compliment—and a challenge. Besides, I figured he'd forget the nickname in a day or two. I didn't know Toby very well yet, because the only name he called me from that day on was Tesla.

With Toby and me it was never a matter of growing closer. We were close from our first afternoon in the Physics Department, our disagreements never more serious than the Einstein / Tesla debate. As time passed, we got to know each other the way only brothers do. We spent our vacations together, at first alternating family visits. When

Toby came to my hometown, Applewood, New Jersey, we hung out at WFMH, the pioneering freeform radio station at Hilversum College, tinkering with their transmitter, soundboards, and speakers, or rode the 88 DeCamp bus into Manhattan for Mets games and free concerts in Central Park. In Stonewall, Virginia, where Toby grew up, we walked the length of "The Old 97's" railroad trestle, swam in Panther Falls, ate hot dogs and five-alarm chili at the Texas Tavern. But by spring break of our sophomore year, we began staying in Butler over vacations, doing the same things we did when school was in session.

And we learned we had something else in common—our dreams.

Toby found a word to describe how we felt about our dreams: *ferocious*. Night after night, as soon as our dorm room lights went out, a second reality began. Each morning at breakfast we'd relate the epics we'd lived the night before. Frightening tales of alien invaders. Nightlong dramas of beautiful heroines and heroic romance. Transformations into fantastic creatures with supernatural powers. Sometimes we woke at the same moment in the middle of the night, relating our dreams until sunrise.

And slowly, over time, an amazing thing happened. We began dreaming the same dreams at the same time. Not identical in every detail, but similar in characters and plot.

The one dream we dreamed most often took place in the future. Everyone had their own computer, with each computer connected to all the others! In our dream, universal communication and creativity were a reality. We loved that dream and knew when we woke, without saying a word, if it had come to us again.

That's how we spent our first three years at Wellston. Programming, playing pinball, and dreaming.

Chapter Three: Paul

The Vietnam War had always been a part of our lives, in college, in high school, as far back as I could remember. My mother was against it from the beginning, when Eisenhower sent the first U.S. military advisors in 1955. Now she represented draft resisters in her law practice. My father, a World War II veteran, took longer to come around, but by the mid-1960s he agreed with my mother. Friends had been drafted after high school, but so far, all made it home in one piece. Like everyone in college, Toby and I were spared from the draft, at least until after graduation, by student deferments. Like most, we opposed the war. But active protest wasn't a reality for two computer geeks.

That changed in 1969. Richard Nixon won the presidency in '68 by promising a "secret plan" to end the war. Nixon, like Lyndon Johnson before him, was lying. Nine months after his inauguration the violence continued, escalating daily. When our senior year began, the feeling in the air was skittish and electric. The mood of returning students and incoming freshmen, buoyed by Woodstock only a month before, dampened quickly with a sense of dread as real and heavy and lead gray as the New England sky. Tensions were briefly relieved, but ultimately heightened, by weekly peace marches to Federal Hill and the J.F.K. Courthouse. And for the first time, Toby and I marched with our classmates under the banner of the SMC, the nonviolent Student Mobilization Committee.

On a Wednesday in mid-October, we boarded a Greyhound filled with SMC members headed for Boston. Abbie Hoffman, leader of the Youth International Party, or Yippies, was speaking on the Boston Common, and thousands of antiwar protesters were expected.

From the fringe of the crowd we could see Abbie, full of the joy of being young, alive, and funny as hell, his Massachusetts accent thick, his voice echoing like a ringing bell. "If you don't believe in revolution, think about our foundin' fathuh, Paul Re-vi-ah. Less than two hundred ye-ahs ago, right here in Bah-ston, he looked up at that old Nawth Church, saw the lantuns burnin'—'One if by land, two if by sea!' So young Paul, he jumps on his motorcycle, poppin' wheelies 'round and 'round Copley Square, shoutin', 'The pigs are comin'! The pigs are comin'!' "

Everyone was laughing, clapping, cheering. Then, up from the Charles River side of the Common, the first tear gas canisters landed. Cops, on foot and on horseback, charged the crowd. In full riot gear and gas masks, their battle line advanced through the choking haze, a double phalanx working its way at right angles from Beacon and Charles Streets, trapping us between its flanks, batons swinging up high and down hard on legs and backs, shoulders and heads.

The crowd shuddered, then broke. Abbie kept speaking, his shouts of "Don't let the pigs break up our meetin'!" drowned out by screams and the clatter and thud of running boots and horses' hooves on blood-stained cobblestones. At first, I stood my ground. But when the nearest cop got within ten yards, I backed away. A girl, no more than fourteen, rushed past me, waving a peace sign poster in the cop's face. "Fucking pig!" she shouted. He raised his billy club. I took one step forward. The girl dropped the poster and covered her head with both hands. I didn't know what I was doing, didn't know what I was going to do, but I took another step toward them. Too slow. And as the club arced above her, gaining speed, the cop's eyes shifted to me, his lips moving behind his face shield.

"You're next!" he said.

I froze.

A man, big and bearded, moved between us, grabbing the cop's arm, catching him off balance, throwing him to the ground.

Toby.

The girl ran left; Toby and I ran right. We crossed the Common, dodging protestors and police, stumbling down stairs, seeking safety in the Park Street trolley station.

The station's dim yellow lighting cast a confusion of shadows as hundreds more pushed down the stairs after us. On the overcrowded platform, everyone was staring at the tunnel for the headlights of an approaching trolley, everyone hoping for escape. The fading smell of oil, ozone, and hot metal, a distant rumble, and a pair of receding red taillights said otherwise. It would be a long wait for the next train.

"Fuck!" a woman yelped, and tumbled onto the tracks. Hands quickly reached out, hauling her up onto the platform. Blood flowed from her gashed forehead, and as the rescuers pushed people away so she could lie down, three boys fought for balance at the platform's edge, then fell. The crowd jostled and swayed, some moving closer to help them, some backing away. A man with hair down to his shoulders and a guitar strapped across his chest stepped on my foot as he stumbled into me. Clawing at the man for balance, finding only empty air as he staggered away, I fell to my knees and pitched forward, hands above my head, too high to break my fall. And for the second time that day, Toby saved me, quickly scooping his big hands under my armpits, yanking me to my feet.

My knees throbbed. My heart felt like it was hammering its way out of my ribcage. And suddenly, my eyes were burning. I rubbed them furiously, squinting through tears at Toby, who was rubbing his, too. Around us, people began coughing and choking. "Tear gas!" someone shouted.

Then everyone was screaming.

In panic, they pushed up the stairs against the wave of people fleeing downward. Toby looked at me, his watering eyes reflecting the station's lights. "We gotta follow the tracks. Walk underground to Boylston Street and the bus station." I nodded, and together we jumped from platform to track, leaving screams, tear gas, and panic behind, running toward what we hoped was safety.

The two-hour bus ride to Butler was the only time Toby and I were together when neither of us said a word.

Chapter Four: Paul

December 1, 1969. Before that night there were lots of ways to get drafted. There were also lots of ways *not* to get drafted. The Selective Service System was good at filling its quotas with poor men, especially poor black men. It was better at finding ways out for rich men, professional athletes, and anyone with money and connections. They got student deferments, employment postponements, and medical exemptions, or secured coveted positions in the National Guard. Of the three future U.S. Presidents who were eligible for the Vietnam War draft, Bill Clinton, George W. Bush, and Donald Trump, none were drafted. Of the four future Vice Presidents who were eligible for the Vietnam War draft, only Al Gore served in Vietnam. The rest avoided military service.

Now, the government told us, things were going to be different. Now draftees would be determined by lottery.

Toby and I sat in the lounge at Parker House, our old freshman dorm. Three-dozen young men, all born between 1944 and 1950, and a handful of young women, milled around, snacking on popcorn and making small talk. The room smelled of stale beer, pot smoke, and unwashed college students. Outside the large double-hung windows it was black, the kind of featureless darkness that accrues in the dead of winter. Inside, bare incandescent bulbs cast yellow light, throwing long shadows into the corner where Toby and I sat, twenty feet from the black and white TV that would soon be the center of attention.

"Shhhhhh!!!" The Parker House president waved his hands at his sides, palms down, calling for quiet, while the dorm's R.A. turned up the TV's volume. The screen showed a bunch of old men in dark suits and ties. They stood next to a big glass cylinder. The cylinder held 366 blue capsules. Each blue capsule contained a rolled up slip of paper, and on each slip of paper was a date, one for each day of the year from January 1 to December 31. Representative Alexander Pirnie, a Republican from New York, drew the first number.

Pirnie handed the capsule to another old man, who broke it open and unrolled the slip of paper. "September 14," he said, and handed the paper to a third man, who said, "September 14, zero-zero-one," and stuck it on a large poster board next to the number 001.

Thirty days from today, on January 1, 1970, every American male born on September 14 in the years 1944, '45, '46, '47, '48, '49 and '50, all of them from age 19 to 26, would be called first to serve their country. For many, that would mean Vietnam.

"No fucking way!" the R.A. said.

Friends quickly dragged him aside, offering reassurances.

"Canada, man. I'll go with you!"

"My brother's a doctor. He'll get you a medical exemption!"

"Tons of guys are getting out as conscientious objectors. Apply for a C.O.!"

The R.A. buried his face in his hands. The lottery continued.

"April 24, zero-zero-two."

"December 30, zero-zero-three."

"February 14, zero-zero-four."

Sometimes a date was called and there was no response, because no one in the room had that birthday. Sometimes there were groans, sometimes curses. When they called, "June 5, zero-two-eight," two friends, one black, one white, pulled out a pack of matches and set their draft cards alight, dropping them into an ashtray to the sound of cheers and chants of "No more war!" and "Fuck Tricky Dick!"

Things had quieted down by the time they announced, "May 9, one-nine-seven."

"Holy shit," Toby said. "That's me."

But before I could say anything, the old man on the TV was pulling out the next capsule.

"August 14. One-nine-eight."

My birthday.

"Hey, cheer up, Tesla!" Toby said, thumping my back with one of his giant paws. "We can sit next to each other on the plane to 'Nam!"

"Let's get outta here," I said, grabbing my coat.

"197 and 198's not bad," Toby said as we walked up Taylor Street to our apartment. The sidewalks were slippery with patches of ice, and our breath sparkled in the night air. "Everyone's saying they won't have to go higher than 150."

"C'mon, Toby. You know that's bullshit. The government's lying about that like they're lying about everything else. We need a plan."

Toby pulled out his wallet, opened it, and took out his draft card, the small piece of paper that, for tens of thousands, had turned into a death warrant. "We could burn these suckers!"

"Yeah, we could, Toby. But we still need a plan!"

"Well, here's my plan. I did four years in my military high school, and I ain't never goin' back. So first, I'm gonna use up every minute of my student deferment…."

"Christ, Toby, we graduate in June!"

"Yeah, and maybe the war will be over by June. But if it isn't, I'm goin' C.O., or medical, or… or… fuckin' Canada!"

"What good will that do? We can't stop the war by running away."

"So what's your plan, Tesla?"

"I dunno. I'll resist. Y'know, not show up for the physical, fight it in court, go to jail if I have to."

Toby rolled his eyes. "You better talk to your mom first. She'll tell you what happens to draft dodgers in prison. They're puttin' 'em in with the general population, the worst of the worst. They're gettin' beaten, raped, murdered. They're commitin' suicide 'cuz it's the only way to escape. And what's the government doin'? Nothin'! 'Cuz that's the way they want it! No, Tesla, you're not goin' to prison. You're goin' to Canada—with me!"

I started to argue, but Toby cut me off with a laugh and another whack on my back so hard it knocked the breath out of me. "Besides," he said, "you like hockey, don't ya?"

Chapter Five: Paul

The memorable events of the long winter of 1969–70 didn't all involve the war. Toby and I spent Christmas break helping IBM technicians link Bruin with the new Engineering Department computer, blacking out half of Butler in the process. On New Years Day, George, the Mozart of the Beef 'n' Bun short-order grill, opened just for us, serving up "Wellston Cheeseburgers," fries, and Dr Peppers on the house. After lunch I played the game of my life on *Fireball*, turning the machine over again and again on a single ball as Toby cheered me on. In the end, *Fireball* quit before I did, dying on the spot, its lights dimmed, bells silenced forever. I grinned triumphantly at Toby. Toby looked at me with awe and delight. "You did it, Tesla. The Endless Ball!" But things to come would overshadow our small victories, as the war overshadowed everything.

Early in January, Toby and I were, as usual, up late working with Bruin. It was past 2:00 a.m. as we finished a new program. The Heathkit radio I built when I was nine rested on a table, tuned to the campus station, WELL. (Toby: "Join the Twentieth Century, Tesla. Get somethin' with transistors!" Me: "They'll never replace the vacuum tube!") Grace Slick's voice, silky and powerful, filled the lab, singing *Lather*, about a man who remained a blissful child while his friends grew up and became soldiers.

Before the last notes faded, WELL's overnight student DJ broke in. "So you want to stop the war? Get yourself over to 5 Hope Street. Student Mobe is training marshals for tomorrow's march on Federal Hill. Every marshal is a marcher for peace; every marcher for peace should be a marshal!"

Toby grabbed his beret. "C'mon, Tesla. Let's go."

It was cold, moonless, overcast, but for once, not raining. Two dozen of us stood, collars up, hats pulled down, feet shifting in front of the house on Hope Street. Four SMC leaders faced us. "My name's Nick Rector," the tall one began. "Tonight we're going to do a little guerilla theater, and when we're done you'll be trained parade marshals. Each group leader has marshaling experience in Washington D.C. and here in Butler. Marshals keep the march going where it's supposed to go, help people with medical problems, and above all, make sure things stay peaceful. You ready?" Hands in pockets, we and the other trainees nodded.

They split us into three groups with one SMC leader in charge of each group, while Rector, who was almost Toby's size, moved from group to group, supervising. In the dark, I hadn't noticed Meg until she stepped forward to lead my group. She stood a head shorter than I, two heads shorter than Toby, her posture straight, eyes gentle, wavy brown hair tucked inside the collar of her Navy pea coat. While other group leaders joked and jostled, Meg instructed her trainees with quiet words and spare gestures. She began by showing us how to make a human wall for keeping protesters on route. Taking my arm in one hand and Toby's in the other, she linked them at our elbows, explaining how, at the last Washington D.C. peace march, she'd stood at the corner of Pennsylvania Avenue arm-in-arm with five hundred marshals. "Only five hundred of us," she said, "but because we were trained, because we were disciplined, we turned the tide of a thousand protesters who'd sworn to break the line of march and storm the White House. And we did it without any violence."

Meg taught us how to deal with freak-outs and bad trips, medical emergencies and minor injuries. On the asphalt of Hope Street she lay on her side, curling into a ball, hands clasped on her head with inter-locking fingers, showing us what to do if the police beat us. When it was our turn to try it, she knelt among us making small adjustments to our hands and feet. Then she had Toby and I play the role of police officers carrying her limp body up the stairs of number 5 Hope as she demonstrated techniques of passive resistance to arrest.

For our "Final Exam," all three training groups gathered, taking turns being marchers and marshals, radicals and cops, simulating our own small peace march down Hope Street in the middle of the New England night. Meg, on tiptoes, whispered instructions in Toby's ear, and stepping aside, he quickly slid to the end of the line. The rest of us continued around a corner onto Angel Street, Meg and I linking arms, directing marchers into the turn. As Toby approached, his eyes snapped back in his head, his bear-size body levitating straight into the air. For a moment he looked like the Peanuts dog, Snoopy, happily bouncing down the street. "Unnhh!" he moaned, and still airborne, acted out a wildly over-the-top epileptic seizure.

Meg and I, moving together as though we'd been doing it for years, gently, firmly, took hold of Toby, controlling first his limbs, then torso, laying him down on the asphalt, kneeling beside him, calmly repeat-ing, "It's okay. You'll be all right. We'll help you. You'll be all right. We'll take care of you." And when he finally lay motionless, Meg looked up at me and smiled.

The real march later that day was calm and peaceful, the crowd larger than expected with a nearly equal number of marchers and marshals. Toby, Meg, and I stood together at our assigned position along the line of march in front of Raymond's Federal Hill Newsstand. Ray Constantino, the owner, padlocked the little stand's shutters, joining doctors and lawyers, clergy and shopkeepers, hard hats and students, blacks, whites, and decorated veterans, all marching against the war.

When the last stragglers passed, the marshals joined the other marchers gathered on the lawn of the Kennedy Courthouse, listening to speeches about poverty, racism, and the war. The keynote speaker,

Pete McCloskey, a U.S. Representative from California, his voice echoing off the building's white marble facade, roused us, making us feel like someone in the government was on our side after all. "This war is immoral, illegal, and indefensible!" The crowd roared its agreement. Then everyone linked arms, thousands of us, singing, *All we are saying is give peace a chance!* And as the crowd broke up, drifting away like a morning fog, Meg, her arms linked with Toby on her left and me on her right, led us up the courthouse steps, positioning us on either side of one of its graceful Ionic columns. Pulling a dented Kodak Instamatic from her coat pocket and handing it to a very surprised silver-haired police officer (who'd been watching us closely), Meg stepped between us, smiling.

The slightly out-of-focus picture of three young college students in long hair, blue jeans, and military jackets, arms linked, free hands flashing peace signs, rests on my bookshelf to this day.

While other student demonstrators walked up College Hill to classrooms, cafeterias, and dormitories, Toby, Meg, and I headed for the Beef 'n' Bun. After lunch, Meg surprised and delighted us, winning free game after free game on *Fireball*'s replacement, the new *Joker's Wild* machine. Toby and I gladly played those free games, adding to them, returning the favor to Meg. We quit with three games left on the machine—"A tribute to the Pinball Gods," Meg called it—but not before putting our hands together like football players breaking a huddle, letting out one final cheer. Annoyed looks from late afternoon diners greeted us as we came through the back-room door into the restaurant. George, scrambling eggs with his left hand, flipping burgers with his right, working his short order grill like Leonard Bernstein conducting the New York Philharmonic, smiled one of his rare smiles, shaking his head, never missing a beat.

Toby and I turned right out the door, heading for the Physics Department. Meg, hurrying because she was late for an SMC meeting, went left. After a few steps, she spun around, and walking backwards, called out, "Hey, party tonight at number 5 Hope. Be there or be square!" Toby and I stopped as though we'd smacked into an invisible wall, looked over our shoulders at Meg, and rolling our eyes, sarcastically chimed in perfect unison, "Seeya later, alligator!"

Chapter Six: Paul

The party began typically enough for that time and place. Meg met Toby and me at the door. I'd only seen her wavy black hair jammed inside her jacket, but now it hung full below her waist. Smiling, she led us across the living room through clouds of smoke. Janis Joplin blasted *Piece of My Heart* from stereo speakers the size of file cabinets. I recognized some faces, mostly SMC members like Nick, the leader of last night's marshals training. A football player I knew from Latin class took a joint from the fingers of his cheerleader girlfriend, holding it out to us as we passed.

"No thanks," I said.

"Where's your helmet?" asked Toby, following close behind.

Meg stopped at the foot of the stairs, introducing us to a short, broad-shouldered man who wore a Vietnam Veterans Against the War button on his faded military jacket. "Kevin's coordinating Veterans Against the War demonstrations with the SMC," she said. I realized Kevin couldn't be more than twenty-five or twenty-six. He looked much, much older.

A second fatigue-jacketed man stood silently, ghost-like at Kevin's shoulder. On his left collar two small holes marked the place where insignia of a United States Marine had once been pinned. On his right he wore the red star of the NVA—North Vietnam's Communist

Army. He was taller, more wiry than Kevin, but there was something similar in the wrinkled squint around their eyes, the unsmiling set of their mouths.

"This is Ian Marley," Kevin said. "We served together at Khe Sanh. When we got out I talked him into coming to Butler with me."

We shook hands all the way around, but Ian said nothing. Meg took his hand in both of hers for an extra moment, looking in his eyes. "It's good meeting you, Ian. I hope we can work together on the next march."

We continued up the stairs, the embroidered hems of Meg's bell-bottoms dancing step-by-step ahead of us. Meg shared a tiny attic bedroom with a phantom roommate named Ruth. Ruth paid rent, using the address so her parents wouldn't know she'd moved in with her boyfriend. The single small window faced north, toward the grimy mill town of Springfield, the worst view in Butler. Meg had three warm cans of Pepsi and a cold pizza waiting for us.

"So Meg," Toby said, halfway through his fifth slice, "you want to spank *Joker's Wild* with us again tomorrow?"

"Can't. I have to get out a big SMC mailing. Want to spend tomorrow mimeographing letters and stuffing envelopes?"

"How much text in the letter?" I asked.

"Just a one-paragraph fundraiser."

Toby, as usual, was thinking what I was thinking. "We can get a bunch of postcard stock. Run 'em on Bruin. No fuss, no muss, no stuff. Cheaper postage, too."

Meg's dark blue eyes sparkled. "You can do that?"

"Hey, we can do anything! We're masters of the machines!"

Then suddenly, the crash of breaking glass downstairs. And a man screaming, "Incoming! Incoming! Victor Charlie! Victor Charlie!"

Meg was first out the door, Toby and I right behind. In the living room Ian, hands bleeding, muscles knotted, held a chair straight out in front of him like a lion tamer, waving it at the football player's terrified girlfriend.

The term *Post-Traumatic Stress Disorder* hadn't yet come into the language. Instead, Toby whispered, "Flashback," followed by, "You keep him busy in front. I'll circle."

As I wondered, *What the hell kind of a plan is that?* Meg stepped between the cheerleader and Ian. "Put the chair down, Ian. We're friends, we'll help...." He charged before she could finish the sentence, and without thinking, I jumped sideways between them, arms raised, waiting for the crunch of the chair.

Toby was faster. His big bear paws swatted Ian's arms, pushing them enough so the chair's legs glanced off my right shoulder. Toby's follow-through carried him forward into Ian, awkwardly shoulder-tackling him to the floor. I recovered, straddling Ian's kicking legs before they did Toby any harm. And as we wrestled on the woven oval living room rug, there was Meg, inches from Ian's face, quietly repeating, "It's okay. You'll be all right. We'll help you."

That's when Ian stopped fighting. First his body stiffened. Then, eyes rolling back in his head, his thin chest and legs began undulating like ocean waves. Meg said, "Are you all right?" He managed one word—"No." Then, teeth clenched, his body began the jerky spasmodic dance of a grand mal seizure.

Toby rolled off Ian's chest looking dazed, out of breath. I continued holding his legs, more gently now. Meg, voice calm, quiet, kept talking, reassuring. "It's okay," she said. "You'll be all right. We'll take care of you," just as we'd practiced the night before less than thirty yards away in the middle of Hope Street.

Later, I'll have no idea how long it took before the shaking stopped and Ian's tongue rolled from his mouth dripping blood and saliva. And I won't remember anyone leaving. But when I looked past Meg's anxious face, I realized the apartment, so crowded when we arrived, was nearly empty.

Nick, the SMC leader, spoke first. "We've gotta call an ambulance, get him to the hospital!"

"You can't do that man." Kevin, eyes big, voice ragged, kneeled behind Meg. "They'll ship him out to the Veterans Administration

Hospital. And the VA will drug him and stick him in a straight jacket. I'm telling you man, he'll die there!"

Nick was about to answer when Meg, in the same voice she used to comfort Ian, said, "Don't worry. He's not going to the VA. We'll take care of him."

The story about the beautiful hippie girl with long blonde hair and a peace sign button who first smiles at, then spits on a young soldier returning from Vietnam, has been repeated so often it's become an American folk legend. I never saw anything like that. What I did see was the awe people in the antiwar movement felt for veterans, especially when they told stories of the jungle war they'd somehow survived.

So out of awe, perhaps more than compassion, we carried Ian upstairs to Meg's bed, and for the next four days, under her direction, took turns caring for him like a newborn, feeding him spoons of applesauce and broth, washing him when in fitful sleep his bladder drained or bowels moved.

Kevin came by each night after his shift stocking shelves at Taylor Market. He talked about meeting Ian during the siege of Khe Sanh.

Like he'd done to the French a decade earlier at Dien Bien Phu, General Giap positioned his army of North Vietnamese regulars and Viet Cong guerillas to cut off all ground approaches to Khe Sanh. By the winter of 1967, the large U.S. base was surrounded. Looking for a definitive military victory, NVA mortars began a continuous bombardment while veteran jungle warriors tested the perimeter. Resupply by air and the will of its American and South Vietnamese Marine defenders were the only things keeping Khe Sanh alive.

Everyone heard the rumor that the American military commander, General William C. Westmoreland, asked President Johnson for permission to lift the siege using tactical nuclear weapons. No one knew what that meant for American troops on the ground, but as the siege continued week after week, most welcomed anything that would put an end to it.

"They'd been shelling us nonstop for three days. A dozen or so of us first and second lieutenants hunkered down in this little underground bunker, dirt falling on our heads every time another round exploded. Some guys are talking, some praying, everybody's scared. And this big guy from Michigan, he starts bawling. I mean really sobbing out loud. Mostly, we're pretending not to hear him. That's when Ian pipes up. 'I've got a carton of Camels here says none of you sopranos can sing your college fight song loud enough to drown out those mortars.' Then he grabs the Michigan guy by the arm, hauls him to his feet. 'C'mon, Wolverine,' he says, 'let's hear your best *Hail to the Victors!*' "

Shakily at first, but prodded by Ian's lopsided grin and encouraging shouts from the other officers, the Michigan fight song carried louder and louder through the bunker, everyone joining in heartily at the end, singing words they didn't know, applauding wildly, pounding the smiling second lieutenant on the back. Then one-by-one each officer stood, defending the honor of his alma mater, sometimes off-color, usually off-key, improvising lyrics about beer, coeds, and rival universities.

"Ian was great. Twice as loud and twice as funny as anybody else, belting out *On Wisconsin*, marching in place, saluting the whole time. He thought he won his own carton of smokes, but he wasn't counting on me."

Kevin waited for Ian to finish before revealing his two secret weapons: a battered Epiphone guitar and an operatic voice that sang the lead in several Wellston musical productions including *Pirates of Penzance*. Accompanying himself on guitar, Kevin upstaged Ian with an unsanctioned, Gilbert and Sullivan-style rendition of *Ever True to Wellston*.

We are ever true to Wellston
'Cuz we love our college dear
And wherever we may go
We are ready with a beer
And the people always say
(Whaddatheysay? a dozen voices called out)
That you can't out-drink Wellston men (And women!)
With a scotch and rye and a whiskey dry
And a B-O-U-R-B-O-N!

When Kevin finished, they realized the shelling had stopped. A cheer went up at the unmistakable sound of a C-141 transport loaded with toilet paper and spare parts, food and ammunition, making its approach and landing on the cratered runway.

"Ian sticks his head out of the bunker then looks down at us, face covered with dirt, grinning that lopsided grin of his. 'The enemy has withdrawn!' he says, 'Guess they couldn't take that Wellston guy's singing!'"

Later, Ian and Kevin shared the Camels, and later still took to sharing everything. Together, they volunteered for another tour, though Kevin couldn't explain why. That's when the Marine Corps surprised them, ordering Kevin stateside to Quantico, Ian to Germany.

"We wrote or called each other every week, making plans for cross-country trips, graduate school, or starting a band. But two months before discharge it's like he disappears. No more letters, no more calls. When I try calling the BOQ at his base everyone acts like they never heard of him."

Kevin wrote their former Vietnam CO, now posted in Germany. He wrote back that one morning Ian hadn't shown up for a staff meeting. They found him lying naked on the floor next to his bunk in the Bachelor Officer's Quarters, his dress uniform neatly laid out on his blanket. The only thing they could get him to say was, "I can't put it on. I just can't put it on."

"I guess our old CO tried getting Ian into the base hospital for the few weeks he had left in his tour, but the sickbay docs said there was nothing wrong with him. He said Ian's discharge was being processed, and he'd be flying stateside within a week."

Kevin got a three-day pass and hitchhiked north to Otis Air Force Base on Cape Cod. On a brilliantly sunny June morning, he stood alongside the runway watching a smoky speck far out over the Atlantic grow until it became the easily recognizable pregnant guppy shape of a giant C-5A Galaxy transport plane. The flight crew seemed only vaguely aware they'd delivered "some jarhead space case," taking twenty minutes going through post-flight routines before opening a cargo hatch. Inside the massive jet, big enough to hold helicopters, tanks, and armored personnel carriers, they found Ian, curled in a ball, completely alone.

"He was dehydrated, hypothermic, terrified. That's how my best buddy, a decorated combat veteran, came home."

Chapter Seven: Paul

On the morning of the third day after Ian's seizure, Toby returned from Taylor Market with tea, honey, and candy bars, and quietly climbing the stairs to Meg's room, found her asleep in the old armchair next to her bed, repeating in her dreams, "It's all right. You'll be okay. We'll take care of you."

On the fourth day, I woke in the armchair finding Ian out of bed, standing over me, covering me with Meg's blanket.

That afternoon, Kevin came to take Ian back to their apartment. Ian was shaky, ten pounds lighter, but looking more peaceful than when we'd met him four days earlier. He hugged me gently, Meg shyly, reserving the biggest hug for Toby who'd patiently done the heavy lifting whenever Ian's clothes needed changing. Then he surprised us with three sentences, more than he'd spoken all week. "I went to college," he said. "On a ROTC scholarship. That's how I wound up in the Marines."

Shaking hands, eyes glistening, we all said goodbye.

After that, we hung out with Meg every day. She joined us for Beef 'n' Bun lunches and pinball, Toby and I joined her for SMC meetings. We felt like brothers—and sister—in arms. Within a month, Toby and I cleared boxes full of *Popular Mechanics* and *Scientific American*s out of our Bowen Street apartment's tiny sun parlor, and Meg, with her boxes full of *New Republic*s and *Rolling Stone*s, moved in. We were always together except when Meg went to SMC leadership meetings or on the rare occasions when we attended class—Meg in the Political Science and English Departments, Toby and I in Physics, Math, and Engineering.

Kevin and Ian dropped by Bowen Street every Friday, Kevin strumming his guitar, his perfectly-pitched tenor leading sing-a-longs of *Runaround Sue* and *The Lion Sleeps Tonight*, Toby and I joining in flat and low, Meg high and sweet, Ian silently lip-synching. Ian's dog, a scrappy golden retriever-border collie cross named Broadway Joe lay next to him on the lumpy sofa, scratching the occasional flea and howling soulfully whenever we strayed too far off key. The he'd jump off the couch and trot into the kitchen where Toby would secretly bribe him with a Hydrox cookie or Pecan Sandy. It was no use though, because except for Ian, I was Broadway's favorite human.

Nothing about the suddenness or intensity of these newfound relationships surprised us. That's how friendships were forged in 1969— quickly, easily, and with unquestioning trust, at least among people under thirty who shared the same hairstyles, clothing, politics, and more often than not, drugs. I didn't know Meg's last name, and I don't think Toby did either. It didn't matter.

Meg's only flaw was her lack of interest in computers. So while Toby and I communed with Bruin, she sat with us quietly listening to WELL and reading the *Wellston Daily Herald* or *Butler Journal*. Sometimes she'd bring a dog-eared copy of *Siddhartha* or *Slaughterhouse Five* and read to us aloud. Sometimes she'd read us eye-opening articles about racism, poverty, and the war. Classmates took to calling the three of us "The Marx Brothers." The new joke in the Physics Department was that no one could tell whether Toby or I was Groucho, Harpo, or Chico. But Meg, obviously, was Karl.

Throughout the winter, despite rising tension and increasingly combative protests, Toby and I continued working with Bruin. Outside of computer linking, our greatest collaboration was on a program we named *Thoroughbred*.

I'd arrived at Wellston convinced that a lack of computing power was the only thing standing between my genius and the creation of a program for consistently picking racetrack winners—computing power Bruin could provide. I piqued Toby's interest by taking him to the track, then hooked him with all those marvelous numbers in the *Past Performances* section of the *Daily Racing Form*. For me, those statistics were useful tools from which we could construct a program. For Toby, they were nothing less than a window into the future, the only place where, as he said, "You can learn from history in order to repeat it." Now, on a chilly March morning, after three and a half years of trial and error, numerous money-losing trips to Rhode Island and its two broken-down racetracks, Narragansett and Lincoln Downs, and four rejected attempts to work on *Thoroughbred* for independent study credit, we were ready.

When Ray Constantino arrived to unlock his newsstand at 5:00 a.m., Toby and I were waiting for him. "Don't you two ever go to school?" he asked as we helped him untie the bundled *Daily Racing Form* the instant they dropped from the delivery truck. While Toby anxiously folded back pages of fresh newsprint looking for the *Past Performances* section, Raymond lit his first Corona of the day, clenching the cigar on one side of his mouth, drinking his morning coffee on the other. I held out a crumpled dollar bill for the paper, but Raymond waved it off, peeling two crisp singles from his own gold-plated money clip instead. "Pick me a winner," he said, palming me the folded bills.

Before sunrise we returned to our keyboards, typing the *Racing Form*'s data into Bruin. Entering the numeric history of each horse's past performances took two hours. *Thoroughbred* took another hour to run the entire nine-race card, weighting and sifting twenty-seven different factors for each of the eighty-six horses racing at Narragansett that day.

At 8:15, as we were ready to print *Thoroughbred*'s results, the computer lab's temperature dropped to 66 degrees, the thermostat kicked on the building's old baseboard heaters, the fluorescent lights flickered.

Bruin's screens went blank.

All of our work, every bit of data we'd spent the last three hours entering, disappeared. *Thoroughbred* disappeared.

Toby bolted upright in his chair. I stood frozen at Toby's shoulder, wide-eyed, holding my breath, too shocked to curse.

Toby recovered first.

"C'mon, Tesla! There's gotta be some way to retrieve it!"

Furiously we took turns typing commands on Bruin's keyboards, discussing options as we worked, communicating as only close friends do, me beginning sentences that Toby completed, Toby mumbling fragmented ideas that only I could understand, trying everything we knew and some things we didn't, all to retrieve *Thoroughbred*. Each of us did what he was best at—Toby tossing out far-fetched options, me reeling them back in, organizing them, making them work. Neither Toby nor I considered giving up, but after forty-five minutes searching Bruin's memory with no sign of *Thoroughbred*, our attempts became desperate, our efforts frantic.

Then Toby said something: "If we could get into the atoms of this machine, we'd find everything!"

"What did you say?"

"I said, if we could get into the atoms...."

And suddenly, *Thoroughbred* reappeared on Bruin's screen with all the data from the *Racing Form* we'd analyzed that day.

Toby sagged in his chair, pulling his beret down over his eyes. I whispered a quiet prayer of thanks to the Computer Gods, and nudged Toby back to life.

At 9:15, an hour after what had seemed like certain catastrophe, *Thoroughbred* printed out four names:

Blue Note

Bam Bam

Sail On Lisa

Tony Anthony

Reading the printout, Toby and I had an odd feeling we'd never before experienced with Bruin. The computer seemed, well, proud. Proud, because with our help, it had resurrected *Thoroughbred*. And proud, because it knew those horses would be winners today at Narragansett.

"Put on your socks and pull up your jock! We're goin' racing!" Toby barreled through the door of our apartment and straight into Meg's room. She sat up in bed, hair falling across her face, raising one fist high above her head, stretching. "Okay," she yawned, "but first I have to find my jock."

The afternoon sky was unusually clear, the air cold and fresh. Silky winter sunlight streaming from the south made shabby Narragansett look as grand as Churchill Downs, the thready grass and harrowed dirt tracks like those at fabled Ascot and Saratoga, and every $1,500 claimer like a direct descendant of Man o' War. But the fans, the fans were pure Rhode Island.

On the macadam apron behind the grandstand, Meg, Toby, and I passed a group of twenty or so middle-age and older men shooting craps. The shooter, down on one knee, clutched a fistful of bills in one hand, a pair of dice in the other. Two lookouts watched for police who knew exactly where the game was, but usually stayed clear.

"I thought this was the sport of kings," Meg said as we walked by.

Toby laughed. "You won't see too many princes here!"

"That's because you guys don't know how to tell frogs from princes," I said.

Inside the grandstand, Rhode Islanders milled about, watching the televised tote board for odds changes, eating hot meat grinders, drinking the creamy milk shakes they called *cabinets*, touting horses, and tipping each other on which owner or jockey had told them, "The fix is in for the seven horse!" Rumor had it there were only two race-tracks in America so crooked that Las Vegas odds makers wouldn't make book on them—Lincoln Downs and Narragansett. None of that mattered to Toby and me though, because none of that mattered to Bruin and *Thoroughbred*.

We cruised by aging touts waving slips of pink and yellow paper filled with "guaranteed winners," making our way straight to the two-dollar window. "Blue Note to win in the first," I said, deepening my voice. Then we took our usual places on the rail at the finish line, awaiting our destiny.

Blue Note, a smallish chestnut mare, went wire-to-wire, going six furlongs in 1:11 and 4/5 seconds, winning by five lengths. Meg jumped up and down cheering while Toby and I feigned calm, acting like two science majors whose lab experiment turned out exactly as we expected.

In the second, Bam Bam, a gangling three-year-old stallion, stumbled out of the gate, trailed the field going around the clubhouse turn, trailed the frontrunner, a gray gelding named Favorite Son, by seven lengths at the top of the stretch. Then Bam Bam got his long legs working together under him, passing horses on the outside, pricking his ears, taking aim at the leader. This time our calm pretense disappeared, all three of us shrieking, "C'mon, Bam Bam! C'mon, Bam Bam!" as he pounded down the stretch, his giant strides eating up turf and closing the impossible distance between himself and Favorite Son.

Waiting for the official result, not sure if Bam Bam had gotten his nose on the wire ahead of Favorite Son, Meg hugged us, refusing to open her eyes until the results were posted and the track announcer crackled through the P.A. loudspeakers, "Ladies and gentlemen, the results of the second race are official. The winner, in a photo finish, is Bam Bam—by a nose!" And with that announcement the three of us began jumping up and down, hugging, Toby shouting, "Never in doubt! Never in doubt!"

We sat out the next five races because *Thoroughbred* had instructed us that they were too close to call. By the time the tape-recorded bugler called the horses from the paddock for the eighth race post parade, we'd calmed down a little, spending some of our winnings on chilidogs and Dr Peppers.

The eighth was the feature race, four-year-old maiden $4,000 claimers going a mile and a quarter on the grass. They were cheap horses that had never won a race, but a touch classier than the $1,500 claimers dominating the rest of the card. Sail On Lisa, a beautiful black thoroughbred with white socks and a white star on her forehead, had been a stakes horse running at Aqueduct, Belmont, and Saratoga until she bowed a tendon in the last race of her juvenile season. Since then she'd fallen on hard times, claimed by a succession of owners, finally winding up here at Narragansett, still without a victory. But *Thoroughbred* figured this New Yorker had way more class than a field of horses who'd never raced outside New England, and the change from dirt to grass would suit her tender ankles.

Sail On Lisa won handily, leaving the other horses fifteen lengths behind, enjoying her first trip to the winner's circle. It was almost too easy.

So far *Thoroughbred* was three-for-three. The only problem was, it hadn't done any better than the pari-mutuel betting pool, picking the same horses Narragansett's regulars had also made favorites. After three winners, the Marx Brothers were up only $20 and the cost of their lunch.

Thoroughbred's pick for the ninth and final race of the day was different. After six years racing the New England circuit, Tony Anthony, a dark bay stallion, had nothing to show for it. Never finishing higher than fourth, which earned him $200 in 1968, he'd lost his last three races by a combined thirty-six lengths. The early line had him at twenty-to-one. The favorite was a crafty old chestnut named Sing Song, who'd won his last three races at six furlongs going wire-to-wire.

But *Thoroughbred* saw something the crowd had missed. In most of his races Tony Anthony broke quickly, then faded badly. In his last race at six furlongs, he reversed form, trailing the field, then passing eight horses in the stretch, making up eleven lengths on the leader. We'd programmed *Thoroughbred* to weight form reversals heavily, and at the longer distance of a mile, it computed Sing Song fading and Tony Anthony coming on strong.

As Toby and I turned from the rail to place our usual $2 bet, Meg called us back. Looking directly in my eyes she said "Put all our winnings on Tony Anthony."

Toby and I were confident in *Thoroughbred*'s choice of Tony Anthony, but we were experienced enough to know he was a long shot for a reason. "Tony's ready, Meg," I said, "but Sing Song's got a lot of speed and three straight wins."

"And $18 buys us three pizzas," added Toby, making the same point in a less theoretical way.

Meg took our hands in hers, turned us toward the post parade. "Look at him," she said. "Look at him."

Tony Anthony was beautiful. But that wasn't the first thing you noticed. The first thing you noticed was his size. He was huge, more like a draft horse than a thoroughbred. He wore nothing but his brown saddle and starched-white bridle—no blinkers or shadow role—the only horse in the field not accompanied by an outrider. Calm as could be, he walked in front of us and stopped. Then, like a knight-errant before the battle, Tony Anthony bowed his head to Meg, and walked on.

Toby turned to me. "Gimme the twenty, Tesla. It's all ridin' on Tony Anthony."

I looked at him, hesitating for a moment before handing over twenty $1 bills. Then reaching into the pocket of my faded Levis, I took out my wallet, removing two more crisp singles. "$2 on Tony Anthony to win. For Raymond."

The starting gate for Narragansett's one-mile oval clanged open directly in front of us. This time Meg was the calm one, expecting victory. Toby and I stood nervously on tiptoes, following the horses as they thundered past. Tony Anthony stayed with the speed horse, Sing Song, running at his shoulder, pressuring him around the near turn and down the backstretch. Sing Song set a blistering pace—six furlongs in 1:11 flat, a track record for the first three quarters of a one-mile race. At the far turn they were neck-and-neck, Sing Song on the rail, Tony Anthony driving on the outside. Pounding down the stretch, clods of dirt kicking up at the field strung out behind them, Sing Song's head bobbed in front, then Tony Anthony's, then Sing Song's. The track announcer's call rose in pitch—*And it's Sing Song and Tony Anthony! Tony Anthony and Sing Song!* Meg was leaping, screaming, "C'mon, Tony! C'mon, Tony!" And without realizing it, Toby and I were doing it too, all three of us jumping and screaming, "C'mon, Tony! C'mon, Tony!"

And maybe, just maybe, that big beautiful horse heard us. And maybe, after a lifetime of losing, he too believed. Because as he flew by us at the finish, Tony Anthony pricked his ears, lunging forward, bobbing his massive bay head past Sing Song's at the wire.

Meg took my face in both hands, kissing me hard on the lips. "And you thought I couldn't tell frogs from princes!" she shouted above the roaring crowd and sudden rushing in my ears.

We waited for review of the photo finish, but didn't need the stewards to make it official. Tony Anthony, the winner, by one flaring nostril.

He paid $34.60 to win, and we finished the day more than $360 richer, our tens and twenties stuffed into my left pocket, Ray's winnings in my right. But before we left Narragansett, Meg insisted on going to the winner's circle, hugging the horse's owner, trainer, and jockey, kissing Tony Anthony on his soft, sweaty nose. And the owner, a sentimental undertaker from Pawtucket who'd stuck with his horse through years of frustration, insisted we join him and his family, posing with Tony Anthony for the official win photo.

Today, Narragansett is a shopping mall, Lincoln Downs, a parking lot. But that win photo sits on my bookshelf next to our picture at the demonstration. It shows me grinning, pockets bulging, Toby clutching reams of green- and white-striped computer paper, and Meg, hands raised high, making the sign for victory, the sign for peace. The picture is a testament, proof that Narragansett once existed, proof we were there, proof we had the time of our young lives.

We caught the next bus to Butler, stopping downtown to deliver Raymond's winnings. "I knew you college kids weren't as dumb as everyone says," he beamed, tossing the change into the Easter Seals bottle he kept on the newsstand counter, tucking the bills into his money clip.

Instead of walking up College Hill to Wellston, we stayed downtown, heading for Maccaluso's, Butler's best Italian restaurant. Celebrating victory, flush with our winnings, the three of us crowded around a table for two in a tiny private room. A glowing candle dripped wax on the red-and-white-checkered tablecloth. Meg and I shared marinated sea snail salad, linguine with red clam sauce and a bottle of Chianti the color of rubies. Toby ordered pizza and Pepsi. For desert,

Carmine, our waiter, brought crisp-crusted cannoli filled with lemon-sweet ricotta dotted with pistachios, compliments of the house.

"To *Thoroughbred*!" belted Toby, raising his Pepsi.

"To Tony Anthony!" Meg answered.

"To the Marx Brothers!" I toasted, Chianti glasses clinking soda bottle.

"To the Marx Brothers!" my best friends replied.

That night I lay in bed thinking about Tony Anthony. Again and again, I replayed the big stallion's thrilling stretch drive, always ending in victory, always ending with Meg's kiss. But as I drifted off to sleep, my last drowsy thoughts weren't about the race or Meg. They were about Toby, my best friend, and what Toby said that morning in our moment of desperation. I can still hear him, as though he were here with me—*If we could get into the atoms of this machine, we'd find everything!*

Chapter Eight: Paul

Toby and I were in love with Meg. There was no doubt about that. And perhaps she loved us, too. But there was no romance or even flirtation between us, because no one wanted to upset the happy balance of our friendship. So as winter became spring without any noticeable difference in the New England weather, it wasn't love that began changing our relationship. It was politics.

While our triad grew stronger, the mountain of American and Vietnamese war dead grew higher, and the ferocity of antiwar demonstrations intensified. Meg came back from each SMC meeting doubting more than ever the possibility that nonviolent methods could end the war.

The equinox brought leaden skies filled with sleet. Meg, Toby, and I returned to Bowen Street from a disappointing afternoon at the Beef 'n' Bun. The machines had beaten us badly, and we were unusually quiet when we found Kevin's letter taped to our apartment door. On United States Marine stationery, he'd neatly printed a short note in indigo fountain-pen ink.

My dear brothers and sister,

I'm sorry to tell you Ian killed himself last night. He rigged a 2x4 from a skylight and hung himself with his web belt. He didn't leave a note.

Between my job and night classes, I can't give Broadway Joe the attention he needs. He always liked you better than me anyway, Paul, so I'm hoping you'll adopt him. If that's okay, I'll drop him by tomorrow.

Don't blame yourselves. He cared for you very much and knew you cared for him, too. It just wasn't enough.

Ian once told me there was something he wanted to give you, Toby, so I put it in this envelope.

Semper Fi,

Kevin

Toby tipped the envelope upside down. A red star fell into his outstretched hand.

Meg stayed in her room for two days. When we knocked on her door she softly said, "Please go away." Our newest roommate, Broadway Joe, lay outside Meg's room, head on paws, unmoving. On the morning of the third day, while we were deciding whether to call her parents, Meg walked quietly barefoot into our living room, sitting down cross-legged between us. Broadway frisked beside her, acting like his old self for the first time since Ian's death. A break in the overcast let morning sunshine through our east-facing bay windows, filling the room with golden rays defined by suspended dust. I remember looking in Meg's gentle blue eyes and seeing something I'd never seen before.

That morning Meg's campaign to get ROTC off the Wellston campus began.

When you sign up for ROTC—the Reserve Officers Training Corps—the government gives you some money for college. In return, you take military science classes, march around the football field, wear a uniform to ROTC functions, and occasionally run an obstacle course.

In the '60s and '70s, you did six weeks of ROTC field training between your junior and senior year. Other than that, you were free to be a regular college student. That was the easy part. The catch came after graduation. That's when you began your two-year, regular army, active duty commitment as a freshly minted second lieutenant. From 1965 to 1972, that often meant you were on your way to lead a platoon in Vietnam. For campus activists, ROTC was an obvious target.

Meg was at the university president's office before 8:00 a.m., waiting there until noon before being told he wouldn't see her. From there she rounded up the SMC leadership, calling for an immediate student sit-in aimed at removing ROTC from campus. They listened politely, discussed earnestly, but in the end agreed that while it was a good idea, it wasn't a priority.

Late that night, Meg sat at our kitchen table, telling us everything that had happened. She'd resigned from SMC and withdrawn from Wellston ten weeks short of graduation. "The war isn't just in Vietnam," she said. "It's here, now. ROTC's got to go, and we're the ones who can make it happen. Frankly, I don't give a damn how it happens, as long as it does happen!"

Toby and I were stunned, and our reaction stunned Meg. Everything about our relationship had led her to believe we'd eagerly join her in anything she proposed. She wasn't expecting discussion, let alone disagreement.

I spoke first. "C'mon, Meg. You don't mean violence?"

"Why the hell not? If there's no ROTC, Ian's in graduate school somewhere instead of a coffin."

While I questioned Meg's means, Toby's response shocked her even more.

"Jesus, Meg, we all cared about Ian. When he broke down, we all stayed with him. I held him like he was a baby while you guys washed the piss and shit off his legs. But blowin' up ROTC or burnin' it down won't bring Ian back or make ROTC go away. Honestly, I don't think it should go away."

He'd said it out loud—blowing up or burning down ROTC. That was still sinking in while Toby continued, on his feet, standing over Meg.

"I went to a military high school, and I hate generals and admirals more than anybody. That's why I don't want all those poor draftee bastards left with only West Pointers and Annapolis pricks in charge. The ROTC guys are the only hope they've got."

We knew Toby was a Richmond Military Institute graduate because he often told us about his recurring high school nightmare, one of the few dreams he and I didn't share. He'd dream he was at the Institute, aware he shouldn't be, but nevertheless trying to get his room cleaned or shoes shined for inspection, praying he'd saved enough bits and pieces of old uniforms so he could dress in the proper uniform of the day when the bugle sounded, *Come and get your beans, boys!,* for first mess. Toby always came to our rooms after those dreams, waking us early, needing our company, needing our friendship to pull him back to the world he lived in now. Those were the only times he wasn't the happy, bear-like Toby we knew. And for hours, and sometimes days, his mood was quiet and somber.

Meg knew that, but her only response was angry silence. He'd hurt her; she was hurting him.

Now it was my turn.

I was born on August 14, four years to the day after Japan surrendered ending World War II. Like most boys of the postwar generation, my childhood friends and I played army using real Allied, German, and Japanese helmets and jackets, canteens and insignia, souvenirs our fathers had brought home after winning the war. I carried the name of my Uncle Paul, missing since the crash of his B-17 Flying Fortress over Nazi-occupied France. Lee, my middle name, came from my father's aunt Leah, who was murdered in a German gas chamber. I grew up with the stories and pictures and horror of the Second World War as a part of my everyday life. I grew up with a haunting question that never went away, was never really answered: *Why hadn't the good Germans done more to stop the Nazis?* Now I was asking myself why I wasn't doing more to stop the atrocities committed by my government against its own soldiers and the people of Vietnam.

"Listen, Toby. Those ROTC lieutenants aren't in 'Nam so they can make things easier on the troops. They're over there to kill people until they get killed—or until they come home like Ian. With ROTC, Nixon's trading tuitions for lives, and as long as ROTC's on campus we're helping him do it. No one's talking about blowing anything up or burning anything down," I said, looking sideways at Meg, "but after what happened to Ian, we've got to do something."

Toby's expression was unusual for him. His face, so young and alive, sagged like that of an old man, and there was the same sadness around his eyes I'd seen on the mornings after his dreams of military school. His voice was unusual too, breaking between words as he struggled to control it. "I know exactly what you're talkin' about," he said, "and you can count me out."

Perhaps because of his military school experience, Toby typically hid behind humor, avoiding commitment to anything. For the same reason, his one unalterable commitment was to nonviolence. I respected and loved him for his gentleness. Because of the history I grew up with, because of the war that began in the shadows when I was in elementary school, growing by my senior year in college into a conflagration that seemed about to consume everyone, because of Ian, I was no longer sure about my commitment to nonviolence. I thought about the night in high school when I heard a TV news anchor saying the death toll of United States soldiers in Vietnam had reached one hundred. What was the body count now? Forty thousand? Fifty thousand? Did anyone even know? Well I knew one thing—I didn't want to be another good German.

And then there was Meg. Toby's feelings were bruised, but he'd bounce back. Meg's hurt was much deeper. I wasn't sure which of my two best friends I agreed with, and unlike them my thoughts about violence were vague, unformed. But in the end I chose Meg, perhaps because I thought she needed me more, or perhaps because I was in love with her.

I still had to give it one more try, though I realized later that I should have waited until Toby and I were alone in the Physics Lab or the back room at the Beef 'n' Bun, waited until everyone cooled off.

"C'mon, Toby," I said, "no one's gonna do anything crazy. Besides, Meg's always backed us. We've gotta back her."

Toby stared at me as though Meg wasn't there. "This isn't about friendship. It's not about who backs who. And I can't do this. Not for you, not for anyone." And turning away from us, he walked out of the kitchen, out of the house, slamming the door behind him.

Meg and I spent the next month visiting dormitories and apartments, teachers and administrators, arguing passionately to anyone who would listen, that ROTC should be banned from the Wellston campus. We talked and talked, through days and nights with little sleep. Students and professors listened patiently and with sympathy, but when it came to taking action against ROTC there was little consensus and less commitment.

For the first time since the day we met on the first day of our freshman year, Toby and I hardly saw each other. We continued our projects on Bruin, but working with Meg made any schedule impossible for me. At the apartment, the Physics Lab, and our home-away-from-home, the Beef 'n' Bun, our paths rarely crossed. After awhile we began leaving each other messages on Bruin, updating and summarizing our newly separate work on computer linking, advising each other about meetings, or simply saying when we'd be having lunch.

Tesla— Review my last entries. I really think I made some progress on the data compression program. Meet me 1700 hours at Beef 'n' Bun for dinner and discussion? Toby

Toby— Data compression program looks good. Ad Hoc ROTC Action Coalition meeting 1730 hours. Can't make dinner. Can you walk Broadway when you get home? Beat the machines for me. Paul

Tesla— Crushed by Joker's Wild. Machines have gained the upper hand. Bruin in open rebellion. Not sure it will leave you this message! Need rescue immed....

Toby— Meg and I meeting with rep from Wellston Trustees tonight.
No time to review latest program changes. Sorry. Be home late. Stay up
and have pizza with us? Paul

Our lives soon fell into this new routine. But no routine could hold
for long when events kept overtaking us and all our plans.

At a time when everyone thought the Paris peace talks were
making progress and perhaps the war's end was at hand, President
Nixon and his Secretary of State, Henry Kissinger, supported a coup
in Cambodia. Lon Nol, the general who replaced Prince Sihanouk, the
leader of Cambodia's monarchy, immediately played his American-
assigned role. On April 30, at Lon Nol's invitation, U.S. and South
Vietnamese troops invaded neighboring Cambodia for the stated
purpose of cutting off Viet Cong and North Vietnamese Army supply
lines. The invasion massively expanded the war, the involvement of
American soldiers, and the bloodshed.

Angry, often violent, demonstrations erupted across the country
and on college campuses in every state. On May 4, Meg and I watched on
television as Ohio National Guardsmen shot thirteen students during
a demonstration at Kent State University. Some were protesters; some
were just walking from one class to the next. Nine were wounded. Four
were dead. On television we heard the names. Allison Krause. Jeffrey
Miller. Sandy Scheuer. Bill Schroeder. The last, a member of the campus
ROTC battalion. We believed the killings were intentional, a message
from Nixon: *Behave, children. Children, behave.*

One after another, colleges called strikes, suspending classes,
exams, graduations, in outraged protest of the Cambodia invasion and
the Kent State killings. Strikers believed all their efforts should focus on
ending the war. Completing courses in chemistry and anthropology,
philosophy and English literature seemed pointless, irrelevant in the
face of mass murder in Southeast Asia and Ohio.

Wellston students voted to strike on the night of May 4. Earlier
that evening in a speech at Franklin Hall, New York Senator Jacob Javits
called for "…an end to U.S. involvement in the Vietnam War, the one
issue which has done more to divide this country than anything since

the Civil War!" After Javits's speech, 3,000 students massed outside Franklin Hall on The Green, a grassy quadrangle surrounded by buildings dating as far back as the first American Revolution. Two lines formed, one yes, one no. The line favoring the strike stretched the length of The Green; the line opposed, half as long.

Meg, no longer a student and no longer entitled to vote, stood with me, holding my hand while I voted "Yes," showing my Wellston I.D. card to the student government representatives in charge. Then we climbed to the roof of Robertson House, watching the eerie lamp-lit election continuing below throughout the night. By a count of 1,895 to 884, the strike was on. On May 5, the Wellston faculty joined its students, voting 247 to 47 in favor of the strike. Final exams were declared optional, freeing most of the Wellston community so we could begin working full-time to end the war. By the morning of May 6, Meg had a newly receptive and galvanized audience of striking students ready to take action against ROTC.

Toby— I typed on one of Bruin's IBM keyboards— *Couldn't find you at home or Beef 'n' Bun. ROTC Action meeting tonight. Meet me at Franklin Hall 2100 hours. THIS IS THE BIG ONE. Paul*

To this day I can't explain why I left that final message. Maybe I hoped Toby would stop us. Maybe I hoped Toby would change his mind and join us. Mostly, I wanted him to be there. If I hadn't sent the message, Toby would have spent a quiet evening with Bruin. Toby wouldn't have come to Franklin Hall, wouldn't have crossed Taylor Street afterward.

Toby would still be alive.

Chapter Nine: Paul

After Toby's death, Meg returned to the SMC, whose members unanimously asked her to represent them on the Strike Steering Committee. She was now a general in an army that had largely deserted. Because of the strike there was no real graduation, just a small subdued ceremony, and by June, most students had left for summer jobs and vacation. Those who remained continued working against the war, but soon Wellston's campus felt like a ghost town.

Cambodia, Kent State, Jackson State. The Strike. The May 9 March on Washington where 120,000 gathered peacefully, protesting the war. At the time, these events and the demonstrations of unity and strength that followed seemed to galvanize student opposition to the war. In fact, they signaled its zenith. Perhaps if those tragedies had taken place in the fall, giving Meg and other activists nationwide three full seasons with a captive audience of students, the movement might have endured. As it turned out, summer's lure was too strong for all except the most committed. By the following fall, troop withdrawals, the prospect of a volunteer army, exhaustion, drugs, and the simple passage of time drained much of the energy from the antiwar movement.

The highest number Selective Service called in 1970 was 195. Toby and I, at 197 and 198, would never have been drafted. The wealthy and well connected, regardless of their lottery numbers, still managed to avoid military service. Nixon, disgraced and driven from office by his orchestration of the Watergate break-in cover-up, would eventually repay a small part of his karmic debt, but that was four years away. Incredibly, the war wouldn't end for another five.

The College of Science held a memorial for Toby in Prospect Park, a small green space at the rundown end of Benevolent Street. On the first warm evening of June, Meg and I, together with a dozen or so of Toby's friends and classmates, stood close by the park's giant statue of Thomas Paine looking south over Butler. The polluted skyline framed the city in fiery sunset, dramatically backlighting our small circle. Dogs growled and tussled at the other end of the park, but Broadway Joe sat obediently by my side. As the evening breeze freshened, carrying with it the smell of fresh-mown clover, a Wellston chaplain led the gathering in the Lord's Prayer, remembered from a time when each grammar school day began with its recitation. Meg and I stood together, faces tight, eyes dry, words unspoken.

The stability of our relationship had been based on the odd-numbered geometry of three. With only two of us remaining, our friendship fell apart. At the summer solstice, Meg moved out of her Bowen Street bedroom and back into the house at number 5 Hope. I left Wellston a week after Meg left Bowen Street, never returning to Butler, Bruin, or the Beef 'n' Bun. I went home to New Jersey with Broadway Joe, but within a few days knew I couldn't remain in the east. Before the turning of the leaves, dog and master made their way to California.

Meg and I stay in touch, exchanging cards each May, from east coast to west, west coast to east. Last year she sent me a photo of herself leaning against the rail at Belmont Park, wavy hair cropped short, a silky mix of spun silver with strands of dark onyx. Neither of us has married. In 1985, a very old Broadway Joe passed quietly in his sleep.

In time I came back to the dream I'd shared with Toby, enrolling at Stanford, earning a graduate degree in a newly minted discipline, Computer Science. IPI, Integrated Processing International, hired me straight out of graduate school. Two years in, I quit, sick of the long hours and sure I could make my living at the racetrack with *Thoroughbred*, my programming skills, and the best computers the era had to offer. Six months later, I was broke and begging IPI for my old job. I guess we just got lucky that day at Narragansett.

Today, I find myself the soon-to-be-retired head of IPI's Internet Innovation Division. My colleagues threw me a surprise goodbye party yesterday and gave me a gold-plated smartphone as a farewell token. I've enjoyed my collaborators and enjoyed my work, year-by-year advancing humanity's digital progress. But the best part of my job has been the time I spend pursuing my own research project without coworkers or supervision. It got two lines in one of IPI's Annual Reports:

Paul Simmons's research into historical data retrieval through Internet electron analysis (HYDRA) is in its infancy, but offers unlimited potential. Commercial applications of HYDRA technology include lost data retrieval, law enforcement computer forensics, and historical research.

I wrote my PhD dissertation on the theory that every entry made on a computer remains fixed in the subatomic matrix of the machine itself. I theorized that, on the quantum level, programming makes changes in the electronic structure of computer hardware, generating a quantum hologram that could be viewed using software I dubbed HYDRA. HYDRA would, theoretically, make any information created on a computer retrievable despite deletions, disc removal, and all other means of data wiping.

The idea wasn't new. Since the early 1950s, psychic researchers speculated that objects in the vicinity of dramatic events make magnetic recordings. Given the proper stimuli, the objects periodically "replay" the events in a manner partially detectable to the senses of observers. This explanation seemed plausible in cases where spectral forms of the ungrateful dead haunted scenes of horrific crimes. Simply put, objects, especially those with magnetic fields, are tape recorders. I argued that this type of electromagnetic taping was more accessible in the case of computers, since the initial events (entries) were already electrical in nature. In my thesis, *The Ghost in the Machine*, I hypothesized that via the Internet, accessing the embedded memories of every computer currently online should be possible.

Of the three professors on my doctoral review committee, one loved my thesis, and one, calling it "fraudulent, facetious, and personally repugnant," threatened to have me expelled. The third had her graduate assistant sign off on it because she was busy writing a grant. On the strength of this shaky two-to-one majority, I barely earned my PhD.

At the party my friends in the Computer Science Department threw for me that night, when they all got a little drunk on rum and Cokes and asked me to stand up and say a few words, I knew who I wanted to thank—

"You've all been great, and I appreciate everything you've done for me—the help with research and typing, the encouragement and support, the No-Doz and coffee. I also want to thank someone you've never met, someone who can't be here tonight. When I was in college a guy named Toby Jessup was my best friend. He deserves this degree as much as I do. Because way back in 1970, he gave me the inspiration for my thesis. In our moment of greatest desperation, when all seemed lost, Toby said, 'If we could get into the atoms of this machine, we'd find everything!'"

Now, at the end of my career, my starry-eyed grad-school thesis is almost a reality. And as I get closer, the dream of that cold, May, New England night comes more often. In the lab HYDRA is a success, retrieving newly erased data from the very atoms of a PC. All that remains is turning the same trick with long-lost entries from a remote computer somewhere on the Net. And for that electronic journey, I know where I'll be going. Back to Butler, back to Wellston, back to Bruin. Back to visit Toby the only way I can.

I log on, beginning my search. I'd read an article in the *Wellston Alumni Journal* about two undergrads who'd discovered Bruin stored in the Physics Department basement, resurrected it, and added internet connections so curiosity seekers could check out the ancient machine. Finding that old colossus doesn't take long. Altered almost beyond recognition, but still there, still Bruin. I initiate HYDRA, and wait.

Program running. Enter date and time of search: *September 23, 1966, 1600 hours.*

Enter password: *Fireball.*

And there we are, Toby and Tesla, typing our first halting entries in COBOL and FORTRAN.

Quickly I scroll through the years. It's all there. The programs. The experiments. The ridiculous course projects. The Engineering Department blackout. The messages: *Tesla— Meet me at the Beef 'n' Bun. Fireball dies today! Toby.* I hardly notice the sunrise over the Sierras through my office window. I see instead lead gray skies filled with sleet. As I used to do so long ago, I spend the night with Bruin and Toby.

Oh man—there's *Thoroughbred!* All of our past performances data for our big day at Narragansett, too! And that's where it disappeared! What were those horses' names? The only one I remember is Tony Anthony. Let's see… the data should reappear in a few seconds. I might be able to figure out why it vanished and how we retrieved it.

Huh. The next entry is from later that day—some grad student running numbers for his physics thesis. Everything else is where it's supposed to be. Weird! Is the real glitch in my memory? Did we print the winners' names *before* the data disappeared? Well, y'know what— HYDRA's a time machine! I'll scroll back, copy the data, scroll forward, and paste it in after the glitch where I think it's supposed to be. I may be messing with the historical record, but who else gives a damn except me. Besides, it's a way better story that way.

Okay… fixed it! A little gift to myself, to Toby, and to my less-than-perfect memory of a perfect day!

I move on. And too quickly, I'm at the end. May 6, 1970. My last entry: *Toby— Couldn't find you at home or Beef 'n' Bun. ROTC Action meeting tonight. Meet me at Franklin Hall 2100 hours. THIS IS THE BIG ONE. Paul.* And Toby's final work, a few more lines on computer linking before he reluctantly logged out, heading for Franklin Hall.

My throat is tight, my eyes damp. A tear slides off my cheek, disappearing somewhere inside my keyboard.

On impulse I type: *Toby— I miss you. Paul*

And instantly a new line appears on my screen: *Tesla— If you miss me so much why don't you get your ass down here and help me with this program? Toby*

I'm too stunned to breathe, tears and throat suddenly dry. I stare at the screen.

Somewhere, somehow, in some subatomic way, have I sent a message back in time to a still-living Toby? Is this possible?

Wait. What about *Thoroughbred*? Did the past performances data reappear all those years ago *because I sent it from the future?*

Think like the computer nerd you are, Tesla, not like some old-fart programmer!

Okay. Take a breath. Someone's messing with you, right? A practical joker. Sure, it's unlikely anyone could hack their way into HYDRA and monitor my work, but not impossible. That could explain this— some IPI young gun's idea of putting one over on the Old Man. Or maybe it's a late-night Wellston prankster.

But Toby's reply didn't come after a pause like it should if someone had read my message and typed a response. It simply *appeared* in the old Bruin memory as though it had always been there, with no time lag between my entry and Toby's reply.

And no one, no one except Toby, ever called me Tesla.

All right, one more test. Something simple, straightforward.

Toby— Is that you? Where are you? What are you working on? Tesla

Tesla— You were expecting Harpo Marx? I'm at the Physics Department working on the computer-linking program. Where else would I be? The question is, where are you, and how are you sending these messages? You've been holding out on me, Tesla! Toby

I sit back, reading Toby's reply again and again, wondering what's going on, picturing Toby waiting for an answer. If some bizarre confluence of HYDRA, Bruin, the Internet and who- knows-what created direct access to the past, science just took one of its rare giant leaps.

But I'm not thinking about science. I'm thinking about Toby. Toby with the black beret and red star. Toby with the wizard's eyes and quick smile. Toby on his way to Franklin Hall to stop a crime. Toby on his way to die.

I can save him. One small change and I can save him.

The dangers of messing with history? Hell, I've read all the science fact and fiction ever written on that subject. For all I know, my *Thoroughbred* hack and first two messages already changed history! And if history has changed, would I be aware of it? As my favorite *Star Trek* engineer, Myles O'Brien, once said, "I hate temporal mechanics!"

But this isn't like saving President Kennedy from an assassin's bullets. Toby was a guy who wanted nothing more out of life than a pizza, a free game, and a powerful computer. And oh how Toby would love *this* world! The world where our computer dreams came true!

The choice is simple. If what I think is happening is really happening, I can save my best friend's life. If I wait, and think, and consult, this doorway may close forever.

Early morning here in California, but for Meg, in New York, the day's half spent. How I wish I could ask her what to do. But I know what she'd say—*Help him. Save him. Give Toby back his life.*

There's really no choice at all.

The keyboard's touch is so familiar I'm barely aware of it. Scrolling back, I look again at the message I left directing Toby to the ROTC action meeting decades ago. Without hesitation I delete the words *Franklin Hall*, filling the empty space before my blinking cursor with a lie. I type a new location, *Burnside House.*

Won't Toby be surprised when no one shows up!

PART TWO

NIGHTMARES

Chapter Ten: Paul

Last night the dream came again. It woke me in a new world, the world my actions helped create, woke me shivering despite Meg's familiar touch, gentle on the rutted scars, despite her warmth and the sweltering Mekong night. I've had the dream ever since that cold, May night. Sometimes a year or more passes without it, sometimes it comes two nights running. Lately it comes whenever I close my eyes, even for the briefest naps.

So many years since that cold May in Butler. In all that time no one has admitted storing flammable CS tear gas in Wellston's ROTC offices. But when our gasoline-filled Molotov Cocktails shattered the building's windows, it exhaled a flaming wind into our young faces.

They say Matt Purdy and Alison Field, the graduate students who joined us, died instantly. Yet as I burned, I saw them fight the flames and lose. Miraculously, their bodies shielded Meg. Otherwise she never could have kicked my legs from under me, rolling me down a grassy knoll, saving my life while burning her hands and singeing her hair.

Campus rent-a-cops arrived first, followed by Butler police. They threw blankets over the bodies, cuffed Meg and me to the chrome bumper of a Plymouth black-and-white. Meg screamed at them, "Take him to a hospital!"

They didn't.

I spent the night naked, untreated, on the concrete floor of a Butler jail. At the 7:00 a.m. shift change, the new sergeant on duty walked by my cell, and seeing me, turned pale, retched, and barked orders at a patrolman.

Later that day, Toby sat by my bed in a windowless room at Butler General Hospital. Images of his visit remain jumbled with pain, delirium, waking nightmares. But I remember the wetness on Toby's cheeks. I remember thinking it must be raining again. I remember Toby, reaching out to touch me, and realizing I was bandaged everywhere, withdrawing his hand. Then, in a hoarse whisper, "I'll get 'em for this, Paul. I swear I'll get 'em."

How strange, I thought, *he didn't call me Tesla.*

The District Attorney dropped all charges against Meg and me the moment my lawyer mother arrived in Butler, demanding the heads of the arresting officers, promising the biggest lawsuit in state history. Recovering from injuries caused by my own actions and the authorities' inaction, took longer.

Meg went straight from jail to my bedside, and except for one weekend when she flew home to see her parents, stayed there until I was discharged a month later. On June 6, a mild, sunny graduation day, she helped me down the hospital stairs and out to Hope Street where Broadway Joe sat barking happily in my parents' waiting Buick. I was going home. Home to Applewood, where Meg and my parents spent the summer taking turns feeding me, washing me, and changing my bandages. By Independence Day, with Meg's help, I could sit on my parents' sun porch watching Broadway play with the neighborhood kids, chasing a Frisbee on Grant Avenue. On August 14, my twenty-first birthday, we celebrated with a carrot cake Meg baked and my first long walk. By Labor Day, I joined the kids on Grant Avenue, tossing my gold Championship Model Wammo Frisbee to Broadway Joe, and on the first cool night of September, Meg said "I love you," and I said "I've loved you since that day at Narragansett when you kissed me *before* kissing the horse," and she leaned across my family's white Formica kitchen table, kissing me for the second time.

The next morning a friend from the Physics Department called. He told us that after graduation Toby used his old military school connections, landing a computer programming job at the Pentagon. We were shocked, but not angry. There was no anger left in us.

All summer, letters to Toby came back unopened, marked *Return to Sender*. His parents responded to my long-distance phone calls with polite promises—"We'll tell him you called." The wedding invitation we mailed wasn't returned, but neither was the RSVP card on which we wrote, "We love you, Toby. Please, please come!"

On an autumn morning so beautiful it filled us with wonder to think God could make such a day, Meg and I were married beneath the rose trellis in my family's yard. Meg, in cascading white satin, night-black hair dotted with late-blooming rosebuds from the garden, without makeup, without doubt, without hesitation, said, "I will."

Even as we promised ourselves to each other forever, the looks on the faces of Meg's parents seemed to ask, *How could our beautiful daughter marry this hideously scarred boy?* But the smiles of the neighborhood kids we'd invited to join the ceremony, the touch of our hands as we slid the simple gold bands on each other's fingers, the pastel blues of the high New Jersey sky, and the deep blue of Meg's eyes washed away all that, leaving only peace.

While our guests ate platters of antipasto, lasagna, and oven-baked Chicken Murphy, Broadway Joe worked the crowd, begging scraps. Kevin, down from Butler with his battle-scarred Epiphone, strolled from table to table taking requests. He serenaded us that day with everything from *Brown Eyed Girl* to *White Rabbit*. And when he came to where Meg and I sat cross-legged on the grass eating scoops of Gruning's French Vanilla ice cream covered with fresh south Jersey blueberries, he sang a slow, soft, *Sugar Magnolia*.

Everyone applauded. Kevin bowed deeply, sliding the guitar to his hip, touching its neck to the hem of Meg's gown. Her father proposed a toast, "To Meg and Paul. May they stay out of trouble!" And before anyone could drink, my father, raised his glass high, adding, "And never stop trying to change the world!"

In the early evening when the last guests said goodbye, Meg and I sat together on the grass beneath the rose blossoms, breathing their delicate perfume, holding hands, talking. Sunset behind maples and elms highlighted the fire on their turning leaves, while Broadway chased after the last of the season's fireflies calling each other with flickering light. The evening grew chill; we held each other closer. And we talked about Toby. His black beret and wizard's eyes, quick smile and endless teasing. Meg cried when I told the story of Toby's Academy Award guerilla theater performance during our marshals training practice parade the night we met Meg on Hope Street. "His acting was only good because of my directing!" she said, and we began laughing, brushing away tears with grass-stained hands until it was time to go inside my gold and brown New Jersey firebrick house, saying, "Good night," and "Thank you," to my parents who'd waited up for us in the kitchen.

Then at last, holding each other, holding each other all night in my old single bed, until the fiery New Jersey sunrise bathed us through the bedroom window.

Chapter Eleven: Paul

I spent that fall and winter volunteering at WFMH, the Hilversum College radio station, and Columbus Elementary School where I'd begun my education. At Columbus, I tutored seventh and eighth graders in math and science. At WFMH, I repaired and upgraded tape decks and turntables. Broadway, who followed me everywhere, quickly became the unofficial mascot at Columbus and Hilversum.

My parents suggested that Meg finish her English degree at Hilversum, but she came home from a visit to the registrar's office with an application for nursing school. "I want to learn something real," she said, and began volunteering at the Applewood Veterans Administration VA hospital the next day. She added a full load of nursing courses in September, but found time to organize fundraisers for WFMH and sit in the Columbus library surrounded by giggling wide-eyed children, as much acting out as reading passages from Dr. Seuss and *Winnie the Pooh*.

We watched the war on the evening news every night, and we grieved with neighbors whose sons returned from Vietnam burned, broken, and strung out, and the ones whose sons would never come home again. But while the war continued, we came to believe our war was over, our life together safe and happy in my childhood home. We woke each morning to the aroma of my father's percolating coffee and went off to bed at night serenaded by the theme from *Hawaii Five-0*, *All in the Family*, *Bonanza*, or whatever hit TV show my parents were watching. We fell into a rhythm, a state of harmony that would last until the following spring, until the day Toby changed the world.

Toby spent his year at the Pentagon rapidly gaining promotion to the highest security clearance levels, learning everything about the government's computers. Coworkers would later recall him as pleasant, hard working, cooperative. On May 7, 1971, one year to the day after the ROTC fire, he wiped clean the memories from the Pentagon's mainframes and disappeared.

Decades later, some call Toby a hero. Most consider him the worst traitor in American history. Perhaps he was neither. Because even though he did it to end the war, did it to save lives, I knew he also did it for me. And Toby couldn't possibly have foreseen the events his act of sabotage would trigger. No one could.

In 1971, the most important function of the Defense Department's computer system was managing material support for soldiers in the field. Controlling from Washington every logistical detail of a war on the other side of the world had been a mistake from the beginning. Now, it was a disaster.

Within days everything began running out. While warehouses in San Diego and Pearl Harbor overflowed with supplies, infantrymen stationed all over South Vietnam in places like Da Nang, Dak To, and Nah Trang had no toilet paper for their latrines, no bandages for their wounds, no bullets for their M-16s. President Nixon called an emergency meeting of the Joint Chiefs, telling them, "Get those fucking supplies to our fucking troops, or I'll have your fucking heads!"

The Joint Chiefs returned to the Pentagon, commanding their computer technicians to take charge of the war's complex logistics. The techs, trained only in how to follow computer-generated orders, began frantically giving orders. With no access to stored data, and using only yellow pads, pencils, and adding machines, overworked, sleep-deprived techs shouted garbled instructions into telephones and cabled contradictory messages to bases and depots around the globe. In seventy-two nonstop hours of work, they dispatched thirty fully-loaded C-5A Galaxy transport planes to Camranh Bay, the giant U.S. airbase in Vietnam, and another thirty empty Galaxies to pick up Vietnam-bound supplies at NATO bases in Europe.

When the first Galaxy landed at Ramstein Air Base in Germany, Air Force ground crews rushed to begin loading the giant plane, only to find its cavernous cargo bay already full. At Camranh Bay, Galaxy after Galaxy touched down with cargo bays that were completely empty.

General Giap, the North Vietnamese Army's strategic genius, seized on the confusion, launching a two-pronged attack. Veteran NVA troops swept southward, while in a repeat of Giap's 1968 Tet Offensive strategy, Viet Cong irregulars struck savagely inside the walls of every southern hamlet and city, including the capital, Saigon. South Vietnam's ARVN soldiers broke first, deserting in panic before the rapidly advancing NVA. U.S. troops fought on, often hand-to-hand, desperately buying time, screaming into their field phones for supplies that never came. Finally, they too began fleeing. But with the NVA pushing south and VC everywhere behind the lines, there was nowhere to run.

The U.S Commander, General William Westmoreland, boarded a helicopter on the roof of the United States Embassy in Saigon, evacuating to the safety of the USS *Enterprise* cruising offshore in the South China Sea. Making one last call to the White House, he begged the president's chief of staff, H.R. Haldeman, to do something. In the background he heard Secretary of State William Rogers angrily shouting at National Security Affairs Assistant Henry Kissinger, and Kissinger screaming hysterically at Rogers. Then Nixon came on the line, shocking the four-star general with his order.

"It was an option we hadn't discussed since Khe Sanh," Westmoreland would write in his memoirs. "But there was so little time in which to decide, we began the operation without giving it a code name. President Nixon loved code names."

From the bridge of the *Enterprise*, Westmoreland ordered the arming and deployment of four B-52 bombers based in Okinawa. As they crossed into Vietnam's airspace thirty-five thousand feet above the

South China Sea, two banked north over the Gulf of Tonkin, laying in a course for the communist capital, Hanoi, and the northern port city of Haiphong. Another flew directly inland for the U.S. airbase at Da Nang, now overrun by North Vietnamese soldiers. The fourth, bound for half-occupied Saigon, was shot down on the outskirts of the southern capital by friendly fire from a panic stricken ARVN surface-to-air missile battery. The three remaining bombers dropped their payloads. Mushroom clouds rose heavenward as nuclear fireballs incinerated Hanoi, Haiphong, and Da Nang, and every living creature within a vast radius of destruction. Radioactive ash rained from the sky.

After that, history changed. While an outraged Congress prepared articles of impeachment, rioting protesters occupied and burned government offices in Washington, San Francisco, Boston, New Orleans, Madison, Memphis, Chicago, and a hundred other cities and towns.

In Butler, students stormed the John F. Kennedy Federal Building. As police and guardsmen fell under a terrifying sleet of rocks and bottles, someone lost control, opened fire. Associated Press newswire photos made two of my old friends briefly famous. Kevin McCabe on the Kennedy Building roof waving an upside-down American flag; Ray Constantino in front of his newsstand, cradling Sarah Bramwell, a Wellston freshman, trying, failing, to stop the flowing blood.

At the barricaded White House, Nixon spent the night of May 17 listening to the sounds of sirens, gunshots, and breaking glass echoing down Pennsylvania Avenue. Henry Kissinger, leaving the State Department in search of the president, found him pacing the White House gallery, talking, arguing, with impassive portraits of Washington, Jefferson, and Lincoln.

At dawn, Nixon convened his cabinet, demanding support for a declaration of martial law and suspension of the Constitution. Instead, led by Health, Education and Welfare Secretary Elliot Richardson, the cabinet unanimously refused. Rising to his feet, screaming at astounded Secret Service agents to "Arrest those traitors!" Nixon, pressing the palms of both hands against his temples, crumpled into his chair. Blood clots from phlebitis in his right calf, shaken loose by age, by stress, by insanity, tiny assassins too small for any Secret Service agent to intercept, end the President's life. The entire drama, down to his last word, "Fuck...." is captured on secret White House tape recorders that Nixon had ordered installed to preserve his every utterance for posterity.

Within the hour, Supreme Court Chief Justice Warren Burger swore in Vice President Spiro Agnew as the 38th President of the United States. Agnew nominated House Minority Leader Gerald Ford, Republican from Michigan, to take his place as Vice President. Agnew's first executive order proclaimed the remainder of May a national period of mourning for the fallen President. His second replaced Henry Kissinger with General Alexander Haig. In response to condemnation from America's allies, threats from the Soviets and Chinese, and violent demonstrations throughout the country, Agnew dispatched Haig to the Paris Peace Talks. His instructions: "End this thing." Vietnam's communists vowed to fight on, but on September 1, Haig and Le Duc Tho, North Vietnam's chief negotiator, signed the papers, shook hands for the photographers. These simple, civilized actions earned them each a share of the Nobel Prize for Peace, a prize Le Duc Tho refused.

Chapter Twelve: Paul

As soon as Meg and I saw the pictures from Vietnam, we knew what we had to do. We had no choice.

Before the seasons turned again, we said our goodbyes, leaving Broadway Joe in New Jersey to live out his days as my parents' faithful companion and protector, leaving our old lives and families forever, leaving for Vietnam.

We volunteered with Healing Hands, a communist-front charity that was building medical clinics throughout the war-ravaged country. Vietnamese doctors didn't want us there, arguing that foreigners with no medical training would be more of a burden than a benefit. Communist Party officials overruled them, hoping the arrival of remorseful Americans would lead to a propaganda bonanza and a torrent of foreign cash. They assigned us to the Mekong River Delta People's Clinic and forgot about us.

For months the clinic wasted time and money treating Healing Hands volunteers for malaria, snakebites, and dysentery. Most returned home, sadder but wiser. Meg and I adapted to our new environment, and proved to be, if not quick studies of medical knowledge, at least eager ones. Meg, with her background in nursing studies and volunteer work at the Applewood VA hospital, won the doctors' trust by day and taught me basic first aid by night. No one expected us to stay, but we did, spending our days fighting losing battles against leukemia, lymphoma, birth defects, napalm burns, and a hundred other horrors. As the clinic's reputation grew, nuclear blast and radiation victims came from everywhere in Vietnam, some walking hundreds of miles. Though prevailing winds saved the Delta from the worst of the radioactive fallout, the place where we lived and worked was still a poisoned land. During the war, the American military saturated the Delta with Agent Orange herbicides sprayed from the air and jellied gasoline napalm bombs dropped from high altitude by B-52 bombers. Their goal was to defoliate vast areas of jungle, depriving the enemy of cover while poisoning its food and water sources. The programs failed, but the tragic legacy of the American chemical weapons campaign lives on. Over half the clinic's patients suffer from Agent Orange-related illnesses or the horrific pain caused by decades-old napalm burns. Thousands of American war veterans, doused indiscriminately from the air, share these afflictions with their former enemies.

So the doctors were correct about us being a burden, at least at first. But the politicians were correct too. Healing Hands became a propaganda goldmine, and its international fundraising efforts brought in tens of millions in hard-currency donations. And there was one more windfall no one had foreseen.

Meg.

In months, her duties progressed from applying Band-Aids to assisting in surgery. She learned everything about the clinic, and everything about Vietnamese history, culture, and politics. She taught herself the intricacies of international fundraising and public relations. While I was struggling with the basics of first aid, the clinic's doctors asked Meg to become its Executive Director. Vietnam discovered Meg; the global media transformed her into an icon. She won the Nobel Prize for Peace. And then she turned it down.

When Meg's not combating bureaucrats in Moscow, Washington, Ho Chi Minh City, or some international relief agency, she tends her patients in the Mekong Delta clinic, her hair, more silver than onyx, roughly cropped around her sun-scrubbed face, her beauty maintained with purpose and commitment rather than lotions and makeup. They call her simply, The Mother. Each day they come from the poisoned rice paddies, and she assures them in ever more fluent Vietnamese, "Doung caw louw. Co houng ca seaw. Theaw louw cha co." Don't worry. You'll be all right. I'll take care of you.

The Vietnamese people survive the way they always have. Like Boxer, the horse in George Orwell's *Animal Farm*, their response to every setback is, *We will work harder.* They accept me because they see, like them, I'm damaged but go on.

Another lasting legacy of Toby's infamy is Section 17 of the United States Code, the Computer Access Security Statute. It sailed through Congress with little political or popular opposition, perhaps because of Toby, more likely because people didn't understand what they were giving up. It barred from that day forward all but a few select corporations and government agencies from developing, possessing, or using computers, allowing access only to those with top security clearance. Within six months, every university in America not involved in defense-related research, voluntarily shut down its computers. Ironically, nothing in that law would have stopped Toby.

Signing the Access Bill was President Agnew's last official act. Two days later, he plea-bargained away the Oval Office in return for dismissal of charges stemming from kickbacks he solicited when he was Governor of Maryland.

The Supreme Court rejected the ACLU's Access Law challenge by a 5–4 vote. Justice Douglas, dissenting, called the law, "...the most grievous limitation of free speech in our nation's history," and, "...a blatant attack on the First Amendment." Justice Rehnquist, Agnew's only Court appointee, wrote for the majority, calling computers, "enhanced adding machines" and commenting, "Surely, not even Mr. Justice Douglas would argue that adding machines have First Amendment rights."

Britain and Japan followed suit. They were scared. Everyone was scared. Soon computers were as rare in the Free World as they had always been behind the Iron Curtain. Computing became the sole province of the military and a handful of corporations. I haven't seen a computer since 1972.

Perhaps these events, the deadly rhythms of history, explain the dream. And why, when it comes, it always leaves me shaken. For thirty years it has remained the same, insisting Toby came to a meeting he never attended, insisting this phantom Toby turned Meg, me, and the other students from our purpose with a single ridiculous sentence, insisting he paid for this intervention with his life.

Despite sporadic media reports of Toby's covert CIA detention, or execution, or death in an accident or by his own hand, I think he's still out there hiding somewhere. If he is, I know he shares the dream with me the same way we shared our dreams in college, and wonders at its meaning like I do.

There's one other dream that comes almost as often. It's a lot like one Toby and I dreamed together in the '60s, only in far more elaborate detail. We're sitting at the Beef 'n' Bun counter. The smell of cheeseburgers sizzling on the greasy grill fills the room. George dumps two plates of crisp, crinkle-cut French fries in front of us. Toby looks up at me, ketchup staining his beard. "Einstein," he says, talking through a mouthful of half-chewed fries. "Definitely, Einstein." He holds up a shiny palm-sized device, and begins sliding an index finger vertically across its shimmering screen. I stare, as images scroll upward with the motion of Toby's finger. First, the iconic photo of the brilliant Jewish physicist, silver hair askew, smiling enigmatically, captioned with the words, "Greatest Genius of All Time." Then six equations that changed the world: Einstein's Nobel Prize-winning photoelectric equations, the basis of quantum mechanics, which led to the development of semiconductors and integrated circuits.

I'm stunned, but recover quickly. "Yeah? Well that's their opinion. But Tesla…."

Toby removes his finger from the device's screen, silencing me with a wave of his hand. Then, his smile mirroring Einstein's, he looks past me into the Beef 'n' Bun's crowded dining room. I turn, following his gaze.

At every table, diners sit holding devices similar to Toby's. Some, as Toby had done, are scrolling through text. Others appear to be typing with their thumbs. Still others are speaking into them or listening absentmindedly through tiny earplugs. That's when it hits me. They're computers! Impossibly tiny computers linked in some way that allows them to communicate with each other and share data at near light speed.

I look at Toby in delighted disbelief. His smile broadens into a grin.

"Einstein," he says. "Definitely, Einstein."

I love this dream.

Meg has grown impatient with my retellings of the dream where Toby stops our three-decade-old crime, but never tires of hearing the computer dream. *Nerds in Paradise*, she calls it. When we walk along the Mekong at sunset looking up at the South Asia sky, I often tell its high-tech story. And when I see the Southern Cross's first star shining in the dusk, I always wish the same wish. Silently, upon the star, I wish that wherever Toby may be, he shares this dream.

After all, we always dreamed that one day, we'd change the world.

PART THREE

MELORA

Chapter Thirteen: Melora

My war began a lot like the one in Vietnam. I didn't know it, because back then I didn't know shit about Vietnam.

Professor Sherman tried to warn me. "I'm telling you, Melora, this Indonesian war, it's turning into a quagmire. Before it's over, we'll all have blood on our hands!"

I had no fucking clue what he was talking about.

It all started when some psycho Indonesian general named Hasan got tired of waiting for the elected president to finish her term, so he arrested her. The CIA backed Hasan because the president was a socialist, but Indonesians backed the president because they'd elected her. China backed her too, so they could stir up some shit. No one believed General Hasan when he promised, "…new elections as soon as our homeland is stabilized."

Demonstrators filled the streets outside the presidential palace— the *Istana Merdeka,* or "Freedom Palace"—in Jakarta. After a couple of weeks, that *cabrón* Hasan got tired of the demonstrators keeping him awake at night and ordered riot police to clear them out. The demonstrators threw rocks at the police, so the police tear-gassed them, and when they tossed tear gas canisters back at the police, the police opened fire. When it was over, twenty-two protesters and three cops were dead. At least those are the official numbers.

On the record, U.S. officials called for restraint. But the tear gas choking the crowds? Made in the U.S.A. The rifles fired by Hasan's thugs? Pentagon-issued M-16s. The bullets mowing down the protesters? As American as apple pie. The general was making a lot of Americans rich. Powerful Americans. So he wasn't worrying about U.S. calls for restraint. Why the fuck would he?

Next came arrests of opposition leaders, suspected agitators, and anyone who'd ever pissed off Hasan. That's when the opposition went underground, got a bunch of AKs and RPGs from China, took the name Red Path, and launched a rebellion. Hasan held a press conference. "My government and the Indonesian armed forces will crush Red Path," he said, "and unlike those traitors, we will achieve victory without the need for foreign assistance!"

His speech was on TV. Somewhere. But I didn't watch it. No one did. I do remember TV's talking heads laughing the whole thing off, calling it the "Rumble in the Jungle."

Then the rebels attacked three provincial capitals, Medan, Pekanbaru and Jambi, Hasan asked the U.S. for help, and President Harriman ordered the Pentagon to deploy a few hundred military advisors. Harriman said, "We have a moral obligation to help the Indonesian people protect their democracy from Chinese-sponsored aggression." That "...after losing Vietnam, Cambodia, Laos, and Chile to communism in the '70s, Angola, Afghanistan, Nicaragua, and El Salvador in the '80s, Somalia, Malaysia, and Venezuela in the '90s, and with Indonesia the next domino waiting to fall, it's time America takes a stand!"

As soon as they got there the advisors called in U.S. air strikes against the rebels, so the rebels ambushed the advisors. Killed a bunch of 'em, too. That's when Harriman sent twenty thousand American boys and girls to protect them. Then sixty thousand. Then a hundred sixty thousand. And finally, Operation Righteous Sword, the Allied Expeditionary Force, an occupying army of half a million.

No one's laughing now.

Sure, there were critics. I remember Senator Wayne filibustering "War Hawk Harriman's" defense spending bill, pounding her fist on the podium, saying, "This war, like every modern war, is about oil!" She kept it up for three days, but when she crumpled into her seat the Senate voted 98-2 to give Harriman the money and let him fund his war.

I wasn't into politics. Still, when Harriman said our security was at stake I believed him. I may not be all red, white, and blue, but I am a U.S. Navy veteran, and I am an American. I was afraid that without our boots on the ground, China would be tempted to use nukes like the Russians did in Afghanistan. And how could America bitch about a couple of tactical nukes shoved up General Hasan's ass? I mean we're the ones who let that genie out of the bottle—Hiroshima, Nagasaki, Hanoi, Haiphong, Danang.

Pacifists, liberals, and old hippies screamed that Indonesia would become the next Vietnam. They'd been screaming that every time Uncle Sam went to war since Vietnam. But they were wrong about Panama, wrong about Haiti, wrong about Kuwait, wrong about everything. Wrong because the White House and the Pentagon learned some important lessons in Vietnam: keep the airpower overwhelming, keep the American body-count low, keep the media rooting for our side. And most important? Keep our all-volunteer military so it's always someone else—or someone else's mother, father, son, daughter, husband, or wife—who has to do the fighting.

So this time, like with the boy who cried wolf, everyone ignored the peaceniks. A march here, a demonstration there—they couldn't even get covered on the nightly news. Only this time they were right. With its heat, humidity, jungles, snakes, bugs, and malaria, Chi-Com supplied guerillas and U.S. supported dictator, Indonesia wasn't the next Vietnam, it was Vietnam all over again. More U.S. soldiers and Indonesian rebels killed each other every day, and every day more Americans realized what Harriman and the Pentagon couldn't admit— no matter how you spun it, none of America's victories had prepared us for a full-scale civil war in the jungles of Asia.

When the Indonesian war began, the network evening newscasts instant-replayed the fighting on videotape. Now, thanks to IPI technology, they broadcast it on TV in real-time. They always start with the bag count—

At dawn, Red Path guerillas killed sixteen AEF Troopers in a savage ambush twenty kilometers south of Jakarta. IPI Operations Officers and RITA are responding with air strikes, and sources report over two hundred militants killed. The following real-time video is the exclusive property of IPI, official sponsor of the Allied Expeditionary Force.

War's expensive. So the only surprise was that it took the Pentagon so long to come up with the idea of selling corporate sponsorships. It works for football stadiums and NASCAR, so why not sell ads for war? IPI's happy to pay for the privilege of plastering its logo on the uniforms of America's fighting men and women, selling patriotism and software in one package. Best of all, they make way more money from the war than they spend supporting it. So what if Vegas lays odds on the daily bag count? Who cares if underground gamers stream the live feed on black-market consoles, keeping score? What difference does it make if a bunch of pervs get their rocks off watching history's first live snuff flick? IPI's making money off that, too.

Good ol' IPI—thy Net is America's salvation!

IPI is shorthand for Integrated Processing International. Hardly anyone uses its real name anymore. Hardly anyone remembers it. But everyone knows the United States couldn't fight the first remote-control war without computers. And ever since the '70s when Congress passed the Computer Access Security Statute, or *C-ASS*, as programmers like to call it, there ain't no computers without IPI.

And RITA? Well, that's on me.

An all-volunteer professional military made it easy for the politicians to get us into this mess without much opposition, but it couldn't have continued for seven years—and counting— without the Temporary Reinstated Draft. Nixon got rid of the draft so he could cut the legs out from under Vietnam War protesters on college campuses. If I don't have to go get killed, who gives a shit, right? And for a while after Vietnam there was no draft. Then in the '70s, President Carter started

Selective Service back up, telling teenagers they had to register, promising they'd never be called because there were plenty of volunteers.

Under C-ASS—no computers for anyone except the military—it looked like local draft boards would be making their lists the old-fashioned way. On lots and lots of paper. Then Congress started handing out exemptions to everyone from university researchers to uniform designers, anyone who could show a link between their work and homeland security. Next came banks, stockbrokers, and credit bureaus that could show a link between their work and big fucking campaign contributions. With IPI lobbying Congress, Selective Service, an agency with no job and no purpose, had no trouble getting its C-ASS exemption plus a billion dollar budget to carry out its non-mission. And what did IPI get? The whole shooting match outsourced to it as a private contractor. Oh, and $122,900,000. Working for IPI's Selective Service Division in those days must have been great. No draft, so nothing to do all day except collect your paycheck and play with your fuckin' hard drive.

In the first Iraq war, with no help from draftees, Desert Storm volunteers kicked Saddam's ass. When the volunteers came home sick, the VA doctors stuffed Prozac down their throats and told them it was all in their heads. They called it Gulf War Syndrome, and it was a big deal. Then the media forgot about it, and so did everybody else. In the next Iraq War, Operation Iraqi Freedom volunteers kicked Saddam's ass again, way worse than the first time. But some Iraqis had other ideas, and the war dragged on for years after Bush's aircraft carrier "Mission Accomplished" photo op. Soldiers, sailors, pilots, marines, reservists, and National Guard volunteers who'd completed their service were forced back into combat by catch-22s. I mean, who knew you actually had to read all that shit the recruiters made you sign? As long ago as that war everyone knew we couldn't protect our friends—or spread our empire— without a draft. But no one, and certainly no politician, wanted to admit it.

When the next war—my war—came in Indonesia, there weren't enough volunteers. That's why Harriman called for "temporary" reinstatement of the draft, the TRD. Congress debated for a couple of months, but in the end they gave him what he wanted. Like there's anyone in Congress who's got the balls to vote against keeping America safe.

Thanks to Selective Service every city in America already had an electronic draft board up and running with long lists of girls' and boys' names turned into ones and zeros. And thanks to IPI, the only paper you can find at Selective Service is toilet paper.

The TRD, IPI, and RITA keep the war going. That's a whole lot of fucking initials for Murder Incorporated. The TRD serves up fresh young bodies, replacing ones burned and broken by Red Path mines and mortars in the countryside, IEDs and suicide bombers in the cities, and friendly fire everywhere. IPI's software guides the missiles, navigates the ships and planes. RITA runs ops, ordering draftees where to go, who to kill, when to die. Together, IPI and RITA fight virtual war from the safety of an ivy-covered New England corporate campus, spilling real blood with virtual ones and zeros, confident no hacker can mess with their net.

Yeah, they're confident. And dead wrong.

Chapter Fourteen: Melora

I should thank IPI. IPI and the U.S. Navy. If it weren't for them I'd be just another e-virgin. Because when I was growing up, C-ASS was fucking strict. No exceptions. So how John Paul Jones Academy, a private naval high school, managed to wangle an old IPI 700 computer out of the Navy, I'll never know. I don't like thinking about how bad my life would have sucked if they hadn't.

When I dropped out of St. Francis High—well shit, it was more like I stopped dropping in—my friend Coop started sneaking me into the academy library so I could hang out with him while he re-shelved books. He was taking a big risk, because the academy, an all-boys school, didn't allow girls on campus. The retired navy and marine officers who ran the place figured there was only one reason a cadet would invite a girl in for a visit, and parents weren't shelling out big bucks for their teenage sons to become baby daddies. But Coop didn't sneak me in for sex. He snuck me in because he wanted me to meet the 700.

Coop showed me a few things a Navy CPO taught him about programming—mostly boring navigation shit—but the first time I touched the keyboard, I was hooked.

Coop felt bad because he thought it was his fault I dropped out. It wasn't. The asshole surfers and skateboarders at St. Francis High targeted me long before I started hanging out with a seaweed sucker from John Paul Jones. Sure, they hated cadets because cadets were different, walking around St. Francis in their dress blue uniforms, not because they wanted to, but because the academy made them. And because *civvies*, as academy kids called the locals, thought cadets were rich. That's pretty fucked up if you think about it—the locals hated me because I was poor.

The ocean. It dominates everything in Florida. The state's west coast, the St. Francis side, borders the Gulf of Mexico. Shelter islands—St. Francis Key, Largo, Clearwater Beach—separate the mainland from the Gulf, creating an inland waterway of saltwater bays. The Gulf is *my* ocean. My mother, Tammy Jo Kennedy, even claims she bathed me in it when Pinellas Water and Electric cut her off for not paying her bills. She's told the story a million times—

"The lowest I've ever been. No light, no water, no husband, no money. And me, all alone with two babies—well Joey wasn't such a baby anymore, but little Melora? Still in diapers and crying all the time. Wouldn't sleep, wouldn't nurse, just cried and cried and cried. I thought there was something wrong with her. But with no money, how could I take her to the doctor? And how could I leave a sick baby to go look for work? And smell? I'll tell you, that baby girl smelled like a pig in church! With no running water in the house, what could I do? So I took that child down to Palm Boulevard, stuck my thumb out—I swear three cars slowed down, then speeded back up when they got a whiff of Melora—hitched out to the beach at St. Francis Key, borrowed a little soap from the bathroom at the Arco station, put my baby in the ocean and scrubbed her down from Albania to Zanzibar! And sweet Jesus, the instant her little toes got in the surf she stopped crying. And by the time she made it in up to her chin, strike me dead if there wasn't a big old grin spreading across her face like silage in a hog trough. I tell you it was a gift from God. So you know what I did? I baptized her right there on the spot. Did it myself—Melora Ocean Kennedy. The middle name? It just came to me. Tammy Jo's thank you to God for making my little girl smile! And there must have been something to it, because from that day on, the only time she's happy is when she's in her ocean!"

Like all Tammy Jo's stories, this one's filled with heroism and inge-
nuity in the face of great suffering, praise for God, reference to herself
in the third person, and bad similes. Like most of her stories, it's probably bullshit. I do remember times without water, times without heat
and light, but I can never remember my mother without an expensive
perm and tint, without makeup, without polished, shiny nails and a
short skirt, without a boyfriend. I also can't remember being happy
except when I'm in the Gulf. The smell of salty air, the grit of hot, white
sand between my toes, the way ocean water holds me, weightless and
warm. I live for that shit.

No one taught me how to swim. I've always been able to breast-
stroke, backstroke, Australian crawl, doggy paddle. Always. My earli-
est memory? Swimming in the surf at my fourth birthday party while
mom, mom's latest boyfriend, and Joey eat cake on shore. At six, I was
kicking twelve-year-old Joey's butt in swim races. At ten, I swam out so
far I couldn't see St. Francis Key's hotels, couldn't hear the surf pounding into the beach, couldn't understand why everyone was hysterical
when I bodysurfed to shore near sunset. They thought I was trying to
kill myself, though no one wanted to come right out and say it. And
when I was fourteen my high school P.E. teacher, out for a day at the
beach with his family, saw me churning through the surf, asked me to
try out for the swim team, guaranteed me a spot. I never showed. *What's
the point?* I thought. *They swim in pools.*

We lived on the second floor of a run-down, clapboard tenement
on a side street half a block off Palm Boulevard, St. Francis's main east–
west strip. Some days in spring and fall the sun rose up from one end
of Palm and set at the other like it was tied to a string anchored in our
living room. A month before my eleventh birthday, I woke to that sun
shining in my eyes through the living room's louvered Florida windows.
Loud voices were coming from the kitchen, and though I couldn't hear
the words clearly, I knew I had to make myself smaller on the couch
where I'd been sleeping, make myself disappear into its lumpy cushions.
The voices kept getting louder until they were screaming. I covered
my ears but heard the crash of the kitchen table overturning, dishes

smashing against the wall and floor. Then mom came out to the living room screaming curses into the kitchen at Joey, dragging her jerk-off boyfriend behind her, his hands clutching his bleeding, busted nose. She pulled him out the front door still screaming, slamming it behind her.

Joey came out of the kitchen a moment later, shaking but under control. "Mel," he said, managing a wink, "I guess we're on our own."

He was only sixteen, but Joey got a second shit job, and then a third, and kept us in our apartment, making enough money to pay the electric bill and put food on the table. Coming up the peeling, white outside stairway one day, pounding on the door because he forgot his keys, getting no response from me, Joey was the first to realize there was something wrong with my hearing. The savings from his shit jobs weren't nearly enough to pay for a medical exam, so he hooked up with some gangster and hustled coke to the rich kids at St. Francis College until he made enough for the doctor and the pale, beige, plastic hearing aid the doctor said I needed because of the slap mom's boyfriend gave me a week before they moved out. I've worn it ever since, even when I didn't have the money for fresh batteries, even years later when I was wealthy and could afford to replace it with one that's better, smaller, closer to the color of my skin.

My hearing was the first thing that got me bullied in school—*She ain't deaf, she's fuckin' dumb!* Then it was my dark Latina looks, the only thing I inherited from my father—*What's another name for Cubans? Saltwater niggers!* My cut-offs and tee shirts, hand-me-downs from Joey, didn't help either—*Hey Diesel Dyke, you lookin' for the men's room?*

Joey always took care of me, but he was only sixteen and working three jobs. He didn't have time to be my substitute dad, and soon he became a dad himself. At twelve, I was an aunt.

It was way later when I first met Coop, early in my senior year in high school. He was sitting at a booth opposite my table at Belasso's Pizzeria working on a large pepperoni, reading the latest *Avengers*. I was taking my time before I ordered, enjoying the aroma of tomato paste, fresh-baked dough and garlic, letting it build my appetite. By that age I'd adjusted to the idea my skin color would get me served last almost everywhere in St. Francis. That wasn't a problem at Belasso's though, because I was their best customer. Mr. Belasso, the owner, even let me wait tables for tips and free pizza. He was at his usual place behind the flour-covered counter, soiled white apron cinched up under his armpits, black plastic glasses balanced at the end of his nose, reading the *Daily Racing Form*. He didn't come over to take my order, but he wasn't a racist. He never took anybody's order. If you wanted pizza, you had to go to Mr. Belasso. I was about to do that when the door jingled. Three girls—*blancas* from my English class at St. Francis High—came in, and spotting Coop in his dress blues, slid over to his booth.

"Hey, seaweed sucker, when's the last time you saw a real girl?"

Coop ignored them. Kept eating, kept reading.

"Maybe it's true what I heard about you academy faggots? That you'd rather do it with each other?"

Still no reaction from Coop.

The middle one, the blonde *puta* who'd been doing the talking, went down to her knees across the table from him, putting herself at eye level with his dick, pulling out a cigarette, waving it in his face.

"Hey, queer bait, got a match?"

Coop looked up.

"Yeah. My farts and your breath."

I had to admire his style. So before Blondie could react, I called out, "Hey, you can get off your knees."

Blondie turned, looking at me, recognizing me from school.

"Oh yeah, island beaner," she said. "Why's that?"

"Because he knows when he's licked."

Coop laughed.

All three girls started toward my table.

Mr. Belasso looked up from his racing form.

"You girls buy some pizza or get the hell out!"

They must not have been hungry, because they hesitated, then headed for the door.

"Hey, thanks," Coop said.

"No big deal."

Coop laughed again, his head tilting left, half way to his shoulder. "What's your name?"

"Melora Kennedy."

"Hey, Melora, I'm Dave Cooperman. But everybody calls me Coop."

I nodded. He looked down at his comic book but quickly looked up again.

"Uh, hey, Melora?"

"Yeah?"

"You want some of this pizza?"

"Pepperoni?"

"Uh-huh."

"My favorite."

And that was the beginning of our friendship.

We hung out together a lot. On weekends, when Coop got liberty, we went and did the only things St. Francis teenagers without much cash could do—movies, pinball, pizza, and Pepsi.

St. Francis isn't like Miami, with its royal palms and rich retirees. It's run down and always has been. The palm trees look like they've got cancer, and the only old people who wind up there are the ones whose Social Security checks are so small they can't go anywhere else and still be warm in winter. I never cared that there was nothing much to do, because until I met the academy's IPI 700, I wasn't interested in much of anything other than the beach. Besides, sitting on the railroad tracks near the academy, sharing a pizza or half-a-dozen White Castle burgers, me and Coop always found plenty to talk about.

Coop told me how he'd grown up rich in a big old Victorian house on the corner of Napoleon and St. Charles in New Orleans. Then one fall day a couple of weeks after his fourteenth birthday, his father put him on a bus for St. Francis and John Paul Jones. There was no hug, no explanation, barely a goodbye. He stayed with his grandparents in Mobile for Thanksgiving. No one told him about his parent's divorce until Christmas.

The first two years at the academy he'd been scared and homesick. He didn't like talking about those times but told me enough, painting pictures of a lonely, violent campus where underclassmen might be treated to a toilet bowl swirly or midnight blanket party—a beating given under a blanket so the victim couldn't I.D. his attackers.

"It was like *Lord of the Flies*," Coop said, "only the grownups weren't interested in rescuing us."

His third year had been better, and now that he was a senior and a cadet officer, with graduation a few months away and college tuition guaranteed by his father's court-ordered support payments, Coop finally felt safe.

Coop's friends accepted me as one of the guys, once they got over their disappointment that I didn't have any girlfriends to fix them up with. And while they were good company, for me, anything I did in winter just killed time until it was warm enough to get in the ocean. Tourists from up north hit the beach all winter, but I always waited until March, when wind and water temperatures climbed together into the 70s. In the meantime, I filled my winter nights with vivid ocean dreams of warm sun, hot sand, and gentle surf. In the mornings, I woke disappointed the dreams weren't real but feeling excited that they soon would be.

When spring came, me and Coop began a new routine. Every Saturday at noon I caught the uptown Palm Boulevard bus. Ten minutes later Coop flagged the driver on the corner of Cyprus and Palm, climbing the stairs, paying his fair, dropping breathless into the seat next to me.

"Hey, Mel," he'd say.

"Hey, Coop," I'd answer.

John Paul Jones reserved Saturday mornings for special tortures—room inspections, personnel inspections, practice parades—and Coop couldn't get out on liberty until twelve. But he ran the long blocks from the academy, officer's cap pushed back on his crew-cut head, black tie flapping behind him. And he never missed the bus.

It sucked when civvies got on the bus and hassled Coop, or when Screwy Louie—a St. Francis crazy who looked and smelled like the Wolfman—joined us on one of his bus-tripping joy rides. At least Louie kept us entertained, shouting swear words and farting whenever the spirit moved him. His favorite expression was, "Blaaaaaaaah—PUSSY!" Coop's roommate, Jim Goldfarb, declared March *Screwy Louie Awareness Month*, composing a song to the tune of *Louie Louie* in his honor—

Screwy Louie, oh baby, we're aware of you
Screwy Louie, oh baby, you've got hair on you!
On the bus or at the park
No one's safe after dark
Because of Screwy Louie
Oh baby, we're aware of you
Screwy Louie, oh baby, you've got hair on you!
The Chamber of Commerce won't take action
'Cuz you're their biggest tourist attraction
Well, Screwy Louie….

Most of our rides west over the toll bridge crossing Boca Grande Bay were quiet and uneventful, except for getting off the bus on St. Francis Key where Palm Boulevard ends and the Gulf of Mexico begins, blue-green, shimmering, endless. That view always got us stoked.

We changed into our swimsuits in the bathrooms at the Bonair Beach Hotel's restaurant, hiding our clothes in steel cabinets where the hotel stored extra soap and paper towels. The rest of the day we spent in the Gulf, swimming, body surfing, and floating on our backs, faces turned up at the burning sun. After an hour or two in the water we'd take a break, walking the beach looking for shells, eating candy and potato chips from hotel vending machines, or lying in the hot sand. But we never stayed dry for long.

When the sun got low out over the Gulf, we'd sneak illegal dips in the Bonair's *Guests Only* fresh water pool, rinsing salt from our bodies, changing back into the clothes we'd left in the restrooms, drying ourselves with paper towels. Whenever Coop's grandparents mailed him a few extra bucks, he'd treat me to a steak or a chef's salad in the restaurant. When they didn't, I'd buy us hot dogs and sodas on the beach.

Liberty ended at 11:00, but we stayed on St. Francis Key every minute we could, catching the 10:30 bus so Coop wouldn't get in trouble. When it was time to leave, Coop always got real quiet. He hated going back to the academy. By the time I'd get home, Joey was out working the night shift, cleaning floors and emptying trash at St. Francis Junior College. My six-year-old nephew, Darin, would be asleep in our one bedroom. But Joey's wife, Diana, stayed up late, smoking cigarettes, ready to talk about the day. So I didn't hate going home the way Coop did, but I did hate leaving the beach.

During the week I went to school. In the afternoons, I waitressed at Belasso's. On nights when Joey and Diana both worked, I babysat Darin, making sure he was in bed by nine, getting him ready for school in the morning. Except for school, my weeks didn't suck. But I lived for my weekends at the beach with Coop.

Chapter Fifteen: Melora

By the end of March, me and Coop had our Saturdays down to a science—bus, beach, Bonair—and soon, sun, wind and water made Coop's skin almost as dark as mine.

On the first Saturday in April, I got up early so I could play with Darin for a while before catching the bus. By 8:00 the temperature was already in the high 70s, promising today we'd get a taste of the kind of heat and humidity that normally didn't come until summer. Joey and Diana surprised me by not sleeping in. For once they were up before me, moving around the kitchen, smoking cigarettes, washing dishes. They were awfully quiet, like they were when they'd had a fight the night before.

After breakfast, me and Darin went downstairs to the weedy lot in front of the apartment, playing tag, and hide and seek. I brought a duffle bag holding a towel and my only bathing suit and dropped it on the sidewalk. The sun kept rising, smaller and hotter. When it was nearly overhead, and drops of sweat sliding down my legs began feeling like tiny ants crawling up, I knew it was time to get Darin inside and head for the bus stop.

"C'mon, Darin, time to go in."

"Aw, Mel, can't we play a little longer?"

"Nope. I've got to get going if I want to...."

My words were cut off by the sound of a closing car door and cheery "Hello!" It was my mom, pretty in a floral print sundress and white high heels, hair streaked blonde and permed curly.

"Hello," she called again, as Darin and I stared at her coming up the walk. I'd seen her often enough in the last six years, knew she married a University of South Florida professor, was living with him in Sarasota. But I never expected to see her here, didn't have time to see her now.

"Look Mom, Joey's in the house. I gotta go."

Her spike heels had been clicking on the cement walk as she came toward us, arms outstretched for a hug. Then she stopped, looking puzzled.

"Melora, honey, didn't Joey tell you?"

"Tell me what, Mom?"

"Well, with Diana expecting a new baby and all..."

New baby, I repeated in my head, but the words didn't make sense yet.

"...that it would be better if you moved in with me."

I looked at Darin, who suddenly started crying. Then back at the apartment toward the sound of a slamming screen door.

"We were going to tell you, Mel. Mom wasn't supposed to come until tonight."

Looking over my shoulder at Joey and Diana standing on the peeling white stairs, pushing at my hearing aid with one hand, I watched Joey's lips carefully, making sure I understood him. Then I turned to mom.

"You gotta be fucking kidding me," I said.

"Melora! You know how I feel about cussin'!"

"Yeah, because you're so fucking high class."

I turned to Darin, avoiding mom's eyes.

"I gotta go," I said, snatching up the duffle bag, pushing past mom.

"Mel, wait!" I heard someone yelling, but I kept walking as fast as I could without running. With my head turned away, I couldn't tell if it was mom or Diana, but for the longest time I heard crying, and knew it was Darin.

The bus was late that day, but when it came I got on, thinking, *Thank Christ they didn't follow me!* Everything would be okay when I got to the beach, when I could tell Coop, when I could let the surf wash off the way I felt. The driver looked at me funny but said nothing. I knew I was crying, but didn't care. I sat on the right side window seat where I could spot Coop when he came running down Cyprus, hat back, tie flapping, waving for the driver to stop.

Thinking about Coop made me feel calmer. After all, wasn't his family even more fucked up than mine? He'd understand. And together we'd figure out what to do. I could live on the beach. I could run away. But I didn't need—didn't want—to think about that yet. I just wanted the blocks to fly by, wanted to see Coop flying down Cyprus toward the bus.

But as the bus approached Cyprus, went by without stopping, I didn't see Coop, didn't see anything at first except flat black asphalt and a fuming heat mirage of pooled water. Looking over my shoulder toward the corner, the mirage cleared and I noticed a group of blue-uniformed cadets standing on the bank of the concrete drainage canal paralleling Cyprus, the one they called Piss Creek. I didn't know what was happening, but I knew I had to go see if Coop was in that crowd.

Pulling the signal cord, I grabbed my duffel, moving to the steps as fast as I could, almost falling when the bus stopped short at the next corner. I jumped from the steps, running back down Palm toward Cyprus and the canal. I could see the cadets clearly, a dozen of them on the bank, still and quiet, and one—no two—down in the creek, one standing knee deep in filthy brown water, the other lying face down. I recognized the one standing—Coop's roommate Goldfarb. I knew the other one was Coop.

Pushing through the crowd, scrambling down the bank, cement ripped my knees. I stumbled into the water, screaming at Goldfarb, "Get him up! Get him up! Help me get him up!" But Goldfarb stood there, eyes blank, towering over Coop like a befuddled giant. Yanking at Coop's shoulder, I realized I wasn't strong enough to roll him over. So I kept screaming at Goldfarb, pulling at Coop, until Goldfarb began moving, kneeling in the water, sliding his arms under Coop at the waist and shoulder, turning him easily, lifting him clear.

Coop's head flopped back, then jerked forward, brown water sputtering from his mouth and nose. He was breathing, alive, but his gashed forehead streamed blood, his left pinky finger twisted at a sickening angle, white bone sticking out of purple flesh like the pit of a half-eaten cherry.

"Holy shit," Goldfarb said, "we've got to get him to the academy, to sickbay."

Looking up at the cadets on the bank, realizing there were fewer of them, I shouted, "Help us get him out!" Hands reached down, grabbing, pulling. "Watch his finger! Be careful!"

We got him up the canal's moss-bearded, algae-covered side. With Goldfarb under one arm and a tall cadet whose name tag read *Varzali* replacing me under the other, they half walked, half carried Coop's stumbling, semi-conscious body down Cyprus toward the academy's sickbay. With each passing block more cadets disappeared down side streets, melting away until only Goldfarb, Varzali, me, and Coop were left.

The nurse on duty, Miss Radford, had us lay Coop down on an infirmary bed, called a doctor, and ordered us outside. Varzali headed to his dormitory, while Goldfarb and me stood waiting in the shadows cast by sickbay's overhanging eaves. The canal's water left us caked in a sticky brown mix of algae and dirt, stinking of used motor oil, stinging my torn knees. I tried catching my breath, but the temperature was in the 90s, and breathing the hot, damp air made me dizzy. Finally, I managed a word.

"Civvies."

"Huh?"

"Fucking civvies. Kids in this town. I fucking hate them."

"What are you talking about, Melora?"

"For doing this to Coop. I hate them. Hate them all."

"It wasn't civvies, Melora."

"Who...?"

"It was cadets. It was us."

I looked at Goldfarb, my eyes wide, not understanding.

"Some senior peons—guys who never made officer—had a beef with me and Coop for sticking them with demerits at this morning's inspection. When they saw us heading out on liberty, they followed, then chased us. It started out in fun—they were laughing and joking, shouting for us to 'go fly a kike'. But when they caught us at the canal it wasn't enough. So they pushed us. I stayed on my feet. Coop went down."

Suddenly, I felt nauseous. I might have thrown up if the sickbay door hadn't opened behind us, Miss Radford calling out, "Mr. Goldfarb, the headmaster would like to speak with you." I followed Goldfarb inside and poked my head into the infirmary. Coop looked restless, but asleep. Miss Radford touched my shoulder. "An ambulance is on its way. You should go home and get yourself cleaned up."

By then it was 5:00, and remembering I'd dropped my duffel on the bank of the canal, I left sickbay and walked across the academy's west parade ground toward Cyprus. The kids restricted from liberty for demerits, academics, or because they didn't have enough pocket money to go out, were lining up for evening mess formation into one small company instead of the usual five. I recognized a few faces, but it was the ones I didn't know who stared after me, while the ones I knew looked away. A carload of civvies roared by on Cyprus, tires squealing, laying rubber, screaming, "Fuck you, faggots!" Inside the old Chevy, backlit by the sun over Boca Grande Bay, I saw a flash of long blonde hair. A few cadets yelled back, flipping birds and Italian salutes, but the officers settled them down, ordering them to attention, marching them off to the mess hall.

I walked down Cyprus alongside the canal until I came to the spot where Coop had been attacked. The duffel was gone. Standing there not knowing where to go, what to do next, I waited.

Then squealing tires behind me, and a girl's squealing voice. "You're gonna die, greaser!" The blonde girl who'd hassled Coop the day we met, hung out the Chevy's window, her pale arm twisting toward me. Two eggs hit the sidewalk, two more my hip and shoulder. I was surprised two thrown eggs could have such force, spinning me around, almost knocking me down. I was surprised how much they hurt. But I'd already cried that afternoon on the bus, and I wasn't going to cry now. Not now, not ever.

Chapter Sixteen: Melora

Mr. Belasso let me clean up at the restaurant and sleep that night on some sofa cushions in the back room. When he closed and went home, when it was dark and quiet, I fell asleep. Sometime before dawn, I had an ocean dream. Only in this one, the sky was dark and cloudy, the waves high and rough. And I was fucking scared. So in my dream, for the first time ever, I stayed on the beach far from where the surf was breaking.

In the morning, I talked Mr. Belasso into letting me work full time. The pay wasn't much, but included my own place in the storage room and all the pizza I could eat.

"What about school?" Mr. Belasso asked me.

I lied. "I finished my classes. I've got enough credits to graduate in June."

Coop wound up in the emergency room where they set his broken finger and put on a cast that went up to his elbow. He missed a week of school but was out of sickbay the following Monday. He didn't much feel like going out on liberty any more, so he signed up to earn merits working weekends in the John Paul Jones library. As soon as he was sure the librarian, Mrs. Oyeda, only came in to work on weekdays, he asked me if I wanted to hang out with him there. And that's how I met the IPI 700.

Instead of spending our weekends on St. Francis Key, we spent them on the old computer, learning more every minute, amazed at what it could do, amazed at what we could do. Coop, pecking away at the keyboard with the fingers of his undamaged right hand, showed me a navigation program he'd improved, adding lines of code taking into account known currents, such as the Gulf Stream. I didn't know anything about computers or navigation when I started, but I liberated a couple of the 700's phone-book size manuals and took them back to Mr. Belasso's. After pulling a few all-nighters reading, and with Coop's help, I was up to speed. Soon I one-upped him, creating a new program that let navigators input adjustments for changing winds, tides, and currents.

Next, I went to work on a program for Mr. Belasso, producing graphs showing exactly how much he could turn down his PizzAzziP pizza oven for each ten degrees the outside temperature rose during the day. I thought he'd laugh, but instead he studied my graphs carefully, lowering the oven temperature three or four times each day, raising it again in the evening. At the end of two weeks he announced, "Melora, this thing you did,"—waving the dog-eared computer paper at me—"it's saving me a bundle on gas and air conditioning!"

"Up to 22% in summer," I said. I figured that out on the 700, too.

Mr. Belasso smiled. And damn, did that feel good!

My favorite thing was when I discovered how to encrypt codes into other people's programs. Coop jumped out of his skin one night when his work disappeared from the monitor, replaced by a message—

DON'T TURN AROUND... THERE'S SOMEONE BEHIND YOU!

Of course once I taught Coop how to do it, we kept surprising each other with messages and pranks.

May passed quickly, the days hotter and longer. After Coop's graduation in June, he'd head home to New Orleans, starting college at Tulane in the fall. I knew changes were coming but tried not to think about them. I focused instead on my days at Belasso's and my weekends at the library with Coop and the computer.

On the first Saturday in June, me and Coop were working on the 700, sharing its lone keyboard, when Mrs. Oyeda walked into the library with a Navy officer. Gold circled the sleeves of his dress blue uniform jacket, with more gold above the bill of his cap and more gold on his fingers—a plain wedding band and a bulky Naval Academy ring. Coop snapped quickly to attention. I didn't know what to do, so I sat there waiting, feeling scared. I didn't think they could do anything to me, but I figured Coop was in some really deep shit.

"At ease, Lieutenant Cooperman," Mrs. Oyeda said. I expected anger, but her voice was gentle. Then came the shocker—"Commander Rusk is here to speak to Miss Kennedy."

How the fuck did she know my name? And why the fuck did Rusk want to speak to me? Was I under some kind of military arrest for breaking the Access Law?

Coop tried standing at ease, but his body looked stiffer than when he'd been at attention. Holy shit, I thought, we're both screwed!

"Miss Kennedy, Commander Rusk is here from the Navy Department reviewing cadets who are applying for admission to Annapolis. While you would not be eligible for one of those appointments, and Mr. Cooperman has chosen not to seek an appointment,"— her eyes shot a disapproving look at Coop, then came quickly back to me—"I've been aware of your, um, activities for quite some time, and decided that it was in everyone's best interest if I showed Commander Rusk your work. As a result, he's interested in talking to you about enlistment in the United States Navy." That's when I noticed a sheaf of green and white computer paper under the Commander's gold-braided arm, printouts from the navigation program I'd left behind in the library.

"The Navy could use someone with your ability, Miss Kennedy." Rusk's voice was deep, with the gentle drawl of Maryland or Virginia. "The recruiter for St. Francis served with me on the *Nimitz*, and if you're interested, I'd be happy to set up a meeting."

Coop, aware I was staring, not saying anything, nudged my foot with his.

"Uh, thanks. I mean, thank you."

Things were moving too fast, and too unexpectedly, but Mrs. Oyeda came to my rescue—sort of. "Mr. Cooperman, let's leave the Commander and Miss Kennedy alone for awhile so they can talk."

"Yes, ma'am."

But when they left, Commander Rusk didn't want to talk. Instead, taking off his jacket and rolling up his sleeves, he sat down at the keyboard, started showing me programming languages I'd never seen and programs I'd never dreamed possible. The Navy was gigantic, and most of the complicated shit the Navy did was done with the help of computers. Not like in my world. If Mr. Belasso needed a fifty-pound sack of flour, he called the flourmill, and in a day or two they sent a delivery guy with the flour. At the end of the month, Mr. Belasso got a bill in the mail and mailed the flourmill a check. When the Navy needed to figure out how many tons of flour thousands of ship's bakers needed each month, how to deliver it to hundreds of ports around the world, and who to pay, the Navy used computer programs. And that was the simple shit!

It was hard to believe any of this was for real, but I had to ask. "Would I get to do stuff like that in the Navy?"

"You bet."

"And would I get out of St. Francis?"

Rusk smiled. "I guarantee it."

"Then where do I sign up?"

Commander Rusk hooked me up with the local recruiter a week later. He was a likeable old Chief Petty Officer named Karcher who seemed happy his former skipper had already made all the decisions about my enlistment—"Greased the skids" as he put it. The paperwork was in order, ready for my signature, the box after the question "High school graduate?" marked "Yes" even though I'd told Rusk I dropped out. On the medical forms my height and weight were correct, but in the test results column the word "normal" had been typed after everything from "Allergies" to "Vision"—including "Hearing."

"Uh, Chief? There are some mistakes here on my...."

"The Commander didn't authorize me to make any changes," Karcher interrupted, handing me a pen. "Just go ahead and sign. I'm sure we can clean up any typos later."

I reached for the pen, my hand hanging in mid-air. "Y'know, Commander Rusk promised I'd be able to work with computers. And he promised he'd get me out of St. Francis."

Chief Karcher smiled. "Miss Kennedy, when you sign this paper, you're in the Navy. You'll go where the Navy tells you to go, do what the Navy tells you to do. I ought to know—I've been following orders for thirty-five years."

That stopped me cold. I barely knew Rusk, and I'd heard stories about women in the military. What if he was some kind of perv? And the Navy? Jeez—I'd never paddled a fucking canoe! What the fuck was I getting myself into?

At least Karcher was honest about giving up my freedom. My freedom—yeah, that was a fucking joke. Freedom to be stuck in St. Francis for the rest of my life. Freedom to work shit jobs. Freedom to sleep on a couch in the storage room of a pizza joint.

But what about Joey, Darin, and Diana? What about Mr. Belasso? I'd miss them, and they'd miss me. I'd miss the Gulf, too, if the Navy shipped me some place like, y'know, Antarctica.

Then I thought about the 700 and how programming made me feel. Smart. Powerful. Alive.

Karcher set the pen down in front of me. "Your call, Miss Kennedy."

I signed. The truth is, I had about as much choice as a draftee.

My enlistment began July 1, soon after Coop's graduation. At first he wasn't too happy—"Jeez, Melora, it's like going to John Paul Jones, only with live ammunition!"—but Coop understood the Navy was my only way to keep programming, my only ticket out of St. Francis.

Me and Coop went back to the beach just once. It was the night before the start of graduation weekend, and I wanted to spend a few more hours working on the 700. But earlier that day, at his last academy mail call, Coop had gotten graduation cards from his parents. Sliding a check neatly from each envelope, he dropped the cards unread into a dumpster.

"C'mon, Melora," he said waving the checks, "let's have one more dinner at the Bonair. My treat!"

Instead of taking the bus, we walked the whole way, arriving after dark. By the time we finished dinner—a surf-and-turf feast of Gulf prawns and steak—it was after 10:00. For graduation week, liberty was extended until midnight, so we took off our shoes, walking the beach one last time.

The sky, clear and cloudless, filled with stars, looked infinite. The air was warm and still. Shoulders touching, we stood together at the edge of the breakers looking out at the Gulf.

"Coop," I said, "I'm going in."

"What?"

"In the ocean. I'm going swimming."

"But you don't have a suit."

"I don't care. I'm skinny dipping."

"Okay."

"And don't look!"

"Like I'd want to!"

A week ago some surgeon had reset the bone in Coop's finger. I knew he couldn't go in with his hand all bandaged, knew he wouldn't anyway. So pulling out my hearing aid, I handed it to him, stripped off my tee shirt, and stepped out of my cutoffs. I didn't stop to see if he was looking as I ran into the suddenly muffled surf and dove head-first into a breaker, swimming and swimming straight out from shore until I couldn't see Coop or the breakers or the beach, only the faintly shimmering lights of St. Francis Key's hotels. I kicked over onto my back, closing my eyes, floating in the vastness of cool, dark, salt water. After a time, I opened my eyes and looked up at the billion billion stars shining down on me, looked east as the full yellow moon rose over the Gulf lighting my way to shore. Closing my eyes again, I whispered two words—"Thank you."

Then, I sensed… something. A shift, a disturbance in the ocean's swells. I flipped upright, treading water, turning a tight circle, scanning the Gulf like a periscope operator in one of those old war movies. I'd come up facing west with the thing I'd felt somewhere behind me, so I swirled in a half-circle to my left until I was facing the rising moon. Its light made a path through the water above and below the surface, like a lighthouse beacon, its searchlight focused on me. Yeah, it was moonlight, and I know this sounds like bullshit, but I swear I could feel heat on my face. I could see something too, once my eyes adjusted, something big, its smooth gray form slicing through the moonlit water, coming fast.

I dove.

It dove with me.

I don't know why I dove, or what I was thinking, but I wasn't scared. I've thought about it a lot, and wondered whether I didn't have time for fear, or if some part of my brain knew my eyes hadn't spotted a dorsal fin. Mostly, I think I was in denial because this was my ocean, the one place where I felt safe. But as I swam for the bottom the fish reached me, first swimming parallel, then swirling around me like a giant cape. That's when I saw its underside, which wasn't gray, but white, white and textured like the slick fur on one of my mother's fake fox stoles. Instead of fins, it had gracefully flapping wings. Instead of dead eyes and gaping jaws filled with pointy teeth, it had a smiling half-moon mouth, surprised little eyes, a pair of inward curving horns. And at its other end, a slender, slinky tail.

It was a devil ray. A beautiful, harmless devil ray.

My hand touched sand. I turned, kicking off the bottom with my feet. The ray turned with me, effortlessly reversing direction. Together we swam upward, like dancers, the ray's wings curling and uncurling around me. I lead, swimming up, down, sideways. It followed. I touched its side with a hand. It touched my hip with its tail.

We danced until I couldn't dance any more, until my lungs were burning, until my head broke the surface. I opened my mouth, sucking in air and coughing up seawater. I guess that's when the ray figured out

I was an alien, a tourist, a visitor from another world, because it broke off the dance and headed out the moonlit trail, its tail waving behind.

I stared after it, treading water until it disappeared.

"That was fucking incredible!" I said. And for the second time that night I looked up and whispered, "Thank you."

I took as long as I could swimming to shore, though I knew Coop would worry. Riding one last wave, feeling sand boiling up in the surf around me, I regained my feet, running the final yards to my waiting friend. He'd talked some beachcombing tourist out of his hotel towel without letting him know it was for a naked swimmer, and held it out for me when I got close.

"Thanks, Coop," I said.

I didn't tell him about the devil ray.

Chapter Seventeen: Melora

John Paul Jones Academy was a really shitty school. But it knew how to do one thing really well—put on a show for tuition-paying parents. Graduation weekend was the biggest show of all, and the Final Parade was the biggest show of graduation weekend.

Picture five companies of cadets in black-brimmed white caps with shiny gold anchors, dress blue coats and starched white pants, Springfield rifles at shoulder arms, officers' silver sabers gleaming. After nine months of daily close-order drill, even the middle-school ranks were straight, two platoons to a company, three squads to a platoon. And other than a handful of kids passing out in the Florida sun, the whole thing was fucking awesome.

The parade ended with the battalion passing in review, platoon leaders commanding "Eyes right!" In the ranks, cadets snapped their heads right, looking over their rifle barrels at parents snapping pictures from the bleachers. Officers' chins turned right too, curved saber blades rising and falling with every stride, eyes hidden beneath shiny cap bills worn low. And as he marched by, Coop lifted his chin, so slightly, and winked at me over the tip of his saber.

Everything was spit-and-polish perfection as the cadets marched back to quarters and parents mingled with academy officials. Coop had told me to leave the bleachers, keep my ears open, and follow the corps, even if it meant missing post-parade cookies and punch. I wasn't disappointed. Rising above the dust cloud made by six hundred spit-shined cordovans marching across Bermuda grass-covered sand, Coop's voice, loud and strong, lead the battalion—

Two more days of shining brass
Then John Paul Jones can kiss my ass!
Sound off!
One, two.
Hit it again!
Three, four.
Sound off!
One-two-three-four-one-two— THREE FOUR!

When the battalion was dismissed, I found Coop, giving him a hug.

"That was great, Coop! All of it!

"Thanks, Mel. Hey, Mel...."

"What?"

"This is kind of short notice, and we've always made fun of proms and stuff, but would you like to go to the graduation dance with me tonight?"

He was looking down at his shoes. Then I surprised both of us.

"Yeah. Sure. It'll be fun."

"Great! That's great! Can you be here at eight?"

I nodded.

"And Mel," Coop said, looking at my cutoffs and tee shirt, then back down to his shoes, "have you got something to wear?"

Taking the familiar walk down Cyprus, stopping at Belasso's, I bathed, shook my savings from the rusty tomato sauce can I kept under the couch, and caught the Palm Boulevard bus downtown to the Paris Faire Department Store. Passing through Paris Faire's automatic door, feeling disoriented by the first cold, perfumey blast of conditioned air, I looked like someone who'd wandered in off the sidewalk to cool off.

"May I help you, dear?" A silver-haired lady whose nametag read "Blanche" intercepted me as I stepped inside the store.

"Uh, I'm invited to this dance over at John Paul Jones, and I need some new clothes."

Tapping an index finger thoughtfully against her lower lip, Blanche said, "What's your budget, dear?"

"Budget?"

"How much would you like to spend?"

"I've got about thirty-five dollars and some change."

Blanche's eyes flickered, but all she said was, "My name's Blanche. And you are…?"

"Uh, Melora."

"Come with me, Miss Melora. I think we can find something nice that fits you… and your budget."

Together we picked out a simple white sundress. It was beautiful, my dark skin giving form to the dress's whiteness. But it was also strapless and pretty low-cut.

"Uh, Blanche, I'm not real sure about going with bare shoulders and, uh, so much showing in front."

"Trust me dear, you look lovely."

I looked at the price tag hanging from the dress's neckline by a pale blue thread. $160.

"Uh oh. Guess I can't afford this one."

"Don't worry about it honey. Today's your lucky day. It's on sale!"

"How much?"

"As I recall, it's $25. Now come with me and we'll get you some makeup."

Blanche took my hand and led me to the cosmetics counter, where she filled a small bag with samples. Dark, sparkly lipstick and powder, eye shadow with a hint of red.

"Let's go to the beauty salon, dear," she said. "I want you to meet my friend Terry."

The parlor was filled with women sitting under dryers, reading *Cosmo* and *Vogue*. Terry wore a powder-blue smock, jet-black hair circled into a two-foot beehive, and incredible inch-long nails.

"Terry honey, this is my friend Melora. She's going to the prom tonight, and guess what? She's the lucky winner of our free makeover contest. Can you work on her right away?"

Terry looked at me, looked at Blanche, looked confused. Then a light went on deep inside that beehive, and lifting her chin, parting her lips with a click of her tongue, Terry said, "Why sure, honey. Let me finish this comb-out, and I'll be right with you."

First, Terry cut my dark hair in layers, bringing it up to my shoulders, washing and rinsing it, making it thick and silky. Then she told me to close my eyes, and after scrubbing my face and patting it dry, began applying makeup like an artist gently dabbing watercolors.

"Need something else," she muttered, digging around in her gigantic canvas pocketbook, coming up with eyeliner and a little tube of sparkles.

"Close your eyes again and don't open till I say. Okay, okay, that's it. Blanche, what do you think?"

"Why, Terry, I declare. You are a regular Moe-nay!"

"Thanks, Blanche, but you brought me a masterpiece to begin with. All I did was a little touch-up work on Miss Mona Lisa here. Melora honey, open your eyes and look in the mirror."

"Wow."

"Is that all you can say?"

"Yes. I mean no! I mean thank you, thank you both!"

"Oh it's nothin', honey. Just be sure you don't so much as sneeze before you get to that prom." Then she looked down at my flip-flops. "Blanche, I hope you weren't planning on sending Cinderella to the ball barefoot?"

"Of course not, Terry. Dear, what size shoes do you wear?"

"Six, I think."

"Isn't that a coincidence? We had a pair of six's returned yesterday. Can't sell them now. Why don't you take them, Melora?"

I nodded.

Saying goodbye to Terry, we walked back to the women's department, picking up a pair of strapped, high-heeled sandals on the way. Blanche was smiling, both hands clutched in front of her as I slipped them on.

"Melora honey, you look so beautiful you should be wearing glass slippers tonight. Now get on home and change into your dress so you won't be late. And if you can, send us a picture of you and your handsome beau at the prom."

"I will. I promise I will."

I was the only girl who walked to the dance. And though I thought my dress was the most beautiful one in the world, I didn't realize until I got there that I was the only girl not wearing a gown, the only girl with no jewelry.

Goldfarb stood in the academy's parking lot helping his date out of her silver Camaro. When he spotted me walking up the asphalt drive, he dropped her hand, dropped his chin.

"Holy shit, Mel, it's you!"

Feeling uncomfortable, unprepared, I thought about turning around, heading home to Belasso's. A crowd gathered near the academy's big iron and glass front door, mostly Coop's friends, staring at me. Goldfarb's date was staring too, looking unhappy.

"Wait till Coop sees you! He's gonna freak!"

And there's Coop, stepping out the door, deep purple orchid in one hand, slender purple ribbon in the other, looking around, spotting me, walking toward me, his friends following, forming a circle around us.

"Geez, Mel, you look amazing."

"You don't look too bad yourself."

"Here... this is... I mean, I got this for you."

Taking my right hand gently with his bandaged left, Coop slid the orchid bracelet on my wrist.

"And this, too. It's part of the Ring Dance Ceremony."

Coop took off his gold class ring, slipping it on the ribbon, tying the ribbon loosely around my neck.

"Ring Dance Ceremony?"

"Yeah. I'll fill you in later. Hey, do you guys mind?"

Coop lead me inside through the circle of staring, jostling cadets, past the quarterdeck and into the academy's candlelit lounge.

"I think we're supposed to go through the receiving line," Coop said. "Is that okay with you?"

"Sure, Coop."

We went down the line, Coop introducing me as we stopped before each of the academy's teachers and their spouses.

"Captain Brown, Mrs. Brown, may I present Miss Melora Kennedy."

"Lieutenant Richter, Mrs. Richter, may I present Miss Melora Kennedy."

Mrs. Oyeda, wearing a simple print dress and pearl necklace, was next.

"It's nice to see you again, Melora, and looking so lovely."

"Likewise, Mrs. Oyeda."

Next to Mrs. Oyeda stood her husband, a salty retired chief petty officer with a round red face and rounder belly. Taking my hand in both of his, he showed none of his wife's quiet classiness, but more than made up for it with the twinkling of his sky-blue eyes.

"C'mon, Cooperman, ain't you gonna introduce me to your date?"

"Sure, Chief. Melora Kennedy, meet Chief Oyeda."

"Nice to meet you, Chief."

"Now, Miss Melora, you call me 'Red'—y'know, like a little red rooster!"

"Okay... Red."

"And you, Cooperman," turning on Coop, still tightly grasping my hand, "you *dog*! Where you been hidin' this pretty little lady?"

"Anywhere I could to keep you from stealing her away from me, Chief."

The chief's rumbling belly laugh made everyone in the receiving line, including Mrs. Oyeda, look away uncomfortably. I thought he was great.

"Better move along, young lady, before I get tempted to leave my happy home!" he said, letting go of my hand, shaking Coop's with a conspiratorial wink, earning himself an elbow to the ribs from his wife.

I could feel myself blushing as Coop made the next introduction.

"Commander Rusk, Mrs. Rusk, may I present Miss Melora Kennedy. Sir, I believe you and Miss Kennedy have met."

"Yes we have, Mr. Cooperman. Pleasure to see you again, Miss Kennedy. This is my wife Maggie. Maggie, I'd like to introduce you to Lieutenant David Cooperman and Miss Melora Kennedy."

Rusk's wife was short, dark like me, but Asian. She looked like the women I'd seen on travel posters of Thailand. Dipping her knees slightly, almost curtsying, she spoke in halting, accented English, the way people speak in Japanese monster movies.

"It is a pleasure to meet with you, Miss Kennedy. My husband has told me you are a genius!"

Stunned, not knowing what to say, I mumbled, "Thank you," attempting my own clumsy curtsy, and before I knew it, was moving on to the next couple in the receiving line.

By the time we finished the last introductions, we were both sweating. "Boy, Mel," Coop said, "am I glad that's over. C'mon, let's get some punch and hit the dance floor."

Coop didn't seem to notice what Maggie Rusk had said, but it was all I could think about as we made our way outside to the west parade ground where a tuxedoed band was thumping out *She's a brick... house!* On the plywood dance floor, Coop's friends and a few guys I'd never seen before kept cutting in. A couple of dads even danced with me! Coop didn't mind, and after each song we got back together, Coop bringing me cookies and punch, dancing with me again or introducing me to friends' parents.

With the ringing of a silver ship's bell, the Battalion Commander announced the beginning of the Ring Dance Ceremony.

"So, Coop, what's this ring thing all about anyway?"

"C'mon, I'll show you."

Cadets were lining up on one side of the barracks' outdoor atrium, their dates on the other. Magnolias bloomed in large wooden planters, their perfume almost overpowering the cheap cologne every cadet had apparently bathed in before the dance. In the center a giant papier-mâché John Paul Jones Academy ring straddled a mosaic tile pond. Gold-painted plywood made a platform through the ring's base, bridging the pond. Giant goldfish the size of kittens swam back and forth beneath it, hiding in the shadows or darting up to the water's surface looking to see what all the fuss was about.

The first couple stepped forward, meeting at a shiny brass binnacle bolted to the atrium's flagstone floor. Inside the compass housing, a glass bowl half-filled with water rested on blue satin. The girl leaned over, dangling her date's ring from the ribbon circling her neck, dipping it into the water.

"Water from the seven seas," Coop whispered.

"Yeah, taken from the men's room five minutes ago!" Goldfarb wisecracked behind us.

The girl stood up straight, glaring briefly in Goldfarb's direction. Then taking her date's arm, they walked together up the platform over the pond, stood together beneath the ring. The guy, a friend of Coop's named Terhune, turned to her, untying the knot in the ribbon, handing her the ring so she could place it on his finger.

"At Annapolis, when cadets are engaged, they pin a miniature class ring on their fiancée," Goldfarb explained, more serious now.

With his ring in place, Terhune put both arms around the girl and began kissing her. No peck on the lips, but a long, slow, real kiss.

"Is this part of the ceremony, too," I asked, "or is Terhune making it up?"

"You bet it is!" Goldfarb answered, poking Coop in the ribs.

"We don't have to do it if you don't want, Mel," Coop added quickly.

"No, I want to do the ceremony. It looks like fun."

"I mean the kissing part."

"Hey, Coop," in my heeled sandals we were the same height, so I could look straight ahead into my best friend's eyes, "if you think I'm going to get up there in front of everyone and *not* do the kissing part, you're crazy."

We split up, going to the end of the boys' and girls' lines. Two-by-two, couples dipped, stepped under the ring, moved class ring from ribbon to ring finger, and kissed. A photographer captured them as they came out the other side.

Sometimes it got funny. Like when one really short cadet, with a high-heeled date, couldn't untie the knot. So standing on tiptoe, his face an inch from her chest, he bit the ribbon through, freeing the ring. Other times it was something else—like the pair who kissed so hard the whole ring shook. And when a kiss lasted longer than a few seconds, the dateless cadets standing around watching would start counting off the seconds, "...21, 22, 23...."

Then it was time for me and Coop. More confident in my sundress than when I first tried it on at Paris Faire, I leaned over the binnacle, watching Coop's ring ripple the water.

"It's not really from the men's room, y'know," Coop whispered.

Linking my arm under Coop's, we walked together to the little pond, up the plywood ramp, and turned, facing each other beneath the giant ring. I stood quietly, watching Coop's eyes intently focused on undoing the ribbon's little knot, looking into mine while I took his undamaged hand, slipping the gold circle with its cut blue stone onto his ring finger. Coop slid one arm around my waist, the other across my bare shoulders, and gently moved a half step closer. Less gently, I put my arms around him, my lips on his, closing my eyes, kissing him.

After awhile I became aware of the chanting around us.

"...88, 89, 90...."

And finally, to the sound of applauding, whooping cadets, we turned from each other and faced the photographer.

The pictures were $5 each. You could order copies, have them mailed to anyone you wanted. Uncrumpling my last two five-dollar bills, I handed them to the photographer and addressed one envelope to myself at Recruit Training Command, Great Lakes, Illinois, the other in care of Blanche at the Paris Faire Department Store.

Chapter Eighteen: Melora

I thought Saturday's graduation would bore the shit out of me. It didn't. It was fucking epic.

Mr. Belasso turned down Coop's invitation to the Final Parade, pointing to the lone picture hanging on the pizzeria's whitewashed walls, saying, "I had enough of that crap in the Marines." I asked him about the picture once, ten grimy teenagers in battle fatigues, draped in weapons and bandoliers of ammunition, standing in front of a huge pile of smoking rubble.

"Huế," he said, as if that explained everything.

"Huh?"

"Huế," he said again.

"What's 'hoo ay?'"

"You know, Vietnam, the Tet Offensive, 1968. Victor Charlie and the NVA's surprise attacks behind our lines."

I had no idea what he was talking about.

"Forget it—it's not important anymore." Then, turning to the oven, under his breath, something about, "Stupid kids. Don't know anything. Wind up just like us."

He did accept Coop's graduation invitation, could hardly say no in the face of the engraved blue and gold card—"Lieutenant David Harvey Cooperman invites you to join in celebrating his graduation from John Paul Jones Academy." So we went together, sitting in folding metal chairs on the academy's south lawn, surrounded by family and friends of the graduating seniors.

First came the speeches. Headmaster. Class President. Valedictorian. Then the guest of honor, a former talk-radio host who'd never served a fucking minute in the military, now Florida's junior senator, giving what sounded like a campaign speech.

"I'm so proud to be here today at this fine military institution, where outstanding young men take the first step on a journey which may end in making the ultimate sacrifice for their country...."

"You ever hear such a load of crap in your life?" Mr. Belasso said, leaning toward me, whispering in a voice I was sure everyone could hear, making parents squirm uneasily around us.

When the senator finally shut up, it was time for the seniors. One-by-one, the commandant called out their names, and they crossed the little riser in front of the academy's gray cement fountain, the same fountain where, one moonless night, civvies—or maybe it was cadets— had poured in detergent and food coloring, treating the corps the next morning to a green, foamy, shimmering mess. After crossing, each cadet saluted with his right hand, stepped forward, took his diploma from the headmaster with his left, stepped back and saluted again, applauded by his family.

When it was Coop's turn, I clapped till my hands hurt.

The commandant worked through the senior class in alphabetical order. There was a long way to go from Coop to Terhune, Wilcox, and Zimmerman, but after Zimmerman, lots of clapping, and a few shouts and whistles, the ceremony was over except for one last detail—the Final Formation. The entire corps of cadets marched from the academy's lawn to the west parade, the one bordered by Cyprus Avenue, Boca Grande Bay, the Gulf, the setting sun, and Piss Creek, the same spot where Goldfarb and I had carried Coop to sickbay two months before.

The cadets formed up in their usual companies, with the exception of the seniors, who gathered instead on the parade's north side in front of sickbay and the little bridge crossing Piss Creek. For the first time since they arrived four years ago, their line was ragged, uneven. Jostling for position before their parents' clicking cameras, they weren't quite cadets any more, not quite civilian teenagers either. Standing in front of me, the commandant, dressed head-to-toe in starched whites stretched tight across his butt like a drumhead, and behind me the faint idle of an airport taxi, the one Coop had ordered, pulling into the academy's circular drive.

An honor guard lowered the flag. The junior class president led the underclassmen in a final salute—"Three cheers for the graduates! Hip hip hooray! Hip hip hooray! Hip hip hooray!"

And the graduates answered—"Three cheers for those we leave behind! Hip hip hooray! Hip hip hooray! Hip hip hooray!," then tossing their white caps high in the air, local kids scrambling to snatch them, but not looking back, never looking back again.

Chapter Nineteen: Melora

On July 1, I said my goodbyes to Joey, Darin, and Diana, and boarded a greyhound for Pensacola. Joey called mom, let her know I was leaving. "She'll be here," he said at our little pizza and Pepsi farewell party. Tammy Jo never showed.

Darin was the only one who cried. "Don't leave, Melora. Whomygonna play with?"

Mr. Belasso drove me to the bus station.

"Thanks for everything, Mr. B."

"Just keep your head down, kid. And never volunteer."

"Some day you'll tell me about Huế?"

"Yeah, sure kid, sure."

Later that night at Pensacola Naval Air Station, less than a year shy of my eighteenth birthday, I slept for the first time on something other than a fucking sofa. It was a cot like the others in my barracks, but it felt like heaven. I was out before the bugler finished taps, out the instant I closed my eyes, sleeping deeply, peacefully, dreamlessly, until reveille.

After first mess, a couple of young women petty officers loaded me and the other Florida recruits in my training unit on another bus, this one a charter. Before noon I crossed the Florida border for the first time. Traveling north across Georgia, heading for Recruit Training

Command in Great Lakes, Illinois, some talked and played cards, most slept or watched the countryside roll by.

At Great Lakes, I got my second haircut in less than a week. Terry at Paris Faire had taken my hair from waist to shoulder, the Navy took most of the rest. I was also back in the classroom, studying naval customs, first aid, fire fighting, water safety and survival, and shipboard and aircraft safety, learning skills I'd never use once in the next four years. From the first day, men and women trained together as they'd later serve together on ships and shore commands around the world. Lectures on the Navy's oldest values—honor, courage, commitment—blended with newer topics—sexual harassment and equal opportunity. The only time the instructors mentioned computers was in a three-hour session on Access Law Compliance that boiled down to one simple message: never discuss anything about computers or computer programming with civilians.

My classmates bitched when they learned I'd been excused from all physical fitness requirements, bitched some more when, six weeks into the eight-week training program, a duty officer handed me orders transferring me to Pensacola to begin "technical instruction." I hadn't made any friends in my training unit, but I didn't give a fuck, because I knew I'd never see any of them again.

At my last Great Lakes mail call, the company clerk called my name. I was surprised to hear it, surprised to open the envelope addressed in my own handwriting and see the picture of a uniformed, slightly dazed looking boy, his bandaged hand resting on the hip of his beautiful date, a girl who looked like someone I'd seen before in another lifetime.

Everyone who joins the Navy dreams of cruising around the world on mighty fighting ships. But I wasn't interested in sailing them or firing their guns. My dreams were about creating the computers and programs commanding the ships—their engines, navigation systems, and weapons.

I thought I'd get to live those dreams when I arrived at Pensacola with orders immediately tasking me to Computer Ops. But soon the excitement of working with our brand new IPI 3000s—machines that made the academy's IPI 700 look like a slide rule—gave way to the reality of using them only for payroll, procurement, and inventory. I got as creative as I could, at first reconfiguring and streamlining programs, later rewriting them from scratch.

My superiors were surprisingly open to new ideas, adopting most of my suggestions, recommending me for promotions and pay raises. But by the halfway mark in my four-year enlistment, I'd gone as far as I could go. I knew there was more important work happening somewhere in the Navy. My best guess was the Pentagon. In Military Net communiqués, I saw hints of computers far more powerful than the ones used at Pensacola. My section chief, a skinny old submariner named Kavaney, who looked like he'd spent too many years on the dry side of a thin steel hull millimeters away from hundreds of atmospheres of pressure, swore he'd used navigation and missile targeting programs that made Pensacola's best work read like *Dick and Jane*. And while John Rusk—newly promoted to captain—kept his word about getting me into computers and out of St. Francis, I never imagined spending my whole enlistment in fucking Florida.

Pensacola wasn't all bad. On leave I could bus to St. Francis, visit Joey, Diana, and their new addition, Damian, and keep my promise to Darin that, "I'll always come home to play with you." On liberty, I could walk to Pensacola's beaches, whose waters weren't as warm as St. Francis Key, but were still the Gulf.

I also picked up a new skill. For a while I dated a guy named Wind. He owned Windance Tattoos, a Pensacola parlor catering to women bluejackets. He asked me out in the middle of tattooing a breaking wave on my ankle, and thinking it would be a bad time to learn how he handled rejection, I said okay. He turned out to be a good enough boyfriend and began teaching me his trade.

My Navy pay was enough to support me, send a check for a few bucks each month to Joey, and put a little away for a rainy day. Tammy

Jo was still shacked up with the professor—a record-setting relationship for her—and that was a good thing, because she wasn't asking me for money. As my tattooing skills improved I spent some savings on my own kit, and Wind started letting me cover for him at the parlor. He'd never been very talkative, but as more and more customers requested me, he stopped talking altogether. That's when I packed my kit and went back to spending free time doing the things I'd done before I met him—hanging out at the beach and busing down to St. Francis. Wind never called to find out what happened, so I guess breaking up was okay with him, too. I did get some free ink out of the deal, including what turned out to be Wind's farewell present, his masterpiece—an orange and black Gulf of Mexico devil ray on my arm with its tail curving up my shoulder.

By the end of my third year, I'd about had it. I was making more money than I ever dreamed possible, but my work was going nowhere. Whenever I complained to Chief Kavaney, he'd shrug and say, "Take it up with the old man."

The "old man" was our C.O., Lieutenant Brent Bosworth, who at twenty-four was less than half Kavaney's age. A reluctant Annapolis grad who'd been appointed to the Naval Academy despite suffering from extreme nearsightedness—Bosworth's great-great-grandfather served with Farragut at Mobile Bay, and every Bosworth since had been a Navy man—the young lieutenant mostly stayed behind the closed door of his office, constructing computer simulations of Civil War battles. Every time I complained, he'd squint at me, eyes swimming behind his giant Coke-bottle lenses, saying, "You're the best programmer I've got, Kennedy. I'll put you in for another promotion." Then turning to the infantry marching across his monitor, waving me closer, he'd proudly shout, "Hey, check it out—I finished programming Pickett's Charge!"

To get me off his back, Bosworth recommended me for officer's training, but Chief Kavaney scuttled the paperwork. "You'll never make ensign," he laughed. "You like *workin'* for a living." Besides, he knew I wanted to write programs, not supervise programmers. So with only a year left in my enlistment, it looked like I was stuck being an electronic bookkeeper.

Coop stayed in touch, writing or calling every month. Life at Tulane was good. He majored in engineering because it was the only subject where students and professors could at least talk about computers. Coop earned extra money waiting tables at the French Market, and his dad still grudgingly paid room, board, and tuition. He never saw his parents, both now remarried, spending time with newer, younger families. Most amazingly, Coop had a girlfriend.

"She's just like you Mel, only good looking."

"Maybe," I said, "but I've got better taste in men."

Writing to Captain Rusk was Coop's idea. I'd been on the phone with him for over an hour, bitching about my work, when he said, "What about that guy who got you enlisted in the first place? Why don't you get his help?"

"The Navy doesn't work that way, Coop. Rusk's in the Pentagon, and I can't go over my C.O.'s head."

"What've you got to lose," Coop said, "your good conduct ribbon?"

Coop's argument made sense. So I sat down that night and wrote to Captain Rusk, asking for help. When a month passed with no reply, I figured he never got the letter or simply ignored it. Then one day Kavaney sauntered up to my workstation with a glazed look in his eyes, saying, "Pentagon brass waiting to see you at the old man's. Snap to!"

Hurrying off to Bosworth's office, figuring this was some kind of joke, I walked through his open door, not bothering to knock, because no one ever did. There stood Bosworth, squirming like a walking catfish in a hot cast-iron skillet. And sitting across from him, tall, handsome, relaxed—Captain Rusk. For a moment I stood there taking in the eagle sewn on his desert-tan flight suit before pulling myself together, coming to attention. Lieutenant Bosworth started saying something, but Rusk silenced him with a casual wave.

"Petty Officer Kennedy," he said evenly, "every bit as imbued with military decorum as I remember. You may stand at ease. Lieutenant Bosworth, I'll be borrowing Miss Kennedy for the next forty-eight hours—that is if she's not too indispensable to your operation?"

"No, sir. I mean yes, sir. I mean...." Bosworth, a man overboard, eyes swimming back and forth between me and Rusk, suddenly regained focus. "I mean, aye aye, Captain!"

Smothering a smile, Rusk looked quickly out the office's one small window as though observing the row of F-14 fighter jets parked alongside the station's taxiway.

"That will be all, Lieutenant," he said.

"Yes, sir. Thank you, sir." And with that, Bosworth snapped to attention and marched right out of his own office. From where I stood, I could see a battle raging on his monitor. Captain Rusk was looking at it, too.

"First Manassas?" he said.

"I believe so, sir."

"It's good to see you again, Miss Kennedy."

"It's good to see you, sir."

"Would you like to take a little trip with me?"

"You're the Captain."

Rusk's face broke into a big smile. "You've got ten minutes to pack, Miss Kennedy. And keep it light—there's not much room in a Tomcat."

"I'll be ready in five, Captain."

On the runway sat a shiny, blue F-14 Tomcat with a ground crew chief barking refueling and maintenance orders at his men, saluting sharply as we approached.

"She's all ready, Captain."

"Thanks, Chief. Will you help Miss Kennedy into a pressure suit while I do my walk around?" Like most aviators, Rusk always made his own final check of an aircraft he was piloting.

"Aye aye, sir!"

Once you're in the Navy—and it doesn't matter whether you're a peon or an admiral, a submarine driver, latrine swabber, or computer jockey—there are things you hope you'll get to do that may never have crossed your mind in civilian life. Number one on that list has got to be climbing into the cockpit of a high-performance jet fighter.

Jane's, the bible of fighting machines, lists every bit of unclassified information you'd ever want to know about F-14s. They're as big as a condo—a $38,000,000 condo. That's partly why the Navy retired them in 2006. The only military that flies them now is the Islamic Republic of Iran Air Force, old ones we sold them before the revolution when the Iranians were still our friends. *Jane's* also lists the specs—from wingspan to payload, weight to radar profile. In combat all that stuff makes a difference. But when you're out for a joyride only one thing matters—speed. And Tomcats are fucking fast.

Multiplying g-forces pinned me to my ejection seat on takeoff as Captain Rusk wasted no time rocketing up to cruising speed. I knew there were computers on this rig, and more computers on the ground guiding it, helping the big fighter's computers and Captain Rusk with navigation, communications, and, had we been in combat, weapons systems. And that meant code. Lots and lots of code. But who the fuck was writing it? Not me, that's for sure. I was killing time writing payroll programs. Somewhere down there, some motherfucker was making magic!

"Miss Kennedy." Rusk's voice crackled in my headset. "See that red handle between your knees?"

"Yes, sir."

"If I say eject, keep your arms and legs tucked in tight and pull that handle. If you answer 'What?' instead of pulling that handle, you'll be talking to yourself. Understood?"

"Affirmative, sir."

"Oh, and Miss Kennedy...."

"Sir?"

"I also left you a plastic bag—just in case."

"Thank you, sir, but I won't be needing it."

I could almost feel Captain Rusk smiling, and I made up my mind right then that I'd choke to death before I'd use that fucking bag.

I thought we might be heading for Washington and the Pentagon, thought it was really cool the way Captain Rusk kept me in suspense. Every now and then he used the intercom, pointing out some landmark—"There's the Georgia Dome off to starboard"—never saying a word about our destination. I spotted the Washington Monument, and Rusk keyed the intercom again, saying, "We'll be coming in low over the Potomac; prepare for landing." That's when I felt really smart, like I'd figured it all out. But as soon as we touched down, Captain Rusk came on again.

"Sit tight, Miss Kennedy. We're only refueling."

In less than half an hour we were airborne again, looking down on Pennsylvania's farmland, New Jersey's slums, and the Manhattan skyline. Other than occasional "Yes, sirs," I hadn't said a word the whole flight. I watched earth and sky, hardly noticing the chatter of pilots and air traffic controllers in my headset. But when I caught sight of the Statue of Liberty, I keyed the intercom, saying excitedly, stupidly, "The Statue of Liberty!" feeling less stupid when Captain Rusk, sounding just as excited, said, "Isn't she beautiful!"

Passing over New York Harbor, out over Long Island Sound, I'm thinking, *Okay, I bet it's the sub base at Groton. That would be great!* But we continued north, then east over Rhode Island, descending slowly toward the unmistakable hook of Cape Cod.

The intercom crackled. "There's our destination. Otis Air Force Base."

Massachusetts? I thought, *The Navy left in the '70s when they closed the Boston Shipyard!*

Rusk taxied to a stop in front of a gray tanker and an orange Geo Metro. A three-person Air Force ground crew jumped from the tanker, immediately beginning work on the Tomcat. The non-com crew chief, a tall, blonde woman whose fatigues looked freshly pressed and professionally tailored, saluted sharply, helping Captain Rusk from the cockpit, saluting again once his feet steadied on the runway.

"Welcome to Otis, Captain. Please let me know if we may be of assistance."

"Thank you, Sergeant. Why don't you help my backseater out of the aircraft. Then perhaps you could direct us to the head. And can you tell me where my wife is?"

"She's waiting inside, sir." Then, a small smile. "Says she can't stand watching you land."

Rusk smiled back. "I've never quite gotten the hang of dry landings," he said. "In fact, it always amazes me how Air Force pilots make it look as easy as hitting the deck of an aircraft carrier."

The sergeant stiffened a little at that, started to answer, thought better of it, perhaps remembering who wore the stripes and who wore the fucking eagle.

Maggie Rusk was waiting inside the weathered gray control tower. Approaching her husband with small, liquid steps, hugging him in a way that seemed, well, grateful. Seeing me behind him she quickly broke the embrace, taking my hand with one of her small hands beneath it and one above.

"Oh, Miss Kennedy, it is so good to see you again. You must honor our home for dinner so we can get to know each other better!"

"Now, Maggie, this is business. Let's not force ourselves on Miss Kennedy."

"Dinner sounds great to me, Mrs. Rusk. I'm starving."

"Oh, that is wonderful, Melora—may I call you that?" I nodded. "And you must call me Maggie. Have you ever eaten Vietnamese food, Melora?"

"No, Maggie, but I'd love to try it."

Captain Rusk, shifting his weight from foot to foot, his duffle bag from one shoulder to the other, was looking a way I'd never seen or imagined him looking—not in command.

"Okay you two, but taps is early tonight. We've got a big day ahead of us tomorrow."

"Of course, dear. You come sit up front with me, Melora," Maggie said, steering me out of the building toward the orange Metro.

The Captain trailed behind, returning salutes every step of the way. Our duffels took up the whole trunk, his legs the entire back seat. Maggie insisted I ride up front, and I soon realized why her husband hadn't objected—Maggie was in charge and objecting would be futile.

After an amazing dinner of chicken, pork, and rice in silky white and spicy red sauces that made my eyes water and my nose run, Captain Rusk repeated his warning about our "big day" and headed upstairs to bed. Maggie and I stayed up talking past 3:00, me answering Maggie's questions about growing up in Florida, Maggie answering mine about her homeland, Vietnam.

The next thing I knew, Captain Rusk, in blue wool civilian suit, white shirt, and red silk tie, was shaking me awake.

"C'mon, Miss Kennedy. Rise and shine."

"I should say goodbye to your wife, sir."

"Forget it. She's asleep. And if you two start talking again, I'll have to take both of you to Pensacola. That'll be a tight fit in the Tomcat."

With the Captain behind the wheel, the Metro was a completely different machine, cruising Route 128 as serene and steady as a luxury car, acting nowhere near like the shit-box it actually was. Rusk took the Natick exit, turning in at a long driveway leading to three boxy, four-story, red brick buildings. A sign screened in simple black letters on a concrete security blockhouse inside the entrance read, *IPI*. The entry was open, ungated, but a plainclothes security guard stepped outside as the Metro approached.

"Good morning, sir. It's good seeing you again," the guard said.

"Likewise."

"May I have your credentials, please?"

Rusk handed him two laminated cards roughly twice the size of standard Navy I.D.s. A Glock holstered beneath the guard's blue blazer bulged into view as he reached for the cards. Studying the I.D.s carefully, he looked at Rusk, then at me.

"Excuse me sir, but would you ask the young lady to remove her sunglasses?"

I took them off, not waiting for Rusk to ask.

"Thank you, ma'am. Here are your credentials, sir. Be sure to keep them on your person at all times. Please be advised that you are authorized for admission only to Building A. Your guest is also required to remain with you at all times during your visit."

"Even in the head?" I joked. No one laughed.

"Please park in lot number two. I'll phone ahead and let them know you're on your way."

Though I passed through security checkpoints every day at Pensacola, there was something about this one that had me sweating. Even Rusk, a Pentagon-posted captain, decorated naval aviator, and former wing commander, seemed uncomfortable. All that changed the moment we opened a pair of smoked-glass doors and entered the middle building, where a round little man with rimless glasses who looked like Popeye's sidekick Wimpy, came running up to meet us. I half expected him to say, *I'll gladly pay you Tuesday for a hamburger today!*

"John, it's so good to see you," he said, pumping Rusk's hand up and down, Adam's apple bobbing with the rhythm. "And this must be Miss Kennedy!" reaching for my hand, giving it the same treatment.

"Miss Kennedy, may I introduce Professor Robert Sherman. At Annapolis, he taught me everything I know about computers."

"Nice meeting you, Professor."

"Please, please, call me Bobby. And from what John here tells me you have much to teach us, Miss Kennedy!"

There it was again. Like the first time Maggie met me and told me she'd heard I was a genius. But this time I wasn't quite so floored. After three years working with other programmers, I knew I was good. Still, this guy Sherman was a professor! So I figured he was blowing me some rainbows.

"Thanks, Bobby. Call me Melora. And you're the teacher, so where do we start?"

Bobby's face lit up like the 4th of July. "Right this way, Melora!"

He led us to a polished brass door and stuck his I.D. into a reader. The door slid silently open. Four feet inside was another door, this one made of dull, flat-finish steel. The brass door closed behind us, and a dim red light came on. I couldn't hear a sound from behind either door. Bobby stepped to the side and put one eye against a raised peephole next to the steel door. There was a green flash, and Bobby made a startled little jump. I'm pretty sure I did, too. The door slid open, and we stepped into another world.

It's weird, but the first thing I noticed was the air conditioning. In Florida that was just a name for noisy machines that made the indoors freezing cold. But here, the air felt *conditioned*. It had a cool, silky quality, like it was the best air that could ever be. It wasn't cold, but it gave me goose bumps.

The next thing I noticed was the lighting. Like the air, it was soothing. I could hear a faint, steady hum, but when I looked out across the room, I realized it wasn't the whir of the AC or the buzz of fluorescent lights. It was the sound of big, mainframe computers, dozens of them behind a glass wall that stretched the length of a football field.

"Holy sh…." I caught Captain Rusk's look out of the corner of my eye. "Uh, I mean, WOW!"

"Wow indeed, Melora!" Bobby said. "You are looking at the largest networked array of IPI 6000 computers, with the most memory, power, and fastest speeds anywhere on earth. The Russians don't have anything like it, and neither do the Chinese. No one does. The programs you were using in Pensacola—the ones you kept improving—they were all created on these machines. And that's a tiny percent of what we do with them. Let's head upstairs where you can see more of IPI and meet the people who work with these modern wonders!"

We didn't see that much of IPI, because looking over the programmers' shoulders took up all of our time. What I did see changed my life forever. The fastest, most powerful computers imaginable, and the smartest programmers and smartest programs I'd ever seen. I always thought the Defense Department's hidden programming, its real programming, the kind of stuff I'd imagined on the Tomcat, happened at the Pentagon. I was wrong. Guidance systems, global navigation, weapons control, electronic intelligence gathering—all of it was happening at IPI. And Bobby kept hinting about something way bigger.

"I can't say much, but our top programmers are working on a project that will revolutionize the way military operations are conducted, something we couldn't dream of without the computing power—and brainpower—we've assembled here at IPI!"

While many of the programmers I met were veterans, everyone at IPI was a civilian. Some worked with screens, some with visors. A few jacked directly into keyboards using some kind of implant behind each ear, connected by thin plastic threads pulsing with light. And the amazing thing was, while their screens flickered with lightning-fast strings of code, they never touched the keyboards.

Bobby introduced me to one of the supervisors, a no-necked former marine named Ted. I asked him about the shiny, round steel plate above his ear, visible under the stubble of his GI buzz-cut.

"We program the computers to recognize and respond to neural commands activated by a programmer's subvocalizations. One end of the interface connects here…" Ted reached behind his ear and touched the implant, "…and the other end goes into a keyboard. The keyboard's for backup. That keeps the bosses happy, but frankly, we never use them. The business end of the connection is here." Ted rolled up his sleeve. Tattooed on his bicep was a toothy, spike-collared, fiercely-grinning, muscle-bound bulldog with sergeant's stripes on one foreleg and a drill instructors hat angled between its ears. I'd seen plenty of USMC bulldog tattoos before—shit, I'd done a few—but I'd never seen a tattoo like this one. Shiny, flickering, iridescent, electric. *Alive.* It looked more like it had been forged from strips of hot platinum and gold than drawn with needle and ink.

Ted saw the look on my face and smiled. "Don't worry, ma'am," he said, "it didn't hurt. Much."

I wanted to take my pants off and show him the ink aquarium circling my legs, but this didn't seem like the time.

"What's it do?" I said. "I mean besides prove that marines are jealous of Navy tattoos?"

Bobby and Captain Rusk looked like they were holding their breath, but Ted laughed.

"They're called subdermal semiconductors. Our implants talk to our tats, and our tats talk to the 6000s. It sounds tricky, but it helps our cybergrammers work up to a hundred times faster than our other programmers. And Marine cybergrammers? We get to leave work early, because we're done about a thousand times faster than anyone."

"At least that's what your girlfriends say."

"Well, ma'am," Ted said, while Bobby covered a cough with his hand and Captain Rusk pretended to look real interested in a nearby computer screen, "I can see you'd fit right in here at IPI."

In that moment, I knew I wanted to be a cybergrammer more than anything in the world. And Ted knew it too.

On the way out I asked Bobby, "How come you're not wired?" He was way too bald to be hiding an implant under his hair the way some cybergrammers did.

"Oh, that's for young people like you, Melora. Cybergramming is far too stressful for an old man like me. I'm still using a keyboard if you can imagine that!"

We stared at him.

"What? Did I say something?"

"Oh, it's nothing," Rusk said. "It's just that in the Navy, everyone uses keyboards."

"I didn't realize... I mean, I guess I've really let myself get out of touch since I retired from teaching and joined IPI. I really miss teaching."

Looking at his watch, looking nervous, pushing his glasses up the bridge of his nose with one hand, a few strands of graying hair off his forehead with the other, Bobby began leading us back to the main entrance.

"They only allow three hours for visitors. Can you join my wife Ellen and me for dinner this evening?"

"Sorry, Professor Sherman. We'd love to, but Miss Kennedy's overdue in Pensacola, and I'm expected in Washington, ASAP."

Shaking our hands, still looking uncomfortable, Bobby said his goodbyes as we reached the smoked-glass doors.

"I am so looking forward to working with both of you!"

On the drive to Otis we were quiet for a while. Captain Rusk spoke first, and for the first time he didn't sound like a captain.

"You must have a lot of questions, Melora, and I appreciate your patience with all this..." taking one hand off the wheel, waving it in a circle, "...mysteriousness. I'm sure you appreciate the necessity for complete confidentiality about the last twenty-four hours and everything you witnessed at IPI."

"Yes sir. But Captain..."

"Yes?"

"...why did Professor Sherman quit teaching?"

With that his grip on the wheel tightened.

"Let's just say IPI made him an offer he couldn't refuse."

"Are they making us an offer we can't refuse?"

Captain Rusk didn't say anything for a long time.

"The Navy's my life, Melora, but I've gone as far as I can go. My first love was fighter planes, but after Vietnam they kicked me upstairs to a desk job. I got a second chance in Iraq and Afghanistan, but I spent most of those wars watching younger guys catapult off the *Eisenhower*'s deck. My second love became computers. But admirals aren't programmers. Besides, Uncle Sam realizes washed-up fighter jocks and would-be computer geeks make for lousy admiral material. No, Melora, I'm retiring at the end of next year, and the only place I can keep doing what I love is IPI. As for you, the answer's simple. Please don't take offense at this, but we both know you'll never be much of a sailor. We also know you're the best programmer anyone's ever seen. From the day Mrs. Oyeda first showed me your work at John Paul Jones, you've been slated for a job at IPI. Because you dropped out of high school, and college was out of the question, your only way into IPI was through the Navy. So, I'm admitting to you that I manipulated your life. I'm also hoping you're not angry about it."

I didn't feel angry, shook my head, letting him know.

"You're sick of the grunt work at Pensacola and I don't blame you. Asking you to write payroll programs is like asking Picasso to paint outhouses. I could transfer you to Norfolk or Bremerton or D.C., but you'd end up doing the same kind of work. I kept you at Pensacola so you could be near your family, and near the beach."

"Did you read that in my personnel file?"

"I put that in your personnel file."

Speeding down the Massachusetts Turnpike, I was trying to take in what I was hearing, trying to figure out what to say next. But Captain Rusk wasn't finished.

"There's one other thing—the only important thing really. There's another war coming. Probably not this year, maybe not next. But as sure as sunrise, we'll be at war inside of three years. For that war, the first real cyber war, IPI needs you, and your country needs you. I need you. So I guess what I'm asking is, are you willing to finish out your last year at Pensacola, then come work with me at IPI?"

I didn't say a thing until we crossed the bridge to Cape Cod, until I could see the Atlantic shimmering as far away as forever.

"I'll do it on one condition."

Captain Rusk's eyebrows rose in surprise.

"Remember my friend David Cooperman from John Paul Jones...?"

Me and Coop started working together at IPI the following summer.

PART FOUR

WAR

Chapter Twenty: Toby

Mmmm. So IPI's hooked a couple of new fish. And that one's good. Real good. Their programmers worked on that autopilot glitch for two years. She (she?) waltzes in and fixes it her first day. They're gonna cyberjack her in no time.

Yup, this one's different all right—she's got imagination. And that makes her dangerous.

Well sweetheart, like the song says—*I'll be watchin' you....*

Chapter Twenty-One: Melora

Working at IPI was *sweet*. My first day on the job I corrected an autopilot program glitch that had stumped the other programmers for weeks. I made cybergrammer in sixty-three days—a record that still stands—then spent a month at the IPI labs in Palo Alto having my implants and fiber optics installed and calibrated, and another month in Natick programming my own subvocalization recognitions. The hardest part was adjusting to the immunosuppressants they prescribed me so my body wouldn't reject the implants, but after a few days riding the porcelain bus, I was good to go. Coop had to make up for a lack of experience and a lot of lost time, but with me coaching him, he made cybergrammer in six months.

Our work was fucking incredible, always new, never boring. Okay, this one time we got bored and played a little prank on the security geeks. Me and Coop had them passing kidney stones, breaking into their "secure" Net, setting off intruder alerts for a different IPI entrance every three minutes. Of course Captain Rusk knew it was us right away, showing up at our workstation with the klaxons blaring and the two of us laughing our asses off.

"Promise me you'll never, ever, do that again," he said.

We knew it was a big deal for a man who spent his life giving orders to ask us to stop acting like a couple of *pendejos*. So we promised.

Maggie Rusk became the mother me and Coop never had, confiding in us, letting us confide in her, taking us in the Geo on road trips to Tanglewood and the Cape, taking us shopping at Quincy Market and Filene's, feeding us ridiculous amounts of food.

Professor Sherman and his wife Ellen filled the role of grandparents, throwing birthday parties for us, buying us everything from London Fog raincoats to goldfish, and having me join them at Disneyworld during one of my trips home to Florida.

I couldn't say the captain was like our father because he was, y'know, the Captain. And now he was a senior vice president and, at least in title, our boss. He was the one who assigned us projects, the one responsible if we screwed up. But me and Coop made sure we never screwed up, and once he assigned a project, Rusk left us alone.

A couple of months after making cybergrammer, I was sitting in the lunchroom eating a microwaved burrito, reading *The Boston Phoenix*. Captain Rusk was in the far corner near the parking-lot-view picture window eating some great smelling dish Maggie packed for him, reading *Barrons*. Usually Coop joined me, but he was out on some secret mission, probably a quickie with his latest girlfriend, a big phony from Wellesley, way too young, way too tall, and way too smart for him anyway. Then in walked this guy Kenneth. Coop called him "Hahvahd," because the first thing he always told everyone was that he went there. Hahvahd joined IPI in the same training group as me and Coop, so Rusk was his boss too, but he hadn't made cybergrammer. He asked me out a couple of times like he was doing me a favor, and I said no. When he asked why, I told him "I only date guys who went to Brown."

Kenneth spotted me right away, coming up to my table, pulling a chair around backward, sitting with his legs splayed like he was riding a horse. Captain Rusk was at his back, hidden in the corner, head bent over his reading.

"Hey, Kennedy, howya doin'?"

"Better a minute ago."

"That's pretty funny. I think you get that sense of humor of yours from the Kennedy side of your family. But y'know what I can't figure out?"

"Everything?"

"No, what I can't figure out is this. Sure, JFK did a lot of screwing. But I can't imagine a Harvard man like him fucking some spic. I mean, getting his cock sucked, maybe, but...."

Before I could move, before I could speak, before I could breathe, Captain Rusk was out of his chair, crossing the room, lifting Kenneth off the floor by his Brooks Brothers lapels, throwing him against the lunchroom refrigerator.

"Apologize."

"Whaaa?"

Rusk grabbed him a little tighter, hoisted him a little higher.

"I said, apologize."

"I... I'm sorry. I didn't mean anything, I just...."

"That's good enough." Holding him pinned against the Kelvinator, feet six inches off the floor, Captain Rusk took one hand from Kenneth's lapel and snapped off the IPI I.D. tag clipped to his pocket. "Don't bother clearing out your work station. We'll mail your personal effects."

"I... I don't understand, sir."

"You're fired, mister. Go home."

One great thing about being a Captain—even civilians can tell when it's time to say, "Yes sir," and follow orders. Sliding to ground level, Kenneth scrambled out the door while Rusk smoothed his own tailored suit.

"You okay, slugger?" he said.

Slugger? Where did that come from?

"Yes, sir. I'm fine. That was great! Thanks! But I don't think HR's going to be happy about your termination procedures."

"When it comes to harassment, they'll have to get used to me dealing with it the old fashioned way."

Even though I knew I could have handled Hahvahd myself, could have told Rusk not to interfere, I realized how good it felt having him act like a father should. So instead, I said, "Thanks, dad." And the captain stopped smoothing his clothes and smiled.

Remember all those Access Law exemptions? You know, like the one Congress gave to credit bureaus? I remembered them, too. So I went to my workstation, jacked in, and added a broken lease, unpaid student loans, and three bankcard defaults to that *hijo de puta* Kenneth's credit history.

Have a nice life, Hahvahd.

Chapter Twenty-Two: Melora

RITA. That's my girl. More like my baby.

Evil bitch.

Real-time Integrated Tactical Analytics. Mainframe computers and programs powerful enough to run a war. Remove the human element with all its biases, neuroses, and hidden agendas. Great idea, right? But what's that saying—the road to hell is paved with good intentions?

The war was already fucked before we brought RITA online. We weren't losing, but we weren't winning. Which meant we were losing.

Every month a different admiral or general showed up at IPI, looked over our shoulders, asked a few dumbass questions. None of them knew shit about computers, and all of them looked scared. They had no fucking clue what RITA could and couldn't do, but they all wanted to believe she could win their war for them. So after every visit they flew to DC and told the politicians RITA was The Answer. And after every visit, the politicians wrote more checks made out to IPI. Believe me, IPI kicked back plenty of that taxpayer money to the politicians.

Toby wasn't the only one who taught me history. The Navy did too—at least their version—long before Toby hacked his way into my life. But Chief Kavaney, veteran of two hot underwater wars and one cold one, told me the military history he thought counted. And the old chief told me straight.

"For my arthritis," he'd say, downing his fifth shot of Wild Turkey in the dark back booth at Spanky's, a Pensacola dive bar popular with us bluejackets. Then he'd go off on his favorite subject. Officers.

"Y'see, Mel, they ain't like us. We just wanna keep our frickin' noses clean and do our frickin' jobs. Officers? They're all on the make. Little politicians hooked on movin' up the ladder, all of them with their noses shoved up the butts of the guy on the rung above them 'cuz that's the only way up, and all doin' it so the guy on the rung below 'em will stick his nose up their butts."

"C'mon, Chief," I'd say, "They're not all like that."

"Not all, Mel, but the good ones hardly ever make it to the top. They can't, because makin' it to the top means stickin' your nose so far up the real politicians' butts that you forget what daylight looks like. It means lyin' about everything to keep the politicians happy, lyin' so much you forget what the truth is. Lyin' about things like what it will take to win a war. Or how many boys and girls are gonna wind up dead. Lyin' about how we're winnin' the war—lyin' to yourself about how we're winnin' it—so the politicians can lie to the voters. 'Cuz if you don't go along to get along, you ain't never gonna get another little star pinned on your lapel."

"I met a good senior officer once. Guy who got me into the Navy. And he was a pilot and wing commander in Vietnam."

"Well sure, Mel. Sounds like a *real* warrior. I've known some great ones in my day. But honestly, those guys ain't shit in the big picture. They ain't shit because they don't have the president's ear. And the only ones who've got the president's ear are the ones who tell him what he wants to hear. The further they go up the chain of command—the higher they climb on that ladder—the less they want to take responsibility. They don't have to win wars, they only have to avoid the big mistakes that'll get 'em fired. So they live their lives terrified they're gonna make a big mistake. At first it makes 'em cautious. That ain't a bad thing, because in the short run, it means less of us get killed. But after awhile, it makes 'em timid. Then scared. Then positively chickenshit. And in the long run, that means a whole lot more of us get killed."

I thought about that while Chief Kavaney ordered another round. This time he sipped at his whiskey, swirling it between swallows so the ice cubes tinkled against the side of the glass, eyes focused on something in the distance, or maybe something in the past. I drank my bottle of Bud, sitting quietly because I felt like saying something now would mean butting in on the chief's private conversation with himself. After a long few minutes, he downed the rest of his drink and shifted his gray eyes back to me.

"Winston Churchill said that if you take the most gallant sailor, the most intrepid airman or the most audacious soldier, put 'em at a table together—what do you get? The sum of their fears. I never thought he was talking about sailors, airmen, and soldiers in the field. I thought he meant the ones who climbed that brown-nosing officer ladder so high they got a seat at that table. And I always thought it was those sons of bitches who lost us that fucked up war in Vietnam. Them and the lyin' bastards in the White House they answered to."

When IPI put Captain Rusk in charge of the cybergrammer group hand-picked to fix the shit-show RITA had become and make the billions Congress had poured into her start paying off, the captain called us together for a meeting. "If you could program RITA to be one thing," he said, "what would it be?"

"Fast," Coop said. "Oh, and sexy!" Everyone laughed at that, the way Coop always got us laughing.

More seriously, Caprice, a girl who'd been hired fresh out of some Ivy League school and made cybergrammer almost as quick as me, said, "Smart."

Ron, the former All American quarterback from Utah, raised his hand to speak, as usual, even though everyone else had, as usual, jumped right into the conversation.

"Down the hall and to the left, Ron," Coop said.

Even Ron laughed at that one, but this time Captain Rusk didn't join in.

"Go ahead, Ron—what's the one thing you'd program RITA to be?"

"Adaptable."

"And you, Ted?"

Ted, the ex-Marine with the bulldog neck and bulldog tattoo didn't hesitate. "Deadly," he said.

Captain Rusk nodded. "What about you, Melora? What one thing would you want RITA to be?"

Coop and Caprice wanted RITA to do what computers were best at—process billions of bits of data at speeds millions of times faster than any human commander and spit out the results so others could act on them. But doing more of what wasn't working and doing it faster wasn't the answer. Ron and Ted wanted something better. So did I.

That's when I remembered what Chief Kavaney said back in Pensacola, remembered his Churchill quote about "the sum of all fears."

"Fearless," I said. "I want RITA to be fearless."

Okay, so given my fucked up childhood, maybe I was projecting. But that's when I decided that RITA might make mistakes, but she'd never be afraid.

So we went to work. And we did it. We made RITA fast. We made her smart. We made her adaptable. We made her deadly. And I made her a cold-hearted-bitch. And I never worried about that, because RITA didn't make decisions, only suggestions. It was up to humans to decide whether to act on them. Flesh-and-blood commanders could always make the compassionate choice if the silicon maiden went too far.

You see, I understood RITA. My problem was, I didn't understand people.

If I'd thought more about what Chief Kavaney said, I wouldn't have been surprised when commanders rubber-stamped RITA's suggestions. Wouldn't have gone along when her suggestions were treated like orders. Wouldn't have been so fucking proud when the generals, admirals, and politicians took the safeties off and let RITA, without any human interference, run everything from recruitment to logistics to ops. In other words, the whole goddamn war.

Of course they trust RITA, I thought. She's better at this than they are. And she's better because we made her that way!

But that wasn't it at all.

Commanders didn't turn the show over to RITA because they trusted her. They did it because they were scared. If they let RITA do her thing and it worked, they got the credit. If it didn't work, RITA got the blame. But if they overruled her and things turned out badly, it was all on them.

RITA had become the sum of their fears.

Chapter Twenty-Three: Melora

I'd never lie and say it wasn't fun working on military systems. It was. For most of our lives, me and Coop never had much money, power, or freedom. Now we had all three. We were making great money. So much money in salary, bonuses, and IPI stock options that I had to jack in to figure out what I was worth.

In some ways it was more fun when the war started. After years of simulations and practice, RITA, our creation, was getting a chance to do her thing in a real war. Every day we got shitloads of real-time feedback from her, and every day there were new programming challenges for us. We kept making RITA smarter, faster, deadlier, and more fearless, and as she proved herself, her role in running the war got bigger.

We never ran Operations—"independent contractors" did that out of Building B next door. At least that was the official word. Everyone knew they were CIA. Half the cars in the Building B parking lot had D.C. or Virginia plates; some had license plate frames from Langley car dealerships. And while IPI's dress code meant everyone wore business clothes, most of us in programming found ways to let our freak flags fly—shoulder-length dreads, ink peeking out from beneath cuffs and above collars, half-shaved mullets, heavy-metal galaxies of pierced ears, lips, noses, necks, eyebrows, and tongues. Not so much over at Ops. Those boys and girls all looked Government Issue.

While they handled what most of us at IPI called "The Show," we knew RITA was the real boss, and RITA was our creation. Ted, Coop, me, and the rest of the cybergrammers programmed scenarios and simulations for every operation, and RITA, weighing every option, every bit of intelligence, every lesson of military history, made every tactical decision based on strategic considerations. RITA learned more from each engagement and did something no human commander ever dreamed of—she remembered all of it. We knew RITA would lose some battles, maybe even on purpose. But RITA would never lose a war. And for me, and the rest of us, it was a blast. At least until real bodies started coming home.

Once a month they shuttled Ops Team Leaders over to our building so they could tell us first-hand about improvements they wanted us to make in our programs. We were all on the same side, but we were also competitive. And arrogant. We didn't like them; they didn't like us. We looked down on them because they were too lame to write their own programs. They thought we were a bunch of freaks and draft dodgers. Mostly, the glitches they bitched about were their own fault, operator errors caused by poor training, laziness, or stupidity. At least that was our opinion.

One time some IPI exec got the brilliant idea she could promote teamwork and increase efficiency by inviting Captain Rusk, Coop, me, and a couple of the other senior cybergrammers over to Building B to watch The Show. I could tell the Captain wasn't happy about it, but he put on his game face and said, "Let's go check it out and see what we can learn." Looking at me and Coop, he added, "And let's all be on our best behavior."

We filed downstairs and onto a waiting shuttle bus. Building B was no more than four hundred yards away, and we could have easily walked, but right from the beginning this operation was going by the book. Our "host," a brown-shoed Company *pendejo* named Mr. Smith—seriously, Mr. Smith—greeted us on the bus. He looked like he would have preferred latrine duty.

"Operations' security protocols begin on this bus," he said.

"When the hand goes up, the mouth goes shut," Coop whispered from the seat next to mine.

Smith heard him, narrowed his eyes like he was making a mental note, and continued.

"You are required to stay with the group at all times and immediately follow any instructions given by IPI security personnel. Everything you will observe today is classified. Do any of you have questions concerning your responsibilities in that regard?"

I felt Coop's hand start to go up, but I grabbed it before he could raise it above the seatback in front of us.

"Very well," Smith said, and motioned for the driver to head across the parking lot.

A gun-toting, Kevlar-wearing security team met us at the Building B door. They scanned our I.D.s and took some headshot video. Coop gave me a look and started to say something, but Captain Rusk cleared his throat, and Coop shut up right away. I knew what he was thinking— this was ridiculous. But locked and loaded M16s held at the ready made sure we knew it wasn't just for show.

Our Programming Center in Building A could have passed for the headquarters of any company that had a C-ASS exemption—desks, chairs, phones, offices, partitions, computers, all brightly lit from above. The Ops Center in Building B was more like the set from some big-budget sci-fi movie. The first-floor hall was lined on either side by closed doors with complicated-looking security locks, but the surprise came when the armored elevator doors opened onto the second floor. As my eyes slowly adjusted to the dim green lighting, I realized that it was really the second, third, and fourth floors, because the ceiling was high above us at roof level. Unlike Building A, there were no windows or skylights, though from the outside it appeared there were both. There were also no workstations, no exit doors, and no stairwells. I figured if someone needed to pee they'd have to get on the elevator and find a head behind one of those locked doors downstairs, because there were no restrooms either. And if there was a fire—shit—we were dead.

A wide central corridor led to four sets of double doorways opening into what looked like four heavily soundproofed IMAX theaters. Smith led us down the corridor and through the second set of doors on our left into Theater 2. The low buzz of shoptalk and chitchat coming from inside stopped as we entered. Smith blocked our passage down the aisle with his broad-shouldered body and motioned us to sit in the first of the three rows of plush theater-style seats at the back. Where the floor leveled out in the front of the room, a dozen men and women in shirtsleeves sat or stood by a row of consoles, keyboards, and joysticks. In front of them, the theater's three-story wall consisted of two rows of eight high-resolution screens topped by one giant screen at least twenty feet high and thirty wide.

Smith sat down by himself in the last row. One of the shirt-sleeved girls made a cupped-hand remark that got a laugh from the guy next to her, squared her shoulders, and looked up at us.

"Welcome to The Show," she said, "where IPI's real work gets done."

No one said anything, but I knew what all of us cybergrammers were thinking—*Screw you, asshole*—and a whole bunch of really creative variations on that theme.

"We've timed your visit today to coincide with a scheduled op. We've got a company of troopers in the field, hard intelligence that our target will be accessible within the next thirty minutes, and a "go" from the Pentagon brass for actualizing RITA's decisions without running them up the chain of command. Operations timetables, are, however, always fluid and subject to change or cancellation. Your job today is to sit silently and wait until the scheduled operation is either completed or scrubbed. When either of those two has occurred, Mr. Smith will escort you to your bus. There will be no opportunities for questions."

So we sat in silence, fidgeting, because when cybergrammers have nothing to do and can't jack in, we always fidget. Meanwhile, at the front of the theater, the Ops guys made a big show of looking all cazh. You know, just another day at the office.

That all changed when five ever-louder beeps sounded through the theater's speakers. Everyone was at their stations, sitting up straight, hunching over, or standing behind seated pairs of operators. The annoying girl stood behind all of them, looking like she was in charge. I jumped a little when the screens lit up, at first just a mashup of green and black, then slowly resolving, the small screens filled with jerky images of dimly lit earth and foliage, the big screen showing an aerial view of moonlit ocean. In Indonesia it was night, and Righteous Sword troopers equipped with night-vision goggles were humping their way through the jungle while Marine aviators launched from carrier decks far out at sea, their every move uplinked to RITA and directed by RITA through the people at the front of this room 9,900 miles away.

If this were a movie, it would have been boring. Thirty minutes of leafy, dripping fronds and heavy breathing interrupted by occasional halts, while whispered queries and terse commands flashed back and forth through the ether at light speed, everything orderly and controlled. But it wasn't a movie, and without realizing it most of us were leaning forward in tense anticipation.

Suddenly, there was a clearing—so suddenly the troopers stumbled into the open before they realized it. Someone, probably the company commander, turned and raised both hands, signaling a halt. At the clearing's center, three-dozen thatch-roofed huts surrounded by tilled pasture. At 4 o'clock a goat pen, at 5 a chicken coop, two outhouses at 7 and two more at 8. Between the troopers and the huts a clear alley at 6 o'clock without so much as a boulder or stump blocking the way.

More whispered consultation, and while I couldn't make out all the words, it sounded like the IPI Ops team, after consulting RITA, was urging the unit's reluctant commander forward into the village in search of a specific target. Slowly, and way too noisily, first one platoon, then another, then another moved forward into the clearing. Part of my mind—the part trained more by running simulations on RITA than by the Navy—knew the troopers were too bunched up, knew the third platoon should have been kept in reserve. Another part of my mind realized I was holding my breath.

Now the chicken coop and goat pen were on the first rank of the troopers' right flank, the outhouses on their left. A goat bleated. A twig snapped.

Then, chaos.

I remember most of what happened after that, but I'm not sure what happened when. A searchlight flicked on atop the chicken coop and swept the closely bunched platoons. Blinded troopers began frantically tearing off their goggles. The first rank disappeared from sight as though a trapdoor had opened beneath them, and many of the second rank stumbled over the first rank. Muzzle flashes lit the goat pen from ground level, and both outhouse doors burst open with a fusillade of rifle fire.

The theater's speakers, so quiet before, erupted with gunfire, screams, shouts and curses, the shrill sounds of men and women under attack. Above the noise, one voice hollered, "Fall back! Fall Back!" The front ranks were pinned down by flanking fire, but the rear ranks began pulling out, turning to direct covering fire as best they could.

This was nothing like IPI's real-time public broadcasts. For one thing, that video was always choppy. For another, our troops always won. I'd suspected those broadcasts were edited; now I was wondering if they were staged.

Inside the tree line, the troopers reformed, directing automatic weapons fire at the goat pen and outhouses, and less discriminately at the huts beyond. Javanese curses and screams filled the theater as the enemy's rifles stuttered, then fell silent. Surviving troopers still in the clearing began shinnying toward the jungle, while from the tree line friendly fire into the village whistled inches above their helmets. Too slowly, the survivors inched their way to safety, some dragging the injured with them, some, the dead.

After a few more rifle cracks from inside the village, and a hail of answering fire, everything fell silent. *Now we'll get those bastards!* I thought. I'm not proud of it, but that's what I thought.

In the silence, a different voice this time, barely under control, crackled over the speakers. "The captain's dead. What the fuck do you want us to do now?"

At the front of the room the controllers huddled briefly around the main console before answering. The HBIC lifted a microphone to her lips.

"Pull out," she said.

"Are you fucking kidding me? We didn't take a shitload of casualties for nothing! We're going in and finish the job!"

"Too dangerous. RITA's calling in an airstrike."

"An airstrike! Listen you fucking asshole, we're on top of the goddamn village. That fucking computer will kill us all!"

"Then you better stop talking and pull out."

"You motherfucker... okay, okay... how much time do we have?"

She looked down at the console. "Less than three minutes. I repeat, three min..."

"I fucking heard you! Jesus Christ!" Whoever it was in charge of the company shouted orders, and troopers began shuffling deeper into the jungle. At their backs, more rifle fire erupted, directed toward their noisy departure. One trooper went down. A lucky shot.

"Medic! *Medic!*"

"No time, goddammit! You two, get up under her shoulders and carry her—double time!"

I was so focused on the smaller screens' grainy images that it took a while until the steadily increasing rumble coming through the speakers made me look up at the big screen. Green-lit jungle was whipping beneath the rotors of a Zulu Cobra attack helicopter flying at treetop level. I recognized it because I worked on the IPI team that developed the targeting software for its weapons systems, including the sixteen AGM-114 Hellfire air-to-surface missiles it carried in wing-mounted launchers. Ahead of the Cobra, I could make out the outlines of three more gunships speeding above the jungle, until, in the distance, there was a clearing. All four choppers plunged dizzyingly at the village, and I closed my eyes for a moment to clear my head. When I opened them the Cobras were so close to the deck, I could see people running for cover, or holding their ground, uselessly aiming rifles skyward at the terrifying howl above them.

I glanced at the small screens. The troopers had barely cleared the tree line, but at least they could count on the Marines to come in low, risking their lives to make sure their ordnance fell on the enemies instead of the friendlies.

"Death from above!" One of the pilots said, her words crackling from the speakers. If there was a reply, it was drowned out by at least a dozen booming concussions as the darkened theater flooded with the light from fiery explosions on all nine screens.

The Ops team worked swiftly, sifting data, adjusting camera angles, and reading RITA's analysis of it all. It took a few minutes, but finally the large screen revealed towering flames where once there had been a village. For a moment, there was silence. Then the Ops team members leapt to their feet, whooping and high-fiving. As for our little troop of cybergrammers, all of us, even Coop, sat in stunned silence.

Captain Rusk stood up. Smith blocked the aisle, but the Captain shouldered his way past him like Smith was a ragdoll and pushed through the theater door. The rest of us followed.

That was the last time we were invited to Ops.

Chapter Twenty-Four: Melora

At IPI we talked about the war, like people everywhere talked about the war. In the beginning, with troop deployments small and White House promises big – *The AEF will be home for Christmas!*—most supported the war without question. As one deadline for withdrawal after another passed and casualties grew daily, people at IPI, like people around the country, started taking sides. But despite IPI's focus on war-related R & D, discussions about the war remained casual water cooler and lunchroom topics. Even when we accessed classified information conflicting with Pentagon reports carefully spun to the media, we still felt like we were merely observers. Only Professor Sherman, who was against U.S. involvement from the beginning, argued that everyone at IPI shared "…personal responsibility to act on our opposition to the war." Everyone ignored him. Including me.

The Navy tapped into patriotic feelings I never knew I had, and also put faces on the warriors. I stayed in touch with the old gang from Pensacola—Chief Kavaney was back at sea on the *Dallas*, God only knew where or how many fathoms deep, and Bosworth, promoted to Lieutenant Commander, shipped out on the *Abraham Lincoln*, running Computer Ops for an entire carrier battle group, probably fantasizing he was Robert E. Lee. My nephew Darin enlisted on his seventeenth birthday, announcing, "I'm gonna join the Navy and kick some Red

Path ass. And when the war's over, I'm gonna learn all about computers, just like Melora!" I encouraged him because, like me, the navy was his only way out. Nine months later he was cruising the war zone on the *Lovell*, a tin-can destroyer.

Politics never interested me, but I understood the connection between what I did every day and what I saw on my TV at night. And now I knew something I hadn't known before my visit to The Show—IPI was sanitizing its so-called livestream of the war. Don't get me wrong, what America saw on TV every night was plenty gruesome. But they never showed dissension among the troopers, only patriotic displays of bravery. And they never showed a clusterfuck like the one we witnessed at Building B. And they never showed a whole village being wiped from the face of the earth because RITA had a bug up her ass about one particular insurgent.

Everything I'd seen reminded me of Mr. Belasso and his Marine buddies, the picture hanging on the wall behind the counter at the pizzeria, his warning about Huế and the Tet Offensive. So that's where I began my research.

After three weeks and a couple of all-nighters reading every Vietnam War history I could lay my hands on, I had to talk to Coop. In high school they forced me to take seven semesters of history, but hadn't taught me a fucking thing about Vietnam. Maybe it was different for Coop in college or at John Paul Jones.

One day during lunch, I asked him straight up, "What do you know about Vietnam?"

"Only that my dad got completely screwed up there."

"I didn't know your dad was in combat."

"Nah, he never did any fighting. He was a veterinarian. They needed someone to look after the guard dogs and all the poor retrievers who got blown up sniffing out landmines and digging their way into Viet Cong tunnels. But whatever the hell happened over there made him start drinking. My mom said he never touched booze before the army."

"Look, Coop, I've been reading all kinds of stuff about Vietnam. You should take a look too."

Coop's face got funny, a twisted up expression I'd never seen before.

"Nah, no thanks, Mel. We've got our hands full with this war." Seeing the surprised look on my face, he added, "C'mon, Mel, we've finally got things going our way. Let's not screw it up." Then he took a last bite of his sandwich and walked off without another word.

My next stop was Captain Rusk's office. Everyone at IPI knew about his Vietnam combat record—nine MIGs killed, countless bombing raids, shot down twice by surface-to-air missiles and walked out of the jungle to safety both times—but they hadn't heard it from him. He never talked about that war, was about the only one at IPI who never talked about the Indonesian War.

I knocked on his door gently, like I always did.

"Enter."

"Hi, Captain."

Captain Rusk was always calm and direct. Usually, he greeted me with a smile. Not today.

"I'm glad you came by, Melora. There's something I've been wanting to talk about with you."

"There's something I've been wanting to talk over with you, too, Captain."

"Do you mind if I go first?" He didn't wait for me to answer. "I'm thinking that mess over at Ops shook you up. Am I correct?"

"Yeah, you could say that. I even thought about quitting."

"Well then, may I say that it shook me up, too? That I also thought about resigning?"

I never expected I'd hear anything like that from Captain Rusk. My face must have showed it.

"I see that surprises you," he said.

I nodded.

Captain Rusk was one of the few people I'd ever met who always looked me in the eye when we talked. Now he looked down at his hands.

"Yes, I thought about resigning. Then I thought about all the terrible decisions I've seen human commanders make. All the stupid, vain, ambitious, corrupt, greedy, bigoted choices humans make every day and the countless lives lost because of them. Whatever mistakes RITA makes, at least she won't make them because of prejudice or self-interest. So I didn't quit, Melora. And neither should you. Quitting won't help. We've got to stay, because we're the ones who can make RITA better."

"I don't think RITA's the problem, Captain. I think it's the war."

He looked up at me, startled, like it was the first time he'd really seen me since I walked into his office.

"Melora, if you don't mind my saying so, you look like you've been burning the candle at both ends."

"More like burning the midnight oil. I've been up reading about Vietnam."

"Oh? Reading what?"

"Westmoreland, Giap, Karnow, McNamara. About the Tet Offensive and Huế."

"That's quite a list. What've you learned?"

"That our war looks a lot like that one."

He could have said many things. What he did say shocked me.

"Does that make any difference?"

"Well yeah, of course it makes a difference. If we've gotten into another fucked-up war we need to get out of it before we kill more innocent people." I'd never cursed in front of Captain Rusk before, and the instant the words came out of my mouth I knew I shouldn't have done it then. But Captain Rusk didn't look angry, he looked icy calm. Which was worse.

"Melora, you disappoint me." *Disappoint him?* "The decision to go to war is a political one. Argue, discuss, debate, and demonstrate all you want before that decision is made. Write your Congressmen, vote for peace candidates, go out and get arrested for trespassing at the Pentagon. But once our soldiers are placed in harm's way, the time for protest is over. People like to say we never lost a battle in Vietnam, including the battle for Huế. But we lost that damn war because too many Americans didn't understand one simple fact—every protest undermined our forces and gave comfort to the enemy."

I wanted to stop, but I couldn't. My words came too fast. And too loud.

"From what I read, we lost that war because we didn't understand anything about the Vietnamese people or their history. Because the French colonials replaced the Chinese imperialists, the Japanese invaders replaced the French, the French replaced the Japanese again, and when Vietnam kicked out the French, we tried replacing them. And all because some geniuses at the State Department were scared of China, who Vietnam hated worse than us, and who these days sells us everything Americans buy!"

Captain Rusk looked at me while I caught my breath, his face and words blank, emotionless.

"Miss Kennedy," he said, "you couldn't possibly know what happened in Vietnam. You weren't there."

The next day I began messing with my work. Nothing anyone could call sabotage, just the kind of mistakes the other programmers made all the time. The kind of mistakes that grafted onto other people's work and snowballed. Nothing that would shake up RITA, because who knew how that might turn out, and nothing that would hurt our troops. Just some stupid fucked-up bullshit because I was pissed with IPI and the fucking war. Kids' stuff, really.

But there was more to it than that.

From the first day in the academy's library with Coop and the 700, all I thought I'd ever wanted to do was write programs. Now I realized I'd wanted more. That program I wrote for Mr. Belasso, the one that let him save money on his air conditioning? Why did I write it? Sure, it was fun. But though I didn't understand it then, there was another reason, too. I wanted my work to make him smile.

I never cared about big stuff, never thought about saving the world. But here I was, a veteran of four years in the U.S. Navy and a dozen more at IPI, living my programming dreams. Only now my work wasn't making people smile, it was killing them.

I was killing them.

Was I taking a chance, risking everything I'd worked for? Maybe. But I didn't think so. I thought I was too fucking smart to get caught, and IPI Security was too fucking stupid to catch me. Coop and Captain Rusk? They might figure it out. But as well as Coop and Rusk knew me, I was sure I knew them better, knew them well enough to continue my little protest in ways they'd never notice. Still, I was afraid they'd catch on, afraid what it might mean for me and the only real friends I'd ever had.

Chapter Twenty-Five: Toby

Somethin's changed. There. There! She's stallin'. She could finish that surface-to-air guidance program in five minutes. But she's stringin' it out, addin' lots of redundant code. And a feedback loop. She never does stupid shit like that!

Why now? Is she sick of the killin'? Has she had enough?

Or maybe she's on to me. Maybe it's a trap. She's the only one smart enough to dangle that kind of bait.

Can I trust her? Can I take that chance?

Chapter Twenty-Six: Melora

*A*RE YOU PAYING ATTENTION?

The words flashed across my visor while music coming from the implant hummed inside my head, some guy backed by a '60s band, sounding like he had a kazoo stuck up his nose, singing some shit about how he wasn't gonna work on Maggie's farm, whoever the fuck Maggie was.

But before I can think about what's happening, more words, stinging words—

THE BAG COUNT: 34,786 Americans dead, 136,255 wounded. 140,000 Red Path and Indonesian noncombatants dead, 300,000 wounded. HAD ENOUGH? STAY TUNED!

And the diagnostic I was running on surface-to-air guidance jammers came back online like nothing had happened.

My first thought was practical, arrogant—no one was good enough to get past my security protocols, not even Coop. Every cybergramming stud at IPI tried hacking into everyone else's work, showing off, playing practical jokes, jockeying for bragging rights over who had the biggest hard drive. But nobody had ever come close to hacking me.

Then I stopped worrying about the messenger, focusing on the message. Instead of "Who?", the question became, "Why?" If IPI Security was on to what I was doing, why not just bust me? Why play games?

I dumped out of the diagnostic program, running every tracer I could think of, making up new ones when the tracers on my hard drive turned up nothing. Keeping at it like I always did with seemingly unsolvable electronic mysteries got me nowhere. At the end of the day, I only knew one thing for sure about the message—as far as the entire IPI Net was concerned, it never happened. And that was impossible.

I didn't sleep much that night, and when I did I dreamed the dream of dark skies and churning ocean waters. I woke wondering what came next.

My mystery hacker didn't disappoint. I got to work an hour early, but the instant I jacked in it happened again—

RINGER PARK, ALLSTON. MIDNIGHT TONIGHT. ALONE.

And again, the message was gone almost before I could read it. The music lingered, something I recognized this time, an old song Boston's classic rock station played every day—Grace Slick singing *White Rabbit*.

Options? Tell Rusk. That's what I'm supposed to do, but I was betting my hacker knew why I couldn't let security start nosing around my files. Try tracing again? If I couldn't do it yesterday what chance did I have today? And at some point, someone at IPI Security would notice all my tracing activity and start asking questions. Talk it over with Coop? Until I began spiking my programs, I always turned to Coop. But even if I wanted to tell him everything, I couldn't, because yesterday he'd taken off to Paris for two weeks with his latest honey.

There really was only one option. Besides, my curiosity was stronger than my fear. Whoever sent that message was planning on taking me through the looking glass. No, more than that, knew I couldn't resist the trip.

Chapter Twenty-Seven: Toby

This is nuts. But at least sittin' up here I can see 'em before they see me. Yeah, right. Like they don't have a million ways of stakin' this place out. Toby, you dumbass, just 'cuz you're good at hackin'—and runnin'—what makes you think you can start settin' up meets with potential double agents like you're some kind of freakin' James Bond?

Well ready or not, there she is. That's gotta be her down by the baseball diamond. The cyber haircut for fiber optics, the way she's lookin' around—yeah, that's her all right. I *knew* she was a woman. And damn if she isn't beautiful, too.

Oh Toby, here you are freezin' your nuts off at midnight in mugger heaven, about to get busted and spend the rest of your life behind bars, and you're checkin' out her legs! Focus, buddy, focus!

Hey, she didn't report the messages to IPI brass. Absolutely no Net activity indicatin' that. Just ran a few tracers. And that's good. Unless this whole plan was her idea in the first place. And that would be bad. She's sure as hell smart enough to pull it off. And... and... and damn—she is *gorgeous!*

Okay buddy, what's it gonna be? Now, or never?

Chapter Twenty-Eight: Melora

Allston isn't a city. It's a Boston neighborhood like Brighton, Southie, and Jamaica Plain. Part residential, part student slum, part plain old slum, it was the kind of place I would have lived if it weren't for my high-paying job at IPI.

Ringer Park is a scary little corner of Allston. I came by first in daylight, checking it out before my midnight rendezvous. Just off Cambridge Street, the main bus route from parts west through Brighton, Allston, and over the Charles River to Harvard, Ringer's bordered to the west by Gordon Street's brick row-house apartments, to the east by Allston Street, a fast-moving two-lane road, and to the south by Commonwealth Avenue, one of Boston's main streets. Sandwiched between Cambridge Street and Ringer's east side there's a crooked, mysterious little Avenue—High Rock Way. Once fine, but now peeling homes straddle a big rock formation overlooking the park, like a small mountain in the middle of a flat city. It was pretty obvious where my hacker would be watching for me.

The park is a mess—every one of its globe lights shattered, tennis court nets shredded, benches cracked and graffiti-covered, trash everywhere. It looks like the world of *Clockwork Orange*. In daylight, students walk their dogs next to gangsters out flashing their colors, marking their turf. By midnight, it's empty.

Not wanting to disappoint my new friend, I stood near the dusty baseball diamond's chain link backstop in plain view of anyone watching up on High Rock Way.

And that must be him, I thought, *or a really big mugger. Strolling down the glass-littered cement path like an absent-minded college professor out for his evening constitutional. He really is big. And my God, he's fucking smiling!*

That's when I recognized the face.

All along I'd ruled out the possibility of an IPI programmer, figuring on some unknown whiz kid at the Pentagon. There weren't any other options. Except one. I knew the face, though it was older, shaved clean, better looking, altered. I knew it because it was the face on the cover of the only *Time Magazine* I'd ever read. The biggest difference in real life was the way his eyes caught the light, almost sparkled. I'd read the article fifty times—May 7, 1996—*The Hacker Who Changed History: Toby Jessup 25 Years Later*. Filled with bullshit about his murder, suicide, and recent sightings at U2 concerts and 7-Elevens, the story might as well have been about Elvis. Six paragraphs in an offset box explained his quarter-century-old raid on the Pentagon, and every time I read it, his genius and daring blew me away. And every time I remember thinking, *What a waste.*

"Uh, hi," he said.

"Hi?"

"Uh, yeah. Hello. How are ya?" Extending his hand. I kept mine in my pockets.

"Look," I said, "I know who you are and what you want, so why don't we get this over with."

"Huh?"

"You're Toby Jessup, and you figured out some way of hacking into IPI—probably on the microwave relays we use for networking. Then you noticed me screwing around with my work. Now you think you'll blackmail me. Well, I'll tell you what—you can go fuck yourself. I'll go to jail before I ever give you anything."

"Look, I'm really sorry about how I had to do this…" rolling one big hand over the other, "…thing, but it isn't about blackmail, and I really admire your work, and…." Looking down, then up into my eyes, his hands coming to rest on his hips. "Can we go somewhere and talk?"

The Modern Cafe is a divey shithole on the little square formed by the angled intersection of Cambridge Street and Brighton Avenue, the kind of place still serving its meatloaf special after midnight. No need to find a dark, private table—they all are.

"Hi, Bear," the waitress said to Toby, giving his arm a squeeze. I wondered how this guy had stayed hidden, figured he probably lived within a block of this place. Letting me know that, well, either he'd been incredibly lucky all these years, or *really* wanted to take me to his favorite restaurant.

"Glad to see you got a little friend with you tonight, Bear. Honey, I'm Ruthie," sticking out a hand, a dozen gold and silver bracelets sliding to her wrist. "I'd have to wait all night for him to introduce us!"

I realized then, for all Toby knew about my work, he didn't know my name, most likely expected me to be a guy.

"Hi, Ruthie," taking her hand, "I'm Jill."

"Hiya, Jill. What's it gonna be for you two? Bear's usual pepperoni pizza?"

Toby coughed into his hand. "Ruthie, uh, Jill, might like something diff…."

"Pizza will be fine, Ruthie," I said.

Toby spotted my hearing aid the moment we entered the dimly lit restaurant, and without giving it another thought, made sure I could see his lips whenever he spoke. I noticed right away, couldn't recall anyone ever doing that before.

So we sat there, me and "Bear," waiting for pizza, him telling me how great it used to be in Boston before they cleaned up the waterfront, building Quincy Market for yuppies and tourists.

"There was this all-night place—Mondo's. We'd take the bus up from Butler at 2:00 a.m. just to eat there. They had a full menu, but the big deal after midnight was the Farmer's Special. Three eggs, toast, hash browns, juice, coffee, ham, bacon or sausage. Ninety-nine cents! When the waitress came over to take your order, she'd say, 'Ham, bacon, or sausage?' like that was the only choice. The grill was a mile long, and they had like three hundred eggs goin'—all sunny side up. And Mondo, he was about four-ten, three hundred sixty pounds. Every once in a while he'd push through the kitchen's swingin' doors, flies buzzin' around him, comin' out to break up a fight, or makin' an appearance like some kind of movie star!"

So I told him about my high school days living and working in a pizzeria.

"Imagine this—pizza, three meals a day and midnight snack—all on the house."

"No way!"

"Way!"

And we were laughing, laughing like two kids out on a suddenly successful blind date.

When the pizza came it got quiet again. I hadn't eaten for two days, and it was delicious, the best in Boston.

"Will you tell me your real name?" Toby said.

"Don't tell me you couldn't hack that information?"

"The numerical coding IPI uses for payroll and personnel makes it a little tough, but yeah, I could've. I just felt that was, like, y'know, invadin' your privacy."

I finished chewing, swallowed.

"Melora. Melora Kennedy."

"Uh… hi, Melora!"

"Look, Jessup…."

"Toby. Please, call me Toby."

Two teenage boys walked past our table, nodded to Toby, and slipped past the greasy blue curtain leading to the kitchen. In ones and twos, people had been coming in and out of the kitchen ever since we sat down. None of them looked like health inspectors.

"Okay… Toby. What's going on back there?"

"Gamers."

"Gamers?" I knew he wasn't talking about Monopoly.

"There's clubs like this all over the city. All over everywhere. They write their own code. They've got drinkin' games, and sex games, and games about little rainbow-colored ponies. But war games are the big draw. Gamers take sides and roll-play, pretendin' they're AEF troopers huntin' down Red Path, or Red Path guerillas matchin' wits with RITA. They get their biggest kicks streamin' IPI combat video from the network newscasts on VR headsets. That, and bettin' on the daily bag counts."

I'd heard rumors, but…. "Where do they get the hardware?"

"Sometimes, they steal it. More often, they buy it on the black market."

"Black market?" I realized I was stupidly repeating everything Toby said. But honestly, by then I was feeling pretty stupid.

"Yeah. That's what happens whenever somethin' people want becomes illegal."

"But where does the black market get the hardware?"

"From every business and government agency that's got an Access Law exemption. VISA, Exxon, the Marine Corps. But mostly IPI."

"That's bullshit! No one can get that stuff past IPI Security!"

Toby leaned back in his chair, laughing. "Are you kiddin' me? The guys in IPI Security are the ones sellin' it!"

I looked at Toby, wondering if he was lying. If he was, I figured he must have been one hell of a poker player.

Three more teenagers came in, nodded at Toby, and headed for the back, walking past a table where a couple of Boston cops sat eating pizza. The cops didn't look up.

"Those cops have to know something's going on."

"Sure they do. But they're gettin' their cut. Everybody's gettin' their cut."

"How about you?"

"Guy's gotta make a livin'. I fix the machines. Program 'em too. And when they get too full of themselves, I sit in on a game and whip their butts, old school."

"Do they know you?"

"Only as 'Bear'. But no one uses their real names. Everybody's named Turtle, or Pitbull, or Switchblade. "

"But don't they know who you are?"

"I don't think they care. Besides, they're kids. They don't know any history. Especially ancient history."

A head peered out from behind the curtains, a girl with red hair and freckles. She looked around the room, and spotting Toby, headed toward our table.

"Hey, Bear."

"Hey."

The girl glanced at me. "She cool?"

"Yeah, she's okay."

The girl stuck out a freckled hand. Her sleeve pulled back, revealing a forearm-covering tattoo of a fur-covered demon, blood dripping from its mouth and a man's severed head gripped in its claws. I didn't recognize the artist, but the work was solid.

"Hi," she said. "I'm Grendel."

I shook her hand. "Hey, Grendel. I'm Devil Ray."

"Are you two here to play?"

"No," Toby said. "Just samplin' the cuisine."

"I'm sorry to bother you, Bear, but some guy calling himself Scorpion showed up from Brooklyn. He's running his mouth about how great the Yankees are and how bad the Red Sox suck—and how bad *we* suck—and he's putting up some sick numbers to back it up. I was hoping you could drop in for a game and teach him some humility."

Toby grinned. "Maybe later, Grendel. Okay?"

"Okay, Bear. And you can come, too, Devil Ray!"

"Another time, Grendel, but thanks."

"Okay. Well, see you guys!"

Grendel skipped behind the curtain, walking right by the cops on her way. One of them looked up, watching her ass as she passed and making some comment to the other cop, who turned around for a quick look before she disappeared. Then they laughed and went back to eating their pizza.

"Do you get some kind of thrill out of this?" I said.

"Outta' what?"

"The risk… for you… I mean… right out in the open…."

"I've learned some things since I went underground. Like that nobody suspects someone who doesn't act suspicious. Besides, she may not be in your league, but if Grendel's life had been a little different, she'd be cybergrammin' right next to you at IPI. Do you know how much it means to me that I get to teach her a few things? It gives me a reason to live."

"Why the fuck are you telling me all this?"

" 'Cuz you asked."

"Then why the fuck aren't you worried I'll walk out of here, turn myself in, turn you in"—two more teenagers walked past the cops' table and through the blue curtain—"turn them in?"

"I'm not worried, 'cuz if you didn't work for IPI, you'd be in the back room sittin' at a black market console you'd upgraded, rewritin' everyone's software and kickin' some gamer's ass."

I could feel my face getting hot, so I looked down, took another bite of pizza, glanced over at the two cops stuffing their faces on the other side of the restaurant.

"Toby, is it safe talking here?"

"Safe as anyplace else."

"Okay, so tell me—what's really going on? What do you want?"

"I think you know."

"I know it's not blackmail. That was stupid."

"What is it then?"

"You've got a plan."

"And what do you think my plan is?"

"To do what you did last time. Only you don't want to risk what happened last time. So this time you'll get your malware and e-mines in place, then blackmail Washington to the peace table by threatening another memory wipe."

Toby nodded.

"It's a great plan. But it won't work."

"Why not?"

"Because they're ready for you. They've spent decades getting ready. I'm not saying I couldn't beat all their safeties, but it would take a long time. And once we delivered the threat, how long would it take them to de-bug? A day? A week?" I paused, realizing I sounded like I was in on the plot. "No, your plan won't work, and you know it."

"If I know it won't work, why'd I risk this meetin'?"

"Because you want me to come up with a plan that will work."

"Can you?"

"Do you understand what you're asking?"

"I'm askin' you to betray your friends so we can save some lives."

Without thinking, I said, "I bet you know all about betraying friends." And like with Captain Rusk and Vietnam, I was sorry as soon as the words left my mouth.

Toby's lips opened slightly, his eyes shut, his face looking sadder than any I'd ever seen.

"Look," I said, "I'm sorry. I only meant that...."

"No, I'm sorry. You're right. I've got no business askin' you to do this, puttin' you in danger like this. I'm sorry. I'm really sorry."

We pretended to eat a little more pizza while avoiding each other's eyes. Toby paid in cash, walked me back through the park to my car.

"I wish this could have been, I don't know, different," he said.

So did I.

Chapter Twenty-Nine: Melora

The day began badly. Six months passed since my meeting with Toby, the war more fucked up than ever, nightmares worse too. I stayed up late, remembering his face, his words—*I'm asking you to betray your friends so we can save some lives.* Long after midnight, I fell asleep on my living room sofa, dreaming this time of fire sweeping across the ocean like a lengthening shadow, consuming everything. I woke, and shaking off the nightmare, thought about coming full circle, sleeping on a couch while my king bed lay empty.

I made a habit of going to work early, avoiding anti-war protesters who'd taken up picketing IPI. Today I wouldn't make it in time.

Hey hey IPI, we don't want your stinkin' war!

Hey hey IPI, we don't want your stinkin' war!

Slowing, I drove past ragged lines of picketers, thinking about rolling up the windows, deciding against it. A woman with long dark hair, about my age, holding a peace sign poster above her head, skipped up to the car looking like someone about to ask for directions.

"Hey Nazi, nice Beemer. How many lives did that cost?"

Then she spit on me.

"You okay, Miss Kennedy?" the IPI security guard asked as I pulled up to the blockhouse. Inside, two uniformed Natick cops were sitting with the other guards eating donuts and drinking coffee.

"Yeah, fine," I said. "No worries."

But I watched in the rearview mirror as I drove away to my reserved parking spot, and saw two guards and the Natick cops leave the blockhouse, push the dark-haired protestor to the ground, and zip-tie her wrists and ankles.

Inside, things got worse. Finding the cybergrammer workstations empty, I headed for the lunchroom, the gathering place whenever something big was up. In the lunchroom, thirty programmers stood, talking all at once. Coop met me at the door. He looked pale, frightened.

"Geez, Mel, where've you been?" But before I could answer, "Did you hear about Professor Sherman? They stopped him at the gate this morning, told him he's fired. Took his I.D. off him right on the spot. When they wouldn't let him in to clean out his desk, he marched over to the demonstrators, grabbed a sign and started picketing. Some security guard made a call, and the local cops showed up and arrested him. While they were cuffing him, he had a heart attack or something! An ambulance took him to Newton-Wellesley Hospital about an hour ago. I've been waiting for you so we could head over there together."

In the hospital waiting room, Ellen sat between Captain Rusk and Maggie. Coop hugged her first, then she stood, hugging me, holding on like she'd fall if she didn't. "Oh, Melora, they say he can't move, can't even talk!"

"It's okay Mrs. S. He'll be all right. We'll take care of him."

Coop went for sandwiches that no one ate. Morning faded to afternoon, afternoon to evening. Finally, Captain Rusk talked Ellen into letting him take her home. Coop promised he'd stay at the hospital, call as soon as there was news. Maggie Rusk, taking my arm, said she'd drive home with me.

For a while, we drove in silence. Then I noticed tears rolling down Maggie's cheeks.

"Don't worry, Maggie, Professor Sherman will be okay."

"I pray you are right, Melora. But something is also wrong between you and the Captain, and I am so afraid it will not be okay. He will not talk about it, but he is miserable."

"We had an argument about the war."

"The war. I should have known. So you told him the war is bad and he gives to you his 'In Harm's Way' speech."

"Worse than that."

"Oh. So it is about Vietnam."

Maggie often talked about Vietnam, but never mentioned the war.

"Look, Maggie, don't worry about it. We'll get over it."

"But I must worry, Melora! John is not happy, you are not happy, and we are family. What is more important to worry about?"

My secrets kept me silent, but as I turned into the Route 128 on-ramp, merging with the late night traffic, Maggie continued.

"John met me touring the Eurasian orphan shelter where I worked in Saigon. He was such a handsome young lieutenant—about your age, Melora. I was just a girl. I do not think he noticed me the first time. But he kept coming back. Not for me. To help. And you should have seen him with the children. They called him 'the big American with the funny hat,' climbing all over him, ruining his beautiful uniforms. So many children, their mothers dead or disgraced, their American G.I. fathers shipped home.

"When the war was over he did everything to bring those children here. The new communist government did not want them, but it also did not want to let them go. And Uncle Sam did not want them either. When John came home and saw the young protesters, children who had so much, he thought of the Vietnamese children who had nothing. I think it broke his heart.

"He got me out two years after the peace. I wanted children right away. But John was afraid. Afraid of the radiation and the Agent Orange, afraid for me.

"He believes Americans should have saved my country. But he has no love for how they tried to do it. And he also believes, as I do, the communists are truly evil. I saw how they murdered innocent people in the South. And John hated them before Vietnam."

"It's okay, Maggie. I understand about the Captain."

"No, no, you must listen, hear the rest."

I nodded, keeping my eyes on the road.

"In 1968, John's commander recalled him from his aircraft carrier. John only wanted to fly, but the Pentagon posted him to Czechoslovakia as the ambassador's military attaché. Before reporting to the embassy in Prague, he traveled to Hungary, Poland, and the Soviet Union. He has told me they were the saddest places on earth. He arrived in Czechoslovakia in time for Prague Spring. Do you know what that was, Melora?"

"No," I said.

"A new leader, a young man named Alexander Dubček, came to power. He was a communist. He did not believe in capitalism or democracy. He saw Russia as the savior of his country in World War II and wished to keep Czechoslovakia in the Warsaw Pact military alliance. It is funny today when I hear news analysts and government officials say he wanted freedom from Russian tyranny. Because all he wanted, all his people wanted, was what they called 'communism with a human face'—freedom of speech, freedom of the press, and freedom of artistic expression. Even that was more than Moscow would allow.

"John tells me Prague was like a breath of fresh air after the other communist countries, a beautiful fairy-tale city filled with workers and artists and young people experiencing their first taste of freedom. He quickly became best friends with his Czech driver, Luboš, who worked for the embassy by day, taking John with him when he read his poetry in the cafes at night. John began staying with Luboš at his flat more often than he slept in his own quarters at the embassy, finding something in this friendship he had long missed since entering Annapolis and the Navy. He even began thinking other systems of government, more humane than the one he grew up with, might be possible.

"Here, Melora, I brought this picture to show you."

I caught a glimpse of the captain, younger by many years, next to another man, pale and slender, about the same age. They were standing in front of a castle out of Cinderella, arms resting on each other's shoulders, smiling.

"In August the Russian leaders met with Dubček and signed an agreement saying Czechoslovakia would be left in peace. Then they invaded. They called it 'The Befriendment.'

"The puppet government ordered John out of the country. He wasn't allowed to say goodbye to his Czech friends or take his belongings. But Luboš came to the train station, finding John among all the other American refugees waiting for evacuation, bringing John's things. And this."

Maggie held the picture balanced on her fingertips.

"John begged Luboš to come with him, promised he would hide him until they crossed the border. Luboš said no, he must stay and fight for his country. He said, 'Tonight I will go out to fight and die.' But he never got the chance. A Russian tank commander shot him on his way home—for the crime of waiting at a bus stop."

Maggie was openly crying now, for a man she never knew. And for her man.

"You must see, Melora, John did not become a soldier to fight, or even to fly. He is bigger, stronger, smarter than most. It has made him believe he must save people. He saved me. He saved you. But John could not save his best friend."

As we pulled into the Rusk's driveway behind the parked Metro, Maggie took my hand in both of hers the way she had at Otis the second time we met.

"Melora, David and you are the only children we have. Make peace with him. Please, promise me you will make peace with him."

I didn't get home until after midnight, and when I walked in the door the phone was ringing. It was Joey.

"Mel, I've been calling you all night." He sounded terrible.

"Look, Joey, can this wait till tomorrow? I'm really beat."

"It's Darin, Melora. Darin's dead."

As I pulled into the IPI lot, the night security guard put down his copy of *Soldier of Fortune* and stepped outside the cement blockhouse.

"Evening, Miss Kennedy. Working late?"

"Just forgot something in my office. I'll only be a few minutes."

"Go ahead and park by the front door. You won't be in anybody's way at this hour."

"Thanks."

"And have a good night!"

I drove slowly to the entrance, walked slowly to my office. I jacked in the moment I sat down, hoping, praying, knowing he'd be there.

HELP ME.

Instantly, a message flashed on my visor, then disappeared.

SAME PLACE.

Toby was waiting in Ringer Park, taking a huge chance for me. Seeing how I looked, he said nothing, walking me instead to a first-floor apartment in an old three-story house atop the rock that gave its name to High Rock Way.

"Around 1890, a dad built this with three entrances, one for each of his daughters. Now it's all carved up into apartments."

In a room off the front door, I could see Toby's computers humming away in the semi-darkness.

"Would you like to take a look?" he said. "I admit, I'm really proud of them."

I shook my head no.

"Melora, what is it? Tell me what's wrong."

"My nephew Darin, more like a little brother, his ship, the *Lovell*, went down off the Sumatra coast. Darin, his shipmates, they're all dead."

"I'm sorry, I...."

I could hear my voice getting angry, loud, crazy. But I couldn't stop. "No, wait. Listen to me! The *Lovell* was hit by a Harpoon missile. Our missile. RITA launched the strike!"

"But why would RITA...?"

"We—I—never programmed RITA to do that. Not specifically, anyway. But I did program her to think—to act—strategically, to protect national security, to protect herself."

"How was she protectin' herself by launchin' a missile at our own ship?"

"Because the *Lovell* was dead in the water. About to be boarded by Red Path. About to have its technology turned over to the Chinese. That technology included RITA downlinks and uplinks, the biggest military secrets we have next to RITA herself."

Toby looked away, thinking, taking it in. Then he put both hands on my shoulders.

"Look, Melora, I can't imagine.... I mean, it's awful! But it's not your fault. Human commanders have made those same kinds of decisions."

"Yeah, but a human commander didn't make this decision. A human commander didn't kill Darin and his shipmates. RITA killed them, the same way she's been killing Indonesians for years. Friendlies, hostiles, what's the fucking difference? RITA doesn't give a shit! And me, Coop, Captain Rusk, all the cybergrammers—we created RITA. We're all fucking murderers!"

I wouldn't have blamed Toby if he hated me for not helping him when it might have made a difference, or took advantage of what had happened to talk me into helping him. I knew he was attracted to me, and I wouldn't have stopped him if he held me, or kissed me, or tried to fuck me. What Toby did instead was lead me to his bedroom, cover me with an old down sleeping bag, tell me to sleep, and then fall asleep himself in the chair beside his bed.

I came to work late that day at IPI. I came to work planning to stop the war.

Chapter Thirty: Melora

I took a week off, heading for Darin's funeral at the Sarasota National Cemetery, the first time I'd set foot in Florida since leaving the Navy and going to work for IPI. Joey, Diana, Damian, and me stood graveside next to the American flag-draped coffin that held what was left of Darin. A Navy chaplain began reading the *Lord's Prayer*, but stopped short when mom and the professor pulled up in a Lincoln Continental. As if things weren't bad enough, Tammy Jo had finally found a family get-together worth attending.

Mom, wearing a black sunbonnet, low-cut black lace top, short black silk skirt, black fishnet stockings and lipstick red heels, got out of the car and threw herself on Darin's casket, bawling her eyes out. The chaplain continued reading, but when he got to the part about, "And lead us not into temptation…" mom took it up six notches, wailing, "He was my grandbaby! My grandbaby!" so loud the chaplain couldn't finish.

I knew it wasn't my place, but I couldn't take it any more. From the looks on Joey's, Diana's, Damian's, the chaplain's, and the professor's faces, I knew they couldn't either.

"Jesus Christ, Mom," I said, "will you knock it off?"

Tammy Jo whirled to her feet, pointing a polished red fingernail at me.

"YOU!" She said. "How DARE you!" The chaplain put a consoling hand on her shoulder, but she pushed it away. "This is all your fault, Melora. If it wasn't for you, Darin would be alive!"

My skin flushed red and hot. *How could she possibly know?* I thought. *All my work on RITA is classified. Everything about RITA is classified. Even the name 'RITA' is classified!*

"Mom, please," Joey said.

"Don't you 'please' me, Joseph! It's Melora's fault, and you know it. Darin enlisted because of her. Then she abandoned him like she abandoned all of you. Like she abandoned me!"

For a moment, I felt better. But only for a moment. Of course she didn't know about RITA. But she was right about Darin's enlistment. Was she right that I'd abandoned all of them the first chance I got?

I looked from face to face, not knowing what to say, almost confessing my role in Darin's death on the spot. "L-look, Mom," I stammered, but Joey cut me off, holding up his hand for me to stop, turning to look at Tammy Jo with eyes blazing, voice like ice.

"Now you listen to me, Mom. You've always hated Melora because she's the opposite of you. Everything she's ever done has been about helping our family. Everything you've ever done has been about you. You're so low you want to make my son's funeral about you."

Tammy Jo started to protest, but Joey continued.

"Professor, you're going to put your wife in that car, and you're going to drive her home. And if either of you ever shows your face around my family again, you're going to regret it."

"Well, I never!" Tammy Jo said, tears suddenly dry as her face flushed with righteousness.

"That's right, Mom," Joey said. "You never."

Everyone watched as the Lincoln pulled away, even the chaplain, who looked like he was praying for God to make him disappear.

Joey took my hand in his. "Chaplain," he said, "will you please continue? It would mean a lot to my family."

The chaplain pulled himself together, reopened his bible, found his place, and began reading.

"But deliver us from evil," he said, sounding like he meant it.

Chapter Thirty-One: Melora

I met with Toby again the night I returned from Florida. We agreed not to see each other more than twice a week, which was still too dangerous. Then I explained my idea.

"The first time we met, I told you they were ready for you, expecting you."

"I remember," Toby said.

"Well, we're gonna give them exactly what they're looking for. Because that's their weakness."

"Oh-kay... and the good news is...?

"The good news is, the programming's nearly impossible, but the plan's simple."

"And the bad news?"

"The bad news is, we're gonna need help. The really bad news is, one of us has to get busted."

The next morning at work, I was exhausted, but I'd buried my fears with Darin and replaced them with purpose. I stopped sabotaging my programs, and my programming improved, even outdoing my earlier work. IPI was pleased, increasing my salary and status. What they didn't know was that every other day or so, I embedded tiny bits of code here and there in the IPI Net. Tiny bits of code that one day would electronically join forces, becoming a dinosaur-sized monster. Toby gave the program its name—*Godzilla*.

The only tough part for me was avoiding Coop and the Rusks, even making sure I missed them during hospital visits with Professor Sherman. Of course I didn't want them catching on to what I was doing, but more than that, I was afraid they'd get in trouble if I got caught. Maggie was upset each time I made excuses for missing a dinner party or shopping trip, and that hurt. Coop seemed as set on ducking me as I was on staying clear of him. And that hurt more.

My twice-weekly meetings with Toby kept me going. His bought, stolen, scavenged, home-built machines were marvels, fascinating me with their ancient monitors and keyboards, junk IPI thought was going in some secure landfill, but was instead being sold on the black market by IPI customers and IPI Security. And while I worked through problems step-by-step, Toby took impatient leaps, like skipping rocks across a stream.

I liked programming with Toby. I liked his stories, too. He told me about the early days of computing and showed me a program for picking racetrack winners he wrote back in the day with Tesla, his best friend from college. He claimed that one time it was four-for-four at some track, but either his memory was foggy or they got lucky, because I can't believe even Toby could've figured out something that complicated with the crappy computer and code they were using.

"Bruin was an IBM 650," he said, "the first mass-produced computer. That was before the Access Law and IPI's monopoly. IBM made only 2,000 of them in the 1950s. Wellston was lucky to get one."

"How many gigs?"

"Gigs? Bruin's memory was on a rotatin' steel drum! Of course Tesla and I made a few, uh, modifications."

Most of Toby's stories came with pictures—photo albums, yearbooks, and newspaper clippings he'd lugged around through decades of running.

From his high school yearbook, I learned that Toby, like Coop, was a military school kid, tall, awkward, looking way out of place with his more spit-and-polish classmates. One whole photo album was from Toby's years living underground. Some pages were filled with boring pictures of towers, monuments and museums, and like every tourist who wastes film instead of buying postcards, Toby couldn't remember where a lot of them were. He did better with the funny ones—"Hey look! That's me standin' in front of the statue of Will Rogers and his horse Soapsuds at the University of Texas. The statue's turned twenty-three degrees to the east so the horse's ass is pointed at Texas A&M!" Even on the run Toby collected stories like that one, stories he could finally share.

Another thing he collected was photos of his favorite pizzerias. Every town had its own pizza page, complete with shots of storefronts, freshly-baked pies, and a very happy Toby, his arm draped around the owner. Montreal, Eugene, Austin, Madison, Providence, and Boston. Even St. Francis.

"Holy shit, Toby—that's Mr. Belasso!"

"Who's he?"

"Remember how I told you about living in a pizzeria when I was in high school?"

"Livin' the dream!"

"Well you're not gonna believe this, but that pizzeria was Belasso's!"

"No way!"

"This is incredible! We might've seen each other!"

"I don't think so, kid. That was before you were born!"

That was the only time Toby ever called me "kid," the only time our age difference ever came up.

"Whatever you say, *old man*, but I think it was destiny."

Another of Toby's albums was filled with clippings from the *Butler Journal*, all dated between May 1970 and May 1971. A lot happened that year. Students gunned down at Kent State and Jackson State. Toby's college, Wellston U., on strike against the war. An arson fire at the Wellston ROTC building with two deaths and unnamed suspects in custody. Vietnam nuked. Nixon dead. One *Journal* photo showed a young man waving an upside-down flag over a courthouse, another, an old man, cigar clenched between his teeth, holding a dying girl in his arms. None of this was history for Toby. It was real, and his stories made it real for me. So I asked him if he knew anyone in those pictures. "Yeah," he said, then turned his head and started blowing his nose. I didn't ask again.

There were two photos he cherished above all others, the ones he kept framed on his desk. One of Toby, Tesla, and the smiley-face girl after a demonstration, and another of the three of them in the winner's circle at a long-ago demolished racetrack. When we'd get stuck on a coding problem, Toby would grab them, one in each hand, and stare at them like he was looking into the past for answers. "For inspiration," he'd say, "and luck." He had other annoying habits, too. Like talking with his mouth full of food. And it wouldn't have killed him to try real deodorant instead of the worthless hippie shit he used. But that deal with the pictures was the one thing that really pissed me off.

Late one Friday we ran into some coding glitches that stumped us for hours. It was taking way longer than it should have because each time we got stuck, Toby had to stop and make goo-goo eyes at those fucking pictures. I was tired, and for the first time since we met I was about to lose my shit. Then, all of a sudden, Toby slapped both pictures face down on the desk so hard I was surprised the glass didn't shatter.

"Fuck this shit," he said. "Let's go for a drive!"

With me at the wheel and Toby navigating, we crossed the border into Rhode Island an hour later. Thirty minutes after that we pulled up to a grey stone wall bordering a moonlit beach. A weathered sign read *Welcome to Jamestown*. Breakers rolled in from the Atlantic. It was deserted. I rolled down my window and took a deep breath, filling my lungs with fresh, salty air.

"I remember this place from college." Toby said. "Wasn't sure I could find it though. Tesla and I used to drive out here, buy a barbecued chicken and some sweetbread at this little Portuguese snack shack, sit on the seawall, and watch the sunset."

"Sounds romantic."

Toby punched me lightly on the arm. "Oh it was, Melora. We'd gaze into each other's eyes and recite luuuvvv sonnets in COBOL and FORTRAN."

Toby laughed. Then he unbuckled his seatbelt and moved closer, looking serious. "Oh Melora," he said, "I'm sorry... but I've got to go in!"

Toby bounded from the car, a big, overgrown, puppy of a man, stripped to his boxers and ran through the sand waving his arms until the breakers swallowed him. *This is nuts*, I thought. *We're gonna get busted for sure.* On the other hand, if we didn't get busted tonight, we probably never would.

I got out of my BMW and sat on the seawall watching Toby crest waves as he swam seaward, then bodysurfed to shore. He was an awful swimmer, and a worse bodysurfer. If he'd grown up in Florida he would have drowned before he turned sixteen. In the moonlight, I could see he'd lost his boxers, but I'm not sure Toby noticed. He stood up, and with the surf breaking around his waist, waved for me to join him. So I took off my tee shirt and cutoffs, put my hearing aid inside a sneaker, and slipped into the water beside him.

"C'mon," Toby said, "I'll race you!"

We swam outward, and within seconds I was thirty yards ahead of him. No big deal, since Toby's freestyle was just a bunch of splashing. I circled back, hoping I wouldn't have to rescue him. When I reached him, he was treading water even though it was only waist deep.

I stood up. After a moment, so did Toby.

"Damn, Melora, where'd you learn to swim like that?"

"I grew up in Florida, remember? On the Gulf of Mexico. Where the fuck did you learn to swim like *that*?

Toby laughed. "In military school."

"Well, whatever you do, don't join the Navy."

The moon broke through the clouds, lighting up our bodies, lighting Toby's eyes like someone had thrown a switch.

"Hey, what's that tat on your shoulder?"

"It's a devil ray. They live in the Gulf."

"Why a devil ray?"

I told him the story, the first time I'd told anyone.

"Cool!" he said.

"Yeah, I thought so."

"But you didn't answer my question."

"What do you mean?"

"What happened with you and the ray, that's fuckin' awesome. But what I meant when I asked you why, was what does it mean to you that's so special you decided to wear it for life?"

I'd never thought about it before, but I answered without hesitation.

"It means freedom."

"Freedom? From what?"

I was surprised Toby hadn't settled for my first answer, or asked me instead, *Freedom to do what?* I was surprised he knew me so well.

"You know, freedom."

"Aw c'mon, Melora. Cut the shit. There's more to it than that."

This time I answered honestly. I answered honestly because I trusted him.

"Freedom from all the bullshit," I said.

Though I was standing there naked, two feet away from him, Toby only looked at the devil ray tattoo, and though he was naked two feet from me, I only looked in his eyes, with that crazy, sparkly blue reflecting moonlight in a way that made it look like the light was shining from the inside out. I knew that look from long hours programming with him—he was thinking, trying to understand, figuring something out. I waited, and fuck, that silence should have been uncomfortable, but it wasn't. Then Toby began nodding slowly.

"Yeah," he said, "I get it."

And I knew he did.

Two nights later I brought my old Windance kit with me to High Rock Way and tattooed a galloping black thoroughbred on Toby's shoulder. He cried like a baby, and twice I had to wave a snapper under his nose, but he hung in until I finished. And I don't know where they went, but after that, those fucking pictures disappeared.

From July to September, everything went so smoothly that, at times, my life seemed almost normal. Other times, I was fucking terrified. That we'd get caught. That we'd fail. That we'd succeed, but the war would keep right on going. That I'd lose my friends, my job, my freedom, my life. That I'd lose Toby.

And Toby? He was fucking thriving. You never heard a guy laugh so much. Or saw a guy eat so much pizza. I lost five pounds, he put on ten. And every time we met he greeted me with a big smile and a bear hug.

Except once.

IPI sent me out to Cal Tech to do some career-day bullshit, so I couldn't see Toby for two weeks. When I showed up at his place, he looked like he hadn't slept since I left. He hugged me for a long time, and I could feel that he'd lost the ten extra pounds, plus a few more. This time there was no smile, but worst of all, it was like the light had gone out of his eyes.

"You look like shit," I said. "What the fuck's wrong with you?"

That brought a quick smile, but not much of an answer.

"I haven't slept much, Melora. Lots of nightmares. I've had 'em off-and-on most of my life. And this one about college, it's the worst. I don't know what it means. Probably nothin'. Besides, I missed you."

At our next meeting a week later, Toby was his old self, programming away while happily singing some crappy '70s pop tune about banging a gong and getting it on, whatever the fuck that means. Meeting our November deadline—chosen because the rainy season always brought the war to a standstill—looked likely. But ever since those nightmares, Toby was slowing us down, spending as much time monitoring IPI Security traffic as he did working on our programs.

"Quit worrying," I told him. "Everything's quiet at IPI."

"Yeah. Too quiet."

Then there was the question which one of us would take the bust. For Toby it wasn't a question at all—he assumed it would be him. He had lots of good reasons, laying them out for me in monologues, joking, leaving no room for disagreement.

"It makes sense, Melora. I've already got a price on my head. If we do this right you could skip away from the whole thing free and clear. Then when I get out in thirty years you can support me in my old age. I'll write my memoirs, and after we get our C-ASS exemption, we can open a little mom and pop computer company—compete with IPI!"

Then he'd get serious, sadness returning to his eyes. "Besides, I'm sick of runnin'."

Normalcy ended the day after Labor Day. The day they arrested Coop.

Staying at work, staying calm, keeping away from Toby that Tuesday were the hardest things I'd ever done. All day everybody was shitting themselves about the arrest. Rumor was that for a long time Security suspected some guy in Programming was sabotaging his work, how they'd traced it to Coop, taking him from his Lexington home in the middle of the night, taking him in shackles. It was bad enough pretending I was as surprised about Coop as everyone else, but at least I didn't have to face Captain Rusk. He'd been called to Washington where I figured he was getting keelhauled over Coop.

As soon as it was dark I drove to Allston, parking on Cambridge Street as usual, making my way through Ringer Park to Toby's. He was waiting for me at the door. We stepped inside and put our arms around each other.

"God, Mel, I'm sorry about your friend. The arrest, the whole thing, it was all on TV."

"I've got to turn myself in, Toby, but I had to make sure you'd get away."

"What are you talkin' about?"

"Don't you see? They think Coop's responsible for what we did. He's my best friend. There's no way I can let him hang for this."

Toby took my arms from around him and held my hands in his. "No, Mel, you've got it all wrong. IPI Security was pretty slick. They kept the whole investigation off their Net because they suspected someone might be snoopin'. But as soon as the news broke I hacked into Coop's hard drive. Melora, Coop didn't get busted for what we're doin'. He got busted for what he's been doin'—spikin' every military program he was assigned."

I understood Toby's words, understanding for the first time Coop's reaction to my comparison of our war with Vietnam and the way he'd been avoiding me ever since. It all made sense now. Coop was protecting me, as I'd protected him.

I looked up at Toby. "This changes everything."

"I know," he said. "We can't wait for November. It's too dangerous. We've gotta roll this week."

"Wait till Sunday," I said. "1:30 a.m. Less IPI security on the weekend, even less after midnight."

"Just like we planned, Melora. I'll launch *Godzilla* and sit tight."

"You've got twenty minutes, Toby. Not a second more. I mean it."

"Don't worry, Mel, I'll get the microwave link open two minutes after *Godzilla* does its thing and long before they start kickin' in my door. They'll get a tap on my phone fast, so you've gotta make the call. Wait two more minutes, give the signal, then run like hell. You'll be in Canada before they know what hit 'em."

And hugging again, holding each other in the darkened apartment, Toby and I said goodbye for the last time.

Chapter Thirty-Two: Melora

I lied about Sunday.

1:20 a.m. Saturday, and I'm at IPI, jacked in and ready.

As usual, Grendel and the rest of the Modern's gamers are getting in last licks, practicing, frying eyes until closing time.

Toby's online, hacked into IPI's microwave relays, running last-minute checks, looking over his shoulder for Security, getting ready for tomorrow. He doesn't know about the memory rod I stuck in his computer's access port while he was on the crapper, doesn't know it's stuck in my computer, waiting. One day early, one subvocal command away from... what? I wonder. Ending the war? Maybe. Prison? Definitely. Saving Toby?

I hope so.

1:22.

Fuck, it's hot in here. I don't remember it being this fucking hot in Florida. First week in September, I'm in cutoffs and a beater, AC's blowing right on me, and I'm dying.

Too bad *Godzilla* alone wouldn't be enough. IPI Security needs someone in custody, a way to believe they've won, a way to look like heroes, a chance to let their guard down and start the victory celebration. In half an hour they'll all be partying.

But not for long.

1:25.

When *Godzilla* blows, the worms I buried will come out of their holes, burrowing their way into IPI's soul, infecting every program I ever worked on. Banks, credit cards, oil companies.

Everything except RITA.

1:30.

It's time.

"Initiate *Godzilla*."

Through my implant, I feel it obeying my command, leaping from the memory rod like a gung-ho paratrooper, dropping behind IPI's lines.

1:32

Godzilla's going apeshit. A crazed, fucking monster made from ones and zeros breathing radioactive fire on everything we built for IPI. Years of work times dozens of people. Not just people—me, Coop, Ron, Ted, Caprice, Captain Rusk.

My friends.

1:35.

Yeah, Security's freakin'. Those drones aren't half bad once you light a fire under their hardware. They're on *Godzilla* like silicon on chips.

Stopping it cold.

Cutting it to ribbons.

Following it back to me.

1:38.

I can count on RITA. RITA's fearless. Can I count on Toby?

What if he went out for pizza? What if he's taking another shit?

What if he tries to save *me*?

Fuck it's hot!

1:40.

Toby thinks he's got twenty minutes. I lied about that, too. No sense letting him get comfortable. He's got thirty, but no more. Me? Five, tops.

1:42.

I never told you I loved you, Toby.

Another lie. I told you once, but you were sleeping. Afraid I'd sound stupid, I guess.

1:45.

Boots pounding down the hall. Even at this hour, guards are up and ready to bounce. Breaking down the door? Well that's fucking stupid. I would've unlocked it if they'd knocked. Probably that asshole Smith's idea.

Oh, shit—they've got live TV newsboys with them?

I hope my hair looks pretty.

Chapter Thirty-Three: Toby

1:47.

What the hell?

My monitor's lightin' up like an aurora! Somethin' big's goin' down at IPI.

Oh God. No! She didn't....

Wait.

Get a grip. Turn on the TV, find out what's happenin'.

Breakin' News? Anchor's sayin' somethin' 'bout an arrest. Maybe it's just some.... Shit! Two guards cuffin' Melora, beamin' live into every livin' room on the planet. And... oh, no! What did those bastards do to her?

Torn fiber optics streamin' down Melora's neck and shoulders. Blood, too! Sendin' a message IPI? Showin' everybody how tough you are?

But son-of-a-bitch—it's backfirin'! Melora's lookin' right in the camera, shoutin', "Give peace a chance!"

Why didn't she wait? We agreed *I'd* get busted. For Christ's sake, she promised she'd go underground!

Melora's the one who figured it out. RITA and the draft. That's what keeps the war goin'. And crashin' the draft will hurt the war without hurtin' the warriors.

Not like last time.

Now all of IPI's Security jocks are online, deletin' *Godzilla*, confident in victory. And for this one moment, while their screens all focus on *Godzilla*'s siege of IPI, RITA's vulnerable.

But only if I move fast.

Twenty minutes, she said. *Twenty minutes!* Oh shit—she wasn't tellin' me that once I launched *Godzilla* I only had twenty minutes until *I* got busted. She meant I only had twenty minutes after *she* launched *Godzilla* and *she* got busted!

1:49.

How much time have I got left? Ten minutes? Less? Shit, I'll never make it!

Oh, Melora! They've got you on your knees, zip-tyin' your ankles! If they hurt you, I'll.... And they've cuffed your hands so far behind your back your devil ray tattoo looks alive, swimmin' for its life!

Freedom from all the bullshit, you said. Oh Jesus, Melora, do you know how deep the bullshit is gonna get?

Fuck, Toby, you're losin' precious time. You screw this up, miss your chance, and she'll....

No. Stop thinkin' about her. Get your eyes off the TV and finish the job, finish what she started.

1:50.

Okay buddy, start breathin', start thinkin'. No way there's enough time, but I gotta try.

Grab the phone. Start dialin'.

One ring. Two. C'mon, c'mon! Pick up!

"Yeah?"

"Grendel, it's Bear."

"Duh! Who else calls the back room pay phone?"

"You ready?"

"Thought it was goin' down tomorrow."

"Gotta be now. Can you do it?"

"Fuck yeah!"

"I've got 1:51. Give me two minutes to set up the link, then hit it."

"You got it."

"And Grendel…"

"Yeah?"

"Run."

"Like the wind, Bear. You, too."

"Count on it."

Grendel giggles, then shouts, "Hey gamers—it's go-time!"

The receiver clicks.

Silence.

1:53.

Okay. The microwave relay between IPI and the Modern's game consoles shows *active*. In another two minutes, I'll know.

1:54.

Grendel's launched *Tet*! They've been practicin' that program for weeks. Now c'mon, kids, play the game of your lives!

1:55.

All over Indonesia, from the biggest cities to the smallest hamlets, Red Path is attackin' behind government lines. It's a Tet Offensive rerun, right out of General Giap's Vietnam War playbook.

At least that's what RITA thinks.

She's runnin' a million checks, lookin' for confirmation, figurin' out how to respond, how to put out hundreds of fires all at once.

1:56.

Now I'll give her somethin' else to worry about—*Virtual Fire*.

Check it out, RITA. I've hacked into Selective Service. And guess what? I'm downloadin' all those digital draft records. Names, addresses, birthdates, social security numbers. I am Red Path, and I am robbin' you blind!

So what you gonna do, RITA? You can't stop me; you got more important things goin' on. 'Copters to launch, troops to deploy, a war to fight with battles ragin' everywhere. And you can't ask Security—they're all busy poppin' champagne corks.

1:58.

Too slow. *Too slow!*

I look at the TV. Melora's gone. Some guy in a suit's answerin' reporters' questions. "There was never any serious threat. This was an isolated incident by an unbalanced young woman, a disgruntled junior programmer trying to get some publicity."

Yeah right, asshole. Spinnin' it already. Bet you had that speech written months ago.

1:59.

I'm runnin' outta time. Eight minutes left to disappear before they come for me. But I can't leave yet. Gotta see how RITA decides.

2:00 a.m.

What's it gonna be, RITA? You just gonna take it? Or are you gonna be fearless, the way Melora made you? You gonna let Red Path steal those records, or are you gonna….

And twenty million electronic draft cards go up in virtual smoke.

PART FIVE

MEKONG CLINIC / APPLEWOOD

Chapter Thirty-Four: Paul

The message came while I was bandaging a child's hand. She'd found an old Claymore mine in the paddies, and despite every warning, being a child, picked it up. The rusted metal cut her fingers deeply, but by some miracle the mine hadn't exploded when she dropped it.

"For The Mother," Quyen said, appearing noiselessly at my side. Though she was nominally Meg's government-assigned administrative assistant, everyone at the clinic knew she was an intelligence agent. In her left hand she had a yellow oversized envelope, the type used for military communications. She didn't hold the envelope out to me, keeping it instead close to her chest.

Six months ago Quyen's mother, Lien, came down from the old imperial capital, Huế, visiting her daughter at the clinic. Politeness, protocol, and Quyen's mother all demanded an introduction to Meg, the famous clinic director, The Mother of Vietnam. Instead of the brief meeting everyone expected, Lien and Meg talked for hours. Bowing goodbye as their conversation ended, Meg noticed the black lesions of chloracne, the mark of Agent Orange toxins, on the middle-aged woman's scalp. Assuring her everything would be fine, Meg asked Lien to stay another day so Dr. Ke could examine her during his weekly visit. The doctor found a tumor in her left breast, and Meg insisted the clinic pay for the operation needed to remove it. The tumor was malignant, but thanks to Meg they'd caught the cancer early, and Lien's chances for survival looked good. But if the communist government thought Quyen was still their agent, they were wrong. She belonged to Meg.

"The Mother's in Ho Chi Minh City," I said, tearing strips of adhesive. "You can leave the envelope with me." Quyen hesitated before setting it on the bamboo table next to the scissors and disinfectant, then left as silently as she'd arrived.

I poured antiseptic on the little girl's thin fingers, and she scrunched up her nose at its sharp odor, but didn't wince or cry out. "You're a brave one," I said, though neither she nor her mother spoke English. The white cotton bandage was too large for her hand, so I trimmed it, snugging it tightly with adhesive tape, hoping I'd made a secure barrier against dirt and moisture, insects and bacteria, aware the hand would probably become infected by this time tomorrow. The clinic had used its last vials of tetanus vaccine weeks ago, and the decision makers in Moscow, our prime benefactors, weren't feeling charitable. I rinsed my hands with disinfectant and bowed to the child and her mother as they bowed to me. Then lapsing into American habit, I waved, and the little girl, giggling, backed out of the clinic's open doorway waving her bandaged hand at me.

Without getting up from my U.S. army-issue rolling chair, a relic from the war, I reached for the envelope, tearing through the official VPA—Vietnam People's Army—seal. A cover sheet addressed to Meg, signed by a government bureaucrat, explained that a message to me from an unknown source had been received on the exclusive military net. The message appeared to be in code, making an investigation necessary, and the Minister of Defence would appreciate "…any light the husband of the esteemed Mekong Clinic Director could shed on the matter." The memo closed with "…apologies to the esteemed Director for the unfortunate delay."

The first thing I noticed when I turned the page was the message's six-month-old transmittal date. But as a flush of anger at the delay began inside me, my eyes scanned the text, its two short words numbing all sensation—

    TESLA— FMH

Chapter Thirty-Five: Paul

Nothing had changed in New York City's Port Authority Bus Terminal. Grime covered every surface of the dingy yellow and black concourse just as it had in 1969, the last time I boarded a bus for Applewood. Worn fluorescent lights cycled slowly, raising eye strain from the subliminal to the fully conscious. The smell of urine and cigarettes would have been stronger if decades of exhaust hadn't so thoroughly drenched the building. Escalators, lines, lockers, commuters, buses, and bums all looked the way I remembered. Even the DeCamp bus numbers were the same. At the ticket window, I reacted with the instincts of a native despite thirty years of Vietnamese formality and politeness, aware there was no need for either in New York.

"88 to Applewood. Round trip," I said.

I'd slept during much of the flight from Tokyo, knowing I'd need my strength, knowing I didn't want to think about New Jersey, at least not yet. But images of my childhood animated restless, jet-lagged dreams.

Somewhere over the Pacific I dreamed of my parents greeting me with warm smiles and loving hugs as I stepped off the 88 in Applewood. Then I woke briefly, hiding tears from a concerned flight attendant as I realized I was only dreaming. My parents' lives had ended years earlier, the news reaching me in Vietnam weeks after their deaths.

I drifted off again.

I dreamed of Columbus School, my old grammar school, the school where Meg and I served as volunteers so long ago. I'd gone there for kindergarten through eighth grade, nine straight years, my longest time in one school, before Vietnam, my longest time in one place.

I dreamed of my childhood friends, the children and grandchildren of immigrants from Italy and Ireland, Poland and Greece, Russia and Hong Kong. The Episcopalian kids came from families who traced their roots back to the Mayflower, families who viewed themselves as the first Americans, but who were descended from immigrants just like the rest of us. The black kids were descended from ancestors, who, less than ninety years earlier, the span of a human life, were born into slavery. Their parents had migrated north from Georgia, Alabama, Mississippi, and the rest of the old Confederacy, looking for factory jobs and freedom from Jim Crow during and after the two World Wars. In dreams my friends were frozen in amber, were still children. In dreams, their names were poetry.

I dreamed of the local college campus, Hilversum, the Lutheran school that made Applewood its home for over a century, and of Timmy Jorgensen, the dean's son, a football player, and for years my friend and protector. Together we'd spent whole days and nights beneath Hilversum's elms and maples, alongside its ivy-covered brick lecture halls and dormitories, playing tennis on its gypsum courts, rooting for its sorry athletic teams, nicknamed "The Flying Dutchmen," and hanging out with college kids at WFMH, learning there was an attitude called "hip," which they were, and we weren't.

I dreamed of a warm summer night, walking Maria Beres, a professor's daughter, home through Hilversum's campus after Independence Day fireworks, stopping at a bench beneath a giant chestnut tree, kissing and kissing until we knew if we didn't leave, our parents would soon come looking for us.

I dreamed of walking home late at night through Hilversum, when crime first discovered my town, because for me, its quiet campus was always safe.

Before the rising sun met my flight in mid-ocean, dreams of New Jersey wavered and melted, then disappeared altogether. Yet as images of Hilversum's campus faded, there was the Wellston campus, two hundred miles to the north. And there was Toby towering over me and the others in Franklin Hall on a cold May evening, dissuading us from arson, paying with his life.

Finding myself in New York, so close to the places of my dreams, I remembered how the morning sun streaming through the jetliner's windows had roused me from sleep in time to see the California coast. I'd stretched, stiff from long hours in an economy-class seat, realizing with a shock that we'd flown far inland before remembering Toby never came to Franklin Hall, remembering he was alive.

The 88 made its way out of Port Authority past hookers and panhandlers—as much a part of New York's West Side as Broadway's famous theaters—through the Lincoln Tunnel, under the Hudson River, out to daylight on the tunnel's western side, the New Jersey side.

I was on Route 3, back in the state where I grew up, within the thirty-mile radius of a circle that encompassed most of my childhood. My father's nine brothers and three sisters populated that circle with more than fifty of their children, the cousins I grew up with in one large, rambunctious, extended family. Tenacious Cousin Harvey, who'd spend hours riding his Schwinn across Applewood, tracking the Good Humor truck on hot summer afternoons, sharing his reward—a peanut-and-chocolate covered vanilla Drumstick—with anyone who asked for a bite. Sweet, smart, beautiful Cousin Angela, who stole Timmy Jorgensen's heart the day I introduced them in eighth grade and married him the day after high school graduation. Generous Cousin Alex, four years older than I, whose gentle soul defied his father's savage beatings.

Over the years the circle had expanded. Harvey in Germany, Lisa and Timmy in Connecticut, the rest in Canada and California, New York and New Mexico, heirs to a generation-skipping migration that brought grandparents from Europe, rooted parents in New Jersey, sent children off again in a new diaspora. Alex, like me, wound up in Vietnam. His father made him enlist late in 1966, arguing that he should, "Ignore that antiwar crap." A sniper killed Alex in 1967, two days' walk from where the clinic now stood.

Only Uncle Joel, still a bachelor, the baby of the family, the uncle adopted by my generation as one of our own, remained inside the old circle. The 88 would pass within a block of his Bloomfield apartment. As much as I wanted to see him, I knew I couldn't, knew I dare not take the chance.

I'd told Meg that after thirty years it was time for me to, "visit the old places and appease the dreams." She didn't believe me. But after so many years at the clinic she was too tired, too distracted to confront me or draw me out as she did so often earlier in our life together. I never showed her the message, and though I wanted to immediately answer its call, I resisted leaving for three months so no one would connect my departure with the communiqué's arrival. I didn't tell Meg the real reason for my trip because I wanted to protect her. I hoped she sensed that, respected that, but her unquestioning acceptance signaled something more, and something less.

I'd dreamed so many dreams about Applewood, dreams far fresher in my waking mind than memories of the place left over from my first twenty-two years. I could no longer tell for sure if my recollections of places, people, and events came from concrete reality or from my dreams, dreams that by their nature seemed mythic, slowly changing my impression of the city where I grew up from that of a simple New Jersey town, a blue-collar, gently hardscrabble melting pot of immigrants, to a place where the play of streetlight and shadow made me hold my breath in the moments before sunrise. A mystic place, a magic place, the place of an idealized past and a dangerous present.

The bus rolled on, down Route 3, past the Meadowlands sports complex, a stadium, an arena, a racetrack where my memory held only vacant landfill and the smell of the Secaucus slaughterhouses. Like millions of commuters, I smiled a dark smile, thinking a New Jersey thought, wondering if Jimmy Hoffa, the Teamster's Union leader who disappeared without a trace, was entombed beneath one of the massive concrete structures. But every thought, every memory, was little more than another way of not thinking about where I was, what I was doing.

The 88 pulled off the highway and onto the streets of Nutley, then Bloomfield's north side, heading for its south side, the side bordering Applewood, past Brookfield Gardens, the dilapidated, overgrown garden apartments where my Aunt Sophie raised two sons, David and Ivan. The three of us had mastered every inch of that complex, exploring each summer the urban wilds of the brook running behind the apartments, contracting body-covering rashes of poison oak and swollen mosquito bites, seeking adventure like it was our religion.

The next landmark was Bloomfield Center, two short blocks from Troy Towers Apartments, home to Uncle Joel. Straining my eyes upward, I looked through the 88's sooty windows, up, up the building's fourteen stories to my uncle's balcony, hoping for a glimpse of him. Too quickly my view was cut off by the Erie Lackawanna Railroad trestle underpass, marking the passage onto Prospect Street, and finally, into Applewood, then quickly past Applewood High School, my high school, and into the heart of the Hilversum College campus.

I stood, hoisting my backpack, pulling the signal cord where Ely Place met Prospect Street. Lost in thoughts, memories, dreams, I hadn't paid attention to my fellow passengers. Stepping into the aisle, shuffling toward the front door like a sailor against the bus's rocking momentum, I began looking at the faces around me. The teenagers rising from the seats across from me were black. Everyone I passed was black. The bus driver was black. I'd spent thirty years in Vietnam. A hundred times each day my pale skin, round green eyes, and dirty blonde hair invited curious stares. I never expected I'd feel that visible, that out of place in Applewood.

The 88 rolled to a smooth stop, the front door folding open with a rush of compressed air. I'd barely reached the weedy sidewalk when the teenager stepping off behind me touched my shoulder.

"Hey, man, got a tissue?"

Shifting my backpack, I fished for Kleenex in my jeans' pocket, handing him a couple. Staring at me, he wiped his nose, dropping the tissues on the sidewalk.

"Change. How 'bout some change?"

I shook my head.

"Don't hold out on me. You got some in that bag."

Another passenger, much bigger, stepped from the bus as it pulled away. "C'mon, Tee," he said. "Leave 'm alone."

Tee stood facing me, smiling. "I'm just playin'. But we be seein' you later on."

Tee crossed Prospect, catching up with his friend, joking, pounding the tops of each other's clenched fists as the big man said, "See the scars on that motherfucker's face? That is *not* someone you want to fuck with!"

I thought I should get moving, walk the other way. But I couldn't stop staring after them. That's when I realized there was no one else on the street. In the middle of what should have been a bustling college campus, there were no people. Just trash blowing down Prospect Street, trash blowing in the light summer wind, trash everywhere, ghostly evidence of human traffic.

I looked around at the old Jersey brick buildings, seeing nothing familiar. Broken, boarded up windows, fallen gutters and downspouts, dead ivy and overgrown weeds. And graffiti. Red, green, black, and yellow-sprayed numbers, initials, and symbols covering every surface. Hilversum, the Lutheran college founded in the century before the twentieth, the lush and pretty campus where I'd kissed Maria after July Fourth fireworks, the safe place to get off the 88 from New York after midnight and walk the last mile home beneath stone arches and rose-covered trellises, was gone, just plain gone.

I walked along Prospect Street past more abandoned buildings. Passing traffic made me feel better, then worse, as I felt the stares from lowered car windows. *What if WFMH isn't here anymore?* I thought. *How could it be? There's no college, no campus, no Hilversum. There doesn't even seem to be a city. Maybe I should wait here until the 88 comes by on its return trip to Port Authority. Maybe I should go home.* The hope of finding something familiar from my past, or from my dreams, the hope of finding Toby, kept me moving.

At the corner of Prospect Street and Springdale Avenue, I came upon Roxy's, a small variety store, and went inside hoping someone there could answer my questions, hoping for some human contact. The store was empty except for the woman behind the counter, who put out her hand and said, "Welcome to Roxy's!"

"Hello," I said, shaking her hand gratefully. "I'm Paul, Paul Simmons."

"How do you do, Mr. Paul Simmons. I'm Roxy, Roxy Warnock," she said, mimicking me with a chuckle. Roxy was thin, the color of cocoa, closer to my parents' generation than to mine, her accent hinting at a childhood in Savannah or Charleston.

I sat at the counter on a squeaky stool, mushroomed aluminum bolted to a round, red, vinyl seat patched and re-patched with duct tape. The counter was old and used, marred and scratched, but like everything in Roxy's, immaculately clean. Any chance its Formica surface would ever shine again had passed, but that didn't stop Roxy from polishing and polishing with a green-striped dishtowel the whole time we talked.

"I'm sorry I can't offer you some food, Paul. The grill's shut down, and I'll be closing soon." The lingering aroma of French fries reminded me I hadn't eaten since my flight.

"That's okay, Roxy," I said. "I grew up in Applewood, and I took the bus in from New York so I could spend the afternoon in my old hometown. I'm wondering if you can tell me what happened to the college?"

"Hilversum's been gone since '94," she said. "A hundred years and they packed up and walked away. Too much crime, not enough students. Biggest thing ever happened in Applewood. Just about closed me up, too, with no college kids around."

"What about the Hilversum radio station, WFMH?"

"I don't know about any radio station. But if it was part of the college, it's sure gone along with everything else. There's no one in those old buildings except squatters, pushers, and copper-pipe thieves."

Roxy saw the look on my face, reached for a scratched but shimmering Coca Cola glass, and filled it from the fountain.

"Be my guest to a soda while you wait for the next New York bus. It stops at the corner around four o'clock. I usually close when my grandsons come by after school, but we'll stick around awhile. We can't stay too late though. We're expected for dinner when their mom and dad get home from work. But Paul, don't miss that bus. The next one isn't until ten, and this neighborhood is no place for anyone after dark."

Slumped at a small Formica table in the back corner of Roxy's, sipping my soda, I waited, passing the time reading a week-old copy of the *Applewood Record*. It was the same weekly newspaper I grew up reading, but much had changed. A story on page four recounted the results of post-war democratic elections in Indonesia, while another heralded the return of a dozen AEF troopers to Applewood with the headline, *They're Coming Home!* The front page covered news of Applewood's own raging war. Lonel White, carjacked from her Renshaw Street driveway. Rasheed Robinson, mugged and pistol-whipped on Central Avenue by two men wearing ski masks. Arraignments of forty county school administrators, teachers, and Board of Education members for conspiring to make false workers' compensation claims.

I tried focusing on my own situation and on Toby, the fugitive. Because of a two-word communiqué, I'd traveled nine thousand miles, twelve time zones, forty-two hours, and arrived finding no Hilversum, no WFMH, no Toby, nothing I could identify as my hometown. But I kept turning the pages, kept reading.

Clean up of a fuel-oil spill caused by the theft of copper pipe from one of Hilversum's padlocked residence halls. The burglary of a dozen new typewriters from the city's public library. And the city council's decision to foreclose on twenty-two hundred homes for unpaid property taxes—that story warranting only four short paragraphs at the bottom of page three.

But then there were the children. Fifth graders Shanna Jackson and Jamaal Whitaker honored at a statewide science fair. Selena Ortiz coordinating Middle Schoolers Against Violence. The Applewood High School valedictorian, the first in a decade who didn't face the military draft, looking serious in cap and gown, diploma in hand, on her way to college with a full scholarship to Rutgers.

There were stories about gang murders and drug busts. I remembered a police sergeant's advice to my father when a brick came crashing through my parents' dining room window a month before they moved to Colorado—"Buy a gun," he said. But there was also news of everyday affairs of everyday people, starting businesses, volunteering in schools, holding charity garage sales, scrubbing graffiti gang tags off signs and buildings no matter how many times they reappeared. And a new mayor, a lifelong Applewood resident, promising to rebuild and restore the city.

There was news of decay and crime. There was also news of hope.

The golden bells above Roxy's front door jingled, and two slender, cherub-cheeked, neatly dressed boys, one not yet a teenager, the other no more than seven, came in holding hands. "Hi, grandma!" they chorused, jumping on side-by-side counter stools, quickly snatching up the two glasses of Cherry Coke that Roxy had set on the counter moments before.

"Terrell, James, say hello to Mr. Simmons. He grew up in Applewood, just like you. He came looking for the Hilversum radio station that's gone along with the rest of the college."

Two sets of deep brown eyes focused on me as the boys realized they weren't alone with their grandmother. Shyly, two voices chimed, "Hello, Mr. Simmons." Then Terrell, the older brother, said, "Mr. Simmons, that radio station, it's still there. Right up the street and around the corner on Glenhaven."

"How do you know that, Terrell?" Roxy said.

"Grandma, I've seen white people coming in and out of there, and heard all kinds of crazy music."

"Are you sure?" I said stupidly.

"Yes, sir, I'm sure."

Roxy beamed at me, wiping her hands on her apron. "I'm sorry I told you wrong, Paul. But if Terrell says it's there, it's there. Looks like you won't make that four o'clock bus after all." Her smile faded. "But you remember what I said about being around here after dark."

I tucked the *Record* under my arm and put my hand out, taking first Roxy's hand, then James's, then Terrell's, enveloping their slim, dark fingers. "Thank you," I said. "How much for the soda and paper?"

"Paul, I told you. You're my guest today."

"Thank you," I said again. Reaching into my pocket, I took out two shiny, aluminum, one-dong Vietnamese coins, handing one to each of Roxy's grandsons. "These are from Vietnam, the country where I live."

"Thank you, Mr. Simmons," Terrell said, palming the coin, sliding it into his pocket.

"Thank you," little James said, staring at the coin's strange, shimmering surface.

"Can I ask you two a question?"

"Sure."

"Where do you go to school?"

"W. E. B. Du Bois School!" they proudly answered.

I'd read in the *Applewood Record* about the renaming of schools for African-American leaders and celebrities. Madison School had become the Ray Charles School. Maple Street School was Reverend Martin Luther King, Jr., Academy. Du Bois School, once upon a time, had been Columbus School.

I turned quickly to the door, but Roxy saw my eyes filling with tears.

"Mr. Simmons?" It was James. "What happened to your face?"

"Quiet, James," Roxy said. "You let Mr. Simmons go."

"It's okay," I said, one hand on the door, the other brushing at my eyes. "I was in a fire."

"Does it hurt?"

"Yes. Sometimes."

James looked at me, looking past the scars, past the pain, looking for clues to something else. "And I was wondering…"—Terrell nudged his brother with an elbow, but James didn't notice—"…are you white?"

There was only the briefest moment of silence before Roxy and Terrell burst out laughing. But James wasn't laughing. He looked serious and solemn.

"Yes, James," I said. "Yes, I am."

Chapter Thirty-Six: Paul

Glenhaven Avenue had once been the most beautiful street in Applewood. Large, elegant homes and cool, soft shade under giant oaks and maples made rounding the corner from Springdale, a busy commercial street, like passing through the entrance to a secret forest. The homes were still there, but with doors roughly boarded, windows barred or smashed. Untended trees dropped branches across roofs and porches. Lawns were dead brown, newspapers and fast food wrappings the forlorn flowers on thorny, dying bushes of rose and azalea.

The corner house looked like the rest. Not one of the larger, grander homes, but big enough, stately enough for the professor's family who built it near the end of the First World War. It shared styles from the past with other Glenhaven homes—Georgian columns, small-paned French windows—and features from their present too. Storm-broken oak limbs hanging from their mother tree and resting on the roof, overgrown weed-filled yard, steel bars across first-floor windows. It looked a lot like the house where Meg and I once sat in a living room stuffing WFMH fundraising envelopes with a dozen other volunteers, listening to John Lennon sing *Working Class Hero* on giant studio monitors. It also looked abandoned.

I didn't feel anything dramatic, no heart-sinking, knee-buckling emotions. I didn't feel anything at all walking up the weed-choked red brick path, up one rotted wooden step, standing before the peeling front door. And seeing the empty doorbell socket, knocking first with my knuckles, then pounding with the side of my fist, and finally hearing the rattling of locks and latches and chains, and at last the throw of a well-oiled deadbolt.

If Terrell and James appeared to me like cherubs, the face I saw in the narrow opening between door and jam was surely that of an angel. Blonde hair, hazel eyes, skin the color of fresh-cut peach. She looked at me through the crack, up and down, carefully, cautiously. Then swinging the door wide, smiling a smile both warm and wise-ass, she said, "It's about time, Tesla. I'm Kelly. C'mon in."

Kelly relocked what looked like at least a half-dozen latches and led the way up creaking stairs, her tight denim jeans, loose denim jacket, bounding ahead of me.

"I'm so glad I got to be here when you showed up. He's gonna freak!"

Jumping the last two steps onto the landing, pushing through a door, she shouts, "He's here!" And before I can follow, a giant blocks the doorway, before I can move, a bear envelopes me.

"I guess I'll leave you two lovebirds alone." Kelly, voice softer than her words, moved past us down the stairway.

There on the landing we hugged each other. We hugged each other until, his big hands on my shoulders, Toby gently pushed me back to arms-length. The passing of years and lots of plastic surgery had changed almost everything about him. Clean-shaven, buzz cut, forty pounds leaner, ears, lips, nose, brow, reshaped. The flowing mane and tail of a thundering black thoroughbred tattooed on his right shoulder were visible beneath the cut-off sleeve of his WFMH tee shirt. But the towering height, bowed shoulders, angled neck, wizard's eyes, were still the same, still Toby. I looked in his eyes and felt something come alive in me, a switch-thrown surge of energy overcoming all the miles, all the fatigue, all the emotions of the past few days. Thinking a thousand things to say at once, I didn't say anything. Toby broke the silence.

"Tesla," he said. "Definitely Tesla."

Toby hauled me against his chest, bear hugging me again. I did the only things I could do—hug Toby back, and for the second time that day, feel my eyes fill with tears. Tears for Toby, our friendship, the dead college, my hometown, the Vietnamese people and the American veterans still dying from cancers caused by a war long over. Tears for myself and tears for Meg, who should have been there with us. Tears, because unlike in my dreams, I could really hold my best friend, miraculously before me, flesh and blood. But tears because I also knew that Toby would soon slip away, this time forever, leaving me again with only my dreams.

At last we let each other go, looked in each other's eyes, saw each other's tears. Toby's new mouth was nearly a straight line, but suddenly the old quick smile was there.

"Tesla, you look like hell!"

The rest of the night was crazy.

Toby spoke first, telling me about his last two years. After exhausting every underground refuge, he'd run to the only place he could think of. A place he'd visited with me during our college vacations. A place incredibly still there, still run by radio radicals.

"Remember Hungary's Cardinal Mindszenty? After the '56 uprisin' against the Russians, he lived at the U.S. Embassy in Budapest, a refugee on foreign soil inside his own country, afraid if he stepped outside the commies would grab him. That's how it's been for me. Cared for by DJs and staffers, program directors and volunteers, never goin' outside, not even at night, the best kept secret in America, the most wanted man of the century."

"That's incredible, Toby! But where does the money come from? Are they supporting you, too?"

Toby laughed, his eyes twinkling. "No, Tesla. Money is the easy part. Kelly brings me the *Racing Form*, I run *Thoroughbred*, and Kelly spends her weekends at Belmont, Aqueduct, and Monmouth Park. I'm supportin' them!"

"No way!"

"Yup, you and I are fuckin' geniuses. *Thoroughbred* works!"

"But what do you run *Thoroughbred* on?"

"Oh, don't worry, Tesla. We'll get to that, I promise."

"You have to show me. You have to!"

"Okay, okay, I will. But enough about your brilliant, famous roommate. Tell me about you and Meg. Tell me everything."

With thousands of words and dozens of photos from my backpack, I told Toby the story of my life in Vietnam. I wasn't surprised Toby knew a lot about Meg. Vietnamese propaganda had fueled her legend, drawing international attention that lead to her discovery by the global media, making her famous for her work, infamous for rejecting the Nobel Peace Prize. Toby thumbed through my pictures slowly, setting aside a Polaroid of Meg standing in front of the clinic at sunset, shoulders straight, face freckled, smiling at the little Vietnamese girl holding her hand, the girl looking up at Meg, imitating her posture and smile.

"May I keep this one?"

I nodded.

And so we sat there, in an upstairs bedroom at the renegade radio station in the middle of Hilversum's ghost campus in the city where I grew up, me in a broken-down leather armchair, Toby lounging on his mattress, swapping stories like two former roommates at a college reunion, WFMH's bizarre programming, nonstop aural performance art, drifting up from the studio, soundtrack for a warm Jersey night. We rambled on about everything. Wellston. Bruin. The Beef 'n' Bun. *Fireball. Thoroughbred.* The ROTC fire. Life in Vietnam. Life in the underground. Toby's strike against the Pentagon. His strike with Melora against IPI, RITA, and the draft.

"Tell me more about 1971," I said, "and tell me about *Godzilla, Tet,* and *Virtual Fire.* Tell me how you did it."

"I'll do better than that. I'll show you." Toby stood and walked to a door on the other side of the room. "Follow me, and I'll take you on a trip to Neverland."

He opened the door and flipped on a light switch. Inside the walk-in closet, one bare bulb revealed a wooden desk, a folding chair, and three bizarre contraptions. I'd never seen such machines, but I knew what they were.

With paper and pencil, words, diagrams, mathematical formulas, and his three fabulous computers, Toby took me through every step, amazing me with his genius, amazing me more with Melora's genius, and amazing myself because I could understand, could follow their sophisticated programming after so many years away from computers. For all the personal things we talked about that night, it was then that I felt closest to Toby, and Toby to me, just two old computer geeks talking about what they loved best.

We'd spent the whole night laughing and joking, and from his first bear hug at the top of the stairs, Toby seemed like his old self, the carefree trickster with the casual southern drawl and twinkling eyes. Now his mood changed, his eyes darkened, his words became choppy and strained.

"RITA was fuckin' evil," he said. "But how could I hack RITA without riskin' a lot of lives?" Toby hung his head, staring down at his big hands. "I fucked up so bad in '71. The nightmares…. After what I caused in Vietnam, I wanted to disappear forever." Then he looked up at me, looked deep into my eyes. "I wanted to die. But there was my country, doin' the same thing all over again in Indonesia. Even worse, with RITA. And who else could step up and do what I could? Anyone who might have a clue was already workin' for IPI, already part of the war machine. Hey, maybe I'm an egomaniac. Or maybe I'm nuts. But I had to do somethin'!"

I listened, not saying anything, not sure whether I was agreeing.

"Then I found Melora," Toby said. "She knew RITA was the smartest, most powerful, most ruthless weapon ever created. She knew, because more than anyone, she created it. But she also knew RITA was nothin' without the draft. Because of her time in the Navy, and because she's so damn smart, she understood that every airstrike had to be followed up by AEF troopers on the ground. That every poor grunt bastard who got killed or injured had to be replaced. And she figured out what I couldn't, that there were lots of ways to go after RITA, but only one where no one would get hurt."

Toby took out his wallet, removed a small rectangle of yellowed, dog-eared paper, and handed it to me.

"Jesus," I said. "Your draft card."

"I kept it all these years. A reminder. When they started makin' teenagers register, I knew there'd be another draft some day, another fucked-up war. So we spiked the draft, burned all those fuckin' virtual draft cards. And because of Melora, we did it without makin' an even bigger mess."

"And you succeeded, Toby. You ended the war!"

Toby shook his head. "No, Tesla, we didn't end the war. That wasn't our plan. Melora and I were just hopin' we could slow things down, point a finger at IPI, make people think, give the antiwar movement a chance. We knew Harriman would order all those kids whose draft records got wiped to re-register, but we had no idea some sorority girl from Oregon would go on TV and refuse. Or that when the FBI arrested her, students on every high school and college campus in America would make her a hero and follow her example. Suddenly thousands of kids are missin' registration deadlines, and there's no way they can lock all 'em all up! Kids from Montana to Mississippi, white collar, blue collar, black, white, Asian and Latino, picketin' draft boards with their parents, chantin', 'Hell no, we won't go!' I wish you'd been here to see it for yourself—millions of people standin' up, sayin' no to war. I think it scared the crap out of Congress. They finally got the balls to confront Harriman and cut off IPI's funding. Harriman saw the handwritin' on the wall, saw a way out and took it. When he called for a peace conference, Hasan could have saved his own ass by agreein'. But psychopaths don't negotiate. I wish some photographer had captured the look on that bastard's face when his Pentagon-paid security guards disappeared and Red Path guerillas waltzed into his office and arrested him!"

"But Toby, what you and Melora did—what those gamers did—it's a miracle!"

"Yeah, pullin' off *Virtual Fire* was a miracle. But the real miracle was everything that happened afterward. It would have been the happiest time of my life—if Melora, her friend David Cooperman, Grendel, and the rest of those kids hadn't been locked in solitary cells. Coop wasn't my fault, but Jesus, why did I talk myself into believin' those gamers could go underground? They caught 'em up in Burlington the next day, takin' on some locals in one last game while they were waitin' for sundown so they could sneak across the border into Canada. They never had a chance. And I swear, I was the one who was supposed to get busted, not them, not Melora. That was our plan, and I thought she agreed to it. When she jumped the gun with *Godzilla*...."

Toby's voice trailed off into awkward silence, the kind of silence that told me I should change the subject. But there was something I wanted to know. Something a whole lot less digital, a whole lot more analog. And I had to ask.

"Tell me about you and Melora," I said.

In the four years we spent together in the '60s, I never saw Toby blush. Now his face, neck, arms, turned a deep red-pink, the color of a desert sunset, making the black horse tattooed on his shoulder stand out, bringing it to life.

"Never mind," I said, laughing, pounding Toby's big shoulder. "I think you just told me everything I need to know!"

But Toby didn't laugh, didn't smile. And my smile faded quickly.

"That's why I sent the message, Tesla. That's why I brought you here."

Toby wasn't a college roommate talking about a girl he met at a sorority mixer. He was an outlaw, and Melora was in prison. And I wasn't in some dormitory. I was in a house full of accomplices, about to become one myself.

Toby's plan was simple. Use Meg's international credibility, her fame, her notoriety. Arrange an exchange.

"I'm the one they want, Tesla. Shit, they've been after me for decades. Melora was the real genius behind the draft sting. Her programs make mine look like the shit we did at Wellston. But they don't know it, don't want to know. They'll never believe some girl they used to work with outsmarted all of 'em. Much better for them if they got whipped by Toby Jessup, history's most notorious hacker. Yeah, they'll make the trade. 'Cuz they can't admit Melora's that important. 'Cuz they want me so bad."

Meg was the key. If she negotiated a deal, Toby in exchange for Melora, Coop, and the gamers, no government would risk the universal condemnation that would surely follow double-crossing The Mother of Vietnam. Meg could assure their freedom and guarantee amnesty for Toby's accessories at WFMH.

Toby's plan was brilliant. And I hated everything about it.

"Toby," I said, "that plan sucks. First, you're tried and convicted before you turn yourself in. Sure, they'll put on a show trial. Stick you in front of the TV cameras wearing shackles. Then put you away in a supermax prison solitary cell for the rest of your life. Or worse, if they call it espionage and give you the death penalty! Second, what if they don't let Melora and the others go? What if they sweep in here and put all your friends behind bars? Sure Meg's a saint, but it's not like Uncle Sam ever worshiped her."

"You should'a been a lawyer like your mother, Tesla—always an argument for everything! But listen to me. The fact is, I *am* guilty. And I'm already in prison. There's at least a chance Melora doesn't have to be. And there's another good reason for tryin' it. The dream."

Toby and I looked in each other's eyes, neither of us saying a word, the only sounds faint Klezmer music coming from the studio and the in-and-out rustle of our breathing. In that moment I knew what I'd always suspected—through all the years and all the miles, Toby and I still shared our dreams as we had in college.

"The dream's real, isn't it, Tesla?"

"Yes."

"You wrote a program that changed everything, created this reality, saved my life."

"Yes."

"I'm not supposed to be here. I died in 1970, just like in the dream. But because I'm alive, Vietnam and Afghanistan got fuckin' nuked!"

"Yes," I said again, knowing it was true, knowing I'd admitted the truth to myself long ago, knowing I couldn't deny it to Toby.

"Well then, we have to fix it."

"I can't!" I said. "You've gotta understand. I haven't touched a computer since college, never developed the knowledge, the skills to do what I did in that other life. I've thought about it, Toby. God, I've thought about it. But the dreams only gave me the vaguest idea how it all worked. And most of the stuff, I don't understand. No, I've thought about it, and if I wanted to, I couldn't do it. No one can."

"Melora can," Toby whispered as the first rays of sunrise shown through his bedroom window.

Chapter Thirty-Seven: Paul

I needed time to think, time to decide. But Toby needed an answer before I left. There would be no safe way to communicate once I returned to Vietnam. Toby, and everyone at WFMH, had to know whether they could count on me, count on Meg. Either way they had decisions to make, and couldn't make them without an answer. But first, there were some questions I needed answered.

"Toby, what can you tell me about Hilversum? About Applewood?"

"I haven't seen much, just the view from this window. Kelly can fill you in. Most of what I know about local history I learned from her. Besides, she's been outside the door listenin' to us all night."

"I have not!"

I jumped up, startled by Kelly's voice coming from behind the door. Toby smiled. The scarred maple door slid open, hinges creaking.

"I took two bathroom breaks and a shower. I'm a stadium concert pro, but you boys almost burst my bladder."

Kelly stood cross-legged, arms out, hands curved as if in meditation. She still wore jeans, now topped by a station tee shirt silk-screened with a harmonica-playing dog. Her blonde hair hung straight, soaked and slick, drops of water sliding down her peach cheeks.

"I made it a *cold* shower after all that steamy talk about Meg and Melora."

Toby blushed again, deeper red this time.

"I can tell you two chatterboxes were never frat boys. Babbling all night about wives and girlfriends, and the 'wild thing' never came up once! But y'all sure went on and on."

"Yeah, Kelly, I guess we're not shy, retirin' types like you," Toby shot back, lips set straight, but eyes twinkling.

Kelly struck a pose, head tilted toward her raised shoulder, index finger demurely touching the corner of her lips, hips thrust to the side. "In finishing school they always taught me the ladies should go and make themselves useful while the menfolk retire to the parlor for cigars and brandy."

"Is that where they taught you eavesdroppin'?" Toby said.

"Well, they didn't define 'useful'. I think that part was left up to us."

The quick smile fought to find itself on Toby's altered lips. "How about makin' yourself useful by telling Tesla what happened to Hilversum and his hometown."

"Let me get this straight," she said, eyes narrowing, index finger moving slowly across her lips, finding the exact center. "Tesla travels like fifty thousand miles...."

"Nine thousand," I interrupted.

"Whatever," Kelly said, waving her hand in my direction, bringing it back to her lips. "All so you could meet with the guy who's number one with a bullet on the F.B.I.'s Most Wanted list, collaborate on a plot to free the fair Melora using the good offices of Saint Margaret of Vietnam, risk arrest and a life-long committed relationship with a hairy cellmate named 'Bubba', and what you really want to talk about is your hometown and how some radio freaks came to be camped out in the middle of a forty-acre ghost campus?"

"I dream about it," I said, as if that explained everything.

Kelly arched one perfect eyebrow, looking serious, thoughtful. "That makes all the difference in the world. Why didn't you say so right at the beginning?"

Kelly thought it began with the Newark riots in '67. "That was *long* before I was born," she said, "but my grandparents grew up in Newark and talked about it all the time. The riots were bad—fires, looting, twenty-six dead, hundreds injured—but what came afterward sucked, too. White people, including my grandparents, ran from Newark and Applewood. Middle-class black people, too. Blockbusting real estate companies went into white neighborhoods talking racism and riots, scared homeowners into selling cheap, then jacked up the prices and resold to blacks. Then banks redlined the neighborhoods and wouldn't loan money to black businesses or homeowners."

"The Newark riots went down the summer after my freshman year at Wellston," I said, "and Applewood had its own small riot the same week. But blockbusting, redlining, white flight—that didn't start in '67. It goes way back. And there were other things, too. Things happening when I was a kid."

I told Kelly and Toby about how New Jersey built a medical center in Newark's mostly poor, mostly black, Central Ward, tearing down acres of tenements and displacing a whole community. "And before that," I said, "the East-West Expressway. They built it when I was in high school. It cut Applewood, Orange, and East Orange in half, demolished the core of all three cities, and continued through the heart of Newark. It let whites in the new suburbs—Livingston, Morristown, Short Hills—breeze to Newark Airport doing fifty-five, avoiding the old cities. That highway destroyed whole neighborhoods, driving out whites and blacks, but I didn't understand what was going on when I was a kid. The history classes I took in college didn't explain it, either. I didn't see it as racial segregation until I met Meg. Most of what I know about segregation outside the south, I learned from her."

"Same for me," Toby said. "When I was growin' up in Virginia, Jim Crow was right in your face. A federal court ordered Stonewall's all-white public pool integrated, so the city filled it with concrete. My boardin' school let in one black kid, but told the rest of us we didn't have to room with him. No one did, and he dropped out in two weeks. When I moved up north for college, I figured I was leavin' segregation behind. At first, I thought the only people Yankees discriminated against were white southerners. Remember how it was, Tesla?"

"Yeah," I said. "A psychology professor from Connecticut asked me how I could stand living with a racist from Virginia."

"I remember that asshole," Toby said, "but I'll bet he never asked himself why the Wellston faculty and student body were well-nigh lily-white. I wasn't askin' either until I met Meg. Her favorite English professor, a black woman, resigned 'cuz Wellston had been a white school for two hundred years. It was still a white school when I graduated."

"And I grew up thinking everywhere in America except the south was like Applewood, and that Applewood was perfect," I said. "Sure, white parents and black parents weren't socializing, and neither were Irish and Italian parents, or Jewish and Protestant parents, or Protestant and Catholic parents. But our schools never needed court orders to integrate them. They'd always been that way. All of us kids hung out together—in school and after school, in little league, at the playground, at each other's houses, at school dances—and all of us were from blue-collar and white-collar families."

"Not in my New Jersey," Kelly said. "When I was a kid, only a few miles from here, the only black guy living in my town played second base for the Mets."

"We knew Applewood was changing," I said, "even in the '60s. You could thumb through my high school yearbooks and see more black kids and fewer white ones every year. White flight became more like white panic. Not everyone moved because their new neighbors were black, and lots of black families were leaving, too. They were making more money and wanted new homes, schools, and shopping malls. By the time Meg and I left for Vietnam, all my old friends and their families, white and black, were gone."

"That caused big problems," Kelly said. "Applewood's public employees—teachers, police, civil servants—they don't live here anymore, and every night their paychecks go home with them. That killed Applewood's stores, and the ones that didn't go broke followed the money to suburban shopping malls where there was more space, more parking, lower taxes, and safer streets. That took away more jobs and more money. Property values crashed and property taxes soared.

Ken, the station manager, he's been at 'FMH forever, and he says that in the '80s skin color didn't matter. Black or white, everyone wanted out."

"My parents gave up in '82," I said, "after the brick through the window, the break-ins, the threats."

"Graft was part if it, too," Kelly said. "Not like that's a surprise in New Jersey, but since I've been at the station it's more like official looting. And the school board, teachers, firefighters, police, none of them live here anymore. That disconnect, plus more corruption cases than prosecutors can handle—blue-collar, white-collar, black, white—wiped out everyone's respect for The Man. The country's richer than ever, but politicians and banks write off cities like Applewood like they're writing off a bad loan they never made in the first place. So how does Applewood make up the difference? By raising property taxes—taxes no one can afford. This piece of crap house? Applewood's billing us eighteen grand a year, and redlining banks won't loan us a penny for repairs. It's the same everywhere in this city. That means more bankrupt businesses, more abandoned buildings. And who do you think's gonna fill that void?"

"Who?" I said.

Kelly looked at me like I'd just arrived from Mars. "Who else? Crips and Bloods, crack and drive-bys. Hilversum gave lots of official reasons for closing, but I saw its last graduation—scared-looking parents, and kids getting their diplomas in front of graffiti-covered buildings. That told the real story. I don't know what it was like here when you grew up, Tesla. I wasn't born yet. I only know that I've heard gunshots in the front yard and gunshots in the back yard. One night, some guys were shooting up the old dorms with automatic weapons—just for fun! I sneak in and out of here every day. If I didn't love the station and love my job, I'd never set foot in Applewood."

"Why doesn't the station move to another city?" I said

Kelly laughed, but she wasn't smiling. "We were planning to move to Hoboken until Toby showed up. He's screwed up all our lives."

"I've got to see my old house," I said. "It's where I grew up, where Meg and I were married. I can walk from here. I mean, if it won't put you in danger, Toby."

"Sure, Tesla," Toby said. "Go see your home. Kelly'll go with you, keep you safe. I wish I could go too. I can still taste your mom's Friday-night roast-beef dinners."

"Oh great," Kelly said, acid edge returning to her voice. "Send the blond girl into the 'hood to play bodyguard for the visiting dignitary. What the hell ever happened to chivalry?"

"Just make sure he stays in one piece. He's the only hope we've got. And Kelly..."

"Yes, m'lord."

"...bring back some pizza!"

When I moved to Vietnam, I brought a photo album filled with pictures of home and family. I never looked at it. Visiting the old places in the four dimensional world of dreams always seemed more real than two-dimensional images on paper.

In some dreams I made my way home heading west through Newark's Branch Brook Park, passing Central Avenue's apartment buildings and shops, crossing Grove Street by Holy Name Catholic Church and All Souls School, cutting through the Columbus School playground, down elm-lined Roosevelt, turning up Grant Avenue at the Presbyterian Church toward North Arlington. In others, I came south from the nearby Bloomfield border, passing Fredrick's Tavern and the A.P. Smith manufacturing plant, under the Erie Lackawanna railroad bridge, following North Arlington all the way.

With Kelly, I walked east down Springdale past Roxy's, within earshot of the Garden State Parkway's steady drone. Turning left at the garden apartments on North Arlington, I asked her, "Do you agree with Toby's plan?"

"I don't have a choice. Sooner or later someone's gonna squeal on him. Or drink too much at a party and brag about how they met the famous fugitive. I can't believe we've hidden him this long. Toby's plan is the only way out of this mess for all of us."

"Aren't you worried about what might happen to you if we change history back to the way it was?"

"I would be worried if I believed any of that stuff. You guys may be Einsteins, or Teslas, or whatever, but I still think you're crazy."

We walked another block past the Methodist Church on Rutledge, the street where Timmy Jorgensen once lived. Along North Arlington, some homes looked much the same as I remembered. Fresh paint, mowed lawns. Brick, wood, plaster. Windows, double hung and picture. Roofs, gray slate and brown shingle. Every style America could muster from before, between, and after the World Wars. The streets and sidewalks looked familiar, too, with kids walking to school, parents driving to work. These were the streets where my friends and I biked and roller-skated, built tree houses in summer, snow forts in winter, hid, and held hands. Timmy and I had a secret route on the long block between Rutledge and Renshaw, where from tree to roof to utility pole we traversed the half-mile from the Methodist Church to Ellen Hoffmann's wooded yard without ever touching ground. I could imagine the children who walked past us discovering our route, enjoying its mysteries as much as we did.

According to the *Applewood Record*'s account, these were also the streets where last week a woman was carjacked from her own driveway. Some of the houses looked like they belonged in a neighborhood where that could happen. Injured, broken, abandoned.

A red Mustang convertible filled with a half-dozen teenagers drove past, the car radio blasting distorted bass. One, sitting high, almost standing in the back seat, pointed, saying, "Hey... white people!" no malice in his voice, only unselfconscious disbelief.

And at the corner of Grant and North Arlington, my home. The place where I grew up, the place where Meg and I were married. The safe and happy place, end-point in so many twilit odysseys, but no longer looking as it did in my time, in my dreams.

Twin white Georgian columns at the front entrance gone, replaced by rough, nailed-in four-by-fours. The century-old indestructible golden brick—no façade, but rather a fort-like foot-and-a-quarter thick—dirty, chipped, crumbling. Leaded French windowpanes opaque with grime. Lawn a mass of weeds and litter. Camellias, azaleas, peonies, roses—brown, dead, hacked down, rooted up. Walking to the yard, standing beneath the ruined rose trellis where Meg and I said, "I will," Kelly, seeing my tears, took my hand, saying nothing.

In my dreams, I often made it to the house on North Arlington only to wake up before entering. Sometimes, Odysseus-like trials and obstacles kept me blocks away. Sometimes, through the power of the dream, I was inside my old house, still magically retained by my parents for east-coast visits, still filled with familiar things, with love, still home. Now, in my old back yard, in a world more angular and concrete than dreams allow, I thought how I could probably jiggle the third French window at the corner of the sun parlor, jiggle it just so, loosening the latch, opening it, sliding myself up and over and into the sun parlor of the obviously empty, unlived-in house, the same way I'd snuck out early or snuck in late so many times when I was a kid. But turning to Kelly, holding her comforting hand harder than I'd realized, looking in her eyes, I said instead, "Let's go. Toby's waiting."

PART SIX

MEG

Chapter Thirty-Eight: Meg

"Meg Wells—do you know what they say about you?"

"No," I said. "I don't even know who 'they' are."

"They say you had it all. Energy, ambition, an Ivy League degree. You could have been a Fortune 500 C.E.O. living in a Park Avenue penthouse. Why choose life in a thatch shack? Why choose insects and snakes? Why choose Vietnam?"

Another perky, fresh-out-of-journalism-school, Diane-Sawyer-wannabe reporter, thoughtlessly asking canned questions. Shiny mauve fingernails absently scratch below the hemline of her black mini. She doesn't realize a fat Mekong mosquito's discovered the new blood in town, boring through her white pantyhose and soft, pale skin. Meanwhile, Paul's busy at the other end of the compound. Like he always is when the media shows up.

"I never graduated," I said.

"What?"

"I never graduated. Never got a degree. I dropped out."

"I didn't know.... I mean the research department never told me. I mean...."

"Look, why don't we get you out of those hose and into some shorts. You must be sweltering. And how about some DEET to keep the bugs off?"

"No, I'm fine. Really. My family camps at Lake George every summer, and Daddy always says black flies never bite me because I'm so sour."

Hearing myself sigh, not much caring if the reporter hears it too, I think, *So it goes.* Like Kurt Vonnegut said in that lecture my senior year at Wellston, *So it goes.*

I made *Time*'s cover twice, once when I won the Peace Prize (*Meg Wells, Mother of Vietnam*), again the following week when I turned it down (*The Woman Who Said No*). Toby trumped me with three cover stories. May 1971, *Electronic Meltdown*, his Wellston Yearbook photo, the one with the beret and star and long dark hair making him look like a cross between Che Guevara and Meat Loaf. Then May 1996, *The Hacker Who Changed History: Toby Jessup Twenty-Five Years Later*, with a ridiculous police artist's composite sketch. Paul and I laughed together over stupid stories of Toby sightings anywhere other than pizza parlors or pinball arcades, but Paul's nightmare returned for months, waking him, leaving him sleepless, drained. And the next time, *Lightning Strikes Twice*, an illustrator's imaginative rendering of a Toby who looked like Brando in *The Godfather*, separated by lightning bolts from the A.P. wire photo of Melora under arrest, bleeding and in handcuffs. After the exchange, we were all there together, a nifty collage of past covers under the banner, *People of the Year – Three Who Changed History*. Paul wasn't mentioned. And Paul was the only true history changer among us.

At the cost of Toby's freedom, I'd rescued Melora, Grendel, and the Modern Café gamers from prison, and gotten the obstruction-of-justice charges against the WFMH co-conspirators dropped. No deal for Cooperman, though. That was one miracle even Saint Meg couldn't perform. The feds called his crimes "unrelated terrorism" and refused to budge. He still had twelve years left on his fifteen-year sentence.

Now it was time for another in-depth feature article in *Esquire, The New Yorker, Atlantic Monthly*, whichever magazine sent this girl into the jungle to find me. Why did they bother? Their editors had already decided what she'd write. Meg's a hero. Meg's a villain. Meg's a hero to some and a villain to others. In the end, what difference did it make?

"Where would you like to begin?" I said.

"At the beginning!" she said, giggling a little, scratching a little more.

"I grew up in Grosse Pointe. Do you know anything about Grosse Pointe?"

"One of my sorority sisters lives there. Do you know Shannon Willey?"

"Kim—or is it Kimberly?" She nods. I'm still not sure which she prefers, decide to go with Kim. "Kim, I've been in Vietnam since 1972. My parents have been dead for ten years. I don't know anyone in Grosse Pointe."

The photographer, who's been swatting mosquitoes and fiddling with his lenses, laughs out loud, chokes it off with fake coughing, nearly drops his camera.

"Oh, I'm sorry," Kim says.

I have no idea what she's talking about. My face, as always, shows it.

"I mean about your parents." Three new welts spread across Kim's knee. Gleaming fingernails scratch.

"Listen, Kim," rising, placing my arm around Kim's shoulders, "I'm not saying another word until you change into comfortable clothes and rub on some bug juice. And Scooter," (I can't believe the photographer, a man of at least fifty, goes by the name Scooter), "why don't you head over to the commissary. They'll fix you up with some lunch, and Kim will call you when we're ready." He nods. I don't know why, but all news photographers love food. Especially free food.

Kim raises her hand like an elementary school kid trying to get the teacher's attention. "Uh, Scooter, I really think we should...." Scooter ignores her, hoists his camera bag, takes off toward the commissary at a run.

"Scooter hates me, my editor hates me, even my interns hate me." Kim and I, in the empty clinic, Kim sobbing hysterically, head on my shoulder, like a child, like a daughter, tears soaking through my khaki shirt, through to the skin above my heart.

"It's okay, Kim. You'll be all right. Besides, they're jealous." Holding her, stroking her bleached yellow hair.

"You really think so?" Kim brightens a little.

"I'm thinking any guy named Scooter is jealous of everyone."

Kim smiles, showing white, straightened teeth. I hold a handkerchief to her nose—Kleenex still an impossible luxury at the clinic—she blows long and hard.

"It's because they think daddy got me the job. They don't know how hard I worked in school, but everyone knows he golfs with the publisher. When they come back from the country club, daddy always drops by my desk and loud enough so everyone can hear says, 'And how's my little ace reporter today? Working on a Pulitzer?' I hate it when he does that! And that's why they sent me here. Everyone says you're a horrible interview,"—not a hint of self-consciousness—"that you never talk about yourself, only the clinic. And they knew I wasn't ready. They sent me here to fail!"

Dabbing at Kim's mascara-streaked cheeks, too late for my ruined shirt. "Have you got your makeup kit handy?" Kim looks up, touches her shoulder bag, nods. "Then let's make a trade. Promise you'll show me how you do your makeup. In return, I'll give you the interview of a lifetime. Deal?"

I stick out my hand. Kim takes it in both of hers like she may never let go, powder-blue eyes smiling above damp cheeks.

"Deal!"

"And I'll tell you what. When we're done, you're going to get that Pulitzer."

Chapter Thirty-Nine: Meg

Sweeping lawns, manicured landscapes. Huge mansions of stone and brick. Castles for the royalty of America's classless society kept safe from Detroit's pollution, poverty, and housing projects by moats of interstate highways and hundreds of blue-uniformed knights. In Mary Margaret Wells' Grosse Pointe castle—thirty-two rooms on six acres—Dad was king. Within its walls he ruled with absolute power. Whether the subject was politics, clothes, or what we ate for dinner, only one opinion counted in my house, and that was Dad's.

My first memory was of watching the Korean War on our black-and-white TV, asking my parents to turn it off, my dad saying "No, you have to watch because your mother and I are watching." My second memory is our first trip to Florida.

I was six. Dad liked to begin car trips at night when "all the trash got off the highways." We piled into our cream-colored Cadillac Eldorado with its gleaming chrome fins and tan leather seats, me in my footsie pajamas clutching a pillow under one arm and Gingie, my Teddy bear, under the other, heading down our quarter-mile driveway for the interstate.

I woke in Savannah.

Me stretching groggily on the back seat, Mom sitting up front next to Dad, Dad driving, Dad smoking a cigar. Even the stench of his El Rey del Mundo couldn't block the smell of Savannah's black shantytown, the smell of rot, garbage, and fouled water. As far as I could see through the Eldorado's half-open rear window, black people, going about their business in seemingly aimless patterns like busy ants on a hot day. And it was a hot day. The sun barely risen and it had to be ninety. In and out of windowless shacks pieced from corrugated cardboard and tin, black men, black women, black babies, clothed in rags, barely clothed, nearly naked. Poverty—no, much more than poverty—poorness, poor people, people with nothing but tin and cardboard, brown water and rotting waste.

"Dad, when we get home, can I call President Eisenhower? I want to tell him about the poor people in Savannah. He'll help them!"

Turning, billowing gray smoke toward me, Dad answers. "Come on Princess, those Negroes aren't doing so bad. Why look—they've got air conditioning."

I looked, seeing no sign of big grey units like the ones that cooled our stone castle on hot Michigan days.

"I don't think so, Daddy. They don't even have real windows, just holes in their walls."

"That's what I mean Princess—*natural* air conditioning!"

Then Dad laughed and laughed. He must have laughed all the way to St. Augustine.

Fifteen years later in Professor Stinson's U.S. History class at Wellston, Stinson's delivering a lecture on politics and society in the 1950s.

"So you see, it wasn't that America didn't have problems in the '50s—poverty, racism, political repression—but those problems were hidden. Most Americans had no way of knowing about them."

Raising my hand from the back of Lafayette Hall, I interrupted Stinson, saying, "I was six years old, and I knew."

Dad graduated from Harvard. He never doubted I'd go there too. Of course he meant the women's college, Radcliffe, but never referred to it, only Harvard. "Hell, for all the donations I've made to get my Meg into Harvard, they should name a library after her!" At dinner parties, birthdays, funerals, Dad let everyone know he was making sure I'd be accepted. And Mom decorated my room with souvenirs from Dad's reunions—pennants, pillows, ashtrays, and plaques—all of Harvard crimson.

Senior year in high school, I went through the motions of a Harvard interview. The interviewer was Brownell "Brownie" DeWolfe, stuffy, arrogant, rude, a classmate of Dad's.

"Do you think I should consider some other schools besides Harvard?" I asked.

"Now Meg, there are no guarantees you'll get into Harvard. But I hope you realize one can't really consider oneself educated unless one has a Harvard diploma."

I'd already completed my Radcliffe, Swarthmore, and Wellesley applications when the high school guidance counselor left a note taped to my locker—

An interviewer from Barton, the women's college at Wellston University, is coming today. I think you should meet her.

She was tall, black, stunningly gorgeous. Like my favorite Supreme, Flo Ballard, only with a PhD in English Literature. I liked her the moment she stuck out her hand, introducing herself as "Evelyn Ruger, as in 'sugar,' last-minute replacement for the rich white lady who normally handles Grosse Pointe." A big, smart woman with a big Afro and bigger personality, my high school had never seen anything like her. As we walked the halls together—Evelyn asked me for a tour—every head turned her way.

"Meg, I like your school, but I sure do feel like the raisin at the bottom of the bowl of corn flakes. I think the admissions people sent me out here because I'm from Detroit. 'Course the Brewster Projects aren't exactly Grosse Pointe."

"The Brewster Projects? Isn't that where The Supremes grew up?" I'd read it in Seventeen Magazine, the only thing I knew about the projects.

"Sure did. I sang with those girls in my church choir."

"You sang with The Supremes?"

"What did I say? And let me tell you something. Mary and Flo—'Blondie' we called her because of her light hair—those girls had the voices. But that Diane Ross...."

"Don't you mean Diana?" I interrupted.

"Sure, she's Diana out here in Grosse Pointe, but in the projects she was plain Diane. Anyway, you couldn't hear her little thing above the other girls. But she'd carry on so, the reverend always put her in the front row to keep her from making a scene!"

I laughed. Everything Evelyn said made me laugh.

When we returned to the lounge outside the guidance office, I asked Evelyn if she went to Barton.

"Be SERIOUS, Meg!" Evelyn had a habit of talking in capitals. "I got my degrees from Detroit and Cleveland State."

"Then why do you think I should go there?"

Evelyn didn't say anything for a while, just looked at me, looked through me with her wide brown eyes.

"The guidance counselor showed me your grades, Meg. Your grades, SATs, all that stuff. We both know you can go anywhere you want. Why, if you're smart, you'll head some place warm, like Stanford or Berkeley. But let me tell you something. Wellston and Barton are changing. They're changing because students are making them change, and making decisions about things that really count—curriculum, admissions, and financial aid. I'm not saying they don't have to drag half the faculty along with them kicking and screaming, but the point is, it's happening. Four years from now when you graduate, there may not be a Barton, because students are working on a plan for equal admission of men and women, coed dorms, and complete integration of the colleges. If you want to be part of those changes, if you want to leave your mark, you should come to Barton."

By the time we shook hands goodbye, I knew where I was going to college.

"Dad, I got an acceptance letter from Barton! That's where I'm going!"

"Like hell you are! You're going to Harvard or I'm cutting you off without a penny. And don't think a princess like you can work her way through college!"

"Dad, Harvard rejected me. Here—read the letter."

Snatching the one paragraph letter from my hand, Dad reads, face turning redder and redder.

"No. This is bullshit! Someone made a mistake!"

"It's no mistake Dad. They rejected me."

"We'll see about that!"

Dad stormed up the stairs to his study, called God knows who, but I could hear him screaming. When he came down, he was angrier than before.

"Those bastards! How could they do this to me! I'll bet it was that prick DeWolfe! It must be him! He's had it in for me ever since the day I was accepted at Harvard Law and he barely made it into BU. I'm going to make that son of a bitch pay if it's the last thing I ever do!"

When I came home from school the next day, everything crimson had been removed from my room. Dad never again uttered the words "Harvard" and "Meg" in the same sentence.

Of course, getting rejected was easy. And it proved one thing— Harvard's Admissions Committee really does read those stupid essays they make you write about why you want to go to Harvard.

Chapter Forty: Meg

My freshman year at Barton I smoked pot, dropped acid, went through three boyfriends. By Christmas I put on fifteen pounds. So I stopped eating. By spring break I'd lost thirty. First semester I made straight As, pulling all-nighters with the help of diet pills stolen from my mother's medicine cabinet. Second term I was on my way to Cs, Ds and incompletes. That's when I got a note from Evelyn. "Please come see me in my office."

In Whitman House, home to the English Department and the most rundown building on campus, I found Evelyn's office in the basement. She didn't waste time getting to the point.

"What is WRONG with you, Meg?"

"What do you mean?"

"Missed classes, missed exams, papers not turned in—I did not traipse all the way out to your Mayflower-riding high school to invite you to a four-year party!"

"I'm doing the best I can, Evelyn. Really."

"You are doing NOTHING! Now I have made you an appointment with the Madeira Point Neighborhood Association. You are going down there tomorrow and volunteer to work with those neighborhood kids. Because if you want to flunk out that's your business, but at least you're going to flunk out because you're spending time doing SOMETHING. Do you understand me?"

I nodded, stunned, not knowing what to say.

"And Meg, you look terrible. You are coming with me this instant, AND YOU ARE GOING TO EAT!"

I wanted a university where students weren't treated like children, where the outmoded doctrine of *in loco parentis* had been cast aside. But by acting like a mother, a real mother, Evelyn saved my life. It was that simple. Evelyn saved my life.

Working with the kids in Madeira Point changed everything. Call it amateur psychology, but I couldn't help thinking, if my parents wouldn't comfort me, at least I could comfort others. I even looked it up in the *Oxford English Dictionary*, the old definition, the real definition—comfort, from the Latin *confortare*, to give strength and hope.

Evelyn only volunteered me for two mornings a week, but soon I was spending part of each day at the Neighborhood Association's Community Center, reading to the Portuguese-speaking children from the Cape Verde Islands, and in time, teaching them so they could read to me. Their parents thanked me with whole roasted chickens and melt-in-your-mouth Portuguese sweet breads. Helped by their generosity and the strictly observed ritual of Friday-night dinners with Evelyn at Grant's Womb, a lamely psychedelic campus bistro, the skeleton my body had become soon regained its form. My grades recovered too, despite, or rather because of the hours I spent off campus. By the middle of my second year, when so many classmates experienced sophomore slump, my name returned to the dean's list, staying there until the events of my senior year made grades irrelevant.

Chapter Forty-One: Meg

Mom and Dad never asked me about my extracurricular activities, so I never told them. They didn't ask about my courses, or major, or friends, or much of anything, but as long as I kept getting good grades, they kept writing checks for tuition, room, and board. Dad would call on Sundays, rubbing it in about Harvard's annual football victory over Wellston, and I'd play along, pretending I went to the games, pretending I cared. Mom wrote me brief notes with the latest gossip from the country club or summaries of her canasta hands, always enclosing a twenty-dollar bill, always assuring me all she wanted was my happiness.

One topic I never discussed with my parents was the war. It wasn't that the subject never came up. Dad's wartime proclamations became more frequent as the conflict, in Vietnam and at home, continued growing.

"The President knows what he's doing!"

"My country right or wrong!"

"They ought to shoot a few of those protesters like they do in Russia! Maybe then they'd appreciate how good we've got it here!"

I never told him how the privileged boys I knew at Wellston all had student deferments, how after graduating, the wealthy ones still avoided serving. Or how older brothers of my Madeira Point kids were coming home from the war sick, injured, addicted. Or never coming home again. I didn't say a thing about rising opposition to the war at Wellston and throughout the country. I kept my mouth shut about my own growing involvement in the antiwar movement. I never rose to his bait. And the checks kept coming, even after I stopped coming home.

One Christmas vacation I learned how sons of my family's country-club friends received exemptions from the draft based on letters written by Dad. "All it took was a few words to my clients on the draft board," he bragged after downing his fourth Scotch. "A few words, and now all those draft-dodging little bastards and their families owe me big time!"

That was the only time I ever slipped.

"Doesn't that make you a hypocrite?" I said.

Dad didn't speak to me again until after New Years, until my mother begged me to apologize to him.

I did.

Dad was an officer on General MacArthur's staff in World War II, serving under him from the Philippines all the way to Tokyo. Somewhere along the way he was awarded a Purple Heart. Dad never talked about it, and I would never have known if I hadn't asked Mom why he walked with a limp.

"He never got angry before the war," she said. "I can't even recall him raising his voice." Then she started crying.

I didn't understand about PTSD. No one did. Besides, World War II vets, the Greatest Generation, they didn't get PTSD, right?

As it turned out, that trip to Grosse Pointe was my last. The day I returned from break, I joined S.M.C.—the Student Mobilization Committee Against The War. Within a month I was living with S.M.C.'s chairman, Nick Rector. My opposition to the war became a full-time occupation, leaving no opportunity, even during school vacations, for traveling home. So I made excuses—"Sorry Mom, I've got to stay here and finish my honors thesis." "Sorry Dad, my roommate's family needs me to housesit for them in Newport."—every day working harder against a war I viewed as being waged by the wealthy against the poorer classes of two countries, Vietnam and America.

In the fall of 1969, marching arm-in-arm down Pennsylvania Avenue with 500 S.M.C. Marshals and 500,000 more opponents of what was now Nixon's War, I felt determined and optimistic, thinking, *We're really going to do it, we're going to stop this war! The people are demanding it, and the government can't stand against a vocal, mobilized majority of its own citizens!*

I didn't realize Nixon had discovered support elsewhere—in an invisible, unpollable, unquestionable "silent majority," a constituency whose support he'd soon be citing for widening the war, bombing civilian targets in North Vietnam, defoliating the jungles of the South with Agent Orange and napalm, illegally wiretapping American citizens, impounding funds appropriated by Congress for wastewater treatment, using them instead for secret attacks on Laos and Cambodia, supporting the overthrow of the Cambodian government, invading Cambodia, sending hundreds of thousands of American soldiers into combat, sending tens of thousands of them and God only knows how many Vietnamese, Cambodians, and Laotians to their deaths. By the time of the killings at Kent State, I couldn't understand why anyone was shocked. If anything, the murder of protesters was overdue—and undoubtedly supported by the silent majority.

But before Cambodia, before Kent State, other things happened, small things in comparison to the war, yet far more important to me, things that changed my life forever.

Despite the war, my "Wellston Experience" (as the University's recruiting literature liked calling it) was a good one. I loved exploring Wellston's ivy-covered campus, from The Green, a grassy quadrangle shaded by ancient elms where students and faculty congregated on old picnic blankets, rapping for hours and playing Frisbee or guitar, to the unfinished glass-and-concrete tower of the new science library, invaded nightly by dozens of students who hiked up its seventeen flights of stairs and huddled together on the rooftop against the chill, passing joints and waiting for sunrise. Climbing through trapdoors, out bay windows, and up fire escapes to the roofs of dormitories, libraries, and lecture halls,

I made it my mission to photograph Butler's sooty skyline from every possible angle, in every season, at every time of day.

Thinking about life after college, planning for law school or perhaps a masters degree in elementary education, I declared a double major in political science and English literature, taking every course Evelyn taught—Women in Literature, Twentieth-Century Poets, and her multidisciplinary course, Black Voices: From Bailey (Pearl) to Baraka (Amiri). Inspired by Evelyn, I began keeping a journal, writing poetry, dabbling in creative writing and ethnomusicology classes.

I continued working with kids in Madeira Point, and their parents asked for my help opposing Wellston's creeping expansion into their neighborhood, where new student housing was driving up rents and driving out residents. From that experience I met Nick and other SMC activists.

I was happy. Evelyn's recruiting promises about Wellston were coming true—a great education and the chance to make a difference. Without ever asking, I assumed Evelyn was happy, too. Leading workshops on racism and poverty, winning praise from the community and student-sponsored awards for teaching excellence, writing articles about feminist pre-revolutionary French poets in her spare time. In my eyes, Evelyn was a rising star. It never occurred to me Wellston might not agree, never crossed my mind recruiting promises made to Evelyn might not be kept.

The only failures I experienced at Wellston came in my relations with men. I had lots of men friends, but romances never lasted more than a month or two. Awkward, uncomfortable, frustrating, and not very romantic—that's how I'd describe them. Sex was brief, unsatisfying, and always accompanied by fears of disease and parental discovery. Fears of pregnancy too, though I was on The Pill. I never discussed it with my boyfriends, but I realized they had similar fears, plus one more: commitment.

Because of my interests and the circles I moved in, it was only natural I should date some of the more radical men on campus. But while they might deliver a fiery speech demanding equality for women, their abstract ideals never carried over to the women they slept with.

Some of my girlfriends experimented in relationships with other women, seeming no more or less happy than those who dated men. Their flirtations and my own experience with men made the idea tempting, but women never held that kind of attraction for me.

Compared to my social life, I thought Evelyn's was perfect. She couldn't have been more than ten years older than I, but to me, Evelyn was a woman, while I was still a girl. Evelyn was a professor, a great teacher, a committed activist, possessed of all the beauty, charm, charisma, and confidence I lacked. And Evelyn's mix of intellectual sophistication and interpersonal earthiness, like Anna Julia Cooper and Tina Turner blended into one perfect woman, made her irresistible to men.

Evelyn loved music—avant-garde jazz, rhythm and blues, straight-ahead blues, and anything danceable. Arriving at parties with a stack of records under one arm and always a tall, handsome black man on the other, colorful dashiki paralleling every full and dangerous curve of her body, heavy brass and aquamarine earrings dangling to her shoulders, she'd immediately abandon her date, heading straight for the stereo, ripping stacks of students' Led Zeppelin and Cream LPs off the turntable, replacing them with John Coltrane (her favorite), Howlin' Wolf, Aretha Franklin, and The Electric Flag.

"Clapton? Page? Don't make me laugh! Now you take a listen to Mr. Michael Bloomfield—that's one white boy who can PLAY!"

And she'd cue up Electric Flag's *Wine*, curling one slender index finger in the direction of her date, taking over the dance floor the way she'd taken over the music, the party, the heart of everyone in the room, jitterbugging with heat and sexuality and abandon, her man coolly laying back behind the beat while Evelyn swayed and shimmied an eighth note ahead, making it seem for all the world like the song was written just for her.

I really was still a girl, a girl who couldn't see beneath the surface of anything.

On the first day of November 1968, the New England weather turned bone-chillingly cold as word swept campus that Dan Reynolds, a popular young writing teacher, was dead. "Bad acid," they whispered at a small, unofficial student vigil for those who knew and admired him. I wasn't one of those. I'd never taken a course from Reynolds, never met him, barely had time to shake my head, muttering, "too bad," and "so sorry," to friends in the Creative Writing Program who revered him. When Evelyn missed our Friday dinner, it never occurred to me the reason might have something to do with the death of her English Department colleague.

"Hi Evelyn!" I found Evelyn behind her desk in the Whitman House basement on Monday. "Where were you Friday night? I waited for you at The Womb for two hours."

I talked for another five minutes, complaining about Professor Modine's Polling Statistics class, complaining about the last SMC meeting, complaining about Nick, complaining about God knows what, before I noticed Evelyn's puffy cheeks, her sleepless, red-streaked eyes.

"What's... what's the matter?" I said.

And then she was crying. And I didn't know what to do. So I sat there feeling uncomfortable, wishing she would stop, finally saying, "I'll come back later when you feel better," slipping out of her office door, closing it quietly behind me.

The next day's Wellston Daily Herald headline read, RUGER RESIGNS ENGLISH DEPT. POST, CITES INSTITUTIONAL RACISM. And she wasn't in her office, and she wasn't at her apartment, and no one knew where she was. I didn't hear a thing until two weeks later, when a letter postmarked Detroit arrived in my mailbox.

> *November 18, 1968*
> *My Dear Meg,*
> *I might as well spit it out. Dan Reynolds and I were lovers. He wanted to get married, but I said no. I didn't want to be known for the rest of my life as the black professor who*

married the white man. I never wanted anyone to know we were together. Well, I don't have to worry about that now.

That's not the only reason I left Wellston. I love teaching you white kids, but I need to teach some black kids, too. And that's not happening, not at Wellston, not fast enough for me. At faculty meetings I can count the brothers and sisters on one hand. And no one on that ivy-covered, lily-white faculty is interested in recruiting more dashiki-wearing troublemakers like me.

You have eyes, Meg, but you couldn't see. When you told me about all your man problems, you didn't notice I never told you mine. When you visited my office, all you saw was the big-time English professor—and sometimes when I looked in the mirror that's what I saw, too. But look again. Look at the bare-bulbed basement hole-in-the-wall they called my office. Look at the paper index card on my door that read, "ASSISTANT Professor Ruger." Six years at Wellston and I was still in the basement, still without tenure, still at the back of the bus.

When Dan died, I had to face facts. There's nothing at Wellston for me except you. And at your age, you don't need me crying on your shoulder.

There's one other thing I've got to tell you. When you find yourself a man, a REAL man, forget about whether he's black or white, blind or crippled, Christian, Jewish, Hindu or Buddhist. Forget about what your parents will think or friends will say. Forget about all that shit. Just grab him and hold on. Hold on like your life depends on it.

I'm sorry for not telling you all this before I left. I hope you understand. But please, don't come looking for me. Write if you want, but please don't come looking. We'll see each other again some day, I know it.

If none of this makes sense to you, well, in the words of the old spiritual, "We'll understand it by and by."

Love,

Evelyn Ruger (as in "sugar")

Chapter Forty-Two: Meg

Evelyn was right about me. At nineteen, I didn't need her crying on my shoulder. But at nineteen, I wasn't old enough to know that.

So I blamed myself.

If only I'd stayed with Evelyn in her office. If only I'd asked her what was wrong. If only I knew how to listen. If only I'd hugged her. Then maybe I could have been there for her, helped her through the grief, helped her keep fighting. Then maybe she would have stayed at Wellston until a student sit-in not long after she resigned turned the tide for minority admissions and faculty recruitment. Then maybe she would have been there for me, for things to come. Then maybe everything would have been different.

If only, then maybe.

My most vivid memories of the months following Evelyn's resignation aren't about school, or Nick, or the war. My most vivid memories are of those four phantom words drifting through daydreams, stalking nightmares—*If only, then maybe.*

It turned out Evelyn was right about holding on to a good man, too, right about everything. Except she never did get to see me again.

I wrote her every month from Butler, and every month Evelyn wrote me from her new home, Jackson, Mississippi.

March 3, 1969

Dear Evelyn,

I'm so excited you're teaching again! You should never NOT be teaching!

So many things have happened at Wellston since you left. It seems like only yesterday we were together at Grant's Womb, but Wellston's been through a decade of change.

The sit-in was a complete success. Next year's entering class will include 11% minorities, and increased recruitment of Afro-American faculty members has begun. An ad hoc committee on curricular reform drafted a proposal for a new Wellston curriculum including optional pass/no pass alternatives to letter grades in all courses, detailed written comments from teachers about students' class performance, elimination of all distribution requirements, and increased emphasis on multidisciplinary studies. And Evelyn, the faculty adopted the entire report! In September the "New Curriculum" takes effect.

Can you stand to hear any more? Well get this—next term Wellston will open its first coed dorm. Maybe the revolution has arrived after all!

I know better than to ask you to think about coming back to Wellston. But PLEASE write me everything you can about J.S.U. I'm serious—it's not too late for me to transfer there for senior year! I'd love any college you love. Besides, Wellston's becoming WAY too radical for me!

1968 was a hell of a year. Reverend King and Bobby Kennedy, the Czech Invasion and Chicago Convention police riot, and for me, your losing Dan Reynolds and leaving Wellston. But it's like you wrote me when you left—"we'll understand it by and by." Because, at last, everything seems to be changing. Our new President, Richard "Tricky Dick" Nixon

*of all people (!) says he's going to end the war. I think 1969 is
really going to be something!*

Love,

Meg

April 1, 1969

Dear Meg,

Don't get any ideas, this is no April Fools letter!

*J.S.U. is wonderful. My students are smart young men
and women, and unlike many Wellston students, they don't
take anything about their college educations for granted. Most
of them work. God only knows when they find time to study.
The administration can be a pain (lots of rules to follow), but
the English faculty is friendly, supportive, and genuinely glad
to have me here. Winter was wet but mild, and spring is here
early—not like Butler's nine months of "The Gray Miseries."
Last but not least, the party music is a LOT better than
at Wellston.*

*But Meg, don't even think about coming down here. You
show up at the Greyhound station with your Yankee accent
asking directions to J.S.U., and those crackers down there will
string you up quicker than you can say, "Goodman, Chaney,
and Schwerner." It may be 1969 in Butler, but here in the land of
Dixie it's more like 1869. And I don't want to hurt your feelings,
but I'm not sure our student body would take to a well-mean-
ing white girl matriculating, either. The way they see it, you'd
be taking one of their spots. I guess both sides in this race thing
got a whole lot of work to do.*

*Your daddy paid for that Wellston degree, and you earned
it. So finish up first, then we'll talk about the future and what
you can do with that high-class sheepskin to change the world. I
have to admit though, I would like to be there to see the expression on your daddy's face when he showed up for your J.S.U.
graduation, or when word about you at an all-black college*

got around Grosse Pointe and they revoked his country club membership! (April Fools!)

Love,

Evelyn Ruger (as in "sugar")

VERY EARLY August 16, 1969

Dear Evelyn,

I'm writing you from Bethel, New York, and the Woodstock Art and Music Festival. Nick and I have been here for less than a day, and it's awful. Freezing rain, hot sun, and mud—lots of mud. Hours pass between performances and the rumor is the bands are refusing to leave the Holiday Inn they're holed up in until they get paid—in cash! Meanwhile, we sit in the mud and wait.

Nick came hoping to meet up with his friends from Yale and do some 'Mobe recruiting. I admit, I came for the art and music. After spending sixteen hours Friday getting here from Butler (I'm sure pictures of the traffic jams are making the news), we're both disappointed. It's impossible to find anyone, there's lots more waiting than music, and I haven't seen any art.

(Continued, Monday morning, August 18, 1969)

I guess I was a little cranky when I began this letter two days ago. Waking up Saturday morning on our soggy blankets, stretching out the kinks from a cold, miserable night trying to sleep in the mud only twenty feet from the stage, looking up at the sunrise over the hill, seeing what looked like my whole generation arrayed on that hillside as far as the eye could see, arrayed in all their wild hair and bright colors, well, that was worth all the hassles.

So Nick gave up on organizing, and I gave up on music and art, and we hiked off and volunteered at the Hog Farm tent, helping out with bad trips and injured feet, even the birth of a healthy baby boy!

I didn't like it when Nick slipped off with one of the women from the Hog Farm, but he thinks that's Grosse Pointe talking and I need to get over it. Meanwhile, I smiled at a guy whose hand I was bandaging, and Nick accused me of flirting just to get back at him. Anyway, everything's been fine between us since, so I'm not going to bug him about it.

Isn't it wonderful, though, that half a million of us spent three days in these awful conditions, and there's been no violence or crime? Not always peace, not always love, but enough of both to keep everyone busy helping each other get through this. I came for the art and music, but I'm glad I got to be part of the helping. I hope they're showing that on TV too, and not just all the acid and grass. I want our parents to see we can do something they could never do, want them to imagine what this would be like if they were here with their beer and martinis.

It's Monday morning, and I just finished bathing in a muddy pond. But a marble tub filled with bubble bath couldn't have felt as good. Almost everyone's gone, and Nick's saying, "C'mon, hurry up, finish the letter when we get home." And though the thought of crashing in my warm, soft, clean sheets back in Butler seems like a vision of heaven, I'm sorry it's over, sorry it's time to leave.

Love,

Meg

P.S. Save this letter. The mud splotches from Yasgur's farm may be worth a fortune some day!

August 30, 1969

Dear Meg,

Yes, I saw lots of Woodstock on TV. The freedom, the peace, the love looked beautiful. But your whole generation? I

*have to ask—in that sea of faces, where were the soul brothers
and sisters? On that stage, where were the soul bands?*

*All right, I don't want to get all self-righteous black
woman on you. I love you, and I'm proud of how you helped
in a tough situation. But next summer, can we PLEASE invite
James Brown?*

Love,

Evelyn Ruger (as in "sugar")

P.S. It is time to give Mr. Nick his walking papers!!!

November 30, 1969

Dear Evelyn,

*I just returned from Washington and the Moratorium
Against the War. You should have been there, Evelyn. This
time it really was our whole generation—and our parents and
their parents, black, white, rich, poor, a half million of us. You
should have been there, Evelyn, because it was the beginning of
the end. Nixon's got to stop this war. He has no choice.*

Love,

Meg

December 15, 1969

Dear Meg,

It's a long road to freedom.

Love,

Evelyn Ruger (as in "sugar")

4:00 a.m., January 10, 1970

Dear Evelyn,

*Greetings from Butler and happy New Year! If it's supposed
to be the dawn of the new decade, why does it still feel like 1969?*

*Right after winter break, a huge ice storm greeted return-
ing students. Trees, power lines, streets, and sidewalks all coated
with thick, shimmering ice. Everything looked so beautiful, I*

decided to go outside and take some pictures. After falling three times and nearly breaking my camera and my neck, I retreated inside and settled for taking pictures from my bedroom window. My favorite is enclosed, a close-up of the finches I've been feeding on my windowsill. With the ground frozen solid under half an inch of ice, the Butler birds were starving, literally screaming for human help.

Now that the ice has melted, the temperature soaring to a balmy 36 degrees, Nick, the other SMC leaders, and I spend every night training demonstration marshals. Marching down Hope Street at 2:00 a.m. might have looked crazy a year or two ago, and may again a year or two from now, but in 1970 it seems pretty ordinary.

Something special did happen tonight, and Evelyn, that's the big news! It wasn't the fight Nick and I had before our new trainees arrived—I can't even recall what we argued about, though it was The Big One, definitely and finally our relationship ender (you saw that coming months ago, and I wish I'd followed your advice sooner). And it certainly wasn't the night's cold, dark, black-and-whiteness. Every night in Butler feels like that, more magical than dreary. (Am I building enough suspense?)

So here's the news: tonight, real magic entered my life.

Most mornings I can't recall faces from the previous night's training. But if I live to a hundred, forgetting everything else I ever experienced, I'll always remember training Paul and Toby, two geeks straight from the College of Science. They didn't say much, but their body language, their eyes, their every gesture, communicated the ease of their friendship, the depth of its comfort, a closeness I've never seen before, let alone experienced. That's what attracted me—their closeness.

I have no idea what will happen next. All I can say is, I can't remember ever feeling so good!

Stay tuned!

Meg

February 6, 1970

Dear Meg,

I'm THRILLED to hear all the news! Nick's a good boy, and he'll be a good man, too—when he grows up. As for the new man who brought all this magic into your life, you left out one little detail. Which one is it, girl—Paul, or Toby?

Love,

Evelyn Ruger (as in "sugar")

March 4, 1970

Dear Evelyn,

As usual, you cut through all my flowery prose and got right to the point: "Which one is it girl—Paul or Toby?"

Since my last letter I moved out of Hope Street and into Paul and Toby's Bowen Street apartment (please note my new address). After today's SMC meeting, Nick pulled me aside and asked—with more than a hint of hurt feelings—whose bedroom I settled in. I told him I have my own bedroom (which is more like a very large walk-in closet), teasing that my relationship with him spoiled me so much I could never consider being with another man.

Asking myself the same question you and Nick asked, I do wonder why no romance blossoms between me and one or the other of these two guys I spend all my time with.

Today we went to Narragansett Racetrack together and won a bunch of money using a computer program they wrote to pick winners! Weird, I know, but the most fun I've ever had. I gave Paul a kiss after our horse won the last race, and I kind of thought something might happen between us tonight. But now he's in his room sleeping, and I'm up writing you this letter. It would be easy enough for me to go knock on his bedroom door, but I can't do it.

So why is that? Of course I did just break up with Nick, and I can't handle another failed relationship. I also realize I might jeopardize Paul and Toby's closeness, the warmth I share, the very thing attracting me to them in the first place. Besides, I can't imagine falling for any guy whose idea of great literature is the latest edition of Popular Mechanics! But the real reason is simpler. Paul and Toby are my friends.

I guess that's not much of an answer, but it's the only one I've got.

In the meantime, something else happened, something more important. It also helps explain how the three of us became so close, so quickly.

The same day I last wrote to you, the day after I met Paul and Toby, a Vietnam Vet named Ian Marley had a flashback and a seizure during a party at Hope Street. Kevin McCabe, the local Vets Against the War chairman and Ian's best friend, told us if we called the Veterans Administration Hospital, they'd drug Ian, lock him up, and throw away the key. So I got Paul and Toby, and together we took care of him. Four days watching over him, feeding him, cleaning him, but we did it! He's okay— thank God!—and back living with Kevin.

What happened was terrible, seeing Ian convulsing and in so much pain. But something wonderful happened, too. Together, we saved him. And I feel like I found my gift. Evelyn, I can save people!

Love,

Meg

P.S. Toby, Paul, and I marshaled together at a peace rally a few hours after I met them at their training session. The turnout was great, more than 5,000, and Pete McCloskey, a Congressman from California (and former Marine!) gave a terrific speech. I've enclosed a picture from the Federal Courthouse steps. Paul's the one with the Mets Cap, Toby's wearing the beret and kind of towering over us. What do you think?

March 14, 1970

Dearest Meg,

Please don't misunderstand me, honey, what you and your friends did was wonderful. But like Reverend Franklin used to say in his sermons at the New Bethel Baptist Church in Detroit, only God has the power to save someone. Maybe your gift is the power to give God a little more time to decide.

As for Paul, Toby, and your picture, the answer's simple— I'd take both those good looking young men in a heartbeat! Can they dance? But you, girl—do you need me to come back up there and start feeding you again? Or should I write to your new friends and tell them to get you out to Grant's Womb on Fridays?

Love,

Evelyn Ruger (as in "sugar")

March 22, 1970

Dear Evelyn,

I'm sitting in my room at Bowen Street. Two days ago Ian killed himself. I've never felt so bad.

You were right, Evelyn, you were so right. I can't save anyone. Every day people are dying in this war and I can't save any of them.

I'm not like you, Evelyn. I don't have your faith that God will do the saving. Because of you, because of all you've done for me, because of all you taught me, I have faith in myself, faith I can do something.

I wish you were here, know you can't be. But thanks to you, I'm ready to stand on my own two feet, ready to act.

Ian went through college on a ROTC scholarship. That's how he wound up in Vietnam. Evelyn, one way or another, Dr. King's way or Malcolm's way, I'm getting ROTC off this campus.

Love,

Meg

March 31, 1970

Dear Meg,

I'm thinking back on all my letters to you, feeling more like my Aunt Martha than your friend Evelyn. No matter what I did when I was a kid, Aunt Martha always let me know it wasn't good enough.

"Look Aunty! Watch me swim!"

"That ain't swimming girl—keep your face in the water!"

"Aunty Martha, let me read to you."

"Child, you read so slow I'll be in God's kingdom by the time you finish!"

"I thought I sang really well today in Church, Aunty. What did you think?"

"You sure don't sound like the Wilson's daughter Mary. That girl sings like a little angel!"

So every time you write to me, it seems like Aunty Martha writes you back. I'm sorry. I wanted to keep looking after you, keep teaching you. But you're not a Grosse Pointe teenager any more; you're all grown up. And while I wasn't paying attention, you were teaching me. Teaching me what it really means to care, care enough to do something while everyone else is looking for the door.

Now I've got to sound critical again. I'm sorry about your friend Ian, but he's in God's care and you're in mine. I wish I could bear your hurt for you, wish I could take away the pain. I can't, but I'm still bound to tell you this: you can follow Dr. King's way if you've got the courage. But Meg, even though you read Malcolm's book and wrote an A+ paper on it in my Black Voices class, you don't know anything about his way.

There goes Aunty Martha again! But I don't mean it like that. It's just that I love you, and I've learned a lot in my life you don't know yet. Like some things we do we can't take back. Ever.

*So forgive me when I sound like Aunt Martha. You're
more to me than someone I love. You're my friend. Please,
be careful.*
    Love,
    Evelyn

Kim held Evelyn's letters, tears sliding off her rouged cheeks onto the
worn, wrinkled pages. I waited, then gently took the letters from her,
dabbing at the moisture with her handkerchief.

"There you have it, Kim. Everything the world didn't know about
Meg Wells, the Mother of Vietnam. The rest, as they say, is history. The
ROTC firebombing, Toby's Treason, the Vietnam pilgrimage, the Nobel
fiasco, Toby's Treason Part II, the major-league trade, Toby for Melora
and a bunch of draft picks. That stuff's been done to death. Now you
know the rest of the story, enough inside information to send readers
running to newsstands, publishers and advertisers to the bank. Enough
psychodrama to keep amateur psychologists and historians busy for
years to come. You know—the op-ed writers who explain the clinic,
and even my relationship with Paul, as a natural extension of Mother
Meg's need to save the world because of her guilt over being born a
rich girl from Grosse Pointe. The critics who say it was inevitable that
when I did fall in love, it would happen only after my future husband
was disfigured in a fire.

"But at least you know it was Evelyn who got me thinking about the
importance of finding a real man, a good man, and holding on to him.
I was thinking about that when Paul, Toby, and I went to Narragansett
Race Track, feeling like millionaires after our big, beautiful horse won,
feeling something that made me want to kiss Paul, feeling something
more when I did. Evelyn's words guided me when Paul helped care for
Ian, and when Paul cared for me after Ian's death, comforting me the
only way I could be comforted, by joining me, following me, helping me
fight the fight until it almost cost him his life. And Evelyn's wishes came
true for me the night Paul and I met—2:00 a.m. January 10, 1970—the
moment he first smiled at me, the night we practiced marshaling in the

middle of Hope Street. That's how I discovered the magic that changes the physical, the emotional, the spiritual, from awkward and unsatisfying to ecstatic and insatiable. It amazes me how in all those relationships before Paul, I never understood what was missing. Love. And after all, isn't that what your readers want, Kim? A love story?"

"OHMYGOD MEG, THAT IS SO BEAUTIFUL!"

And again, Kim's crying. And God help me, I'm crying too, turning away, making sure Kim can't see.

"C'mon, Kim, don't do that. After all, if we leave out all the stuff about Vietnam, the stuff your readers don't want to hear, the story has a happy ending."

"I don't care about readers. I want to hear your story. The whole story, happy ending or not."

"Okay, but if you want the rest of the story there's only one way to get it."

"I'll do anything! Just tell me!"

"How long are you supposed to stay here?"

"One more day."

"Then spend it working with me at the clinic."

Chapter Forty-Three: Meg

I might have been happy living the rest of my life with Paul in New Jersey. For the first time I had a real home, a loving family, and a man I loved. But when I saw the pictures from Vietnam, I had to go. It was as simple as that. If you'd asked us, we might have said we'd stay a couple of years, like a Peace Corps hitch. Neither of us was prepared for what we found.

Even without the nuclear attack, Vietnam would have been a disaster. Decades of war, famine, the North's "victory," Agent Orange, disease, malnutrition, political reprisals, imprisonments, murders, and new wars with China and Cambodia. The U.S. and its allies washed their hands of the whole situation. Only the Soviet Union offered aid, but the aid offered was mostly military. A week after we arrived, the government official in charge of our small western relief effort gave a rousing speech.

"Our Soviet comrades only desire is to help!" Then muttering under his breath, "To help themselves." The next day he disappeared.

We spent our first months in Saigon—newly renamed Ho Chi Minh City, though to this day everyone except government officials still calls it Saigon—creating a relief program for Amerasian orphans. These were kids fathered by American soldiers with Vietnamese mothers. No one wanted them, and the communist government wanted its western volunteers out of the way, working on something unimportant without sacrificing their propaganda value. Within six months my group had adoption programs up and running in Israel, France, and Canada. Impressed with my work, Information Ministry officials, the same people who took Jane Fonda on her tour of the Hanoi Hilton prisoner-of-war camp, began exploiting my public relations potential. That's when they sent me, Paul, and the others to the Delta. What better people to tell the world about the horrific health and environmental effects of the U.S. Agent Orange aerial defoliation campaign than the brave, selfless American volunteers.

When the Information Ministry realized the Americans were more interested in actually bringing aid and comfort to the people of the Delta than in attacking their own homeland, the government assigned an assistant to spy on us, and forgot we existed. Decades later the Vietnamese government is as surprised as we are that we're still here.

The first time I traveled the road from Saigon to the Mekong, the obvious parallels to my family's Florida trip didn't strike me. I was too much a foreigner, too focused on differences in appearance and culture, differences between life in postwar Vietnam and life in America to see the obvious similarities. Years later, returning to the clinic from a European fundraising trip, riding in the air-conditioned comfort of a Zlin limousine on smoothly paved U.S. Army-built roads, feeling more like a privileged native than an expatriate American, passing endless rows of scrap metal shacks, that's when I remembered.

Their skins were lighter in color than the blacks of Savannah, and the women carried their burdens balanced on bamboo poles instead of in metal buckets, but as in Savannah, the children were skinny and barefoot, the men shirtless, the heat and odor of poverty stifling. I wondered if the poor of Savannah still lived like the poor of Vietnam.

The Mekong River Delta looks nothing like the way it's portrayed in American war movies. It is hot, it is humid, but it's more than a big river running through dense jungle. It's farmland, important farmland, the Vietnamese agricultural equivalent of the Mississippi Delta.

Mekong farmers raise rice and peanuts, and like farmers every-where their greatest ally and greatest enemy is water. From May to

November torrential monsoon rains flood the Delta, wiping out crops, eroding soil, erasing whole villages. Unlike their brothers and sisters on the Mississippi, farmers of the Mekong also battle land mines, unexploded aerial bombs, Agent Orange poisoning, and malaria. Many suffer from disabling war injuries. So Oxfam and the other relief agencies help with soil conservation, flood control, and sustainable agriculture, the health of the land. Our clinic treats chronic illnesses, infectious disease, and bodies separated from limbs by explosions, the health of the people.

Working at the clinic, even for a day, is a life-changing experience. Kim finished her day the same way all visitors do—hot, tired, in tears.

"I don't care what the publishers or editors or advertisers or readers think. I don't care what my father thinks! I'm quitting the magazine! I want to work for you, Meg! Here, now, if you'll take me."

"If you really want to help, go write my story. But write about the clinic, too. I've got a file drawer full of press releases no one's ever bothered to publish. You can copy everything right from there."

"But I want to work with you! Learn from you!"

"Look, Kim, let's be honest. You don't belong out here in the jungle. But after you file your story, if you still want to help, we sure could use someone with your connections for fundraising."

"I'll do it! I swear I'll do it! But I'm coming back. I mean it!"

"You'll always be welcome. But before you win that Pulitzer, we've got to get Scooter's face out of his feedbag so we can do the photo shoot. Then it's time for you to deliver on your part of the bargain."

"What do you mean?"

"You've forgotten already? My makeover!"

"Okay, sit still, a little more lip gloss, a touch more eye shadow, a dash more perfume... right... there. And some sparkles. Oh, you don't know about sparkles! Just close your eyes. That's it! Okay, you can look in the mirror!"

Kim held up the little surgical mirror, the one we use when we're looking for shrapnel inside wounds. Dark red lips. ("Better with your hair and complexion than the pinks I use.") Cheeks flushed and sparkled to match, eyes dark and mysterious, eyeliner, eye shadow and mascara so subtle you hardly know they're there. And yet... and yet.... "WOW! Kim, I don't know what to say" (looking down at my newly lacquered fingernails), "I mean I haven't worn makeup since... since... I don't know. But you're a GENIUS!"

"All I did was bring out your natural beauty. And honestly, Meg, I think the results show you should be making yourself up more often now that you know how."

"Well, ya' know Kim, out here in the Delta, I mean, well, thank you. Thank you a lot."

Kim gave me a big hug, knelt next to her suitcase and began digging. "You'll need one more thing if I can find it in this mess. Ah, okay, here it is! It's a little tight on me, so it should be perfect for you. It's real silk."

A short, sheer, scarlet nightgown.

"Go ahead, take it!"

"But how will I return it?"

"It's a present, silly!"

And now I'm hugging Kim.

"Thank you, Kim. I mean really, thank you. It's hard to explain, but I want to do something special."

"You don't have to explain a thing. I mean I'm a woman, too, aren't I?"

"How'd the interview go?" (Paul, sprawled on our futon, looking down at his bedtime reading, a dog-eared, three-year-old copy of *Science Digest*).

"Not bad. How was your day avoiding the interviewer?"

"Oh c'mon, Meg, it's you they want. And besides, I..." (looking up at me), "I... I... Meg! You look... you look great! I mean, you always look great, but you REALLY look great!"

"That darling girl from the magazine gave me a little help" (lying down beside him, touching his face with mine), "but I'm still me."

"I don't want anyone else" (kissing me). "But is this some occasion? I mean it's not our anniversary or something, is it?" (reaching out to douse the oil lamp).

"No, you big romantic" (kissing him back). "I decided that if all this becomes nothing more than a dream, tonight I'm making sure whenever *you* dream, you'll dream about *me*."

"I'll never forget our life together. Never."

"I believe you, Paul. And neither will I."

(Paul, looking sad). "I hope this doesn't put a damper on what you've got in mind, but I tried contacting Melora again today, and she wouldn't talk to me. I don't think there's any way she'll run HYDRA."

"Nothing can put a damper on what I've got in mind" (holding him close, drawing his arm away from the lamp before he can reach it). "Leave the light on. And leave Melora to me."

And kissing again, the time for words passes.

"Mother, are you all right?"

Quyen, our spy/assistant's voice through the thin thatch door. Paul and I stop, holding our breath.

"Everything's fine, Quyen," I say. "We're fine."

"I heard noises...." (A little embarrassed, uncertain what's going on inside the hut). "I want to make sure the Mother is safe."

And we're giggling, like college students caught in the act by a roommate.

"The Mother's fine, Quyen, really," Paul answers. "And next time we'll hang a necktie on the doorknob."

A moment's hesitation, then, "What is a 'necktie?'"

And we're laughing, laughing louder and longer than we've laughed in years.

Later, long after Kim's silken nightie fell carelessly to the bamboo floor, when the oil lantern's glow softened to invisibility, Paul and I lay in each other's arms, catching our breath, then sleeping.

And like our first night together in New Jersey, the sun's rising, huge and red on the horizon, bathing us in warm morning mystery. For Paul, asleep long after he normally wakes, a dreamy, peaceful smile gracing his wounded face, nightmares replaced by one shared dream, a sweet dream, as I promised. For me, my own contented smile. But for me, the day also begins with purpose, with work to do.

Paul was right about Melora. It won't be easy. But with the passing years, I understand my true gift. With decades of practice I've honed it, refined it, perfected it. Not the gift of saving people, like I wrote Evelyn about so long ago, or the gift of giving God more time to decide. My gift is simpler, less angelic. Call it leadership, persuasiveness, or the courage of my convictions. Call it manipulation. For better or worse, my gift is getting people to do things, whatever things I decide need doing.

I know my own history. I persuaded Paul and Toby to help care for Ian the day after I met them, talked Paul into joining me, first in agitating, and later, along with the others, in arson. He gave up everything he loved, complicated machines mostly, following me to Vietnam, following my dream instead of his own. I've enlisted countless governments, corporations, and charities as clinic sponsors, energized hundreds of volunteers, even turned the official Vietnamese government spy—with a little help from the spy's mother—into my personal guardian. My gift turned Kim from sorority/society girl into dedicated savior of those who lack everything she's spent her whole life taking for granted.

Yes, I understand my gift. And on my next trip to Saigon, at the beginning of the rainy season, I'll see Melora, get her to do what must be done.

Chapter Forty-Four: Meg

When Paul returned from New Jersey, he was quiet, distant, making me realize how quiet and distant he'd been for so long I couldn't remember when the warm, outgoing Paul had disappeared. He explained Toby's plan, answering all my questions about our old friend, leaving the details of the exchange up to me.

Of course it worked. The F.B.I. couldn't wait to get its hands on Toby, the Most Wanted who had eluded them for so long. With only a year left before Grendel and the other gamers came up for parole, the Justice Department had no problem sweetening the deal with their early release. Dismissing obstruction charges against WFMH's staff came easy—no one wanted to tangle with their New Jersey lawyers and the A.C.L.U. Freeing Melora was a political plus, quieting groups that had sprung up demanding her release, groups that had never forgotten Vietnam War hero Captain John Rusk's impassioned trial testimony on Melora's behalf, testimony that ended his career. In the press conference explaining the deal, the Attorney General quoted Rusk's description of Melora as "...a bright but naive young woman acting under the Svengali-like influence of a cynical, notorious terrorist."

For the Vietnamese government, granting Melora asylum meant a public relations and intelligence bonanza. Pictures of me greeting her at Ho Chi Minh Airport made the front pages of newspapers and magazines from New Delhi to New York. And after a couple of months' rest and recuperation, military commanders put Melora to work in their antiquated computer center where, Quyen reported, she updated the operating systems and training, for all practical purposes taking charge of the entire operation.

So the U.S., Vietnam, Toby, Paul, maybe even Melora, got what they wanted. The funny thing was, for the first time I could remember, I found myself wondering, *What do I get out of this?*

Paul wouldn't tell me much about the other history, but I knew that if Melora recreated HYDRA, sent a message back in time, she'd rescue Vietnam from a nuclear holocaust. She'd also send Toby to his death.

And me? I'd lose thirty years' hard work, all the differences I'd made, the international reputation I'd earned. I'd lose Paul. I'd lose Toby again.

Years ago, when I saw Toby's picture paired with Melora's on *Time's* cover, I felt… surprised. Not surprised he resurfaced, destroyed the draft, monkey-wrenched the war machine a second time. No, I was surprised that Toby, in my memory a grungy, twenty-year-old, pizza-loving geek, actually had a girlfriend. And surprised I felt jealous.

Paul never complained, but I knew he wasn't happy, knew he was meant to spend his life among computers, not in some third-world unelectrified jungle. And while I loved the children of the clinic, I always hoped for children of our own. Yet waking more and more often, trembling, soaking in sweat I couldn't explain merely by the Delta's tropical climate, I understood it was too late. That's why somewhere along the way, with the help of daily hardships and crises, the numbing reality of daily routines, my passion faded.

Then suddenly, there's Toby—the accidental activist, man of mystery, glamorously unstoppable, excitingly uncatchable. If Paul was meant to spend his life among machines, hadn't Toby become the kind of man I once imagined spending my life with? Yet instead, here was this beautiful young woman who'd obviously been much more than mere partners in crime with the dashing, tattooed fugitive, the man who could have been mine so long ago.

Quyen's sources reported to her, and Quyen reported to me, that since Melora's arrival she'd become friends with several techie colleagues, many of whom had once worked with U.S. military forces in the South. Melora easily bridged the language barrier that took me decades to overcome. For her and her new friends, language apparently consisted of long strings of ones and zeros.

Communicating with Paul and me was another matter, friendship out of the question. From her first day in Saigon, Melora made it clear she had no interest in seeing me, answering my cheerful questions in monosyllables, then looking directly in my eyes, saying simply, "No one ever asked me what I wanted, so I don't owe you anything."

Melora tolerated Paul, perhaps because of whatever Toby wrote in the letter Paul brought her, perhaps because she wanted to learn everything she could about Paul's New Jersey meeting with Toby—"Was he okay? I mean healthy and everything? Did he tell you how we did it? Does he understand why I did what I did? Is he angry at me?"

After reading Toby's letter, she listened while Paul explained about history, HYDRA, and his dreams. She looked at him silently for a long time, reread Toby's letter, and said, "If all we need to do is get Toby to the ROTC action meeting, why can't we change the message, send him the meeting's correct location, but add something like, 'Stick around afterward for free pizza'?"

"We know what changing history did the first time," Paul said. "Three nuclear bombs dropped on Vietnam, two on Afghanistan. Toby and I agree, we can't take that chance again."

"So you've decided. Toby has to die."

Paul could barely answer.

"Yes."

That's when Melora turned her back saying, "You haven't got enough imagination to make something like this up."

Six months passed without a word from Melora. Then she called Paul to Saigon, making it clear I wasn't invited, grilling him for ten and twelve hours at a time with questions about HYDRA, many of which he couldn't answer. Another six months passed, and another, every attempt Paul made to contact her rebuffed by members of Melora's growing entourage. Then, two years to the day since her arrival, Melora summoned Paul again.

"Thanks for letting me past your honor guard out there, Melora. You've done well for yourself the last two years—your own office, your own assistants, your own computers...."

Melora noticed Paul's eyes looking hungrily past her at the monitor on her desk and jacked in her cybergrammer headset before replying.

"Two years while your best friend rots in prison," she said.

"Two years you've been free, Melora, so you could do what he asked."

"Look, Tesla, I didn't bring you here to talk. I brought you here to show you something." And almost inaudibly, under her breath, Melora said, "Initiate HYDRA."

Paul looked past her again, past her to the monitor. And just like in the dream, he saw his and Toby's old Bruin entries scrolling down the screen, stopping at Paul's final, altered, history-transforming message.

"Melora, that's incredible! You did it! Now we can change the message, change history, make things the way they're supposed to be. I wish we could tell Toby. He's right about you—you're a genius! But can we wait a little before you send the message? I'd like to talk to Meg, explain more about what may happen."

Then, subvocally, Melora uttered a single word.

"Delete."

And looking up from her monitor, past Paul, out her window at the cloud-filled sky, she said, "Now you don't have to explain anything."

Paul pleaded with Melora to change her mind. She answered with a single sentence— "Leave, or I'll call someone who'll make you leave."

Paul and I realized Melora loved Toby, held us responsible for his imprisonment, blamed us for wanting her to kill him. But I thought there was something more, something I could never explain to Paul.

Yes, I was jealous of Melora. That's why I wasn't surprised when I realized Melora was jealous of me.

Chapter Forty-Five: Meg

The rainy season begins with a huge storm backing up out of the South China Sea, crossing the Gulf of Tonkin, slamming into the southern peninsula with hundred-kilometer gusts and sheets of rain. The helicopter trip to Saigon is one long roller coaster ride, and with zero visibility, there's nothing for me to do except meditate, pray, and rehearse the coming conversation with Melora.

At Vietnam's equivalent of the Pentagon, a two-story French Colonial wood-frame building filled with men and women in khaki seated behind American-made steel desks, a tall young lieutenant greets me, bowing, welcoming "the esteemed Mother to our ministry." Yet his demeanor is cold, a far cry from the effusive welcomes I usually receive at government offices. Driving home the point, he assigns a mere corporal to escort me to Melora's quarters. The young soldier knocks on Melora's door, but on the command "Enter," spoken in perfect Vietnamese, I step past him, opening the door, quickly closing it behind me, leaving the non-com outside.

"Hello, Melora."

Melora lies stretched on her bunk, clothed in a khaki tee shirt, cutoffs, and sandals soled with tire tread from abandoned U.S. Army jeeps. She's been waiting, no doubt warned of my arrival, reading the glossy American magazine in which Kim's article appeared, and jacked into the computer on her desk, running what looks like a pinball program.

"Well, if it isn't Motherfucking Teresa. What brings you out of the paddies? Come to lay hands on my sick computer?"

I answer, in control as always, as always sure what to do, sure I can talk Melora into doing it, too.

"No, Melora. I'm here to ask for your help."

"I read your big interview, Meg." Rising from her bunk, holding the magazine between thumb and forefinger like something unclean.

"And?"

"And funny how you relate every detail of your glamorous life story—I mean, shit, I thought you were gonna tell everyone what color panties you wore to your first demonstration—but you got amnesia between the night you met Tesla and the morning you arrived in Vietnam."

"No color."

"Huh?"

"No color. I wasn't wearing panties."

"Fucking hilarious, Meg."

"Is that a problem?"

"Yeah, I'd say it's a problem. Unless you think that little ROTC fire was funny. Or maybe you've forgotten. But Toby remembers, and he told me everything."

"What's 'everything'?"

"How it's your fault the whole thing happened. How you got poor lovesick Tesla to follow your stupid plan, got him and the others burned up for nothing, turned Toby into a criminal avenging his best friend."

"Toby never said that."

"Come on, Meg. Everyone knows that if it wasn't for you, Tesla's in one piece, Toby's a free man, Hanoi isn't a radioactive slag heap. And what did you give up, Saint Meg? A fucking Nobel Prize? That's a lot of guilt for one spoiled little rich girl to carry around all these years. Must be gettin' heavy. So fuckin' heavy you need my generation to clean up your generation's mess."

"You're lucky you had my generation making messes for you to clean up. You wouldn't like the world we were born into."

"You never gave us a chance to find out."

I stop, take a breath.

"So... you think Toby's still in love with me after all these years?"

Melora's head jerks around, eyes wide. I'm glad, seeing her look surprised, off balance. Anything's better than her anger. But in the next moment her dark eyes flash.

"You want to save all your Vietnamese victims, but the only way is with a computer. And you can't even find the 'on' button."

"That's why I saved you."

Her eyes blaze again, then turn smoky, flat, opaque.

"Toby carried two things with him all those years he was hiding. Do you know what they were? Pictures of you, and him, and Tesla."

"And every time you saw them you got angry because you couldn't be part of something so important to him."

"I never worried about you and Toby. I never worried because I knew he could never love some stupid e-virgin. And I knew you couldn't love anyone who didn't have cancer, or leprosy, or was at least deformed."

If she's sorry about what she said, she shows no sign.

"Look, I don't care what you think of me. I don't care what you think about Paul. But if you care about Toby, do what he asked."

She says nothing for a long time. I'm thinking she won't answer at all, as Paul warned me. But slowly, softly, she at last begins speaking.

"You think I don't know anything about *your* war, about Vietnam, Cambodia, Kent State, Jackson State? About you brave college kids going to classes, keggers, and, oh yeah, peace marches? Well I know this much. If you women hadn't always been so busy doing whatever your men wanted, you might have ended that war in five years instead of twenty."

"Is that what this is about for you? Showing your independence?"

"What's it about for you, Mother Meg?"

"Putting things right. Making them the way they're supposed to be. Sparing the Vietnamese people—and maybe the Afghans too—generations of birth defects and radiation poisoning. Stuffing the nuclear genie back in its lead-lined bottle."

Melora looked up at me, angry, disgusted. "Isn't it really about your guilt? Because it was you who caused all this, you who talked Tesla and the others into setting the fire. If your friend, the English professor in the article…" waving the magazine in my face, then tossing it in her waste basket, "…Evelyn—if she'd been around she could have talked you out of it. She wasn't. One more thing you fucked up. Because of you she leaves, Tesla gets torched, Toby wipes the Pentagon's computers to get revenge. Doesn't that make it your fault America nuked Vietnam?"

"Yes."

"Now you want me to sacrifice Toby to atone for *your* sins?"

"Yes."

"So I give up Toby, Toby gives up his life. And what do you give up Meg? Your shot at fucking sainthood?"

I can't say anything. Can't speak. Just feel tears on my cheeks, feel myself crying, in front of Melora, her eyes bright, satisfied.

"Well, Meg, you can go fuck yourself."

We sit together while I cry and Melora plays video pinball, sit together in silence as time passes and monsoon winds howl outside her window.

Finally, I speak.

"Toby and Paul aren't the only ones who have nightmares. Except I don't have to close my eyes to live mine. They're there, every day, right in front of me at the clinic. And I can't escape them by waking up. Ever wonder why Paul and I never had children, why none of your coworkers have children? Because we're afraid. Afraid they'll be little monsters with two hearts or two heads. Afraid the radiation in our breast milk will make them vomit and bleed, dissolve before our eyes the way children do every day in this country. So hate me if you want, but if you care anything about the people you call your friends, spend one day working at the clinic. One day. Then you can tell me to go to hell."

Melora looks at me, thinks for a moment, jacks out of her cyber headset. "Okay. I'll come to your clinic. For a day. But after that, I don't ever want to see you, or Tesla, again."

I leave without saying another word, walking quickly, afraid Melora will back out of the bargain we struck, afraid I'll upset its delicate balance. But halfway down the empty hall I turn around, meaning to apologize, to tell Melora, *I'm sorry*, tell her, *Don't listen to me, forget the clinic, forget everything I said, live your own life.*

At the door I hear sobbing and know it's too late. I hear sobbing and know Melora's made up her mind. I know I'll have my way. But unlike with Kim and so many others, if I open the door, offer her my shoulder to cry on, there will be no comfort there, no strengthening for her, only humiliation. So instead, I turn away.

Chapter Forty-Six: Meg

At the next new moon, Melora came to the clinic. Any day now she'll have HYDRA up and running, send the message, set history on its proper course. The price I pay, the price Melora pays, the way Melora hurt me, the way I hurt Melora, the hurt yet to come, none of that matters. Because Melora changed her mind, as I knew she would. She'll change history, as I knew she would. You see, that's my gift. Getting people to do things, whatever things I decide need doing.

It's funny how even now my thoughts turn to my parents. All that cruelty directed at bending a child to their will. I guess I've become like them, after my fashion. Bending people to my will, less brutally than my father, more openly than my mother, more successful than either of them.

Melora says she won't give any warning. I wonder, will I feel anything when I blink out of existence? I spend my time tending to the clinic, enjoying the ritual of my monthly visit with Quyen's mother, making up for time I lost—will lose—with Paul, putting jealousy to rest in a downy bed of renewed passion. And Paul, as used to be his way, said the sweetest thing—"I don't need makeup or the nightie. I only need you."

Kim? She's halfway across the world, Pulitzer in hand, as I promised. She kept her promise, too, a convert to the cause, raising money for the clinic among the rich and famous. The big interview changed her life, but I can't say I would have been so free with intimate details of my history if I didn't believe in my heart that before too long none of this history will exist, including the interview.

Even so, Kim never asked, and Melora never asked, so I didn't bother telling them what happened to Evelyn. If I had, they'd know Mother Meg doesn't always get her way. Besides, why spoil a happy ending?

May 5, 1970

Dear Evelyn,

Yesterday Ohio National Guardsmen murdered four students at Kent State. We watched it on TV. Everyone's shocked but me. God help me, Evelyn, but I'm not shocked. I've been expecting it.

Wellston's going on strike. Last night 3,000 students gathered on The Green. Two-to-one they voted in favor of the strike. I stood with Paul, holding his hand while he voted. Then we climbed to the roof of Robertson House, watching the vote continue until dawn. Paul thought I couldn't see his face in the dark, but I could, and he was crying.

I've been up for three days straight helping organize protests, fundraisers, and community education programs. At night we meet in Franklin Hall, endlessly discussing what to do about ROTC.

It's so cold here in Butler. I can't remember a May this cold. And I miss you, Evelyn. We all do. We miss you, and we need you.

Love,

Meg

May 13, 1970

Dear Meg,

Cold is not a problem here in Mississippi. May in Mississippi is more like August in Butler. And it's not just the weather that's hot. The students, the faculty, the police, the politicians—everyone's hot, and getting hotter.

Every night carloads of rednecks roar through campus screaming racial slurs. Every day student protests get bigger and more unruly. I was home in Detroit during the '67 riot. That's what this feels like. Hot, very hot. And like somebody's going to make a mistake.

If you can stand a little good news, here goes. Yesterday the custodian came and put a new plaque on my door. It reads—not Assistant Professor, or Associate Professor—but, PROFESSOR Evelyn Ruger. I make half the money I did at Wellston, but at least I'm doing at as a FULL Professor. My students are throwing me a party as soon as things settle down.

For a girl from Grosse Pointe you're doing fine up there without me, and I want you to know I'm proud of you. But don't THINK about writing me until you've had a good night's sleep and a hot meal! And don't worry, Meg. We are going to end this war!

Yours truly,

Evelyn Ruger, (as in "sugar")

Professor of English, Alexander Hall, Jackson State University

Evelyn's letter reached me after the news. On May 14, police sprayed the Jackson State campus with bullets, firing three hundred rounds into Alexander Hall. Miraculously, they added only two more names to the list of four from Kent State, the list of tens of thousands from Vietnam. Phillip Gibbs, a twenty-one year old pre-law student, and James Green, seventeen, a high school senior taking a shortcut home from work.

Evelyn's name wasn't among those reported in the *Times* as killed or injured, but two days later the *Detroit Free Press* ran her obituary. A meter maid found Evelyn slumped over the steering wheel of her '66 Chevelle. The coroner's report said she died from a stroke suffered while rushing to campus during the gunfire.

When Paul's doctors upgraded his condition from critical to stable, I called my parents. "I want to come home," I said. My father wouldn't speak to me; my mother wired me plane fare. But I didn't go to Grosse Pointe. I went to see Evelyn.

In Detroit's New Bethel Baptist Church, the same church where six years later two surviving Supremes, Diana Ross and Mary Wilson, would return for Flo Ballard's funeral, Reverend Franklin, Aretha's father, presided over the ceremony. He'd asked Evelyn's friends and family to bring music they shared with her. After his eulogy ("Dear God in heaven, you took this beautiful child from us too soon! But she's in your sweet care now. So look after her, Jesus. Evelyn was one of our best!"), the Reverend invited everyone to play Evelyn's favorites on an RCA portable set up next to her casket. For the next hour, sounds of the Temptations, Miles Davis, and Reverend Franklin's famous daughter flowed through the church, warming Evelyn's friends and family, letting them visit with her one last time.

My turn comes. I leave the wooden pew, marching up the aisle past all those dark faces, the white girl from Grosse Pointe, feeling like a cornflake in a bowl of raisins. I've brought a dog-eared copy of John Coltrane's *A Love Supreme* that I stole from WELL's record library at Wellston. Setting it on the platter, lifting the tone arm, carefully placing the stylus in the black vinyl groove, I wait, not ready to look at Evelyn, not ready to say goodbye. Except for crackling from the RCA's speakers, everything is silent, even the crying stops.

As Coltrane's soaring saxophone prayer fills the church, the mourners join him, erupting with "Hallelujahs" and "Praise Gods." I find my lips moving, my voice growing louder, rising above the others, joining them, leading them, simply repeating Evelyn's name—"Evelyn!

Evelyn!" And Coltrane sounds for all the world like he's playing just for her.

That's when I look beside me into the open casket. And there's my friend, dressed in a white satin gown, looking beautiful, looking like a Supreme.

PART SEVEN

MELORA

Chapter Forty-Seven: Melora

Meg was right all along.

"Spend one day working at the clinic," she said. I stayed for six months. Changing bedpans. Changing bandages. Changing my mind.

I would've stayed longer, but the Minister of Defence ordered my ass back to Saigon to fix some programming glitches in People's Army surface-to-air missiles. Personally, I'd spend that money on education, or medical care, or shit, I don't know, pizza. But after what Vietnam's been through, who can blame them?

So Meg was right. Or maybe that woman's a fucking *bruja*. Either way, I'll never see her again. Or Tesla.

Or Toby.

In Saigon, the timer I set is counting down. HYDRA, Tesla's many-headed monster, up-and-running right under the nose of my CO, a party-appointed *pendejo* who can't tell a microchip from a potato chip. Hacking into IPI's Net and finding Bruin was easy. Wellston still accepts IPI blood money, still links Bruin to their Net. They say it's for historical research, but the real reason is no one ever gave enough of a shit to cut the link. Besides, with Toby in prison and me half a world away, why not let their guard down? They caught the bogeymen, so who the fuck do they have to be afraid of?

In my office at the Defence Ministry, Tesla's last message, his first message, the real message, is loaded on my computer and ready to drop. When Tesla changed it, he didn't know where it was going. I do. To 1970. To Bruin. To Toby.

Will it prevent my war? Will it keep Coop, Grendel and the others out of jail? Will it save Darin's life? Tesla doesn't know. He doesn't know what will happen to me. He only knows there won't be any nukes dropped on Vietnam or Afghanistan. And he knows Toby will die.

I could change my mind. Try another way. Try to save him. Haven't slept in months thinking about that one. Tesla's got his dreams, and I've got fucking nightmares. But I could send a different message, right? I've thought of hundreds of them. And then what might happen? Wars? Famines? Pandemics? Peace and love? Or maybe the fucking Martians attack.

I don't know. I can't know!

Oh, shit. I'm so fucking weak. That's why I set the timer and got outta Dodge. The hydrofoil from the port in Saigon to Vung Tau took ninety minutes, long enough so there's no fucking way I can turn back in time. The fare was cheap, too. Especially for a one-way ticket.

The South China Sea isn't the Gulf of Mexico, but Vung Tau has four good beaches— Front, Back, Pineapple, and Paradise. The humid air smells sweet and salty, the sand hot beneath my feet, the breakers churning. Looks like I'm spending my last day in Paradise.

Forgive me, Coop. Forgive me, Maggie. Forgive me, Captain Rusk. You deserved better. You too, Tesla. Even you, Meg. I never apologized for shitting all over you.

And forgive me, Toby, for doing what you asked.

I pull out my hearing aid, the one Joey bought me when we were kids in St. Francis, and stick it in my pocket. Stripping off my tee shirt and stepping out of my cutoffs, I ignore the staring tourists and run into the suddenly muffled surf, diving headfirst into a breaker, swimming and swimming straight out from shore, until I can't see the tourists or the breakers or the beach. I kick over onto my back, closing my eyes, floating in the vastness of warm, clear, salt water.

Then, I sense… something. Something big, its smooth gray form slicing through the water, coming fast.

I dive. It dives with me. I look, and through the salt-water's sting, I see it.

It's different from my Gulf of Mexico devil ray. Bigger. Way the fuck bigger. Fifteen feet long. No horns, but a wide scoop mouth and white belly, spotted, like a dog.

I dive deeper, not sure if it's following. My hand touches bottom, hair floating around my face, plastering down against it as I turn and kick upward.

There he is, five yards away, undulating his huge body, staring at me, wondering what the fuck I am.

Is he dangerous?

Does it matter?

I swim upward, spinning as I swirl past him.

C'mon, *diablito*, we're running out of time. C'mon—dance with me!

PART EIGHT

TOBY

Chapter Forty-Eight: Toby

"How's he doin' that?"

I was so surprised, I said it out loud. I'd pulled up Tesla's last message. But as soon I read it, a new one appeared!

Toby— I miss you.

Damn! Did Tesla figure out how to send messages through the Engineering Department link? Helluva way to break the news!

Okay, Tesla, how 'bout this—

Tesla— If you miss me so much why don't you get your ass down here and help with this program? Toby

At first no response. Then—

Toby— Is that you? Where are you? What are you working on? Tesla

Well that's a head scratcher. He knows where I am, he knows what I'm workin' on, and he damn well knows I'm dyin' to find out how he's doin' this!

Tesla— You were expecting Harpo Marx? I'm at the Physics Department working on the computer-linking program. Where else would I be? The question is, where are you, and how are you sending these messages? You've been holding out on me, Tesla! Toby

No answer. Tesla's lettin' the drama build!

But ten minutes go by, and there's still no answer.

Okay, I get it. He wants me to figure it out for myself!

So I scroll back to the message that was waitin' for me when I logged in, lookin' for clues.

Toby— Couldn't find you at home or Beef 'n' Bun. ROTC Action meeting tonight. Meet me at Franklin Hall 2100 hours. THIS IS THE BIG ONE. Paul

In the blink of an eye *Burnside House* replaces *Franklin Hall*. And in the next instant *Franklin Hall* reappears, replacin' *Burnside House*.

Tesla's gotta be workin' over at Engineering. But that doesn't explain the instantaneous appearance and disappearance of entire sentences. If he's makin' changes through the link with the Engineering Department computer, deletions and additions should be occurrin' after a pause. Maybe he imbedded the changes directly into entries he made on Bruin before I got here, programmin' them to appear only after I logged in, playin' one of his practical jokes and tryin' to freak me out.

No. Not Tesla. Not lately anyway. It's been a while since he joked about anything. But still, it's just like him to bust my balls and make me wait until I see him at the meeting!

The meeting. Thinkin' about the mystery of how Tesla programmed the shiftin' messages was a lot easier than thinkin' about what they said. And thinkin' about the meeting made me remember the nightmare.

Last night's Richmond Military Institute dream had been particularly vivid, especially bad. Everyone in their rooms, shinin' shoes, shinin' brass belt buckles, tightenin' Windsor knots in black neckties, hurryin' down dark corridors and stairwells to mess formation. Then fire. Fire and smoke. In the hallways, in the stairwells, smoke and panic. And screamin', screamin' for help. There, there at the foot of the officer's ladderway, in dress khaki, Tesla, Tesla on fire, burnin', burnin', callin' out through smoke and flame, "Toby! Toby!" Then another voice behind me. A woman. A beautiful woman with chopped black hair, quicksilver wires danglin' from behind her ears like *Star Trek* jewelry. A woman I'd never seen before, yet familiar, important to me, illuminated by fire, pointin', cryin', cryin' out, "Save him! Save *him!*"

Nightmares always come after the phone calls.

"Toby Jessup, please."

"Speakin.'"

"This is William."

"What do you want, Willie."

"The usual, Mr. Jessup."

"Are you ever gonna to tell me your real name?"

Silence.

"Okay, okay. Here's my report. But I'm tellin' you, this is the last time. Understand?"

"Go ahead," Willie said, makin' it sound like a threat.

"The ROTC Action people are gettin' some support 'cuz of Cambodia and Kent State. Kent State wasn't your idea, was it Willie?"

"I'm listening."

"Anyway, I don't think you've got anything to worry about. I'm pretty sure I can talk 'em out of doin' somethin' stupid."

"It doesn't matter. We'll be ready for them."

"What the hell's that mean?"

"Is there anything else?"

"No. No, that's it. But I mean it, Willie. I've kept my part of the deal for four years. I'm a month from graduation, but I'm done. Finished. No more. Ya' understand, Willie?"

"Thank you Mr. Jessup. I'll be in touch."

And the son of a bitch hung up.

It seemed so fuckin' harmless when the commandant called me into his office. I was a senior, and he knew I'd been accepted at Wellston, knew my family didn't have the money to pay for it. The note said he wanted to meet with me, "…to talk about some scholarship opportunities." But when I got to his office he wasn't there. A brown-shoed, blue-suited civilian sat behind the desk instead.

"At ease, Mr. Jessup. Have a seat."

I hadn't been standing at attention.

"Mr. Jessup, my name is Mr. Duke. I've got a proposition for you, a way to help you get through college and serve your country while you're there."

"I told the commandant I'm not interested in ROTC."

Duke smiled. "Yes, Mr. Jessup. I'm aware you have no interest in a military career. That's not at all what I had in mind."

His proposition was simple. "Have you read about the radical groups forming on college campuses?"

"I've heard of SDS."

"There are far worse organizations than SDS, Mr. Jessup. There are students who want to burn buildings and plant bombs. There are students who want to rob banks and use the money to buy weapons. There are students who want to kill people. All in the name of peace, Mr. Jessup, all in the name of peace. The only way we can stop them from bombing and burning and killing, from trying to destroy our way of life, is with information."

"So what do you want me to do?"

"Nothing complicated, son. Go to college, take your courses, go to football games, go out on dates. In other words, be a regular college student. And report what you see and hear to us."

"Who exactly is 'us'?"

"Us, Mr. Jessup, are the people who are offering you a free ride to Wellston University."

Talking myself into making the deal was easy. I wanted to go to Wellston. I couldn't afford it on my own. And besides, I was a nerd. I'd never meet any radicals, never have anything to report. I was screwin' Duke and his pals good. I'd get my tuition paid, and they'd get nothin'. If that's the way they wanted it, that was fine with me.

Except four years had passed, and the whole world was different. I was different. And it wasn't fine with me any more.

When I woke from last night's dream, I was hot and sick, my heart racing, stomach churnin', like I was gonna puke. I could still hear Willie, no emotion in his voice—*We'll be ready for them.* My head felt like someone had shaken one of those little plastic dioramas filled with water and fake snow. But when the snow settled, I knew, more than ever, that violence never helped anything. Knew that after Cambodia and Kent State the war would have to end soon. Knew I had to do somethin', say somethin', to stop the two people I loved most in the world from makin' a terrible, dangerous mistake.

I never say much at meetings. Just listen, joke around, suggest ways we can use Bruin. But tonight's different. I'll have to speak up, have to find the words. And after the meeting, I'll tell Tesla and Meg, tell them everything. I hope they'll forgive me, hope they'll understand.

Alright. Gotta head out soon, but I'll type in a little more code on the linkin' program before I leave. I wish I could stay here all night. Continue workin', continue life as it might have been before Mr. Duke, before Willie, before this whole fuckin' war.

But that's history. And I can't change history.

8:45. Time to pull up my socks and put on my jock. Time for the meeting at Franklin Hall.

Standin' in the doorway, feelin' the chill of the cold, May, New England night, I flick off the lights. And turnin' to Bruin one last time, for no particular reason, say, "Goodbye."

PART NINE

PEACE

Chapter Forty-Nine: Paul

Last night the dream came again. The war, the ROTC meeting, the fire. Toby, Meg, Melora. Butler, Applewood, the Mekong clinic. The dead. Students like Bill Schroeder, Allison Krause, Jeffrey Miller, Sandy Scheuer, Phillip Gibbs and James Green. American and Vietnamese infantry, marines, aviators, medics, and nurses, remembered on walls and war memorials. Ian and thousands like him whose names grace no monuments but who died serving their country nonetheless. And civilian victims whose only memorial was the anguish of their families. The dream left me awestruck at the sight of towering mushroom clouds from nuclear explosions that never happened, yet did happen, could happen again, in any version of history I choose. And at the end, it woke me, clutching at my face in a nightmare of pain, feeling scars that aren't there, scars from a different lifetime.

Yet despite my nightmares, I welcome the dreams. I welcome them because they've been my guide.

Paul Atreides, the hero of Frank Herbert's *Dune*, saw the future so precisely, saw it so many times, he could pilot an ornithopter even after going blind. I've lived history so often in my dreams, I can almost move safely through life with my eyes closed. Yet this time I've had to be careful, living exactly as the dreams tell me, making the same choices, the same mistakes I made the first time, making sure I don't upset the course of history again.

Even so, I must have messed up. America went metric in 1975. Disco never happened. The Watergate DNC office didn't get burgled. Or the cover-up succeeded. Either way, Nixon finished his second term, got his *Four More Years!* Made the most of them, too. Recognized China, passed the National Environmental Policy Act, abolished the draft, and legalized gay marriage. Go figure.

The wars go on endlessly, but since Nagasaki, thank God, no one's dropped another nuke. So far.

I've tempted fate a couple of times. I developed a Web browser named *Toby.* And though I promised Melora I'd never contact her, a promise I've kept, I have followed her camouflaged electronic trail. It wasn't easy, because if it were, the FBI and Interpol would have found her years ago. She goes by the name Blackbeard and spends her time hacking into securely firewalled corporate and government networks around the world, leaking their secrets online. The only trace she leaves behind is a Polynesian-style graphic of a Gulf Coast devil ray. She's so far underground even I can't find her physical location, but in case she has dreams and comes looking for me, I left her a clue: I created an app for training novice programmers, naming it *Melora.*

For all that, I'm glad the dream takes me no further than this moment. Because now, I'm free.

One last time I read the message on my screen: *Toby— Couldn't find you at home or Beef 'n' Bun. ROTC Action meeting tonight. Meet me at Franklin Hall 2100 hours. THIS IS THE BIG ONE. Paul*

With regret, with sorrow, I exit Bruin's memory, bringing HYDRA up on my monitor.

Press "Delete."

A new message appears: *Are you sure you want to permanently delete this program?*

Yes, I answer. *Yes.*

And that's it. Decades spent fulfilling the dream's mandates. And now, at last, with whatever time I have left, I can pursue my own dreams.

Retiring from IPI is the first step. The young guns running the company won't miss the old fart once-upon-a-time legendary programmer, will be happy they don't have to fire me. Many years and many millions spent researching HYDRA, a failed program. No mention in the annual report, just one line in the profit-and-loss ledger under the column headed *Adjustments*.

IPI stock options have made me a wealthy man, and if my 401-K ever runs short, all I have to do is visit Santa Anita or Golden Gate Fields. I have my dreams of Toby and his *Thoroughbred* programming tweaks to thank for that. I also have my programs, *Toby* and *Melora*, and thanks to IPI, the knowledge, capital, and experience to market them. But the thought of staying in California, emulating other successful Silicon Valley businesses, becoming the next IPI, feels hollow. And with no dreams to guide me, the hard part will be finding inspiration elsewhere.

In the middle of the mild California winter, inspiration arrives. A copy of the *Applewood Record* sent by my Uncle Joel with a note—
I'll bet this brings back memories!

In part it was the article about thieves stealing copper pipe from Dickens Hall on the abandoned Hilversum campus, heedlessly spilling hundreds of gallons of heating oil, costing the city thousands of dollars to clean it up, dollars the city didn't have. In part it was the story about WFMH closing its studio in the old house on the ghost campus, moving to a renovated warehouse in Hoboken. Mostly it was the front-page picture captioned, "Citizens clean graffiti." And there's Terrell, James, and Roxy scrubbing gang tags from a W.E.B. Du Bois School wall.

That night I hopped the redeye into Kennedy, caught a taxi to Port Authority. I can't imagine what twist of history led to its transformation. Antiseptically clean, classical music soothed, I barely recognize the old bus terminal. At least the commuters, and bus numbers, haven't changed.

"Number 88," I told the ticket clerk. "Round trip to Bloomfield."

This time I don't ride the bus all the way to Applewood. Instead, I pull the signal cord at Bloomfield Center, walking the short block to my uncle's apartment, surprising Joel as he finished his morning bagel and coffee. This time I'd tour Applewood as a passenger in my Uncle Joel's midnight blue Sedan deVille.

"Look over there, Paul—Hilversum's old chapel. Remember when we went to Dean Jorgensen's investiture with your friend Tim? It used to be beautiful."

I look, seeing only boarded windows, graffiti-covered brick. Whatever events led to Port Authority's rebirth, Applewood was still the place of my nightmares, unaffected by history's return to its original path. Apparently my hometown was screwed no matter what happened.

"Turn up Springdale," I said. "I want to grab a Coke at a luncheonette I remember."

"I don't think there's anything left in Applewood you remember," Joel says. Then he spots Roxy's. "Well, I'll be a son-of-a-gun! How did you know?"

We walk through the jingling door. Roxy's waiting behind the counter, polishing it with a green-striped dishtowel.

"Can I help you gentlemen?"

"A couple of Cherry Cokes would be fine," I say.

"Okay, but you should keep an eye on that fine car out there. Some of these kids around here, well, you know."

We nod while Roxy sets the sparkling soda glasses before us, and two more further down the counter. "For my grandsons. School's out, and they'll be here any minute."

Though he thought my idea was crazy, Uncle Joel helped arrange my schedule for the next three days, making phone calls, setting up meetings, chauffeuring me, joining me while I mixed nostalgia and business.

First came a hastily arranged conference with the energetic Applewood mayor.

"Mr. Simmons, what you're proposing could mean a lot to this city, show people we're moving forward, give kids a chance to make a decent living without moving away."

"Applewood has a lot to offer, Mayor Barkeley. Fifteen minutes from Newark Airport, twenty to midtown Manhattan, and forty acres of buildings and building space on the old Hilversum campus available at bargain-basement prices. I don't know why more businesses aren't jumping at the opportunity. But you understand, I'll be starting small. Only a half dozen employees. And there's no guarantee we'll succeed."

"I hope this won't offend you," Barkeley said, "but Applewood doesn't need a white man to save it, and it doesn't need a miracle. It needs opportunity. That's why I'm prepared to offer, subject to City Council approval of course, substantial tax incentives if you decide to locate your business here."

"Mr. Mayor, when I call the police or fire department, I'll expect them to come. When I hire graduates of Applewood High School, I'll expect them to be well educated. That's why I expect my company to pay its full share of taxes."

A broad smile spread across the mayor's bearded face as he extended his hand. "Welcome to Applewood, Mr. Simmons. Welcome home."

Two nights later, Joel and I celebrated signing a lease for the old WFMH building, contracting with Roxy's to provide weekday luncheons for my employees, hiring Roxy's brother Curtis to keep an eye on my new headquarters until I move in, hiring Terrell and James as chief testers of the educational software I plan to market. Over dinner at Nicastro's in Newark's Italian North Ward, where the Chicken Murphy is as spicy and tender as I remember, the nutmegged biscuit tortoni in fluted paper cups every bit as cool and creamy, we toast the speed with which my new dream is becoming reality.

I raise a glass of ruby-red Chianti. "To the future, to success, to TDI—Tesla's Dreams Incorporated."

"L'Chayim!" my uncle replies, "To life!"

The next day we tour W.E.B. Du Bois School, Terrell and James proudly guiding us to the beautiful old auditorium where I once played Tiny

Tim in the fifth-grade production of *A Christmas Carol*, where I now answer students' questions about careers in programming. After meeting with the principal, scheduling a school field trip to Tesla's Dreams for one year in the future, Uncle Joel and I say goodbye to Terrell and James. Walking down Springdale, over maple-lined Roosevelt, we check the stately tree where, as a sixth grader, I carved Ellen Hoffmann's initials inside a heart together with my own, finding the once slender letters "E H" and "P S" spread inches wide. We head up Grant Avenue to the corner of North Arlington, where we're joined by a real estate agent friend of Joel's.

"It's obviously been vacant for some time, seized by the city for unpaid taxes. But other than a couple of broken windows it's in good shape. And the asking price is very reasonable. Would you like to take a look inside?" she says, offering me a key.

"I don't need a key," I say, answering her puzzled look by simply jiggling the third French window at the corner of the sun parlor, jiggling it just so, until it slides smoothly open.

Since returning to Applewood, I've done everything with the constant help and company of my Uncle Joel. Now I find there's something I have to do before flying to California to sell my house, pack my few belongings, sell the IPI stock options that will help me follow my dreams. One last phone call I have to make alone.

"Hello?"

"Hello, Meg?"

"Paul?"

"I'm across the river in New Jersey."

"Oh my God! I don't believe it! How long will you be there? Can I see you?"

"I was hoping you'd say that. I'm staying with my Uncle Joel in Bloomfield. Do you think you could take a bus in tomorrow?"

"Paul Simmons, you are unbelievable! You think you can call out of the blue, expect me to drop everything and hop on a bus to New Jersey?"

"I'm sorry. I thought...."

"I don't care what you thought. I've waited all these years, and I'm not waiting another day. I'm coming now, and that's final!"

Chapter Fifty: Paul

Now that history has returned to its proper course, my thoughts race forward to the future, to Meg. Even so, a part of me still lives in that other history, the history I helped create. Over the years, I've thought about the events leading up to the ROTC fire—the unanswered questions about flammable tear gas, and why police arrived so quickly but medical care arrived so late. Knowing the answers lay in information shared, decisions made, actions taken *before* history veered from its original path, I investigated. With my level of access, with my hacking ability, I didn't bother with Freedom of Information Act requests. I went looking, found what I needed, learned the truth about my best friend.

The worst thing for Toby must have been keeping his secret from Meg and me. And though I've never found a smoking gun, I'll always believe he paid for that secret with his life.

So what will I tell Meg when I see her? About Toby, about Melora, about us? Will she think I'm crazy?

I've learned the dangers of keeping secrets, of not trusting the people I love to understand what's in my heart. So I'll tell her the truth. All of it. And I'll speak the words I was afraid to say so long ago.

But where will I begin? At the beginning, or the end? In the altered past, or the unknowable future? Or with last night. That was only yesterday, and I remember it best—

Last night the dream came again....

Acknowledgments

Virtual Fire is an unusual book. I began writing it in 1995. With the help of *hundreds* of volunteer readers, I completed it in 2019. Something close to a full list of contributors appears in my 2015 novel, *The Speed of Darkness—A Tale of Space, Time, and Aliens who LOVE to Party!* Additional thanks are due to those who stuck with the project from beginning to end, especially Forest, Sky, and Margie, and those who came later and helped with finishing touches. Fond memories of high school and college classmates and all of my "Columbian School Kids" gave life to *Virtual Fire*. Darin Varzali, Dr. Damian Jorgensen, Lyndon Duke, Heather Henderson, JoAnne Linkner, Kate Donovan, Erika James, Joel and Terry Narva, Mark and Alice Duffy, Paul Machu, Susan Castillo, Barbara Sullivan, Kathie Rivers, Melora Kennedy, Brent and Peggy Bosworth, WFMU DJ Kelly Jones, Brown University Archivist Raymond Butti, my first editor, the late and much beloved Russell Becker, my sister Karen Lee, and my parents, got *VF* running strong out of the gate. Author Lisa Brownell, Dr. Andrew Elliott, Denise Jessup, Dr. Lynne Oland, Bill Goetz, Jennifer Boudin, Mireille Machu, and Thomas J. Sylwester gave it second wind on the backstretch. My entire Writing Group and Beta readers *extraordinaire* Kevin May, Geoff Henkle, L.J. Bousquet, Stephanie Deverts, and Wendy Watson, along with my Marketing Group led by noir author Valerie Brooks, and cover designer Ana Grigoriou-Voicu, aimed it toward the finish line. First Lady of Grammar, editor Mary Oberst, brought it home a winner, and Audio book narrators David Cooper, Lelia Zsiga, and Karen Lee Sobol, and Audio Producer Forest J. Sobol, gave voice to my words. Much thanks and much love to all of you!

EXTRAS

FictionFire

The Vietnam War: Additional Sources

Nonfiction

The Vietnam War: An Intimate History
by Geoffrey C. Ward and Ken Burns

Vietnam: A History
by Stanley Karnow

A Rumor of War: The Classic Vietnam Memoir (40th Anniversary Edition)
by Philip Caputo and Kevin Powers

Dispatches
by Michael Herr

Hue 1968: A Turning Point of the American War in Vietnam
by Mark Bowden

Siege of Khe Sanh: The Story of the Vietnam War's Largest Battle
by Robert Pisor and Mark Bowden

When I Turned Nineteen: A Vietnam War Memoir
by Glyn Haynie

War For the Hell of It: A Fighter Pilot's View of Vietnam
by Ed Cobleigh

Fire in the Lake: The Vietnamese and the Americans in Vietnam
by Frances FitzGerald

Winners & Losers: Battles, Retreats, Gains, Losses, and Ruins from the Vietnam War
by Gloria Emerson

How We Won the War
by Vo Nguyen Giap

The Long Gray Line: The American Journey of West Point's Class of 1966
by Rick Atkinson

When Hell was in Session
by Admiral Jeremiah Denton and Ed Brandt

When Heaven and Earth Changed Places (Tie-In Edition)
by Le Ly Hayslip and Jay Wurts

The Latehomecomer: A Hmong Family Memoir
by Kao Kalia Yang

The Girl in the Picture: The Story of Kim Phuc, the Photograph, and the Vietnam War
by Denise Chong

Fiction

Saigon: An Epic Novel of Vietnam
by Anthony Grey

The Sorrow of War: A Novel of North Vietnam
by Bao Ninh and Frank Palmo

The Things They Carried
by Tim O'Brien

Matterhorn: A Novel of the Vietnam War
by Karl Marlantes

Graphic Novels

Dong Xoai, Vietnam 1965
by Joe Kubert

Such a Lovely Little War: Saigon 1961-63
by Marcelino Truong and David Homel

Movies

Hearts and Minds (1974)

The Deer Hunter (1978)

Coming Home (1978)

When Hell Was in Session (1979)
Apocalypse Now (1979)

Platoon (1986)

Full Metal Jacket (1987)
Hamburger Hill (1987)

Good Morning, Vietnam (1987)

Heaven and Earth (1993)

We Were Soldiers (2002)

The Fog of War: Eleven Lessons from the Life of Robert S. McNamara (2003)

Journey from the Fall (2006)

Last Days in Vietnam (2014)

Links

The Draft Lottery Broadcast, Dec. 1, 1969 – https://www.youtube.com/watch?v=XhLbysRh8XY

Results of the First Draft Lottery. Find your draft number and see whether you would have been drafted – https://www.calledtoservevietnam.com/blog/information-about-the-vietnam-era-draft/the-results-of-the-first-draft-lottery-dec-1-1969/

Selective Service Today – https://www.sss.gov/About/Quick-Facts-and-Figures

Napalm and Agent Orange – https://vietnamawbb.weebly.com/napalm-agent-orange.html

Music

New York Times Article: *I Served in Vietnam. Here's My Soundtrack.* –

https://www.nytimes.com/2018/03/13/opinion/vietnam-war-rock-music.html

The Vietnam War Antiwar Movement: Additional Sources

Nonfiction

Give Peace a Chance: Exploring the Vietnam Antiwar Movement: Essays from the Charles DeBenedetti Memorial Conference (Peace and Conflict Resolution)
by Professor Melvin Small and William D Hoover

Vietnam and the American Political Tradition: The Politics of Dissent
by Randall B. Woods

Witness to the Revolution: Radicals, Resisters, Vets, Hippies, and the Year America Lost Its Mind and Found Its Soul
by Clara Bingham

Born on the Fourth of July: 40th Anniversary Edition
by Ron Kovic and Bruce Springsteen

Steal This Book
by Abbie Hoffman

Revolution for the Hell of It: The Book That Earned Abbie Hoffman a Five-Year Prison Term at the Chicago Conspiracy Trial
by Abbie Hoffman and Reverend Billy

Kill for Peace: American Artists Against the Vietnam War
by Matthew Israel

Selma to Saigon: The Civil Rights Movement and the Vietnam War
(Civil Rights and Struggle)
by Daniel S. Lucks

The Catonsville Nine: A Story of Faith and Resistance in the
Vietnam Era
by Shawn Francis Peters

Hardhats, Hippies, and Hawks: The Vietnam Antiwar Movement as
Myth and Memory
by Penny Lewis

The Kent State Massacre: The History and Legacy of the Shootings
That Shocked America
by Charles River Editors

Four Dead in Ohio: Was There a Conspiracy at Kent State
by William A. Gordon

The Report of the President's Commission on Campus Unrest;
Including Special Reports: The Killings at Jackson State, the Kent
State Tragedy. (Physician travelers)
by United States President's Commission on Campus Unrest

Fiction

The Risk of Being Ridiculous
by Guy Maynard

Hocus Pocus
by Kurt Vonnegut

Five Freshmen: A Story of the Sixties
by Steven S. Kussin

Leaving Kent State
by Sabrina Fedel

Graphic Novel

VIETNAM
by Julian Bond and T.G. Lewis

Movies

Coming Home (1978)

Kent State (1981)

Born on the Fourth of July (1989)

Links

Jackson State Shootings – https://libcom.org/history/
jackson-state-shootings-1970

Video

500,000 March on Washington – https://www.youtube.com/
watch?v=fv7Gk-Pg7Rw

A Vietnam War veteran speaking at an anti-war protest in
Washington – https://www.youtube.com/watch?v=wkJ2aIRQl-I

Music

Country Joe McDonald: *I-Feel-Like-I'm-Fixin'-To-Die Rag*
https://www.youtube.com/watch?v=-7Y0ekr-3So

Phil Ochs: *I Ain't Marching Anymore*
https://www.youtube.com/watch?v=gv1KEF8Uw2k

Jefferson Airplane: *Revolution*
https://www.youtube.com/watch?v=KigBEoBxhmE

Jefferson Airplane: *Lather*
https://www.youtube.com/watch?v=vO-J7F4vPtg

Electric Flag: *Killing Floor*
https://www.youtube.com/watch?v=Tq3NwCHm-4U

Edwin Starr: *War*
https://www.youtube.com/watch?v=01-2pNCZiNk

Creedence Clearwater: *Fortunate Son*
https://www.youtube.com/watch?v=N7qkQewyubs

Creedence Clearwater: *Run Through the Jungle*
https://www.youtube.com/watch?v=bf_xZVhaAKs

James Brown: *Say it Loud, I'm Black and I'm Proud!*
https://www.youtube.com/watch?v=eb_1NNdf_30

Bob Dylan: *Masters of War*
https://www.youtube.com/watch?v=exm7FN-t3PY

Buffy Saint-Marie: *Universal Soldier*
https://www.youtube.com/watch?v=DbKa2gapq_M

The Animals: *We Gotta Get Outta This Place*
https://www.youtube.com/watch?v=wJVpihgwE18

Crosby, Stills, Nash & Young: *Ohio*
https://www.youtube.com/watch?v=TRE9vMBBe10

Other Reading

Prague Spring
So Many Heroes
by Alan Levy

Redlining, Blockbusting, and Segregation
The Color of Law: A Forgotten History of How Our Government
Segregated America
by Richard Rothstein

Reveal, from The Center for Investigative Reporting: *Kept Out*
https://www.revealnews.org/topic/kept-out/

WFMU Freeform Radio
https://wfmu.org/about/

IBM 650 Computer
https://en.wikipedia.org/wiki/IBM_650

Meet the Author

Mendy Sobol is a former attorney, law school teacher, and college ice hockey coach. He dreams of traveling via teleportation, yet often uses a rotary dial telephone. Find out more about Mendy at http://www.mendysobol.com/ and on his Facebook page at www.facebook.com/fictionfire/.

Interview

You began writing Virtual Fire in 1995. Why did it take so long to finish it?

Believe me, that wasn't my original plan. I completed a first draft in 1999, and after several revisions, copyrighted it in 2003. I always loved the characters and story, but it was a first novel. As in many first novels, I was telling a story I *had* to tell, as opposed to telling a story I *wanted* to tell, and I was eager to move on. In 2015, I published *The Speed of Darkness*, finished writing a volume of speculative short stories, and began work on my next novel, *The Eternal Blue Sky*. During those years, I often set *VF* aside, but just as often reopened the file and wrote a new passage or rewrote an old one. I'd learned a lot about writing during those twenty years, and each time I returned to *VF*, I saw new problems and new ways to fix them. The United States' continuous involvement in foreign wars and the legacy of the Vietnam War also motivated me to keep working on it until it was ready for publication.

Is Paul Simmons's narration early in the novel autobiographical?

Anyone who knew me in college would laugh at that idea!

In *VF* I drew on my experiences and those of my friends more than I've done in later works. Like Paul, Toby, and Meg, I was a college student in 1970, and like them I spent many afternoons at the racetrack.

Like Toby, I graduated from a military high school. Like Melora, I love the ocean. Unlike Paul and Toby, I was a Creative Writing major and never used a computer until 1995. The first draft of VF was handwritten and later rewritten on my first desktop computer. Each of the VF narrators includes bits of me and other people I've known, but VF is *not* autobiographical.

What motivated you to write *Virtual Fire*?

In the early 1990s, I was coaching a college ice hockey team. Two of my players, Darin and Damian (still close friends), asked me what it was like going to college "in the '60s." Some of their teammates saw it as a magical time of peace, love, and solidarity, while others pictured a bunch of drug-crazed hippies burning down buildings.

I wrote them a short story set in 1969, entitled *Dreams*. It was about two friends, Paul and Toby, training as antiwar parade marshals in the middle of a city street in the middle of the night. In 1990 that would be weird, but in 1969 it seemed normal.

One day over lunch, I read *Dreams* to Darin and Damian. As the story expanded, my parents and their friends read it. As it grew into what became *Virtual Fire*, my kids and their friends read it. I've always hoped that regardless of generational differences or views concerning the Vietnam War, VF will increase understanding of divisions that affect us to this day. I believe the power of friendship and the power of dreams can overcome those divisions and bring us together in pursuit of a more peaceful future.

You said you had little experience with computers when you began writing *Virtual Fire*, yet computers play a big role in the story. How did that come about?

By the 1990s, computers had become part of the culture for college students, so it made sense that fictional computer wizards from the past would be more interesting and relatable. As I learned about computers, computers became more interesting to me, and their role in the story grew. That worked out well from a speculative fiction / science fiction and character development perspective. Leaving messages on an IBM 650 is complicated, so I took some literary license with that.

You've written about coincidences affecting your writing. Did any coincidences play a role in *Virtual Fire*?

In *VF*'s first draft, I wrote that Toby died three days before his May 9 birthday. For Paul's birthday, I chose August 14, the date World War II ended. In a draft written two decades later, I added a chapter about the 1969 draft lottery. That's when I discovered the randomly drawn draft numbers for Toby's and Paul's birthdays were 197 and 198.

We picture writers slaving away in isolation. Is that what the experience of writing *Virtual Fire* was like for you?

Not at all. I love writing. For me, writing fiction is like going on the coolest vacation ever and meeting fascinating creatures—human or otherwise—who surprise and inspire me.

Dozens (and with *VF*, hundreds) of people have generously read my work and offered ideas that made it better. I wish I'd kept a list of the friends, family members, editors, and strangers who contributed to *VF*, but because I didn't, let me say right here that I love and appreciate all of you!

What are you working on now?

Two new novels. *The Eternal Blue Sky* is a BIG space opera about genetic engineering, intergalactic warfare, space-faring hippies, and the descendants of Genghis Khan. The other novel will—hopefully—amuse more F. Scott Fitzgerald fans than it enrages!

Introducing

If you enjoyed
VIRTUAL FIRE
look out for
THE ETERNAL BLUE SKY
by *Mendy Sobol*

Not to know what has been transacted in former times is to be always a child. If no use is made of the labors of past ages, the world must remain always in the infancy of knowledge. — Marcus Tullius Cicero

Everybody needs his memories. They keep the wolf of insignificance from the door. — Saul Bellow

Eric Stratton sat alone on the porch at the top of his stairs, an old man warming his wrinkled face in the waning sunlight of the last mild day of Indian summer, anticipating the daily visit of Regan Hollady, his only remaining friend from the Naval Academy and the many campaigns of the Dream Wars.

She was late.

Eric waited, something he was not good at. Soon enough, a solitary figure appeared, walking along the path that led to Noahstown and formed a border between the Gobi Plain and the Great Magnolian Forest. Eric raised one hand, shielding his eyes from the sun, and squinted.

It wasn't Regan.

Without looking away, he reached into the worn leather holster that lay across his lap and withdrew an antique but fully functioning, perfectly maintained sweep laser, leveling it at the approaching figure. The young woman hesitated.

"I'm here to see Captain Stratton," she said.

"Why?"

"Because he knew my great-grandfather."

She started walking toward him again. As she reached the steps he could see, even through the pale luminescence of his cataracts, that she was very young, just past her teens, and very beautiful. Her face was pie-plate round, her skin without blemish. She was tall, well over six feet, and her dark hair, unevenly cropped above her ears, curled upward revealing twin galaxies of colorful piercings. Her lips were thin, his favored type for kissing, and her eyes translucent green with flecks of gold. Her loose overalls hid the precise features of her body, but Eric only had two skills, and one of those relied on the ability to discern an attractive figure regardless of apparel. Her figure, he could easily see, was uncommonly attractive. Her perfection, because it was perfection, was simultaneously disarming and unnerving.

Eric gestured toward the folding chair next to his, the one he'd set out for Regan.

"Take a load off," he said.

The girl took one step toward the chair and stopped.

"Are you going to put away the piece?"

Eric lowered the sweep laser to his lap but didn't return it to its holster.

The girl dropped into the chair. She'd been walking a long time.

"What's your name?" Eric asked.

"Jenny," she said. "Jenny Harvard."

A heartbeat after she finished speaking, Eric raised the laser, pointing it directly between the girl's lovely green eyes.

Jenny looked away from the laser's barrel. The corners of her pink lips turned upward in a smile, revealing perfectly straight, perfectly white teeth. For a moment Eric thought she might laugh, but he also thought there was a deep sadness in her impossibly pretty, unsmiling eyes.

"You can put the laser away," she said, "I won't bite."

Eric leaned toward her, nostrils flared, loudly sniffing once, then again, more in the manner of a canine than a retired warrior. He leaned closer, sniffed a third time. Not even a hint of spoiled milk or cloying perfume, just the intoxicating smell of a beautiful young woman on a warm fall afternoon.

"I said I won't bite, but you look like you might."

"How?" Eric asked.

"How what?"

"How did they fix you?"

"Gene resequencing."

"Prove it."

Jenny hesitated, but only for a moment. With her eyes still looking off toward the forest's dark evergreen canopy, she reached behind her, untying the straps on her overall bib and lowering it to her navel, revealing firm upright breasts, smooth light-brown aureoles, and nipples pointing skyward toward some distant star.

"I appreciate the offer," Eric said, "but at my age it might be dangerous."

Jenny's smile grew wider, and for a moment her eyes brightened, too.

"Given your reputation, Captain Stratton, I might be tempted. Unfortunately, that's not the point of this peep show."

Eric smiled, but his index finger remained on the sweep laser's well-worn trigger.

"Look closer, Captain. Please."

Eric did as she asked. Even if the girl was trying to distract him, he was confident he could pull the trigger before she attempted anything, and even if he couldn't—well hell—it still might be worth it.

Then he saw it. A comet-tail spray of acne beginning at a point in the middle of her right breast, disappearing into the shadow between her breasts, and reemerging up the side of her left breast in a two-inch band of gravelly pimples.

For the first time since the girl appeared at the end of his driveway, Eric relaxed, breathing more deeply now that he no longer needed to keep his breath under control. His smile grew warmer as he raised the sweep laser upward and to his right before taking his finger off the trigger and returning it to his lap. He was a little disappointed, though not surprised, when Jenny raised the overall bib, covering her chest and tying the denim straps behind her long, lovely neck.

"What kind of resequencing?" he said.

"Viral."

"Rough treatment. Why not biochemical or nano-mechanical?"

"Rough on my mother," Jenny said. "She let the doctors infect her when she realized she was pregnant. Bio or nano would have been easier. Safer too. But viral offered the best chance for success."

"Looks like it was worth it."

"For me, yeah. Not for my mom."

"What happened to her?"

"She nearly lost me from the infection, almost died herself. But when the treatment was complete, she still had the craving. They'd corrected the nature, but couldn't fix the nurture."

"Where is she now?"

"She waited until I was born, waited, my foster mother told me, until my scalp broke out with cradle's cap. Then she ate a bottle of sleeping pills."

"Huh," Eric said, "a Beaut with integrity. That's rare."

"Thank you for your sympathy, Captain Stratton."

Eric reached over, roughly grabbing Jenny's hand.

"You listen to me, Jenny Harvard, I don't have any sympathy for Beauts. If you knew how people suffered, how many of my friends had to die! All I can say is I wish every one of those Beaut bastards had your mother's guts."

Jenny placed her hand gently over Eric's. Her skin was soft and cool, and ever so slowly Eric loosened his grip and looked away.

"I apologize, Ms. Harvard. To me, your family name is the most profane word you can imagine. Worse than that, it is blasphemous. But you weren't around for any of the history, and none of it's your fault. Your name is a curse, and bless your mother for trying to lift the curse from you. You can't possibly understand how great a blessing that is."

Eric started to pull his hand away, but Jenny gripped it more firmly. Reaching across with her other hand, she touched his cheek, turning his face gently toward her.

"I want to understand," she said, "that's why I found you. History is one lie on top of another, but I believe you'll tell me the truth."

Jenny and Eric sat for a while, warmed by the light of the golden sun as it journeyed ever lower across the eternal blue sky. Every so often Eric looked away from the horizon, beholding instead the youth, beauty, and as he now knew, *near* perfection that was Jenny. Yet beneath that, Eric sensed something unseen, and it was that something, more than her youth or beauty or near perfection, that stirred an almost forgotten yearning to again be young, invincible, and looking forward to the limitless future.

They made small talk—how long had Eric lived on Magnolia, was it always this hot here, how long had it taken Jenny to find him, had she come all this way alone—until Eric said, "Look Jenny, you've traveled a long way and put up with God knows what to find me. But the Dream Wars, the Taran Holocaust, they're no short story. They're more like *Gone with the Wind*, *All Quiet on the Western Front*, and *The Naked and the Dead*, rolled into one. I could think of worse things to do than holing up in my house all winter talking to you, but at your age you should have better things to do than sitting around listening to an old soldier telling lies. And that's another thing—you came here looking for truth. What the hell do I know about truth? I spent most of my life chasing women and killing your ancestors. Is that the kind of truth you're looking for?"

Jenny laughed, a lovely laugh, deep and throaty, the opposite of her clear, no-nonsense speaking voice. "Why thank you, Captain Stratton. I believe I will accept your invitation!"

"What are you talking about?"

"Your invitation for me to spend the winter on sunny Magnolia listening to your, uh, war stories."

"Jenny, do you know anyone on this planet? Do you even have a place to stay tonight?"

"I was hoping you might hook me up."

"Okay, tonight you can stay here, floor or couch, your choice. It's too late to find you a room in Noahstown, anyway. But tomorrow you're outta here, understand?"

"Perfectly, Captain. But tonight, should I be worried? I mean, your reputation…." Jenny, looking scandalized, brought her fingertips demurely to her lips.

"Ms. Jenny Harvard, if I believe in anything, I believe in sex—that it is good, and decent, and the one true gift whatever gods may be have granted to relieve the suffering of humankind. But I also believe in sin, and perhaps the worst sin of all comes from blaspheming the sacredness of sex. No one should be held accountable for their thoughts—it's only actions that have consequences—and if an old man like me were to act on his thoughts and take advantage of a young girl like you, that would truly be sinful."

"It's settled, Captain Stratton. I accept your invitation to stay the night, but on one condition: you will begin the story of the Dream Wars as soon as we finish eating the dinner I hope you'll let me prepare for us."

Eric grunted, "Fair enough. But don't get too comfortable. Tomorrow we find you a boarding house."

Eric looked down his driveway, squinting against the now-setting sun. "Hmff, guess she's not coming today after all."

"You were expecting someone?"

"An old friend. She stops by most days. Maybe you scared her off."

"I told you I wouldn't bite, but I never said I wasn't scary."

Something about Jenny did scare Eric. Not like her infamous great-grandfather, or the other Beaut monsters of the Eight Families, but something deeper, more profound. He wanted to ask her right up front, because that was his way, but he was afraid she'd be offended, afraid she might leave. This feeling was something new for him, and he admitted to himself how much he wanted her to stay, especially now that Regan wasn't coming.

"C'mon," he said, "it's getting dark. Let's go inside and I'll show you the galley."

Eric holstered the sweep laser, almost forgotten on his lap, and genteelly extended his arm to Jenny. Jenny slipped her arm in his, and together they stood and turned toward the house, leaving the first chill of evening behind.

Eric's home was small, tidy, and functional, well suited to a retired Marine and confirmed bachelor. The front door opened into a living / dining room, with a kitchenette on the right and a magnoliawood table and four chairs on the left. A hallway led to three rooms at the back of the house, an office and a bedroom joined by a full bath with tub and shower. The entire space comprised no more than six-hundred square feet, but white magnoliawood walls, large windows facing barren fields at the back and sides and lush forestland at the front, a wraparound porch, and an arched ceiling capped by a widow's walk, gave the house an open, spacious feel. Glossy, high-resolution photos of nebulae and auroras dotted the walls, interspersed with pictures of places Eric had visited and friends he had known. Visitors asked why he didn't display his many commendations, and Eric would respond by saying he'd run out of money framing his more numerous reprimands. If his guests looked more closely, they would have realized that other than its tidiness, nothing about Eric's home gave away his military background.

Eric pushed back from the table, working a toothpick between two of his molars. The girl was a terrible cook—burned toast with canned tuna smothered under heated mushroom soup—but at least it was a hot meal, more than he'd have bothered with.

"Where do you want me to begin?" he said.

Jenny turned from the little sink where she stood washing the last of their dishes. "Growing up in the displaced persons camp on Maracca, the whole subject of the Dream Wars was taboo. The missionaries who taught history classes in the refugee school called it 'a difficult, war-torn period that ended in the destruction of Tara and the ascendancy of Serene Khatun and the Magnolian Empire.' But that didn't explain why the camp guards would spit at us and mumble about 'the fucking Beauts.' And whenever we asked the adults questions about why we were there, they'd say, 'some things are better left alone.' Most of them were so spaced on suppressor drugs, it was a miracle they could talk at all. Later, when Serene Khatun dissolved the camps, I got off Maracca on the first shuttle that would take me. But wherever I went it was the same story—no one wants to talk about the wars, and the history vids are a joke."

Eric sat silently, listening, not wanting to betray the emotions stirred in him by Jenny's story, half wondering why, and half knowing he was holding back for her sake.

"So I guess I'm saying, I'd like you to start at the beginning, wherever you think that is."

Eric already knew Jenny well enough not to ask if that was wise, if it weren't perhaps better to let the ghosts sleep. She wouldn't have chosen him if she didn't want to hear it and hear it straight.

"Okay," he said. "Chapter One."

There is a field, a hot, dusty field several hundred acres in size, a rare open space, an inexplicable break in the vast, dense, green of the Great Magnolian Forest. From his vantage inside the tree line at one end of the clearing, Eric sees a swirling dust cloud. It grows larger, consuming the field, spreading to its edges and into the forest. His eyes blur with dust and he is choking. He cannot see, but he can hear—pounding hooves in the thousands, crossing the field, away and then back, kicking up the

*dusty turf in great clods that soar high into the air and fall again, explod-
ing in clouds of dirt and pebbles that shower over him, stinging the bare
flesh of his face and arms. He flinches, covering his eyes. The horses are
moving toward him; he can hear their snorting and high-pitched whin-
nies, see their green-tinged coats, smell their panicked sweat. He raises his
arms, shouting, "Yaah! Yaah!" and the horses reverse direction, moving
in concert like a wayward flock of geese, galloping away from the woods,
away from safety, into the center of the clearing.*

*In the distance, a monotonous droning sound grows louder, closes
on his position.*

*His back turned to the clearing, he is running, running along a slen-
der, weed-choked trail, the afternoon light filtering green through the
forest's canopy, woody tendrils grasping at his ankles, thorny branches
scratching his arms and face, leaving red-beaded welts. Not far to go
now, but his lungs burn and legs turn to wood, with the droning louder,
closer, rising in pitch, until ahead, only fifteen yards, the trench's outline,
and Regan, waving urgently. Props beat the air directly overhead, but he
is slowing, his legs stumbling as he pitches forward the last few steps, an
awkward airborne pirouette, falling into Regan's outstretched arms as
she reaches for him, rolling forward with his momentum into the covered
ditch, underneath and then on top of him. The props, quieter, more distant
bass than treble, muffled by the huddled sweating bodies stretching into
the semi-dark distance on either side, the warm earth beneath his shoulders, the dripping, meaty fronds above, and Regan hard on top of him,
elbows digging into his chest, flattened against him, breathing hard and
hot against his neck. Everything is hushed except for Regan's breathing
and the syncopation of his own harsh gasps.*

*One sharp warbling whistle. And another. And another. And another.
Until the air is so heavy with shrieking noise there might never be room
for any other sound again. Until suddenly, the whistling is consumed by
the first concussive detonation and the next and the next and the next
and the next and the ground heaves with explosion after explosion and
great clumps of earth falling on the thick magnolia leaves and branches
above his head sifting downward raining him with dirt and shrapnel*

whistling through the forest and sizzling through the trees overhead drip-
ping magnolia-scented sap hot and sticky on his arms and chest whistling
bombs whooshing rockets strafing endless lead explosions and hot gushing
sap soaking his shirt and dripping down his cheeks, blinding him.

Abruptly, it stops. A blink, an instant, a heartbeat of total silence, like
deafness, not even the sound of Regan breathing. Eric raises his head next
to Regan's cheek and listens. The props are faint. His ears ring, a muffled,
high-pitched tone. The droning fades. The planes are gone. Along the
trench the soldiers lift their heads and listen. All is silence.

Except the horses, the horses screaming....

Eric's head jerked forward, a prop a few feet above him. A moment's
panic. *Whoomp whoomp whoomp.* The ceiling fan, its broad blades
churning slowly through the warm night air in his darkened bedroom.

"Fuck."

Eric lifted the soaking sheet from his body, braced himself on one
elbow, and twisted his legs over the side of his bed. Still sitting, he pulled
off his t-shirt, then boxers, slowly sliding them under his buttocks and
down to his knees. Only then did he stand, a little unsteadily on his
bowed, arthritic, varicose-knotted legs, letting his underwear drop
to the floor around his feet and wiping the beaded perspiration from
his arms, chest, stomach, and thighs with the already damp t-shirt. He
stripped his sheets, placing them across the back of the chair next to
his night table, setting them out to dry along with his shorts and shirt.
He took fresh sheets from the dresser and remade his bed. He did all
this without much thought, going through the motions of an often-re-
peated routine.

The next step was using the bathroom before going back to bed,
but this time he paused.

"Got to think about the girl," he said. "If I go in there, it'll wake
her up."

Eric stood for a moment, naked, unsure, measuring the pressure
in his bladder against the hours left in the night.

"Aw the hell with it," he said, and lay down on his bed, hoping he could hold his water for the three hours left until dawn, hoping Magnolia, and her dreams, and his past, would let him rest, at least for the remainder of the night.

The next day Regan dropped in while Eric was drinking his first cup of coffee and Jenny was still asleep. These days there was a little sugar swirled in the cocoa of Regan's hair, and she wore it collar length instead of cut above her ears. Other than that, she looked to Eric as though she'd barely aged from her academy days. Her eyes were still the darkest blue, her posture erect, her mind sharp. The shopkeepers and clerks in Noahstown enthusiastically told Eric how great he looked, but despite the cataracts, Eric could see his reflection in mirrors, and unlike people, mirrors didn't lie. His hair, while thick and wavy, was completely silver. In contrast with Regan, Eric's gray eyes appeared cloudy, his frame bent with arthritis, and his memory—at least of recent events—forgetful. Some years ago he'd unpacked his old dress blue uniform. Twenty frustrating minutes later he gave up all hope of buttoning the jacket's gold buttons or zipping the pants' fly. Regan, he was certain, could still fit trimly in hers.

"I missed you yesterday, Regan."

"Not much, from the look of things."

Before bed, Jenny had borrowed a set of pajamas—the pants almost shorts length on her—washed her very feminine undergarments in the kitchen sink, and hung them to dry in the middle of the living room. She'd chosen the floor of the back room over the couch in the front room, so Eric threw down some pillows and an old featherbed for her. She fell asleep before he closed the door behind him. That was eight hours ago, and she would sleep for twelve more, not arising until Eric had supper on the table.

Eric wanted to talk about the girl, but Regan was in a hurry.

"I just dropped in to say goodbye. I'm heading offworld for a few weeks."

"What's up?"

"Great niece fell in with some stoner refugees from Cascadia. Got herself arrested on Athena, and you know how tight-assed those Athenans are. Naturally, the mayday goes out to Auntie Regan. Never a dull moment in the Hollady family."

"Regan, I've got a visitor."

"No shit, Eric."

"Not just any visitor—a virus resequenced great-granddaughter of the big Beaut bastard himself."

"Harvard?"

"Yup. Jenny Harvard, to be precise."

"I hope you smelled her."

"More than that. She's got pimples." Eric made a snap decision not to tell Regan *where* the girl had pimples.

Regan whistled. "Eric Stratton and a Harvard under one roof. I must be hallucinating."

"She wants me to tell her the history, Regan. The real history."

"So this one's a masochist instead of a sadist?"

"I don't think so. But still, there's something about her…."

"So what are you gonna do?"

"I don't know. I mean she's a likeable kid."

Regan lifted Jenny's polka dot brassiere between her thumb and forefinger. "I'll bet she is. And beautiful too, even with pimples."

"Not bad, but nothing special."

Regan laughed.

"Well, what do you think I should do, 'Auntie Regan'?"

"Tell her, Eric. Tell her everything. Kid's got a right to know. More than that, her generation needs to know."

"What am I supposed to do with her in the meantime? She hasn't got a place to stay, doesn't know anyone on Magnolia, and everyone I know would as soon spit on her as rent her a room."

"Let her stay here, Eric. It's safe, and she can keep an eye on you while I'm away."

Eric bristled. "I don't need anyone 'keeping an eye on me'!"

"Then do it for my sake. I'll feel better knowing you've got company. Besides, I'm sure you won't mind keeping your eyes on *her*."

Eric hadn't won an argument with Regan in years and knew he'd already lost this one. "All right, if that's the way you want it, she can stay. And I'll tell her everything, like you said. But if this blows up, I'm blaming you."

"Why should this time be any different?"

Regan turned toward the door.

"Hey, Captain Hollady, where's my goodbye hug?"

For a long moment the two old friends embraced, till Regan broke it off with a peck on Eric's cheek.

"So long, Captain Stratton."

"So long, Captain Hollady. Oh, and Hollady—try not to shoot anyone while you're on Athena."

"And you, Captain Stratton, try for once in your life to keep it zipped. She may be a beauty, but she's still a Beaut. Even as small as it is, you wouldn't want it to get cut off, would you?"

Also by Mendy Sobol
THE SPEED OF DARKNESS—A Tale of Space, Time,
and Aliens Who Love to Party!

CHAPTER 1—GEIGER

Roy Geiger accepted his appointment as First Officer of Grissom Base on Jupiter's fifth moon, Io, the same way he accepted all his accomplishments—with a complete lack of ambition. Roy's childhood neighbor, Jeffrey Graham, was always the ambitious one, the leader. Geiger was the sidekick, the second banana, the loyal best friend.

Had Roy grown up next door to anyone other than Jeff in their side-by-side mirror-image Florida homes, he never would have sought a scholarship to attend St. Petersburg's Honor Naval High School, Admiral Farragut Academy, never received one of the school's two appointments to the United States Naval Academy at Annapolis, Maryland (Graham got the other one), never achieved the rank of Lieutenant Commander, never been posted to Jupiter's giant volcanic moon Io as second-in-command—to Commander Jeffrey Graham.

Now they sat together at the Grissom Base officer's mess—Graham at the head of the table, Geiger at his right hand, eating breakfast and looking out at a vista neither of them could have imagined when they were children.

Gus Grissom Base rested within the shelter of Daedalus, an almost perfect bowl-shaped crater, twenty-six kilometers in diameter. With almost no atmosphere to obscure it, the 360-degree view around Daedalus's rim was crystal clear and dramatically spectacular. Starting thirty feet below the crater's surface, Daedalus had been built upward toward its rim, level upon level. After almost three decades of steady growth, in what was acknowledged as humanity's greatest engineering achievement, the entire caldera of Daedalus was ringed with mining offices, science laboratories, military barracks and luxury hotels. Development had been somewhat haphazard and unzoned, more often than not determined by the transfer of large numbers of credits into the off-earth bank accounts of highly placed officials. But everyone wanted a view, and by unspoken agreement the outward surface of every level was faced with specially tempered glass, like ever-larger rings milled from diamonds. At sunrise, Grissom Base looked like a giant, glittering, crystal punchbowl.

"Long way from Florida, eh buddy?" Graham asked.

"I still miss those sunsets over the Gulf of Mexico, but sunrise on Io is not bad, not bad at all."

"And first mess beats those cold grits and fried eggs they used to serve at Farragut."

"Roger that, Commander, but I sure could go for a glass of real Florida orange juice to wash it down!"

Geiger spooned himself a second helping of "Pancakes a la Io," the mess chef's breakfast specialty. Io's low gravity made them extra light and fluffy.

"Well, Roy, duty calls," Graham said, pushing back from the table. "I am outta here."

"You're gonna miss sunrise."

"Have to. Engineering requested my presence over at the minehead, ASAP. Something about stress fractures in some of the structural supports."

"Sounds serious, Jeff. Want me to come along?"

"And keep you away from all that paperwork that's been piling up on your desk? Not on your life! Besides, that's why they pay me the big bucks!"

"Suit yourself, Skipper. But I really don't have anything pressing this a.m., so I'm thinking I'll pass the time drinking coffee, watching the sun rise and contemplating my duties as an officer and a gentleman."

"Duties like hitting on Ensign Deyo?"

"Commander, I am shocked at your lack of faith in the dedication of your loyal first officer. I assure you the lovely ensign was the furthest thing from my mind. But now that you mention it…"

"Still no luck, eh?"

"As our new interstellar neighbors the Djbrr are so fond of saying, 'Failure is merely a prelude to success.'"

"Even repeated failure?"

Geiger shrugged.

"Well, don't let that paperwork slide too long, Roy. I've got a feeling this stress fracture thing will require another mountain of it today."

Graham got to his feet as Roy groaned.

"That all you got to say for yourself, sailor?"

"Yes sir. I mean, no sir. I mean…aye aye sir!" Geiger leapt to his feet, snapping to attention and saluting sharply.

"Carry on then, young man," Graham said, returning Geiger's salute and striding toward the mess hall door, "and try not to do anything today that will embarrass the United States Navy… or your commanding officer!"

Geiger lounged in his swivel chair, taking a sip of steaming black coffee, contemplating the silence. The hour before dawn was one of the few quiet times on Grissom Base. Graham always made a point of waking Geiger with an intercom call ninety minutes ahead of reveille so they could work out, then enjoy breakfast together before the junior officers began filing in. Every morning Geiger grumbled his way out of bed, but he never rolled over and went back to sleep. Rising early also gave him, in theory, extra time to catch up on paperwork, (the scourge of every First Officer in the fleet), an opportunity Geiger routinely ignored. The Navy may have replaced sailing ships with starships, he thought, but it would never replace paperwork. To Geiger, that meant paperwork could always wait until tomorrow.

Through the mess hall door he could hear steps approaching down the passageway. That would be Ensign Deyo. Bright, ambitious, fresh out of Annapolis, and, as Geiger was almost constantly aware, quite attractive. Liz Deyo was always the first of the junior officers to arrive at every function. "Be a heckuva commanding officer some day," Graham had once remarked. Geiger agreed. Working with Jeff all these years, Roy knew a good commanding officer when he saw one, though he had no such ambitions for himself. What he was, and what he wanted to be, was one hell of a great second in command, maybe the best in the fleet. While he may have let the paperwork slide a little too often for his C.O.'s liking, he never let Graham down on what they both considered his primary mission—backing up his C.O., as Graham had backed him since elementary school.

"Morning, Liz."

"Good morning, Commander."

"Are you here early for the sunrise, the chow, or my charming company? After all, it is Friday the Thirteenth. Could this be my lucky day?"

"Just trying to get a head start on my work, sir," Deyo said, sliding a pocket computer from her tunic and setting it on the mess hall table next to her plate.

Geiger groaned. "All work and no play, Ensign?"

Deyo ignored him and began spooning salad and home-fried potatoes on her plate. *No pancakes for someone who spends as many hours in the gym as Deyo*, Geiger thought.

Just then the first rays of sunrise crept over the far rim of Daedalus, shining directly into the officer's mess like diffused golden laser beams. On the other side of the crater, 180 degrees from where Geiger stood, the day's mining operations had begun. The drill-head threw fine particles of sparkling red Ionian clay and Palomino sand high into Io's thin atmosphere, turning sunrise into a spectacular, silent fireworks display. Jeff would be over at the mine by now, missing the wondrous sight they usually enjoyed together each morning.

Then Roy noticed something strange, something he would see when he was awake and asleep, in daydreams and in nightmares for the rest of his life. The slightest V, a notch in the crater rim at the drill head, allowing a premature and temporarily blinding blast of full sunlight to flicker out across the crater and into Geiger's eyes. Roy blinked, clearing his vision, and watched as the notch grew, deeper, wider, with astonishing, shocking, horrifying speed....

VISIT MENDY SOBOL'S FACEBOOK PAGE AT
www.facebook.com/fictionfire/
FEATURING
BREAKING NEWS
FORTHCOMING RELEASES
LINKS TO AUTHOR SITES and FAN FICTION
EXCLUSIVE INTERVIEWS
EARLY EXTRACTS and COMMENTARY

FOR INFORMATION ON SPECIAL OFFERS,
GIVEAWAYS, AND OPPORTUNITIES TO SUBMIT
AUDIOBOOK AUDITIONS
JOIN OUR EMAIL LIST AT
www.mendysobol.com/